A NOVEL BY SHEY STAHL

Published in the United States of America
ISBN-10: 1479315923
ISBN-13: 978-1479315925

Warning: This book contains adult content, explicit language, and sexual situations.

Cover Art: Allusion Graphics, LLC and Elaine York
www.allusiongraphics.com

Interior Design and Formatting/Proofing:
Elaine York, Allusion Graphics, LLC

The Champion is a progression book that captures the essence of this sport and what it means to be a championship team. It takes these characters we love so much from being the kids they were, to the adults they become, through a vivid and affectionate portrait of racing on the edge, both on and off the track. There's no big climax as I've had with the last few stories, but more of a real life display of their lives and hurdles they faced through pit stops.

I'd like to thank my badass readers! They are the best and pimp my books like champs. Thank you.

The Boy and Honey Girl, I couldn't do this without your support along the way.

My sister, I love you for everything you do for me even if you never answer my text messages.

My parents and the rest of my family—your support means everything.

Linda Knight, oh, Linda, I couldn't do this without you, and you know that. Regardless, you're the best and always here to talk me through everything and out of the ridiculous. I laugh every single time you write, "Took out semi." That right there shows my maturity in all this.

And finally, my racer boys who help with all the terms and that includes, my husband, whose mechanic expertise is greatly appreciated. Axel, Billy, Kasey, Joey, Justin, Trey, and Cody, thank you, boys.

For my mom. Childhood should be a child's best memories. A lot can be said for a child's memories and because of you I will hold them with me forever.

All compromise is based on give and take, but there can be no give and take on fundamentals. Any compromise on mere fundamentals is a surrender. For it is all give and no take.

-Gandhi

Table of
CONTENTS

A Champion – A champion is said to be an individual or team who has defeated all opponents in a series, event, or race.

The morning brought with it grief and regret, but also answers as to what might have gone wrong.

My wife—my wonderful, understanding, and supportive wife—stood beside me, watching the crowd gather in the stands of Charlotte Motor Speedway.

It was times like these that I looked at my life, my family, my team, and wondered why?

Why them and not me, or us?

Racers like me were used to deciding their own fate on a track. That wasn't to say outside factors didn't play a role, but usually your destiny, which was dependent on the outcome of a race, was held in your hands.

As a racer, your home was the track. It was where your love for racing was formed and where you cultivated it into something great. It was where nothing else mattered but the dedication, passion, confidence, and ambition. These were the only traits that I believed set a racer apart from others. Until today.

Racers were not born racers.

Sure, you may have had some innate ability within you that drove you down this career path, but it wasn't a gift. It was a natural inclination for speed, competition and tact—for pushing yourself beyond your comfort zone, taking risks, and striving to be the best.

Over time you nurtured these to become a champion in the sport that had consumed your entire life. Success and respect in the industry wasn't just handed to you.

I was a champion. The racing community was looking to me for answers. They wanted me to help them through this tragic time.

But could I?

Lisa approached Tate and me standing on the grid. The tears in her eyes reflected what the racing community was feeling. "Jameson, can you give the speech this morning?"

This was something that countless hours on the track and in the garage never prepared me for. Consequently, I realized that titles, trophies, and driving abilities were not, in fact, what set a champion apart from other racers. The true test was now.

You see, every now and then, a racer came along, and his talent wasn't defined by the trophies or his ability. What set him apart was what defined him in the blaring spotlight.

It was ordinary men doing extraordinary things.

Still, the questions remained.

Could I?

Window Net – A woven mesh that hangs across the driver's side window to prevent the driver's head and arms from being exposed during an accident.

Living with Jameson was difficult.

The only person I'd ever lived with was Charlie, and those two couldn't have been more different. Jameson was constantly leaving his clothes everywhere, shoes in the oddest places, and I didn't think he understood where the garbage was or that we had one. I even went as far as making a sign that said, "Hello, I'm the garbage can."

Didn't work. He still set his empty beer bottles on the counter and trash on the counters. I didn't understand. Even Lane put shit in the garbage, but my husband at twenty-three, couldn't.

Honestly though, Mr. Jangles kept his litter box tidier than Jameson did our kitchen.

Since we had just gotten married, I decided to wait at least a few weeks before I brought this up to him. We were still in the honeymoon stages. There was no sense in ruining that.

I'd always wanted to have a huge family dinner. Now clearly, I wasn't rational when I had the idea that this would all go smoothly. I must have been high as shit.

What happened that evening was hard to describe.

After we arrived home from the small honeymoon and the championship awards banquet, Jameson assured me the real honeymoon would come after the baby was born, and we could really have some fun. The naughty wizard (my nickname for myself) envisioned broken furniture and clothes hanging from ceiling fans—the good ole Pit Lizard days before I looked like a whale.

At eight months pregnant, I thought I would never see my feet again let alone a pair of single digit jeans.

Once at our home on Summit Lake, I decided I wanted everyone together for Christmas. I also decided to have this whole Christmas dinner disaster without Jameson's knowledge. Nancy offered to help, as did Alley. So I thought no problem, right?

Wrong again.

It started when I convinced Jameson we needed to drive to Olympia the day before Christmas Eve and go to Bed Bath and Beyond so I could get dishes to cook with. That was one necessity our home was not stocked with. We were currently eating off paper plates with plastic forks.

His response, "I don't think so. I have no desire to go to a Bed or Bath ... or whatever else they sell. What the hell does the Beyond part stand for?"

Ignoring him, I continued. "I need dishes," I told him, sitting next to him on the couch as he flipped through the channels. "This house has nothing in it."

"That's not true." He took another drink of his beer, nodding his head toward the kitchen. "There are paper plates in there."

"I need dishes for Christmas dinner."

His head slowly turned toward me. His facial expression was hard to read, but it was something similar to the time I told Charlie to take a flying fuck when I was thirteen because he wouldn't let me pierce my nipples.

"Why?" he finally asked with a sour edge.

"EveryoneiscomingoverforChristmasdinner," I blurted out as fast as I could and began to run away but was quickly stopped by a death grip on my wrist.

"Come again, Sway?" His eyes narrowed. "For a second there I thought you said everyone is coming over for Christmas dinner."

I swallowed. It was as though I was trying to swallow over a boulder in my throat.

"I did."

He was silent. No words, nothing; he just stared at me, his expression tense, fixated, and quite frankly, it frightened me. I was also almost certain he wasn't breathing.

I felt the need to explain, and when that didn't work I did what any normal knocked up woman would do. I cried.

"Shhh ... shhh ... it's okay, honey," he soothed, rubbing my arm and then swiftly pulled me against his chest when it became apparent that the tears wouldn't end without some sort of physical assistance. "I just ... don't like my family that much. What would make you think I would want them all at our house at the same time?"

I cried some more. "I just want everyone together before they aren't anymore," I wailed like a child.

That did him in. He knew I meant Charlie and agreed to my plan—with a stipulation.

"If those fucking twins spill anything ..." He eyed me carefully. "I'm shutting the entire operation down."

After my break down, we made our way to town for materials and maybe even some drugs for my husband. I wasn't sure there was any other way to control him if we had both our families together.

"What the fuck is that?"

"It's a ... actually ... I have no clue. Let's go find the plates." I began walking away from the kitchen gadgets and over to the dishes.

Jameson threw his arm around my shoulder.

"Yes. Let's find these dishes you speak of and get the hell out of here. I hate shopping."

We were shopping like a normal husband and wife, and it was

nice. Aside from his attitude and the occasional second glance at Jameson, most everyone was leaving us alone.

Seeing as he'd just won the series championship in his rookie season, there was no shortage of recognition anywhere we went.

"Plates ... yes." Jameson smiled. "Hey, look ... beds. How clever with the name and all."

"Get off that, it's for show only." I started to look around the store to see who was watching.

"No, they're not. Why else would they put them out here but for testing?" His eyebrows waggled.

"I don't think so sport, get up." He only sprawled out further. "They're for show only."

"Come over here." His voice was dripping with sex—sex that I desperately wanted. These last few days I had turned him down just because I was so uncomfortable.

"No, I'm not getting into trouble."

Even though the thought of a quick qualifying lap on that bed, in public, was incredibly enticing, I did not want to go to jail and become someone's bitch. First of all, I didn't need any more tattoos and second, I wouldn't look good with a buzz cut.

"*Wife* ... I think given the terms in which we are here ... you should be nicer to me," he hedged, reaching for me.

"*Husband,*" I yanked him up by his shirt. "We're here for dishes."

We didn't get up and eventually started making out on the show bed.

"Excuse me," a timid voice whispered beside us. "I'm going to have to ask you to get off the bed. It's for display only."

I looked over my shoulder to see a tiny red-haired girl smiling down at us, her innocence radiating in her flushed appearance.

"See ... I told you," I muttered.

Jameson gave the young girl a lopsided grin, trying to earn her forgiveness with his looks. I slapped him on the side of the head.

"Let's go, champ."

He groaned but followed.

Eventually we settled on some new dishes and cookware. It came in handy to share a brain at times—it meant that we agreed on almost everything that went into our house. I say almost because Jameson refused to let me paint the baby's room a soft blue. He seemed to think he needed something a little more manly. We settled on a tan color.

"Now ... I need to go to the grocery store."

"I don't think so," he told me, putting the bags in the Expedition. "I hate grocery stores. Too many people,"

"Fine." I smiled. "I can go by myself."

"I don't hate it that much. "

Whew, I'm getting good at this!

Since the incident with Darrin, if Van wasn't with me, Jameson refused to let me go anywhere by myself, and knowing his feelings toward the accident, I couldn't blame him.

After the grocery store, we picked up Lane so that Alley and Spencer could finish their Christmas shopping. I also thought this was their plan to get us some parenting experience. I didn't feel the need to inform them of what happened to Logan's hamster, Blubber. No one needed to know about that homicide as I was never formally charged with anything.

Lane never stopped talking—I was actually a little worried that he hadn't taken a breath on the way home.

"I'm hungry," he announced when we walked into the house, tossing his coat over his shoulder.

What should I feed him?

What does one feed a three-year-old? What do you feed babies?

I really needed to do some research.

I reached for Jameson's favorite, blueberry Pop Tarts. You can't go wrong with Pop Tarts, or can you?

"What's Pop Tart?" Lane asked, appearing by my side.

Jameson lifted him up onto the counter while we both stared at him, confused.

How could a kid not know what a Pop Tart was?

"What's a—" I was in shock. "You poor child!" I pulled him into a hug. "What kind of world are we living in when parents don't feed their kids Pop Tarts?" I grabbed his chubby little cheeks and squeezed, his adorable pink lips pushed together. "Please tell me you've at least had Eggo waffles?"

I let go so he could speak.

"Duh ... Uncle Jay eats those all the time."

Jameson smiled, ruffling his hair. "They're fucking delicious, that's why."

"Jameson!" I gasped. We really needed to work on this language issue we were having. "You better hope he doesn't repeat that around Alley," I whispered to Jameson, handing the toasted Pop Tart to Lane.

"You know ..." Lane began, his eyes twinkling with mischief. "I not say if you give me something."

I still found it adorable when he missed words.

"Wow," Jameson laughed lightly, his shoulders shaking with the motion. "He learned younger than Spencer and I did." Reaching around to his back pocket, he pulled a dollar out of his wallet. "Will that work?"

Lane's eyes gleamed as he took the said dinero from him. "Yep." He jumped off the counter, Pop Tart in hand.

A few hours later, after we got everything put away, Jameson was keeping Lane busy as I prepared everything for tomorrow's festivities when I heard our doorbell ring.

I was not prepared for who was at the door.

"Look, Jameson ..." I swung the door open both annoyed and concerned, "... our *neighbors* came over to welcome us to the *neighborhood*."

Jameson appeared around the corner with Lane on his back.

"Oh really, who—" He stopped mid step when he saw Dana Sloan, his harmless but peppy stalker fan, standing there with Cooper Young, a guy I slept with in high school. Let's just say neither one of these people he wanted to see. Ever.

"You have to be shitting me?" Lane reached around Jameson's

shoulder and held his hand out.

"Nope, not shitting you." I smiled at Dana. "They made cookies. We can eat them later."

He gave me a look that said no way but nodded.

"How long have you two lived next door?" I asked, trying to mask my discomfort with the entire situation.

"Oh, we just moved in about a month ago," Dana beamed. "We're just renting, but we're hoping to buy it now." You couldn't miss the meaning behind that.

"How long do you plan on living here?" Dana asked and then began talking about something else and then back to another subject. She was all over the place. You couldn't keep up with the speed in which her mouth was moving. "You didn't answer ... how long do you plan to live here?"

"We didn't say," Jameson replied. That was all he said.

We stood there in awkward silence before I decided to fill it.

"So, we were just leaving," I hinted, reaching for my coat.

Jameson had quickly disappeared, but Lane was now counting his money on the kitchen stool.

Goddamn him, he left me alone with these assholes.

"Well, we were just about to head out so ..." my voice faded again, hoping they'd take the hint.

We weren't really going anywhere, but I had to get them to leave somehow.

"Okay ... I made you some cookies." Dana pushed a plate of chocolate chip cookies at me. "I know they're Jameson's favorite."

They weren't. Everyone who knows Jameson knows that oatmeal raisin is his favorite cookie.

"Mmm ... yes ... he can't get enough of those *chocolate chip cookies*," I emphasized the chocolate chip cookies part rather loudly for no particular reason at all.

Cooper and Dana both looked at me as if I'd completely lost it, but at least they finally left, after telling me a shit load of times that they loved our house and Merry Christmas. They all but skipped off the porch, hand in hand.

"Weirdo," I heard Lane say off in the distance.

"Jameson?" I called climbing the stairs.

"Yeah," his voice sounded muffled and distant.

"Where are you?"

"Who's with you?"

"It's just me, asshole. Where are you?"

"In the kitchen."

I waddled my ass back into the kitchen. It was the only way to walk these days. I wouldn't say how much weight I'd gained because it was just downright embarrassing, and I was pretty sure even an elephant, that was pregnant for two years, didn't gain this much weight.

"Are they gone?" he asked, but I still couldn't see him.

"Where are you?"

The pantry door swung open, and he and Lane barreled out with water guns and soaked the shit out of me.

I was prepared, though. I knew this would eventually happen after he bought those goddamn things the other day. I quickly maneuvered my sea lion ass to the sink and drenched them with the sprayer.

The impromptu water fight ended on account of flooding in our brand new kitchen and left Jameson, Lane and me laughing and soaking wet in almost an inch of water.

As we were mopping up the floor, well Jameson was, I was looking out the back window at the lake where Cooper and Dana were waving to us from their paddle boat.

"We have neighbors, Sway," he leaned against the cupboards. "Peppy, stalker neighbors."

"What they doing?" Lane asked, looking out the French doors in the kitchen, his tiny arm stuck inside a bag of Cheetos.

"It appears these assholes are stalking us," Jameson told him, stealing a couple Cheetos when Lane walked over to him as he sat on the kitchen floor. Lane held out his hand and plopped down on his lap. Jameson in turn handed over another dollar.

"We should get a security system installed."

"We already have one, but we're for sure installing security cameras and a barbed wire fence," Jameson added.

"Barbed wire is tacky."

He looked up at me from the floor with a contemplative expression. "You're right ... make it an electric fence, more reliable anyway. It might keep Spencer out, too."

Lane looked up from the cookies he stole off the counter. "I need milk." A couple pieces of cookie flew out of his mouth onto Jameson's arm.

Jameson tried to keep his cool, but if you knew him, you knew that nearly anything on his skin repulsed him and chewed up cookies crumbs were no different. He calmly set Lane on the ground next to the saturated pile of wet towels, stomped to the bathroom, and closed the door.

"What's wid him?" Lane asked, his bright blue eyes curiously looking in the direction Jameson had gone.

"He has issues with stuff on his skin," I explained, wiping the chocolate from his face with one of the towels off the floor.

Lane seemed to contemplate this for a moment before smiling. "Dat could come in handy." I could almost hear the "muahahaha" chanting in his head as he walked into the living room, Cheetos and cookies in hand. It was at that moment that I became aware that Lane was exactly like Spencer.

I spent the rest of that evening preparing everything for tomorrow with a giddy high. Since he was diagnosed with metastatic brain cancer, I knew my dad, Charlie, wasn't going to be around much longer, and I desperately wanted everyone together.

I also knew it was a horrible idea ... but what wasn't a horrible idea for *any* family to all be in the same house at the same time? We were all completely crazy, but families were window nets, as Jameson called them. They kept you from falling out of the car completely.

On Christmas Eve, our entire family arrived around two, and it took me a good hour to get Jameson to even come downstairs. Before he did, I found the need to warn the twins, also known as my half-brothers from hell. They were pretty much the worst children ever, and I frequently referred to them as the Lucifer Twins.

"Listen, you two." I grabbed their little cheeks in my hands, squeezing. Two sets of chocolate eyes watched me carefully. "Stay away from Jameson today," I told them. "I'm only looking out for your safety. What the hell are you doing?" Lucas was bouncing up and down like he had to pee. "Stop moving."

"I need to pee," he replied, reaching between his legs.

"Then pee." I sighed. This parenting shit was exhausting. "In the bathroom," I specified when he grinned.

I spent most of the morning with the women of our families cooking this meal. When everyone was finally eating, I was pleasantly relieved. I enjoyed cooking with the girls as it was a nice change.

I didn't cook with Jameson any longer. Why?

Because it was easier to do it myself. Just simple tasks like making a sandwich was so in-depth. He would start out by saying, "Where's the bread?" Then he moved on to, "Where's the peanut butter? And the jelly? How much peanut butter do you use? How much jelly?" Do you put peanut butter on both sides? Do you cut it in half? Wait, do you toast the bread first?"

See? It was exhausting.

Who knew making a peanut butter sandwich was a ten-step process.

When everyone sat down to eat, I felt like a load had been lifted from my shoulders, or maybe it was that I wasn't on my feet with my balloon belly sticking out.

Kyle and his girlfriend, Elle, who in not so many words called me fat earlier today, came over. Justin and Tyler showed up with their girlfriends, who seemed nice enough and did not call me fat. They said I was glowing and beautiful, and I wanted to kiss them but didn't. I enjoyed Justin's girlfriend, Ami, and enjoyed talking pregnancy with her for a while as she just found out on Thanksgiving she was expecting.

Van came over, which made me happy. I felt like he was part of our family now, and I wanted him to know he was. Since the incident with Darrin last fall, Van wasn't more than a mile away from us at all times—it was reassuring.

Even though I was a little nervous about tonight, I loved having everyone together. I couldn't remember the last time our entire family and friends were together under the same roof—aside from the wedding. Any time you put family together, it could be a good evening or a *very* bad evening where someone got hurt or the cops are called. I wouldn't rule either out just yet—it was still early.

After collecting more food, I sat back down beside Spencer. On the other side was Jameson with Logan across from me.

"What did you say, Spencer?" Nancy asked, her eyes glancing around the table apprehensively.

I had no idea what they were talking about.

"I told him to suck my dick. I wasn't helping him," Spencer replied. "It was a dumb idea from the start. He had no idea what he was talking about."

Nancy gasped in horror and covered Lane's ears as he was silently building his mashed potato volcano, his brow creased with determination.

"I didn't, Mom. I didn't do it," Jameson told her in defense, holding his arms in the air as if in capitulation. She looked somewhat relieved. "I told him to fuck off," he finished.

There was another gasp from Nancy as she once again covered Lane's ears. He must have heard, though, because he held out his hand to Jameson, who handed over another dollar bill without thinking.

Spencer replied with something else and nudged my shoulder. I couldn't understand him. There was so much goddamn food in his mouth, so I just shrugged. He popped another deviled egg in his mouth, laughing.

"Well, this is a lovely meal, Sway," Jimi said with a smirk. "It's a nice table, too."

I knew instantly where he was going with that statement as did my overreacting, quick-tempered husband.

Jameson, who had been building his own mashed potato volcano, looked at his dad next to him. "What the fu—" He stopped when he realized Lane was waiting for the slip. "What did you say?"

"Darn it," Lane laughed.

"I said this is a *nice* table you guys have." Jimi's voice was laced with innuendo.

Jameson glanced over at me with suspicious eyes.

"You ... were they ... *no* ..." His eyes flickered back to Jimi who was grinning widely. "You have to be fucking kidding me!" He threw his wallet at Lane and stalked away. "This is fucking bullshit! We're getting a new table, Sway."

"What's he so mad about?" Emma finally realized we were all gaping at Jimi and Nancy, who had long since turned a bright shade of red.

"Way to go, Jimi," Charlie praised, patting his back.

"What are they talking about?" Lucas asked. He'd been just as clueless as Emma that we had just found out that Jimi and Nancy did the horizontal mambo on our dining room table since we humped on theirs once.

"Jameson's mad because they did—" Logan began.

In a complete shit move, I kicked Logan under the table to get him to shut up. Yep, I resorted back to schoolyard survival with a six-year-old. When he cried, I felt like a complete asshole ... until he cackled and ran into the family room where Jameson had disappeared.

I had my reasoning for kicking Logan; the last thing we needed was for Lane to start asking questions. Lane was still innocent; give him a few years and Spencer would surely destroy that, but I refused to do it myself.

Once dinner was done and we'd moved on from the conversations of Nancy and Jimi on our table, Jameson returned to the kitchen. He'd been holed up in the family room playing video games with Lane and Justin, avoiding everyone else.

"You have some serious making up to do," he said to me, lifting my chin so he could press a kiss on my lips.

"Yes, yes, making up ..." I placed the last plate in the dishwasher before closing the lid shut. "Lots of making up."

"That's right." He nodded, walking back into the family room where Van was wrestling with the twins.

Van came in a few minutes later, breathless from the exertion. "Thanks so much for dinner, Ms. Sway," he threw an arm around my shoulder. "You sure can throw down a meal." His other hand rubbed his belly leisurely. "I may need to move in now."

"Thanks Van, did you get enough to eat?" Alley and I put the final touches on the dessert buffet we'd created on the center island.

"Yes, definitely ..." His gaze shifted as Alley carried the brownies over. "Wow ... look at that." His eyes widened as he took in the sugar insanity.

Van quickly gathered a few brownies and other treats before making his way into the movie room.

Jameson snuck back into the kitchen, wrapping his arms around my waist and pulled me outside with him.

"Now ..." His lips captured mine. "For that making up you have to do ..." The cool winter air mixed with his warmth breath, causing me to shiver as I melted into him.

Before Jameson could hold me to the making up, Charlie and Jimi stepped outside onto the patio with us, laughing like Cheech and Chong in *Up in Smoke*. I was almost positive that was playing in the movie room now.

"What's wrong with them?" Jameson asked in a very melodramatic way, running his hands through his hair, stepping away from me.

I watched them for a moment and knew something was wrong.

"I have no clue." Something was bizarre about the way they were acting.

Frustrated, Jameson threw his hands up in the air. "I'm not ... there's ..." He seemed to search for his words for a moment. "...something wrong with them. They don't usually act this way."

"I think they might be on something," I deduced after Charlie chuckled once, his pupils dilated to the point you couldn't see the chocolate of his irises.

"Oh my God," Jameson balked, examining his dad—who was currently peeing on the side of our house while Charlie laughed hysterically.

"They're *definitely* on something," was my final assessment.

"What though?"

"Jimi, were you out here with Charlie earlier tonight?" I asked him after he put his junk away. I had no desire to see my father-in-law's camshaft.

"Yep!" Jimi replied with a grin, slinging his arm around Charlie.

At the same exact moment, they both turned to look at one of our palm trees as though it said their name.

"Oh my—"

Jameson groaned. "They're fucking high, aren't they?"

"Appears that way," I answered with a giggle of my own. This was funny to me.

"Hey," Charlie turned to Jimi. "Do you think there's any of that dip left?" he asked as Jimi helped him up the steps leading into the kitchen.

Jameson shook his head. "Could this night get any worse? I told you this was a bad idea, Sway."

"Jameson."

He turned sharply on his heel. "Don't *Jameson* me, and don't give me that face," he told me matter-of-factly. "Listen to me next time."

"Jameson, shut up." I shook my head slowly, walking over to the patio table to pick up the beer bottles scattered around.

"Don't tell me to shut up."

"I just did."

"Well ... don't."

"Are we really going to argue about this?" I spun around on my own heel to face him.

"Yes," he began and then stopped when I looked up at him. "I'm going to get a beer," he mumbled, retreating.

He was right—this was a bad idea, maybe even a horrible idea. So far this evening, Logan spilled fruit punch on our living room floor, Aiden knocked over an entire carton of milk in the kitchen, Jimi and Nancy had sex, at some point, on our table, Spencer told Jameson to suck his dick, twice, Charlie and Jimi were high and laughing while currently enjoying the desserts, and Lane was making money off everyone and their potty mouths.

When I walked back into the kitchen where Alley, Spencer, and Jameson were standing, I was met with Jimi and Charlie laughing uncontrollably.

"This is too funny." Alley reached for her camera on the counter. "I have to get some pictures."

Jameson left the room while Alley took pictures. I had half a mind to lock myself in the bathroom for the rest of the night.

Another hour later, Jameson finally returned with an armful of beer cans that I assumed he, Justin, and Tommy had drunk. He shuffled through the kitchen, placing the beer cans in the recycling can, his shoulders slumped forward and a set scowl on his face, grumbling words no one could understand. The French doors leading out to the patio slammed behind him.

"What's his problem?" Spencer asked, walking in with Aiden.

"He just doesn't like you guys." I shrugged. "That's all."

"Did you know Dana is their neighbor?" Emma asked Alley, giggling. Just then, Jameson walked back inside, his cheeks flushed from either the cool air or his annoyance.

"No shit?" Spencer laughed. "That's awesome."

“Fuck off,” Jameson told him and walked upstairs.

“Jeez, what the hell is his problem?” Emma balked.

It was only Christmas Eve. Just imagine tomorrow with all of us and presents involved. It may have been too much, but it’d been a while since I laughed this much.

Lying there in bed, I realized that I might have over done the whole “up on my feet” thing these last few days because *now*, as I laid there, I was feeling it. My back was aching, I was cramping, my legs hurt, and I had to pee badly.

From around twenty weeks pregnant, I’d been on restricted bed rest due to pre-term labor. Being up on my feet wasn’t exactly what was allowed.

“Jameson…” I tried to gently push him off so I could go to the bathroom.

He wasn’t budging.

“Jameson, if you don’t get the hell off me I will piss myself in this bed. And not only is that gross, but you will then be lying in piss, so GET OFF!” I yelled, trying to push him off again.

“Noooo … Mom. It’s not my turn to wear the bunny suit …”

What did he dream about?

I pushed him again.

“Grrr …”

Did he just growl at me?

Suddenly, kneeing him in his timing gears was looking tempting as the adorable flailing spaz started kicking me in my bladder. If you didn’t know, timing gears were gears bolted directly to the camshaft. And the camshaft, well, that was my word for a penis.

“JAMESON!” I yelled, feeling the vibrations of my voice. I should feel bad that I just yelled at him, but seriously, he was practically lying on top of me. I was eight months pregnant and had a baby pushing on my bladder. I understood he was tired after the Christmas Eve we had, and we had to be at his parent's early in the morning, but damn it, I needed to pee!

"Grr ... *need* ... sleeeppppeee," he mumbled as he rolled away.

Once he rolled off, I didn't have time to laugh at him. I was now starting to dribble pee down my thighs as I got out of bed.

As soon as I stood, I peed all over the carpet.

Shit, that was just embarrassing.

"Damn you, Jameson ..."

If he would have let me out of bed when I needed to go, this wouldn't have happened.

I also couldn't understand why pregnancy was so disgusting?

I mean, so far I hadn't seen anything good about it. People said pregnancy was beautiful, but I thought that was just a crock of shit. My ass was huge. My ankles looked like they belonged to Shamu or one of his distant relatives, and I couldn't sleep. And I was pretty sure I changed my underwear at least four times a day from the lack of bladder control. And let's not forget about the lack of sex this last week because I honestly felt too damn fat to be even remotely interested in Jameson's camshaft anywhere near my crankcase. After all, that camshaft was the reason I had all these problems. I used to be attached to him, but now ... I wanted to *detach* him.

While walking into the bathroom, I was momentarily distracted by the fact that my thighs were rubbing together—something I hadn't noticed until now and yet another dislike to add to my "growing list."

Jameson must have woken up to my grumbling, which I thought was internal, but apparently, once again, was not.

"Sway, why did you pee on the floor?" he asked, wiping his eyes to focus on me.

I hadn't realized what time it was, but I glanced at the clock and saw that it was only four o'clock.

"Because you're an asshole and wouldn't get off me," I snapped and waddled to the bathroom with a towel between my legs. I slammed door behind me, hoping to wake him up.

He chuckled. My husband chuckled at my misery.

Jerk.

When I sat down on the toilet, more pee came out, and more and more. It was an endless flow of fluid. I wondered if I had any bodily fluids left.

When I thought I was done, I started to get up. When I stood, a gush came out, but this time it appeared to be tinted pink.

Confused about this, I reached for the pregnancy book on the back of the toilet and skimmed through the pages. I found what I needed since Emma had tabbed the pages of labor for me.

That's when I went through the checklist for the signs of labor.

Back ache ... check.

Cramps ... check.

Discharge ... check.

Sudden gush of fluids ... double check.

Scared shitless ... triple check.

Standing there reading these signs of labor, I realized I was now standing in yet another puddle of water and scared shitless.

This couldn't be happening.

"Oh, Jameson," I yelled from the bathroom like I was calling a dog in from outside.

He didn't answer.

If he thought he was sleeping through this, he was out of his damn mind. This was one shit storm I wasn't handling alone.

Opening the door to our master bedroom, I tossed the book at his head, not caring at that point if it hurt him or not. Of course, it hit him in the back of the head with a thump.

"Ow ... *fuck,* Sway, why in the hell did you do that?" he asked, rubbing his head and glaring. "That hurt."

I must have looked rather hideous, because when he looked at me, his mouth dropped open in shock.

There I was, with just a bra on, standing in the doorway to our bathroom in a puddle of water. My hair probably looked like a haystack, and I'm pretty sure my nipples were leaking again. I checked just to make sure ... yep, leaking.

Great, now I needed to change my bra, too. I threw my arms up in the air once again, frustrated with my lack of body control.

"Mmm, since you're up …" Jameson reached for me, pulling me onto the bed after I put on a new pair of underwear. "You have some serious make-up sex to do."

"My water broke."

"I'll get you a new one," he said, yanking me down. "Back to the make-up sex."

"No, I'm serious. My water broke."

"And I told you I'd get you a new one tomorrow. Get over here." His expression of lust changed rather suddenly when he felt my lack of body control leaking on him. "Did you pee on me?"

"What are you?" I slapped him across the face. "I told you my water broke!"

"Well, shit …" He took in my appearance again, comprehension flashed when I turned on the light and untangled myself from him. "Are you …?"

"Either that or I've expelled my body weight in piss. Get your ass up!" I yelled, walking over to the dresser to find some clothes to wear.

Jameson was rambling incoherently and pacing across our bedroom as he tried to find clothes to wear. It wasn't long before I was staring at him naked, and the reality of the situation hit me. I was in labor and couldn't be focusing on a camshaft.

After all, that camshaft was the reason I sprung a leak in the first place.

Bell Housing – A cover, shaped like a bell, that surrounds the flywheel and clutch that connects the engine to the transmission.

Every time I thought about going into labor … I didn't think it would happen on Christmas Day nor did I expect it would be anything like *this*. I wasn't prepared for the pain and I wasn't I prepared for how unprepared we were.

Jameson was wound up, and I was a basket case with an egg—the egg being the baby, if that didn't make sense.

"It's fucking freezing out here!" Shivering, Jameson rubbed his hands together once he was inside the car.

"Jameson, just calm down," I glanced down at his bare legs and giggled as we sat in the Expedition.

"I am calm. This is my calm." His eyes narrowed, as I continued to giggle and pee a little.

"Is that so? If you're so calm, where are your pants?"

He sighed in defeat when he looked down and realized why he was so cold. "Shit."

He came back a few minutes later, still complaining.

"I've eaten entirely too much ice cream these days … my pants don't even fit!"

"Jameson?"

"Yeah?" He glanced over at me, digging the keys out of his pocket.

"Those are *my* pants."

"Shit."

He came back again, another five minutes later, still complaining, but this time he looked even more agitated.

"Jesus Christ, did you buy these for me? I mean ... I know I've gained a few pounds this off-season—no thanks to you and your ice cream—but fuck. What's with the kangaroo pouch?"

"Those are *mine*!" I yelled. We were never going to make it to the hospital at this rate. "You should change and wake the fuck up! Put your own goddamn clothes on!"

He sat there staring at me for a moment like I'd lost my mind. He'd lost his mind, not me.

"You really should change." I motioned with my hands to the water still trickling out of me. "We need to go."

"You think?"

I punched his shoulder. "Don't be an asshole."

When he came back, he was finally wearing his own jeans and in a completely different mood. I began to think he'd smoked some of Charlie's pot.

"Okay, let's do this!" he proclaimed, pumping his fists in the air and starting the truck.

"This isn't a pep rally. Calm down."

"I'm being supportive. There's a difference."

"Is that so?" I snorted. "I couldn't tell."

"You don't have to be so harsh. I'm only trying to be encouraging."

"How about you focus and drive to the goddamn hospital!" I snapped, slapping the back of his head. "That would be supportive."

He glared. "Stop hitting me."

"Since I will be popping a child out of my crankcase today, I will do whatever the fuck I want." I slapped him again. "Now drive!"

"You should be nicer to me. *I'm* the one driving."

I sighed heavily. "No, you're not driving. You're sitting here wearing one of my maternity shirts and arguing with me about being nicer to you." I pointed to his shirt and leaned back in the seat, as his eyes drifted to his shirt. "You should look in *your* closet for *your* clothes. I don't know how many times I have to tell you, but mine is the one on the left, not yours."

Smugly, he got out to change his shirt and came back with a muffin in hand and another bottle of water. I reached for the muffin, rolled the window down and tossed it in the driveway. "I can't eat, so neither can you, asshole."

After a good twenty minutes of this bullshit, we finally made our way to St. Peters Hospital in Olympia, only to have Jameson go the wrong way, twice, and then ask to stop at Burger King because he was hungry.

My response went something like this: "Go ahead, but if you eat in front of me, I will chop your dick off. No lie."

He didn't stop, but he did complain the entire trip about how he was starving and that I had no right to throw his muffin out the window. I had no sympathy for him or his stupid muffin.

On the way there, I called our family and let them know we were heading to the hospital and wouldn't be there for Christmas morning. Instead, we'd be bringing our son into the world if we stopped arguing long enough to actually get there.

I still couldn't grasp that this was it. For the past few months, I had imagined what this would be like—going into labor. Now that it was finally here, I had no idea what to do. I was a nervous fucking wreck and muffin boy beside me wasn't any better.

Spencer and Alley were already in Olympia so they were the first to arrive, although I didn't want Spencer anywhere near the hospital when I had the baby.

I was frightened enough thinking a child was supposed to come out of my crankcase making it the size of the Grand Canyon.

That shit would never be the same.

Dr. Sears met us on the labor and delivery floor as soon as we arrived. After getting us settled in a room and hooking up the monitors, he sat down to give us the news.

"Sway, your water has broken."

Well, at least I knew I didn't pee; that was slightly reassuring.

"I need to do an exam," he said, putting his gloves on.

Immediately I felt Jameson's hand tense around mine when he checked my cervix. I was sure this was awkward for him to watch. Who would want to watch another man stick his fingers inside his wife's crankcase to check her bearing alignment?

Definitely not Jameson.

When the doctor hadn't moved his hand as quickly as my over-bearing husband wanted, Jameson shot him a glare.

"Are you finished yet?"

Dr. Sears ignored him and delivered the news I was dreading. "So it looks like you are fully effaced and dilated to a five. You're measuring at thirty-four weeks, and the baby looked great on the last ultrasound. If everything goes okay, we should have him in your arms this evening depending on how your contractions progress. It looks like we'll have a Christmas baby!"

This should have been good news to me, but the word contraction was haunting me. I didn't like that word—feared it actually.

"What are contractions?" I asked with a hesitation a mother-to-be shouldn't have. I skipped certain parts of those pregnancy books for a reason. *Denial.* "I mean ... I understand they're like cramps, right?"

"Yes, Sway." Dr. Sears laughed, but held some concern for his patient and her being a dumb shit. He was probably wondering if he should call social services now in fear this child shouldn't be with someone like me. I would if I was him.

"The contractions are what *push* the baby out."

"Do they hurt?"

His brow furrowed, and his eyes darted between Jameson and me.

"Well, I've never had a baby, but from what the women I treat say, yes ... badly."

"Can't you just knock me out?" I whined.

"No, we don't do that these days."

"Shit."

I looked down at my bulging belly and wondered why he couldn't have magical powers and just magical-power his way out of me.

Jameson reached for my hand, pulling it to his lips. A small smirk appeared across his lips as though he was thankful he wasn't the one doing this.

"It's okay, honey," he had the nerve to say. "You'll do fine."

"Do me a favor," I told him, pulling my hand away. "Don't say that. For the sake of my sanity through this, do not say everything will be fine." I motioned to my stomach. "There is a watermelon trying to squeeze out of my crankcase right now. IT IS NOT FINE!"

He laughed. Fucking laughed.

I tried to keep Jameson and myself calm as the nurses went to work, but clearly, I was freaking the fuck out. Jameson wasn't doing *any* better. I swore to myself at one point if he ran his hands through his hair one more time I was going to junk punch him.

Usually, I found this sexy, the whole stressed Jameson, running his hands through his wild hair, but right then, it was irritating the hell out of me, which was precisely why Spencer wasn't allowed in the room.

He and Alley showed up a little while after we got here, and Spencer decided it was appropriate to eat a breakfast sandwich in front of me while I was, in fact, starving to death.

"I wouldn't go to sleep tonight if I were you," was my response.

"I forgot how scary you can be," he replied, backing away.

I kicked him out to the waiting room after that. He reluctantly left after making more than one reference to my crankcase and the fact that Jameson would need a GPS to navigate his way around after the baby came out.

How Alley could stand him was beyond me.

Emma stepped in for a moment and teased Jameson about not having sex for six weeks after the baby was born.

"I'm not talking about my sex life with you," Jameson replied harshly. "That's inappropriate."

"It's not inappropriate," she told him, taking a drink of her mocha, which pissed me off because I really wanted coffee. "I'm your sister, not your mother. We can talk about sex."

"No, no we can't. We're not close," he went on to say. "That's *not* something we talk about."

Emma started crying. I had no idea why, but she left. It might have had something to do with the fact that Jameson just told her they weren't close, but I couldn't be sure, and I really didn't fucking care at that moment. My insides felt like they were being ripped apart, spark plug by spark plug.

"You should go comfort her," I told Jameson who had just picked up a magazine.

"Why?" He didn't look up but shook his head. "I don't want to talk to her."

"Because you made her cry,"

"She's a girl," he said. "Girls cry."

Another contraction hit me, and I swear on all that was holy my fuel pump gave way.

"I'm never having sex with you again!" I yelled in the midst of the contraction. "I'm serious this time."

Jameson threw me a frantic glance. "That's a bit drastic. Don't you think?"

"No ... I don't!"

"Just calm down ... everything is ..." my murderous glare cut him off. "Sorry," he mumbled and looked out the window.

"Merry Christmas!" Spencer walked in wearing a Santa Claus hat with Tommy behind him. "Smile for the camera."

I can imagine what that picture would have looked like.

I turned to Jameson. "If I stabbed Spencer with a fork, do you think I'd get arrested?"

He shrugged.

"No, Emma didn't. Just make it look like an accident."

He grabbed Spencer by the sweatshirt he was wearing and flung him toward me.

"Here, hold out that fork, and I'll trip him. Problem solved."

Spencer left after that.

"Good plan, honey." I high-fived him. "I like the way you think."

"We make a good team," he agreed.

Nancy and Jimi came in after that just to say hello and wish us good luck and Merry Christmas. I kept adjusting my blanket to make sure Jimi couldn't see anything.

He noticed, and just like his sons, felt the need to embarrass me.

"Sweetheart," he drawled out slowly. "I'm damn near fifty years old ... I've seen it all before."

Jameson realized what I was covering up.

"That doesn't mean *you* need to see it!" he barked at his dad, handing me another cup of ice chips. "Stop looking."

"Okay ... well ... we will be in the waiting room," Nancy announced and leaned down to kiss my forehead. "You look great."

"You don't have to lie."

"Yes, I do," she smiled and patted my shoulder. "After almost thirty years of being married to a Riley ... you'd learn to lie as well."

Charlie was the last to come in and didn't stay very long once the contractions started to pick up, and I began to sound like a drowning feral cat. He did wish us a Merry Christmas and sent me into another emotional frenzy when he gave me a heart-shaped locket he'd given my mother when I was born.

It took me a good hour to recover.

When the narcotics kicked in, I started to calm my inner demons and the need to junk punch my husband abated. That was a good thing if I wanted more kids in the future.

Suddenly I was relieved to have this wonderful man by my side. I knew it was the drugs talking, but I was grateful regardless.

He held me and ran his fingers through my hair as they put the needle in my back, whispering that he loved me. He added, "Even if you did throw my muffin away," with a hint of resentment.

Once the contractions increased, and I started to feel like I was having the baby any minute—Jameson freaked out and left the room, which brought me to another round of hysterics.

Alley stepped in to take his place and said that Aiden was comforting Emma but just told Jameson if he didn't get his ass back in here he was going to junk punch him for me.

There was a lot of threatening punches going on today.

I thought poor Emma was freaking out because she saw how much pain I was in and that Jameson said they weren't close, but came to find out she was freaking out at the gowns they made you wear.

Some days I couldn't believe I married into this madness.

Alley sat there comforting me. The more I watched her, though, the more I realized something was incredibly different, besides the fact that her hair was back to one color.

"What is up with you? You are all perky and cheerful."

"Nothing," she smiled. "This is exciting. You're having a baby ... like *really* having a baby."

"So everyone keeps saying." I rolled my eyes. "Why are you excited?"

"I'm uh ..." She smiled widely.

"You just found out, didn't you?" Yesterday she had the sneaking suspicion she might be pregnant again.

Alley nodded with a smile. "But let's not focus on that right now. Today is about you guys and this little guy coming out of you."

I didn't like the phrase, *coming out*. It reminded me of some kind of alien movie or some shit.

Jameson came back in a few minutes later, looking smug, and a little frightened that Aiden also threatened to junk punch him.

"What *happened* to you?" I seethed.

"I'm sorry," his head hung. "I got scared."

"You got scared? The Jameson I married is a force of nature ... passionate, determined and focused, and never second guesses himself." I had no idea where the words were even coming from—they kept flowing. I was possessed. "What happened to you? You've gone soft on me."

He leaned over, kissing my forehead as he whispered he was sorry once again, ignoring my silly rant.

I, of course, pumped full of so many narcotics, forgave him.

I was too scared not to forgive him. I honestly thought I was going to die. All I kept thinking about was on top of how bad this all hurt, from now on everything would be different. The world no longer revolved around Jameson and me, but it would also include another human being who had needs. This wasn't a hamster or Mr. Jangles. I couldn't forget to feed him or bathe him; he would have real life needs, and I was pretty sure I was not qualified for it and neither was Jameson.

Jameson moved closer and sat behind me in the bed so he could wrap his arms around me.

"I don't think you guys gave me enough crack." I was referring to the epidural as crack. "I think I may need more of the crack."

"Just breathe, honey," Jameson whispered to me when I started pushing.

"No! I will not breathe until I get more crack!"

"We can't give you any more," Dr. Sears told me with his head between my legs. I felt like asking him how the view was. "Sway, the baby is crowning. You need to push and breathe."

I slammed my legs shut, the slap of my thighs echoed throughout the room.

"What the fuck is crowning?" I asked frantically. "That does not sound good. It's not normal, is it?"

"Yes, it is normal," he told us, and I say *us* because when Dr. Sears said the word crowning I felt every muscle in Jameson's body clench in horror. "The baby is ready to come out, just push!"

"No ... I don't want to do this anymore!" I wailed, clawing at Jameson.

"It's a little late for that. Sway, you need to push. If you don't push, the baby will go into distress. Please, push," he urged.

In a simple gesture to calm me, he rubbed my thigh, but Jameson didn't take it as a simple gesture.

"Do you mind not touching my wife's leg like that?" he growled.

"I'm only trying to get her to push so your child can be born," Dr.

Sears answered.

"Do that without touching her," Jameson suggested.

"Physically impossible, Jameson," Dr. Sears shot back. "Now both of you concentrate, the baby is crowning."

"Stop saying that word!" Jameson and I yelled together.

The word was just disgusting and made me think of ... never mind ... I won't even repeat what I was thinking—just use your imagination.

Dr. Sears laughed.

"Do you want to see?" he asked Jameson.

"Uh ... no ... that's all right," Jameson replied timorously.

"I don't blame you," I said to him.

People said childbirth was a beautiful thing ... another crock of shit in my book. It was sweaty, painful, bloody, gooey ... did more need to be said? It wasn't beautiful to me. It was disgusting.

I tried to practice my breathing and actually calm myself, but I only resembled something out of *The Exorcist*. At one point, Jameson actually looked afraid of me. If I could just calm down, I could act like a normal version of myself and everything would be okay, but I was freaking the fuck out.

Jameson was perspiring like a professional soccer player behind me.

"What are you on?" I asked him in between pushes. "You're dripping."

"Sorry ... this is intense." He was panting almost as much as I was as he wiped sweat from his forehead.

I turned a little to look at him. "Hey, asshole," I whispered harshly. "Just imagine what I'm going through."

He let out a nervous chuckle and ran his hand through his hair.

When I actually started pushing, we had to kick Spencer out for trying to see if he could help given he had the skills needed to catch a baby with his experience on the pit crew ... *fucking jackass*.

I was absolutely horrified that Spencer might have gotten a view of my crankcase that I threw the closest thing I could find at him. He was now in the ER getting stitches above his eye because the closest thing I could find happened to be a camera. I threw it pretty hard, but could you blame me?

I felt like I'd been pushing for hours when I felt an insane amount of pressure. Dr. Sears pushed on my stomach to turn the baby slightly. Jameson had his head down next to my ear, whispering words of love and adoration, which just annoyed me. His head didn't shoot up until we heard a cry shriek through the room.

"Here he is!" Dr. Sears announced, holding him in the air. "It's a boy!"

And there, flailing around like our tiny adorable flailing spaz was our son, covered in the most disgusting gooey mess I'd ever seen. In the beginning of the pregnancy I thought of him as a parasite—this just confirmed my thoughts. He actually looked like one.

I burst into tears as I turned to see the shock on Jameson's face as he looked at him. I couldn't get a good view of the baby yet. All I saw were flailing arms and legs. I thought he'd be crying, but after the first couple cries, he stopped.

My heart sank thinking something was wrong with him.

"Is he okay?"

Jameson's nervous eyes followed our little boy until they brought him to rest in his arms. Jameson turned to show him to me as he pulled the blanket down off his head. "He's fine, honey."

It was the most beautiful sight I had ever seen in my life. Even with the goo still coating him in spots, I could see the shock of silky rusty hair lying on his head in an unruly mess of waves. He wasn't a parasite after all.

"Sway, look at him, he's beautiful. He blinks and everything."

The tears in Jameson's eyes said it all as he placed our infant son in my arms.

Despite this beautiful image, I kept focusing on the fact that he didn't understand that babies blinked.

What did he think they did?

I wondered what he would do when he found out they pooped, too.

Those concerns disappeared when Jameson brought his free palm to my face.

"I love you," we both whispered together, feeling the moment.

We stared in awe at this tiny creature that was now ours; and the nerves, fear, exhaustion, and medication set in ... and I vomited all over the place.

Relief swept over me the moment I was positive everything was okay. When I looked down at him, I could see so much of Sway, but there was no denying that color of hair—my hair, my mother's hair.

Sway shooed me away to take pictures of him before he was whisked away to the NICU for some tests. I got pictures of him being weighed and measured. Then a nurse took a picture of me holding his hands and kissing his tiny feet and forehead. As I snapped photos, I noticed that he also had my long fingers and my exact lips. It was like looking into a mirror.

When they took him away, Sway begged me to tell our family the good news. I went out to the waiting room to find them all waiting anxiously.

"Well?" Emma ran over to me. She looked happier.

At least she calmed down after her little emotional breakdown. I still kept my distance from her just in case she felt the need to hit me again.

"He is fine. He's in the NICU for now, but if he does well, he'll only be there for a couple of days."

"We want details!" Alley shoved my chest.

"Okay, Jesus." I got them to all sit down as I began to recount the delivery, including the parts where Sway freaked out.

I looked to see my mom and Andrea wiping a few tears from their cheeks.

My dad, while rolling his eyes, passed a nearby tissue box to her, and then she passed it on to Alley and Emma who were apparently having issues as well.

"He is little at five pounds, two ounces and seventeen inches long. They do have him on a little bit of oxygen, but the doctors say it's probably just temporary."

I handed the camera off to my mom who sat in between Emma, Andrea, and Alley. They cried over each picture, and I noticed Charlie sitting quietly off to the side.

I went sit next to him and nudged his leg. "You happy, Dad?"

He smiled and nodded.

"Yeah, I'm just so ... relieved." He shrugged and looked down at his feet. "I'm relieved I was here, and they are both doing well."

"I know what you mean." I was about to say more until Emma spoke up.

"Hey, Jameson, what's his name?" Emma asked, looking up from the pictures.

I smiled. "We haven't decided yet."

Everyone had been asking for weeks what we'd name him, but we had yet to agree on one. I knew what I wanted, but I wasn't so sure Sway would be okay with it.

Lane snuck on my lap.

"He cute?" he asked curiously.

"Yeah, he's pretty cute." I smiled at him. "Are you excited to have a cousin?"

"Sure am!" he announced. "I'm gonna get him a gift."

He then grabbed Spencer's hand and walked toward the gift shop.

Spencer glanced down at him as they waited for the elevator. "You can get him anything you want—just no cougars. His dad will go apeshit."

"Noted," Lane said, nodding.

A few hours later, I sat there quietly watching my beautiful wife sleep as I rocked our newborn baby. He was handsome—no surprise there—and perfect. His features reminded me of myself, but I could see Sway in there as well. He was a perfect mix of the two of us blended together.

He seemed to have my exact hair color and texture with loops that flung out at the ends. You couldn't tell what his eye color would be, but I assumed he'd have green since both of us had green. One thing he did have that I found particularly adorable was Sway's nose. Sway had an adorable button nose, which our son now had. *Our son.*

It felt almost anomalous to think I was now a father.

He looked up at me and, in that moment, I knew just like his mother, I could never deny him of anything. Sway was everything to me, and I never knew that I could love anything as much as I loved her until our son was placed in my arms.

He instantly had me wrapped around his finger; my reason for existence had just doubled. Nothing else mattered more than these two. Not racing, not the championship, nothing.

I gently rocked him, humming softly. Soon, he wormed his way closer to me, just as Sway always did, and fell asleep.

My eyes focused on Sway again. Her lips were pushed out into that adorable pout she had when sleeping, her cheeks flushed from the exertion she put forth today. She was beautiful, and she had just given me the best Christmas gift anyone could have possibly given me.

She made me a father. Winning the championship this year had nothing on this feeling.

"You know, kid," Charlie said, holding the baby against his chest. "Your parents are stupid sometimes, but the smartest thing they did was bring you into this world."

"Wow, Dad, thanks ... I think." I adjusted the blanket surrounding me to hide away the funbags.

"Sway, it's not the destination you choose. It's the journey you take to get there."

"What does that even mean?"

"Fuck if I know. I saw it on a commercial ... I think. Or maybe it was a billboard?" His brow furrowed in confusion. "Or maybe it was in a fortune cookie?" Charlie's memory was fading these days so I wasn't surprised he didn't remember. "Regardless, it seemed like a responsible bit of wisdom."

Just then, the baby sneezed and Jameson's frantic eyes met mine. "He sneezes, like a tiny human."

Charlie looked over at me, concerned. I felt the need to explain.

"Apparently Jameson thought we were having a non-human baby who doesn't sneeze or blink."

Charlie responded, "You two should take a class or something. Maybe a book would help."

Alley and Spencer, along with Lane, were the next to come in.

Watching Lane with his cousin was adorable. He tried to be so gentle with him when Spencer just tried to toss him around. This also caused a brawl between Jameson and Spencer that Aiden had to separate.

I was too distracted by the size of my funbags to care about their stupid brawl. It was like magic; the funbags seemed to have grown in a matter of hours. "My boobs are huge!" I announced to no one in particular. "Like really huge ... is that normal?"

"It's awesome," Jameson replied, gawking at them as Alley held the baby.

Alley snorted. "You won't think it's awesome soon ... she'll kill you if you touch them."

A few hours later, it was just Jameson and I with the baby. It was nice to finally be alone with my boys—on Christmas.

I loved thinking of the idea that we had a child together.

To some people it might've just been a baby. But it was more to me. Just his tiny presence in our world was a big deal for us. We had been through so much in these last nine months, and to finally have him here, healthy, was such a relief. I also took comfort in the fact that I was no longer Jameson's pit lizard. I was his wife, his wizard.

And together, under not so ideal circumstances, we created another life that brought us closer than ever. We were one person.

There were so many words I would use to describe what Jameson was to me, most of which wouldn't do us justice. We had a bond that never wavered or faltered. Sure, we argued relentlessly at times about things as insignificant as muffins, but we had a bond. It was a bond that had been built on friendship, love, tragedy, loss, and so much more. He had become my soul mate.

Jameson sat there quietly, holding the baby, looking over the book Dr. Sears gave us on caring for him, and I daydreamed about fairytales.

"Jesus Christ, it's like a gremlin; he comes with instructions, Sway." He tossed the book aside and focused all his attention back on our son. "You're adorable, little buddy," he cooed.

Charlie was right. We needed to take a class.

"We should decide on a name," Jameson murmured, brushing his fingertips over our son's flushed cheeks.

"I know what you want to name him," I whispered, watching them together. Seeing my husband holding our newborn son was enough to send me into another round of complete emotional hysteria, but I held back.

Jameson laughed and let out a whoosh of air. "Am I that transparent?"

"No," I smiled, reaching for his hand. "You forgot we share a brain."

"You're okay with it?"

"I think it's a perfect name for him."

He maneuvered his way into the bed with me, placing the baby in my arms.

"Merry Christmas, honey," he whispered before placing a tender kiss on my forehead and leaning down to kiss the baby.

My heart nearly stopped when he said our son's name for the first time.

Corner Weights – This is the distribution of a car's weight among the four wheels. Managing corner weights is very important to handling.

"And Merry Christmas to you, too ... Axel Charles Riley." Jameson placed another kiss on his tiny forehead.

Axel let out an adorable little whimper and snuggled closer to me.

The nurses had taken off his oxygen so we were finally able to cuddle him without tubes in the way, and all I wanted to do was snuggle with my boys on Christmas.

My boys.

When I looked back at my life this time last year, everything about it was different.

I wasn't lying in the arms of my dirty heathen, and I wasn't holding our newborn son. Even though it'd only been a year, a lot could and had changed in that year.

In 365 days, 52 weeks, 8,765 hours, or 525,948 minutes your life could change completely.

What you once believed in, you didn't anymore. What you once loved, maybe you didn't anymore. What you never thought was possible had suddenly became possible in those 365 days, 52 weeks, 8,765 hours, or in those 525,948 minutes of the best and worst year of your life.

"I can't believe we're parents now," I said softly, leaning my head against his chest.

Listening to his steady, slow breathing I traced the planes of his chest, remembering what we had been through to get to right now. It may have been one of the best years and the worst years of my life mended together, but the reality of it was this—lying in a hospital bed with my dirty heathen and my flailing adorable spaz.

I was one *proud* Mama Wizard.

Jameson stroked my face. "Me either ... I'm actually a little worried about it. We don't have a clue what we're doing," he told me with a wary expression he'd had a lot these last few days.

The truth was—we didn't have a clue.

I glanced over at the parenting books on the metal tray next to me.

"We should read those." I looked up at him, and I almost burst out laughing at his expression of complete disgust.

He groaned.

"Those books don't make any sense. Who wrote them anyway?" His eyebrow arched. "I bet they don't even have kids."

"Did you even read them?"

"Well ... kind of," he grinned. "I'm more of a *hands on* type of guy." He leaned back against the bed with his fingers linked behind his head and an amused look on his face.

"Since you're so hands on ..." I handed him the baby. "I think he needs a diaper change."

You could literally see the blood drain from his face.

"I haven't had to change him yet ... Mom did it earlier and then the nurse."

"You said you were hands on ... get to it."

He took Axel in his arms gingerly. "Seriously?"

"Yes ... I can't get up."

Jameson had this look on his face as if I'd just asked him to commit a murder with me. Slowly, he turned on his heel and placed the baby on the changing table.

I could get up, but I was being lazy, not to mention I felt similar to that Michelin Tire guy, the only difference being my rolls were fat, and his were tires ... I think.

I couldn't believe how everything turned to a jelly-like substance after the baby came out. Why couldn't that just come out with the baby? This was something I'd never understand I guess. Now I understood why plastic surgeons were so busy with tummy tucks.

"Where are your diapers, little man?" Jameson asked Axel in the cutest voice I think I'd ever heard him use.

Axel simply let out a whimper again but didn't cry as Jameson began to change his diaper, all the while providing the baby with a commentary of what he was doing, which I found incredibly endearing.

Watching my husband with our son was probably right up there with feeling him touch my stomach while I was pregnant. I felt unbelievably close to him now.

All those years of being his pit lizard, I was so much more now.

Jameson, as though he could hear my thoughts, tilted his head at me with a wink.

I giggled when he held Axel up, and the blanket fell off, leaving him in just his diaper, blinking at Jameson. I almost said, "Hey, look, he blinks!"

"What are you doing?"

"Putting clothes on him."

"It'd help if you actually had clothes—that's a receiving blanket."

Jameson held up the blanket, examining it. "Well, no wonder I couldn't find the arm holes."

I giggled again and reached for the parenting books.

Our families stayed away that night and let us enjoy our baby together, alone. The nurse insisted we shouldn't sleep with the baby, in fear we'd squish him.

Did we listen? No, we slept in bed together, all three of us.

Being a mother was something incredible.

Aside from the physical abuse they put you through in the beginning, oh, and the late night cravings, and the smells of awful gas that you thought could never come from you. There was also the bloating, the gaining weight, mood swings, swelling, tiredness ... should I continue?

And then you have labor that quite literally made me rethink my gender selection.

What the fuck went wrong there?

Regardless, after that horrendous experience, you were handed this child. A brand new child. A child who had never experienced all the wrong that could happen in the world.

I'd heard people tell me that the child you had was the one you were meant to.

Did the child know that?

Or was it something where when they were assigning parental units, he got the short stick?

I honestly didn't think he would have chosen me willingly.

All that aside, I was handed a baby and expected not to ruin him.

I also couldn't understand why they didn't come with a manual. A car, any electronic device, hell, even my toaster came with a fucking manual. Why couldn't a child?

So there you were ... sweating like a pro wrestler and staring down at this tiny child who drew the short stick, hoping he couldn't sense the fear. And then their eyes opened, and you saw all those fears slip away.

After all, they were new. There was plenty of time to brainwash them into thinking you *did* know what you were doing.

The next morning our families arrived. This was another scenario where the result was not at all positive.

Five minutes after Alley and Spencer arrived with Lane, Jameson and Spencer were arguing about a football game on the TV, Alley was holding Axel and cooing non-stop to the point where it was actually annoying me, and Lane was being the cool little dude he was and making sure I had everything I needed. That part was enjoyable.

"Do you need ice?" he asked, ready to run to get it.

I looked at the full pitcher of ice and smiled at him. "You know ... I think I could use a little more, buddy."

He smiled, and off he went to find more.

What was not enjoyable was the fact that I just wanted to sleep in my own bed. I had also started breastfeeding, and Axel, being just like Jameson in every possible way, wanted to eat non-stop.

Shit went south when Emma showed up with a stuffed cougar for Axel. Jameson kicked her out, which damn near caused a fistfight between him and Aiden and then Spencer got involved. All three of them had to be escorted out by security.

Tommy, holding a bundle of flowers, stopped by as Jameson chatted with security.

Leaning forward, he kissed my forehead and snuck a glance at the baby in Alley's arms.

"He sure is cute."

"Thanks." I smiled up at him, adjusting my blankets. Tommy was not seeing the foodbags.

"Here," Alley offered, "hold him."

I laughed a little when he nervously held his arms as Alley handed Axel to him.

"We definitely know who the father is." Tommy laughed, looking at Axel's loops of rusty locks.

"Yeah, there's no denying that color."

"You know," he whispered when Alley began talking on her cell phone. "I'm really happy for the two of you. I was beginning to think I was going to need to knock some sense into you two."

I smiled. It was funny to me that everyone around us saw the changes occurring over the years between Jameson and me, but *we* ignored it.

An hour later, Jameson came back with ice cream and chocolate.

Of course, I forgave him. He had chocolate. I also thought the fight was somewhat entertaining.

It wasn't long, and I was feeling like I hadn't gotten the chance to snuggle with my son. It'd been a full twenty-four hours since he was born, and I think I'd gotten to hold him for maybe an hour. He'd been passed around so much I thought for sure he'd have motion sickness.

Jimi and Nancy couldn't believe how much Axel resembled Jameson as an infant. He even had the same scowl when things didn't go his way, which happened a lot. I wanted to tell him, "If you think this sucks, kid, wait until we take you home. At least there's supervision here."

When I finally did get to hold him, I spent hours surveying him. I memorized every little detail about him, from his rusty loops of hair, his adorable chubby cheeks, his cute button nose, his long fingers, and the tiny little rolls on his legs. Everything about him was perfect, and we created him.

It was hard to believe that what started out as complicated had brought us this perfect little being.

For only being born at thirty-four weeks, he was incredibly healthy—*tiny*, but healthy.

Aside from when he was delivered, we'd yet to hear him cry. The nurses assured us everything was fine, but it just seemed strange to me that a baby wouldn't cry. Even when he was hungry, he just simply let out an adorable flailing whimper.

Charlie came later that night, and Jameson stepped out with Van to get a real meal.

I loved that he and Van went out together. Van spent his fair share of time holding Axel as well, which sent me into a full-blown emotional shit storm. Much like the times I decided to watch *Father of the Bride* and the day Jameson and I got married.

I couldn't imagine how he must feel seeing us together as a family, knowing his was gone.

All this reminded me of the fact that the man currently holding my baby was dying. In the days following the wedding, Charlie's appearance was shocking. He was losing incredible amounts of weight, his eyes had dark circles under them, and some days he couldn't even form a complete sentence.

Today was a good day.

"He is beautiful, Sway."

"He is, isn't he?" I gleamed. I was one proud mama wizard.

"You havin' more?"

"I think I'll wait until I've actually left the hospital before that happens," I told him with the same enthusiasm I exuded after being told I had to go through labor in the first place.

I knew Jameson and I'd probably have more; after all, we did make one adorable flailing spaz.

"Don't worry, Axel Charles," Charlie assured him, "your parents are crazy, but they're pretty cool."

Axel stared at him as though he knew he was in for an interesting life.

Of course, I started crying watching my son and my father bonding. I was emotional. I cried at everything the last day or so. I thought this would have ended when he was born, but no such luck—in fact, it was worse.

The following day, I was released to go home, which was awesome. I hated staying in the hospital after having to spend so much time in one when I was pregnant with Axel.

Leaving was another story altogether.

It took Jameson, Spencer, Aiden *and* Van to figure out how to put the goddamn car seat in the Expedition. How this was so complicated was beyond me.

Once in the car and ready to go, Jameson was the doting father he'd become these last few days and had Axel so bundled up from the snow that I couldn't see anything but his tiny eyes.

"I think he's too hot," I told Jameson when he started the car.

Jameson turned around to look at us in the backseat. "*Nah* ... he's toasty."

"His little cheeks are red."

"'Cause he's toasty. I'd rather be toasty than cold."

"How do you know that's what he'd want ... maybe he likes the cold?" I suggested.

"No ... he doesn't," he said evenly. "Now let's go."

He then proceeded to pull onto Ensign Road at five miles per hour. Here was a NASCAR Champion driving five miles per hour because his infant son was in the car ... how ironic was that?

I made him stop at Norma's on the way home so I could get a hamburger. I was starving from that ridiculous shit they called food in the hospital. I was actually amazed some people didn't die just from ingesting that shit.

When we pulled into our driveway on Summit Lake, our entire goddamn family was waiting for us.

Jameson and I just sat inside the car for a few minutes, watching them, before Jameson turned around to look at us in the backseat.

"We're never going to get them to leave, you know that, right?"

"Let's just play nice, for now."

"So you say ... I'm tired." His head fell against the steering wheel. "This has been exhausting. I just want to go to bed."

"Really?" I challenged, smacking the back of his head.

"Sorry," he replied softly, ignoring my eye contact.

"That's what I thought. Now help us out."

With the help of my annoyingly protective husband, we made it inside the house and prepared ourselves for an evening with our family.

Jimi and Nancy brought over Papa John's pizza for everyone. I think I devoured half a damn box just by myself.

"Go get Lucas," I told Jameson after I finished feeding and changing Axel for the third time tonight.

Axel was constantly hungry and then constantly pooping. It was an endless cycle. Most parents said to be prepared for no sleep. Well, they should warn you that when they were awake, all they did was shit and eat.

Occasionally they cried.

"Why?" Jameson looked at me confused, his eyes following Lucas down the hall.

"He's wearing my maternity bra," I told him, rocking Axel in his room. "It's weird."

Jameson took off to find Lucas.

I was *not* impressed with Logan and Lucas that evening. They were either crying or laughing. I couldn't understand how two six-year-old kids could be so annoying.

Around nine that night, everyone finally left, and we were once again alone with the baby.

You know that feeling you got when everything was right in the world—you're calm and collected?

That was not us at all, especially when it came time to bathe him that night. Andrea and Nancy offered to stay, but we were adamant that we could do this on our own.

Halfway through the bath, I was ready to call them.

We had more soap and water on us than the baby, and let me tell you, we had an abundance of water and entirely too much soap for one baby.

Poor Axel just whimpered away. It was evident he sensed we had no idea what we were doing.

"You have too much soap on him," I told Jameson while he tried to wash his baby boy parts.

"No I don't."

"Yes ... yes, you do."

"No, I don't," he stated firmly, turning to glare at me, holding our soapy baby in the air.

What did Axel do? He peed mid-air all over Jameson.

This made me happy.

"Apparently *you'll* need more soap," I told him, handing over the soap and giggling hysterically.

My giggling turned to shrieking when Jameson turned Axel on

me.

I was now the one being peed on while Jameson laughed his ass off. This made me unhappy.

"*Whaaa* ... *whaaa* ..." Axel started crying and momentarily shocked us.

Momentarily because he was still peeing on us.

"See ... he doesn't like his mommy peed on." I smiled at both of them, holding a towel up to cover the stream.

"I'm sorry, little man," Jameson set him back in the water. "Mommy asked for that." He turned to look over at me, amused. "Husband one. Wife zero."

"Oh, hell no, we're not starting that again."

"Yes ... yes, we are."

For being only four days old, Axel made the most expressive faces. The one he was currently making made me smile. It was a set scowl at Jameson, and kind of resembled the one Jameson gave most people. He wasn't impressed with our argument. I guess I wouldn't be either, if I was naked in a bath, and the two people who were supposed to be washing me were arguing.

Eventually we finished the bathing ritual. I couldn't believe how much work these tiny humans were.

So far today, I got up, fed him, burped him, changed him, and then rocked him to sleep. I must have done that ten times.

Once I finished, and he was asleep for a nap, it started all over again a few hours later.

It was exhausting. I felt bad for women who had twins or triplets, or worse, six babies.

What were they thinking?

I didn't get any better at being a new mommy. In fact, I thought it took a turn for the worse after a few days. I couldn't understand where the normal version of me had disappeared to. It was like she was on vacation.

"Is that normal?" Jameson asked me.

"Is *what* normal?"

"The crying ... it can't be normal." He ran his hand over the back of his neck. "Can it?"

"What the fuck did you think was going to happen when we had the baby?" I snapped. "They cry."

"Well ..." He lifted my chin for me to look at him, tears falling down my cheeks. "I would expect it from the child ... not from you."

"I'm sorry!" I wailed. "I have no clue what I'm doing, and neither do you!" The baby's diaper was on backward, how that was possible was beyond me. You'd think he would have noticed when he put the straps on. This was our fifth day as parents, and one would think we would have been getting into the swing of things, but no. "I'm so tired. Last night I tried to breastfeed Mr. Jangles, thinking it was the baby. Imagine my surprise when I felt fur and him purring. I just need sleep!"

What did Jameson do? He started laughing.

"At least you didn't try to breastfeed me," his face became completely serious. "That would have been ..." He paused for a moment. "*Awkward.*"

I slapped his shoulder. "Can't you breastfeed? I need some sleep."

"Not happening. I don't care if Aiden thinks he can. I'm not doing it," he told me, taking the baby from me while I continued to cry. "But I *will* feed him the milk you've been pumping," he offered, looking down at me as I fixed my bra, gazing at the enormous foodbags. "They're huge."

"Don't remind me." I pushed them together for fun. "They resemble Dolly Parton's breasts, only full of milk."

Jameson just laughed and carried Axel out of our room so I could get some sleep in our new Egyptian cotton sheets Emma purchased for us.

And if you've never slept on Egyptian cotton sheets, you're missing out.

The following day, Jameson and I were supposed to do an interview with Maggie Summers from *SPEED*. Alas, there I was, hiding in our master closet from Dana.

While organizing my shoes by color out of pure boredom, I heard Jameson enter the room and open the door, smirking.

"Why are you on the floor? Get up." He reached for me. "The reporter will be here soon."

I put my fingertips to his lips, with a "Shh," and then mouthed the word, "Dana."

I didn't need to say much else.

"Who let her in?" he seethed in a flat but timid voice.

He was still scared of Dana, his peppy stalker fan, and for good reason. The woman had some stalker issues for sure.

"Emma."

"I'll fucking kill her." He went to stand, but I pulled him back down with me.

"If Dana sees you ... she won't leave."

His chin jerked up as he thought for a moment. "Good point. I know where Emma lives. I can pay her back later."

Emma and Aiden recently purchased a house together in Mooresville, next to the one Jameson had built for us. Jameson was not happy about that by the way. This was also why we planned to live in the Summit Lake house this year instead of the one in Mooresville. Sure, Jameson was going to spend the majority of the year on the road, but once Axel was a couple months old, we planned on traveling with him.

After much discussion following Axel's birth, we decided I would step down as General Manager at the track for now and concentrate on being a mom. Jameson hired Andrea to take over, which turned out to be a better idea. She was better at the planning than I was.

"How long has she been down there?" Jameson groaned, throwing one of his shoes at the wall.

"Ten minutes, maybe." I leaned back against the wall, pulling one of my black heels from under my ass.

He looked around the closet. "Where's the baby?"

I held up the monitor. "In his room with Lane."

We could hear movement on the monitor so I turned it up and listened.

"There, there, baby Axel. I take care you," then Lane started humming softly to him. "Me not allowed to pick you up so I just rock you." Lane let out a little giggle. "You sure are cute."

Both Jameson and I smiled listening to Lane pacify Axel who had started his little whimpering. He reminded me of a little puppy with the whimpering.

"How the fuck are we going to get out of here?" Jameson finally asked after thirty minutes in the closet together.

"I'll go check to see if she's gone yet."

I army crawled out of the closet and peeked over the stairwell to see Dana closing the door behind her.

Thank God.

I wasn't sure how much longer I could contain Jameson in the closet without resorting to sex, which wasn't an option. It had only been a week, and I had no fucking clue how in the hell the two of us would make it five more weeks without sex.

It was easier when I was on bed rest because he was gone for the majority of it, but now, he was home and constantly giving me these looks. The ones that had me wanting more than just reciprocating motions.

Testing for the upcoming NASCAR season would be starting up again after the New Year, so that would distract us, but it was going to be interesting.

Spencer and Aiden already placed bets on who'd crack first. Assholes. I only said that because their bets were against me.

Maggie showed up shortly after Dana left, and we did the interview along with a shit load of pictures for their magazine spread.

Jameson and I both hated being in the spotlight, but it came with a championship for him.

"Would it be possible to get some of you with the baby?" Maggie asked once the interview was completed.

"No," Jameson said in a hard, tight voice. "No pictures will be taken of Axel." I looked at him quickly and saw that his expression had turned violent.

"Why?" I whispered.

He didn't answer at first, just scowled. Maggie was on her way out before he finally murmured, "I don't want him exposed to all this just yet. The time will come when he can't escape it, but for now ... I want him to just be ours."

I understood him completely. Axel was innocent, and he was ours. The public hadn't seen him yet, and when they did, everyone would want pictures of him.

On New Year's Eve, we all gathered at Charlie and Andrea's house.

Jimi and Nancy were still in town, so once again, just like Christmas, all of us were together under one roof.

"Where's Charlie?" I asked Andrea when I walked into the kitchen. I'd just given our sleeping little boy to Alley to hold while the boys played some stupid drinking game I was sure would end in a fight.

Andrea gave me an apprehensive glance.

"Sleeping," she said softly while chopping the lettuce for the salad.

"Is he all right?"

I watched silently as she started to speak and then stopped, placing both hands on the counter.

"He called me Rachel last night when he woke up, and now he's confusing the twins ... I feel him slipping away Sway, and I just can't stop it. I've heard the doctors, and I've seen all the scans. I know we don't have long, but to think of it happening now ... scares the shit out of me." She leaned forward, her eyes darting around the room. "I can't handle those boys by myself."

"Don't look at me for advice," I told her, holding my hands up. "I mistook my cat for a kid and tried to breastfeed him."

Andrea laughed as Nancy walked into the kitchen.

Nancy reached over and rubbed my back as she walked past me. "Van says to tell you that he's on his way; he got stuck in traffic."

I laughed, reaching for the mushrooms to cut them.

It was as though Van had become my other child—even though he was older than me. I was constantly worried about him. All this worrying led to one thing. I insisted he move in with us in the guest apartment above our garage.

With the help of Jameson, he did. Since his wife and little girl had died, Van hadn't been around much of anyone. When I first met him, he was withdrawn but sweet. But ever since Axel was born, Van had become more open and welcoming with us all. He had no one but his parents and in-laws, and now he had us.

The more time he spent around Jameson, Spencer, and Aiden, though, the more he resembled a Riley.

All of that aside, when it came to our safety, Van was all business, particularly when it came to Axel now. Anywhere we went these days, Van was with us, with his eyes fixated on the baby and me.

Charlie was up around seven and smoking pot in the backyard when the Lucifer twins tried to go out there with him. Andrea had to explain that he was taking his medicine and they should not be around him.

Lucas threw a complete fit that resembled the kid from *Problem Child*. The only difference was Lucas had brown hair, not red.

"I just want to go out there with Charlie!" Lucas screamed.

This went on for a good hour, the Lucifer twins throwing fits over everything. Lane watched in amusement, and when Axel finally woke up from his catnap, he too gazed at them.

At least that was what I thought. The kid couldn't see more than a foot in front of himself, though, so he was probably staring at Jameson and me wondering what in the hell went wrong when he was assigned his parental units.

Thoughts of finding him a therapist resurfaced. I'd need to get on that sooner rather later.

Van finally showed up and joined the drinking game the boys were playing. I couldn't figure out exactly what they were playing, but I also never took the time. I spent most of my time feeding Axel and handing him around to everyone.

I wondered if they ever got motion sickness from all the handling. I knew if someone passed me around like that, I'd be hurling all over them. But I wouldn't mind being all swaddled and warm like he was. I wouldn't mind being rocked to sleep either—that did look appealing to me.

After a few hours of all this madness, we decided to stay here tonight with the roads being icy and Jameson drunk to the point he was now slurring his words.

"Three ... two ... one ... Happy New Year!" we all yelled together as we welcomed the New Year.

Jameson turned to me, smiling, and pulled me hard against his chest. "Happy New Year *wife*." His voice was low and gravelly, and I was shaking. It was hard to believe that just his voice could set my body on fire, but it did, or was it the lack of sex that had something to do with it.

"Let's go to bed ..." he suggested and began kissing down the side of my neck, pulling my sweater away, nipping at my skin.

"We can go to bed ... but you need to keep your hands to yourself, mister." I poked his chest.

His hand came up to rub the spot I poked, still smirking. "We can do *other* stuff ... we're good at *other* stuff."

He had a very good point there. If anything, the two of us had *other* stuff down to a fine art.

"You mean like reciprocating motion?" I asked with a giggle.

He growled pushing me against the wall in the hallway. "*Fuck*, honey ... don't tease me."

Once inside my old room, we were settled on the bed in a very heated over-the-clothes make-out session with reciprocating motion with a little porting of the heads, but to be fair, the clothes were quickly disappearing. His hands were so sure, so strong, and so completely inescapable as he moved against me.

"*Whaa ... Whaa ... Whaa!*"

Great timing, kid!

Jameson sighed. His head fell forward against my collarbone, but his hips continued to move against mine, wanting more, but so did Axel as he let out another cry.

"Seriously?" he grunted, still moving.

"Get used to it, Daddy." Pushing against his shoulders, I flashed him a smile that resembled Bob Barker from *The Price is Right*. "We're parents now."

Jameson just laughed and laid back against the headboard, adjusting himself.

I retrieved Axel from the bassinet, and when I picked him up, he made his signature puppy whimpering and snuggled closer to me. Laying him on the bed, I prepped myself for breastfeeding.

"I can't look at those." Jameson said and looked away. "I'll get distracted again."

I giggled while Axel whimpered again and started rooting his head around, searching for his foodbags. When I got him situated, he went right to town.

"Wow, he was hungry." Jameson's eyes got wide as he watched our son eat.

I laughed. "He's always like this when I feed him. He acts as though I'll never feed him again." My eyes met Jameson's when his hand was still on my ass, caressing it. "Kind of like *someone* else I know."

"Point taken," he grumbled and waited for me to finish feeding our son.

Although once the feeding, burping, changing, and rocking was finished ... the *other things* were dealt with. Many times.

As I said before, everything had changed.

In 365 days, 52 weeks, 8,765 hours, or 525,948 minutes my life had changed completely.

Then it started all over on New Year's Day, and who knew what this next year would bring.

Rebound – In shock absorbers, a rebound adjustment is a change to the dampening of the shock on the expansion stroke.

"I know you don't want to leave us, but it's your job," Sway told me as we stood in Axel's bedroom discussing my schedule for the next few weeks. "I understand." Her hand came up, brushing my hair away from my forehead. January had flown by with testing, and racing was now starting again.

"I know ... it's just hard now. I want you guys with me."

This last month since Axel was born, I had spent every minute I could with the two of them, enjoying the chance to finally be a family; even if it was only for a month, I'd take it. I'd take any moments I was given.

"We will be in Las Vegas with you," she offered.

"It's just not the same. Last year you were there at Daytona." I shrugged, looking down at my feet. "I just ... wanted you there, as my wife. It's lame, I know—"

Her finger silenced me. "It's not lame, Jameson. I know exactly what you mean."

I almost forgot how well she actually knew me.

We both turned to look down at Axel when he whimpered. Sway had him buckled in his car seat.

"What's on him?" she asked, examining his hair.

Kneeling down, I took a closer look. "I'm not sure ... it looks like ... you have to be fucking kidding me ... LOGAN!" I yelled after him.

Lane turned to Sway with an arm full of Legos.

"I not do that." He smiled. "Can I hold him?"

"Sure, buddy, just let me get this peanut butter out of his hair," Sway replied while I ran after Logan.

I found him hiding in our pantry, snickering to himself as he ate peanut butter with a spoon. I grabbed his scrawny arm and pulled him out, sitting him on the counter so I could look him in the eye.

"Listen to me," I growled. "Stop acting like an asshole."

He held out his hand.

"I don't think so. I only give money out to kids I don't want to corrupt. You start resembling a normal child and *maybe* I'll watch my mouth around you."

"He wanted peanut butter," Logan replied trying to defend his actions.

"He can't even talk. What would make you think he wanted peanut butter?"

Logan shrugged carelessly. "He whimpered."

"He always whimpers."

"Sorry," he finally said and reached for the peanut butter.

I snatched it before he could take it again—trying to restrain myself from laughing at his scared shitless expression. "No, no, you're done with the peanut butter."

This babysitting shit was hard work. How our family thought we could handle a newborn baby, the Lucifer twins, and Lane all at once was bullshit.

Lane was okay ... the twins were not. They hardly classified as *normal* children.

It was the day before I had to leave to Daytona for Speedweek, and the last thing I wanted to be doing was babysitting these shits today, but Andrea had to take Charlie up to Seattle for a doctor's appointment, and Alley and Spencer were at the doctor, as well, getting an ultrasound.

Logan had long since passed out next to me, but Lucas was another story. It was now close to nine o'clock, and I thought for sure he'd be asleep by now but no such luck.

I was almost certain he had this plan that if he annoyed me long enough I would eventually cave and give him chocolate so he would leave the room. You'd think at some point logic would have set in and I would have recognized a pattern, but no, I chose to ignore it. Ignorance is bliss.

"Is everything okay?" Sway asked, carrying Axel into the family room, amused I'm sure.

I shot Lucas a warning glare.

"Yes, everything is fine," I told her, feeling as though I might have gotten the situation under control, and not wanting to miss any more of *Dog the Bounty Hunter*.

The minute she walked in the kitchen, Lucas started whining again that the tape was hurting his arm. I hadn't had much experience with kids before, but was intuitive enough to know things were not going well.

I was blissfully engrossed in my show while simultaneously contemplating a career choice in the bounty hunting and pretending Lucas wasn't doing anything out of the ordinary besides jumping on the couch and looking for some sort of attention. I ignored him. He wasn't going to get attention from me. I was trying to watch a goddamn show and not think about Speedweek fast approaching.

Then he jumped off the couch, untied himself, and tossed the remotes directly at me. One hit me in the forehead, and the other hit the wall behind me, knocking over a glass on the end table.

Once I got hit in the face, I lost it.

"I warned you once," I told him, carrying him kicking and screaming up the stairs. I set him on the bed where they were going to be sleeping. "Now ... go to sleep."

"I'm not tired," he countered and sprung to his feet.

"Well, I suggest you get tired." I closed the door behind me, praying that Axel never acted like them. If he did, I would be sending the little asshole to boarding school as soon as permitted.

When I finally made it to bed that night, Sway was fast asleep with Axel. He was snuggled up against her chest in our bed, nuzzling his foodbags. I couldn't blame him. I wished I was doing the same.

Mentally, I was preparing myself for racing again, but emotionally I wanted to be here, with my family. This off-season had brought with it another reason for me wanting to be home with my family. *Axel.*

I lay there awake, watching my son and wife sleep, remembering these last few weeks with them. Between testing and being pulled in every direction possible by my sponsor, I was still able to find time here and there to be with him and Sway.

I couldn't tell you how attached I was to them. Not a minute went by that they weren't both in the back of my mind.

As careful as I could, I wrapped both arms around them and was asleep before I knew it.

There was the most annoying sound in the world disturbing my sleep, and it wasn't stopping.

I opened my eyes and blinked steadily into the darkness of the motor coach only to see my phone was blinking on the nightstand.

It was back to reality and entirely too soon for me.

Once I arrived in Daytona, I was in race form once again. Though I missed my family, I loved racing, and there was no denying that when I was at the track. It was in my blood and would be forever.

What I didn't love was the newfound fascination everyone had with my personal life.

It seemed everywhere I turned people were asking how my married life was or how my son was. I wouldn't mind telling them, but I also knew my words were never my words. Everything I said these days was misconstrued into something else entirely. So I kept my mouth shut.

I was always in a shitty mood when I had to get up early, but when

I was away from my family, it was worse.

Once I was surrounded by the obligations of the day, I was grumpy and that was never a good thing. Just ask Emma who was currently shoving posters in my face while I glared at her.

"How many more of these do you have?"

"Just sign them, asshole," she replied with a smile, handing over another.

Standing outside my hauler, I looked down the row of eighteen-wheelers lined up along the paddock. It was nice not to have to walk as far this year.

All the haulers in the paddock were lined up by the previous season's points. This meant I was now first in line instead of last like last year. Made for less walking, that's for sure.

I had some time to kill after my interview with ESPN—before the race started—so I sent Sway a text message, which she didn't return. It just made me miss her even more because I imagined she was incredibly busy with Axel, and it made me want to be there for them.

Speedweek flew by just the same as it did last year. The Budweiser Shootout seemed to blur right into the Duel 125s with all the sponsorship commitments I had, along with the unending amount of press. I was never alone these past few weeks, and if I was, I was sleeping, alone.

Sway couldn't bring Axel to the race so she stayed home, which was incredibly frustrating, but I knew I needed to get used to it.

I thought I'd said this before, but each season, rules changed, drivers changed, owners changed, and sponsors changed. The beginning of the season was a time for change.

Even the name of the series had changed sponsorship.

Since 1972, the Cup series had always been referred to as Winston Cup. Now it was being called the Nextel Cup Series.

The new season brought with it rookies needing to prove themselves. I went easy on them because not only was I in their shoes last year, but I was trying to be the better man this season and not such a hothead.

That newfound optimism ended when I had a run-in with Gibson Racing's new driver, Colin Shuman.

His first remark to me when we met at the drivers' meeting was, "So you're the chump who couldn't stand up against Darrin?"

"Don't pay him any mind," Bobby Cole, my teammate with Riley Racing, told me.

Not only was I appalled by the irreverence of Colin Shuman, I felt like someone had punched me in the stomach at the mention of Darrin's name, and, therefore, I reacted as such.

"Shut the fuck up," I told him as I took a few steps in his direction. Bobby and Tate had to grab me by the arms. "You have no idea what happened, so I suggest you keep your goddamn mouth shut."

Kyle was by my side in an instant along with Mason, Aiden and Spencer.

Immediately, I was thinking that this season would be a repeat of the shit I went through last season with Darrin, but it wouldn't be ... I refused to let it be.

The reporters were relentless with the questions about Darrin, and how I'd dealt with it over the off-season. The questions also swirled around my personal life and marriage to Sway, all of which I answered with the same answer.

"It's great."

As far as I was concerned, that was all they needed to know.

Before long, I found myself inside the car waiting for the green flag.

"Let's have a good day out here, bud. We are the defending champions. Let's show them what we're made of and start this season off right," Kyle, my crew chief, said as I finished adjusting my belts.

"Ten-four."

"Pull your belts tight. It's a long race. We've got five hundred miles so take your time."

Envisioning the race in my head as I always did, my thoughts drifted to Sway and the baby. I wondered what they were doing right now and was frustrated that I wasn't able to hear her voice this morning.

Last season during my rookie year, I had something to prove to everyone coming into the Daytona 500. Though that hadn't changed, it was a different kind of establishment. It was showing everyone I was a champion.

I wasn't optimistic, and I certainly wasn't hopeful, as you can't be in racing. Instead, I was sure.

When you thought about it, as a race car driver, your education never ended. Other drivers would school you any chance they got so you always had to be on your game. Every race, every track, every turn was a test of endurance, skill and disposition, a chance for you to demonstrate how much you knew and how much you have left to learn.

On tracks like Daytona and Talladega, you would run wide-open, holding the throttle down the entire lap. The only way for you to go faster was by drafting. The lead car would cut a hole in the air while the other cars drafted behind. You could either ride the free air all day—using less fuel—or you could use it as a passing tool.

If you were passing, when you'd gotten momentum, you could swing out and pass. Sounded simple but it wasn't. Drafting was a mysterious game. You either knew it or you didn't. It took practice to learn how the air moved over the cars and the feeling of the way the car moved through that air. Some never figured it out, just like some never figured out the grooves in dirt racing. It was a talent or an art, if you will. There are times when you think you've got it figured out and one wrong move of just an inch and you've been schooled by the superspeedway. You know nothing.

Kyle and Mason talking strategy interrupted my thoughts during the warm-up laps.

"Stick with Cole and Harris. It's our best chance at getting to the front."

"Green flag this time by," Kyle told me. "Push Harris in front of you, line up behind him."

Once the green flag dropped, I was on a mission. Tate and I worked together to move to the front. Daytona was a track that required drafting. If you fell out of line, you were hung out to dry.

I was running third, behind Shuman within a few laps, and I wasn't all that surprised we went from our nineteenth starting spot to third in twenty laps. Drafting does that. My car was awesome, and I was ready for him. Colin was too obvious with his movements so I could tell he was going to block me high. His movements were jerky and predictable, and he was nervous given it was his first Cup race and he knew I was faster.

Tate, who was lined up behind me, tapped into my frequency. "I'm with you when you go."

I could feel beads of sweat trickling down my face under my helmet, even with my cool air system; I was sweating like crazy.

"Outside at your door," Aiden announced. "Middle two. The ten and the ninety are with you."

I could see Austin Kennedy in my periphery, but I was just a fraction of a second quicker, and that was all I needed to pull in front of him going into turn two.

Austin darted in behind Cole two positions back in the draft leaving Shuman out to dry.

Every muscle was burning from the exertion of racing at Daytona as I fought each second not to fall out of the draft.

"Fourteen coming strong behind you," Aiden said.

Had I ever mentioned how much I hated seeing that number fourteen again? I was sure with my dislike for the actual number, you could gather Colin and me would never be friends.

Some five laps later, I was not expecting Shuman to take the air off me some and send me into the wall with his kamikaze drafting.

"Fourteen never lifted. Hit the wall in turn four, right side flat," Aiden told the crew. "Twenty-nine outside ... clear ... keep it low."

Way to start the season!

I immediately thought to myself: nothing was worse than spending the entire off-season preparing for the new season only to wreck the first race out.

Of course, this pissed me off. I flashed a few hand gestures and pushed against him when the caution came out with my mangled car. I was amazed I was able to drive it away after that.

"Asshole!" I yelled and bumped him once more. He pushed back, offering his own hand gestures.

It wasn't a friendly hello.

I was almost positive this would result in some words with NASCAR after the race and possibly some words with Shuman, which I'd be ready for after his earlier comments.

Kyle came over the radio as I pulled onto pit road. "Calm down, bud, we can still pull through with a decent finish here."

Aiden was also yelling something I couldn't quite make out about me being out of control, but because of all the commentary on my behavior my dad was now contributing to the conversation.

"I wonder if I could drive without the radio?" I asked myself during the pit stop.

"You copy, Riley?" Cole asked once I made it back up front after pitting twice to repair the damage.

"Fourteen at your door ... clear," Aiden interrupted.

"Ten-four, I think we should hold up," I said to Bobby. "The track's changing out here,"

"I agree. I was tight and now I'm loose. If we could get some momentum we could stretch it out."

"Stay with me, I think we can make it to the front if we stick together."

Kyle kept yelling for me to keep myself in check because I was extraordinarily aggressive the rest of the race, as were Cole and Harris. I couldn't help it, and apparently neither could they. First race of the season and this Shuman asshole was already trying to take me out like Darrin.

Cole and Harris, after last season, were protective of me on the track. It explained their aggression.

Anytime you add a new driver into the Cup series, they earned that rookie strip to be taken off their car. At this rate, Shuman wasn't earning his.

Gibson Racing really knew how to pick drivers.

Cole, Harris, and I made it to the front, but it wasn't enough to compete with Paul Leighty.

"Good job, bud. Way to pull through with a good finish," Kyle said as we crossed the finish line.

We managed to snag a fourth place finish, and just as I expected, NASCAR officials, along with Tate, Bobby, and Colin Shuman immediately surrounded me.

I knew I was driving like an asshole. I was all over other drivers being intentionally antagonistic.

Tate shook his head next to me, knowing what my reaction would be to this.

I flashed a quick smile at him and pulled myself from the car, all while Shuman wouldn't shut up. Like I said, Gibson knew how to pick 'em.

"I see marriage hasn't calmed you down," he smarted off. "Looks like your girl needs to put out for you, relieve some of that pressure so you don't drive like an asshole all the time."

I didn't say anything, just walked toward Tate as a NASCAR official followed close behind me. I knew I'd get myself in trouble if I said anything. I didn't know why he would feel the need to bring my wife into this, but the mere thought of it had me seeing red, and worse was the fact that this eighteen-year-old kid didn't seem to realize I was about to kick the shit out of him if he didn't shut his mouth.

"Don't tell me she stopped putting out already?" he snorted as he smiled cockily following me.

The red overruled, and I stopped thinking and started acting. I ripped my gloves and helmet off and started throwing punches at him. This kid was clearly an asshole and needed to be put in his place.

I didn't appreciate his remarks and thoughts on my private life.

I was only trying to teach him a lesson, school him off the track.

Tate did nothing but stand back and watch while an official pulled me off him. When I looked back at him, I realized I did some pretty decent damage, too. I was sure I'd broken his nose with the amount of blood coming from it, and maybe bruised his ribs a little. I was hoping I had cracked a couple.

Along with the ever-present reporters, the NASCAR official was in my face instantly, threatening to suspend me, which then caused me to start yelling back at him because, goddamn it, he was standing there the entire time. He was close enough to hear him taunting me.

Apparently, in NASCAR's rules, taunting doesn't equal an ass kicking ... who knew? I guess I didn't read that section of the rule-book. It must be under "detrimental to the sport" but taunting was not. But I'll tell you what. That detrimental to the sport shit was sure beneficial for them as the screaming fans still in their seats right now watching this will attest.

Kyle and Spencer pulled me away from the official who I was about to show the same lesson to. It took both of them to pull me away, forcing me toward the NASCAR hauler.

"What the fuck is wrong with you?" Kyle snapped, pushing me forward.

"He ... that ... he was saying shit ... and I ... *fuck*!" I couldn't even string a damn sentence together. I'd lost it once again. Just when you thought you had control over yourself and everything you learned had taught you something, you realized once again, you were no different than any other animal and always fighting for survival.

"Stop this shit!" Kyle said incredulously, yelling in my face. "I thought you would have learned with Darrin!"

Kyle knew better than to get in my face, or maybe he didn't. Either way, it just riled me up even further.

The fact that I was away from Sway, that it was the first race of the season and some kid tried to fuck with me by talking shit about my wife, had me in somewhat of an emotional, hormonal, testosterone, and adrenaline-ridden mess.

"Don't ever mention his name around me again, Kyle," I warned, jerking my arm away from him.

"Calm down," he huffed and stalked inside the hauler.

After a few deep breaths, I headed inside to face the fire.

Shuman was leaving just as I walked inside. We exchanged a heated glare, but other than that, he avoided me and for good reason.

I chuckled to myself that he was holding a towel to his face.

After a few minutes there, fuming with Kyle, Lisa opened the door and motioned for me to come in. Kyle waited as she didn't want to see him yet.

"It's good to see you, Lisa." I kicked my feet up on her desk after I took a seat in the leather chair to the left of her desk.

"Feet down, Riley," she snapped but smiled despite her clipped tone.

I was surprised to see I was joking around considering my shit-tacular mood.

"First of all ... congratulations on the baby," she smiled. "I hear he's cute."

"Pft ... look at his dad ... why wouldn't he be cute?"

She smiled and clicked her pen obsessively. "I see fatherhood hasn't calmed the Rowdy Riley down, has it?"

"Oh, *please*, that fucker was asking for it."

"Regardless, just because you're a champion, doesn't mean you can go around starting fights. You need to act like a champion. Going out there and roughing up the rookies is not the way to conduct yourself. Especially after last season."

Of course she would refer to last year.

Everyone seemed to like to remind me of what happened as though I forgot. Every single time I looked at my wife, I was reminded. Every time I looked at my son, I was reminded. And every time I looked at the championship trophy, I was reminded of how I got past it. Why they thought that reminding me would be beneficial to me, when I constantly reminded myself, was stupid.

I stood immediately, my temper rising again.

"I didn't start it!"

"Sit down," her glare had me sitting. "I know you didn't start it, but I'm not going to put up with shit this season. Act like an adult. Walk away for once."

I had no comeback for that one because when I thought about what I just said, I was acting like a child. I only nodded after that as she told me I was being fined, but she wouldn't issue probation if I kept out of trouble.

I left after that, only to be stopped by my dad.

"Where have you been?" he asked, following in step beside me.

"Uh ... bathroom?"

"Bullshit," his eyes narrowed. "You were in the NASCAR hauler, weren't you?"

My eyes flickered to his, but I kept looking straight ahead while a group of fans approached us. I shrugged once. "I just wanted to say hello to Lisa."

"Yeah ... I'm sure," he replied signing autographs beside me.

"You wanna catch some dinner before I fly home?"

I hadn't had seen much of my dad since New Year's. He left right after the holiday to prepare for the World of Outlaws season. Their series actually started in late January as opposed to mine that started in February. Being the owner of the team I raced for, he must have thought his presence was needed at the first race.

The fans around us distracted him so I asked again, "Dinner?"

"Sure," he agreed nodding. "How're Sway and Axel?"

I felt a smile graze my lips.

"Good. I can't wait to see them." I smiled even wider when I saw she was calling me. I hadn't seen her and Axel in nearly three weeks, and I couldn't wait to get home tonight.

"I bet," my dad smiled and shook his head as I answered my phone.

Blister – An overheating of the tread compound resulting in bubbles on the tire surface.

"I've had a good forty-two years, Sway," Charlie said randomly, his breathing labored as he lounged around my family room. "I've done everything I wanted to do."

"Don't talk like that, *Dad*," I told him, throwing a cookie his direction. "I don't want to think about it."

I knew by his appearance it would be any time now, but just as I had always done, I denied it. Avoided it. I'd perfected denial to the point where it worked well for me.

Emma had flown in this morning so when Charlie started talking about dying, she was bawling.

"Stop it," I whispered, throwing a cookie at her as well.

"I'm trying ... it's just that ..." she burst into tears again and shoved another cookie in her mouth.

I'd been into baking this week and had made four dozen oatmeal raisin cookies as well as a pot roast today, alone.

I received a Kitchen Aide as a wedding present, and I was making use of it. It was as though, by baking, I was trying to keep my mind off the fact that my dad only had days left, and my husband was across the United States.

"Okay." I threw my arms up in the air. "I can't handle either one of you right now. Stop this."

They both stared at me like I'd lost my mind, and I was fairly certain at this point I had between the lack of sleep I was getting and my new obsession with baking.

I had a hunch when Charlie came over here this morning that he came for a reason.

Again, I was in avoidance.

It was Sunday afternoon, and the race was in the pre-race ceremonies when Jameson came on the television. Axel, though he couldn't see very well, turned his head in the direction of the TV when he heard his daddy's voice. His brow furrowed in concentration.

I listened carefully as he talked about the off-season and his expectations for this coming season.

"I spent most of my time with my family. I've been testing in Phoenix, Loudon, and Atlanta, but other than that ... it was just enjoying my wife and son."

The announcer laughed at his wide grin, as did all of us.

"So you got married and had a kid all in the three month off-season, busy weren't you?"

"Yeah ... I was." He waggled his eyebrows at the end of his lewd statement, and I wanted to punch him.

Emma and Charlie laughed.

I hardly thought that was appropriate but giggled anyway.

"Do you have a chance at winning here today? Win the championship and come back and win the Daytona 500? How cool would that be?"

Jameson threw his head back and laughed.

"Yeah ... it'd be pretty cool. We weren't that great in qualifying, and our last practice run we changed the setup quite a bit so we'll see ... you never know. Daytona is tricky. You can be leading one minute and the next you're running forty-third. It's the luck of the draw and how well you partner up with other drivers in the draft."

"What do you think of these rookies this year having been in their shoes last year?" Neil asked Jameson.

I could tell by that point Jameson was done with the interview, but he continued to give his attention to the reporter while simultaneously signing autographs for the swarm of fans surrounding him.

"Well, I've only met a few. I met Colin Shuman this morning, and I can't say I was impressed but ..." Jameson shrugged. "I know when I started ... it was all about finding your groove and proving yourself, and I suppose that's what they're all workin' toward this race."

Jameson turned away from Neil, making it clear that the interview was done.

Before Neil walked away, Jameson did send us a quick hello.

"I just gotta say hello to my beautiful wife and son at home. I love you, honey, and I'll see you guys tonight."

I cried and reached for the cookies in front of me.

Most of the afternoon went this way with Charlie talking randomly about death in between his catnaps and leaving Emma and me in tears.

I wasn't sure how much more either of us could take without snatching his weed from him just to relax. Believe me, if it wasn't for breastfeeding, I would have taken it when he first walked in the door this morning.

Charlie woke up soon after the race was under way and watched with us for a little while before he fell asleep again.

In my gut, I knew this was the end, and that made the day even worse.

After watching a few reality TV shows with us, Andrea picked him up to take him home, and I made sure I gave him an extra-long hug goodbye, as did Emma.

"I love you, Dad."

He smiled, a real smile, one I hadn't seen since he saw Axel for the first time.

"You've made my life what it is, kid," he told me and kissed my cheek before he left. "I love you."

Closing the door behind him, I was met with Emma and a mouth full of cookies.

"How fucking sad can one afternoon be?" she wailed, cramming another one in, then started choking on them as crumbs flew from her mouth.

"Stop putting them in your mouth while crying," I replied, smacking her back. "You'd think you would have learned that as a child."

Axel was still in his bassinet in the family room so Emma, currently choking, and me, crying, walked back in there and flopped down on the leather chair.

"I know that was his goodbye ... I just know it," I mumbled, reaching for the remote next to me.

"I know, right. I feel the same way," Emma agreed reaching for Axel, still coughing.

"Why don't you wait until you've stopped coughing," I suggested, handing her a glass of water, taking Axel from her.

"Good idea."

Axel whimpered as he usually did, snuggling into my arms.

He'd be two months old next week, and every day he reminded me a little more of Jameson.

He hadn't lost any of his rusty loops of hair. Instead, it was thicker and hardly tamable. His eyes were lighter as green hues began to peek through. The best part was that he was gaining weight.

The first month we had a hard time getting him to gain any weight, but now he was packing on the pounds, and I was losing them from breastfeeding, which I loved.

I should clarify. I loved losing the weight. I hated breastfeeding.

Who in their right mind would want a child using their nipples as a feeding device?

I got that it was supposed to make you feel closer to your child, and was incredibly healthy for the baby, but I really didn't enjoy it, at all.

Let me explain the bad sides I discovered. When I first started, it was excruciatingly painful. It was as though he felt he needed to bite down on my nipples to get any milk out. I tried to assure him this wouldn't help matters, and all he needed to do was suck, but I was almost positive he had no clue what the fuck I was talking about.

Then, after he got the hang of sucking for his food, my nipples began to crack and bleed. Not enjoyable … at all. I wasn't sure what he got more of, blood or food.

"Do you have any milk?" Emma asked, heading for the kitchen for more cookies.

"Yeah … look in the side door." I smiled. "Make sure you grab the one in the carton, not in the bags."

Axel whimpered, letting me know he was ready for his dinner.

I would say that breastfeeding was getting easier, but I still wished he were a year old so I could stop.

Later that night, Emma and I cuddled in bed with Axel watching a *Friends* marathon when my phone rang. I figured it was Jameson letting me know he'd be home soon, but I was surprised and sad to see it was Andrea.

My heart was immediately pounding in my chest uncontrollably when she asked, "Sway?"

I handed Axel to Emma knowing I couldn't hold him right now. "Yeah it's me, what's up?"

She paused, and right then I knew what it was. "Andrea … please don't …"

"I'm *sorry*, Sway. I'm … I …" She hesitated as her tears broke through. "I'm sorry, sweetie."

I stared at my feet, frozen with shock, my mind resisting her words.

Without collecting my thoughts, or gathering my composure, I called Jameson, while simultaneously throwing up.

I felt the rush of adrenaline course through my body, waiting for him to answer. The burning started in the pit of my stomach, bubbling to the point where it felt as though it was acid, destroying me, and crippling me where I stood. My arms and legs were tingling, trembling with a nervous energy and pain.

I tried to speak when he finally answered, but all I managed to say was his name as Emma held me.

"Jameson ... please ..."

"Sway?"

All I could hear on the other end was crying—hysterical crying. Instantly, I was thinking something was wrong with Axel or maybe she was hurt somehow. "Sway? What's going on?"

There was still no response, but I could faintly hear Emma's soothing tone comforting her.

"Jameson?" Emma took the phone.

"Emma," I sighed in relief that someone was there with her. "What's going on? Is something wrong with Axel?"

Emma let out a strangled sob. "It's Charlie."

Oh, God!

Dad was still standing beside me, though he was now on the phone with Wes, lining up flights for us.

"All right, we'll meet you there. Thanks Wes," he hung up and motioned for me to follow him.

"Emma? Is Charlie ..." My voice failed me. I couldn't bring myself to speak over the lump lodged in my throat. "Did he ..."

"Yes," she managed to squeak out and continued crying. "He's ..."

She didn't need to say it, I knew.

Before I left three weeks ago, he was fading fast. I knew it was only a matter of weeks, but I wanted to be there for Sway when it happened.

I finally had to hang up with Emma. She and Sway weren't making any sense.

I called Andrea to make certain she was all right.

"Jameson?" Andrea answered meekly on the first ring. "Are you okay?"

Am I okay? Seriously? How could she be worried about me right now?

"Andrea, Emma just called."

"I know ... I called Sway," she told me in a hushed voice. "It's Charlie. He's gone—I'm sorry."

I felt as though my heart broke into a million pieces and someone punched me at the same time.

Oh, God, how I want to be with my wife right now.

Dad sensed what had happened and started frantically rubbing my back, assuring me we'd be there shortly as I leaned against the side of the hauler for support. I couldn't walk.

"Are you okay, Andrea?"

"I don't think it's sunk in yet," her voice cracked. "The boys are at the neighbor's, and Nancy just got here. Van is bringing Emma and Sway over."

"Okay ... I will be there in a few hours."

It took four hours and one speeding ticket to reach Elma, but we made it. Tears couldn't be helped when I saw the complete look of devastation on my wife's face.

How much more would this woman have to endure in her life?

I shook my head in disgust that, once again, I wouldn't be able to protect her from this. I had no control over what happened to Charlie or her mother. All I could do was be there for her—be the husband and father to our child that she needed.

When I walked into the living room of her childhood home, I couldn't believe how many people had already gathered there. Tommy was there, Mallory and Bryce had shown up, and even Justin and Ami were already there. Our support system was gathering.

I searched the room and saw Sway in the corner, sitting in Charlie's chair, holding Axel. Her eyes were swollen, her face flushed, and her shirt was soaked from her tears.

I instantly ran to her.

"Sway ..." I breathed, clutching her tightly.

Nancy took Axel from her as Sway wrapped her arms around my neck.

I needed to get her home, away from everyone. It was evident by her appearance she needed to be alone right now and not in a room full of people.

Nancy reached for her, as well.

"I've got her, Mom. Emma, get my keys." I was careful as I could be, gently picking her up. I was clutching her so tightly I was afraid she couldn't breathe, but she only held me tighter, clinging to my chest. I was trembling, struggling to gain some sort of self-control for Sway's sake. She needed her strong husband, not the emotional wreck I'd been on the flight home.

"Make it stop," she pleaded. "Please ... make the pain stop."

I wanted to make it stop for her. I'd give anything to take the pain away.

Alley pointed at her watch. "Jameson ... what are we going to do? You have an appearance tomorrow in Charlotte."

"Cancel it," I growled. I couldn't believe she would think I would do it after this.

"It's not that easy, Jameson. It's for your sponsorship with Simplex on the sprint car team. You requested this one."

I spun on my heel to face her.

"Cancel the goddamn thing, Alley!" I pulled Sway closer. "I can't even believe you'd think I would leave right now."

It wasn't right for me to yell at Alley, but my wife needed me. For once, I'd be there for her.

I wasn't going to deny her, not now, not ever. I wouldn't care if my career ended. None of that mattered.

What mattered was in my arms, begging me to take the pain away.

"Dad," I tried to keep my voice even and controlled. "Can you please call Simplex for me and explain ... I can't leave her. See if Justin can fill in for Rockingham this weekend," I requested, taking a deep breath to calm myself. I looked at my mom holding Axel tightly against her. "Mom, can you guys take Axel tonight?"

We hadn't left him with anyone yet, and though the idea scared me, Sway didn't need to worry about having to take care of him.

I carried Sway to the car and drove her back to our house on Summit Lake, never taking my hands off her. I wasn't letting her go.

She tried her hardest to control herself the entire way, but at some point, I realized it was a doomed effort for her.

When I pulled into our garage, Van was there, pacing back and forth.

"Is she okay?" he asked in a concerned voice, his eyes examining her. "Can I get you anything?"

I only nodded as he helped me get her inside.

"If you need anything ... just let me know," he offered.

"Thanks, Van. I really appreciate everything you've done for us."

I quickly scooped Sway up and took her straight to our room. As we reached the bed, I pulled her into my arms and silently rocked her.

This seemed to have brought on a new round of weeping, and all I could do was hold her. It was all I wanted to do. She took all of her emotions out on me, and I hoped my being there was at least some comfort to her while she was in pain. She cried loudly, and I was glad we were alone.

Sway's tears were relentless, and she cried much longer than I would have suspected; but then again, I was surprised it wasn't longer.

Christ, she'd just lost her father. Who wouldn't be crying?

All throughout his sickness, when she finally found out, Sway remained positive. I knew this was the front, her denial, but that was Sway—always had been. When she was hurting, she smiled, never letting you know it was killing her inside.

As I held her that night, sometimes she would quiet slightly, only to pick up with more force. I was at a loss, trying to comfort her with quiet murmurs and loving strokes. Mostly, I just held her, as that seemed to be the best option at this point.

Every tear that slid down her cheek was like a knife with serrated edges stabbing me in the heart. It was more than I could stand to see her in this type of pain.

When she finally fell asleep, her tears didn't stop.

I watched her all night. My own pain, I could handle. Hers, I could not. This was almost unbearable.

The sun finally rose, and a new day seemed to finally dry the tears.

She had quit crying by the time she awoke, though I knew it would be temporary. When the disorientation from sleep wore off, she would remember what happened, and the pain would come again.

"Hey," she cleared her throat. "Where's Axel?"

I stared at her intently. She *seemed* better, but I couldn't be sure.

"With my mom. Are you … all right?"

"I'm fine," she insisted, as though she was trying to convince herself.

I grabbed her face in my hands, forcing her to look at me. Her eyes were swollen and red. I gently ran the tip of my thumb over her lips.

She looked at me intently, tears filling her eyes again.

"I'm so sorry, honey," I soothed, rubbing her back and rocking her back and forth on our bed.

"I just … can't believe he's really gone," she murmured into my chest and then burst into tears again. "I don't want it to be real."

"I wish it wasn't real," I told her and pulled her closer. "I really do."

It was real, though, and we had to deal with it.

Blown Motor – This would be a major engine failure, like a connecting rod going through the engine block. Blown motors usually produce a lot of smoke and steam.

"Thanks for everything you guys have done," I wailed against Nancy's shoulder, as she and Jimi both hugged me tighter. "I've always felt like you two were my second set of parents."

Jimi, Nancy, and Emma had taken care of everything for us with the funeral. I could hardly function let alone plan a funeral.

If it weren't for Jameson and Axel, I'd probably still be curled up on the floor by the phone.

Had you ever heard that saying, "Everything happens for a reason?"

What a crock of bullshit that was.

Shitty things happened to good people all the time—Charlie, my mom, Van. And good things happened to shitty people—Darrin.

What seemed to cross my mind the most was how was I supposed to feel about this? Was I acting the way I should? If not, how was I supposed to react?

The man I looked up to my entire life, who raised me on his own, was dead. As in gone ... forever ... never coming back. I would never see him at the track again. I would never walk downstairs from my room to see him engrossed in the Sunday paper and eating Coco Puffs or a maple bar donut with chocolate milk.

I glanced out the small window next to me and watched everyone who passed on the street below, going about their daily lives.

Did you ever wonder what they were thinking? How their lives were going?

I did.

I wondered if they faced the same day-to-day shit that everyone else had to. Did some people have it easier? From up here, from a perspective, everything looked fine as if nothing in their life was shitty.

But from what I'd learned, people displayed their emotions differently, and generally, something about their lives was shitty in some way. They were just hiding it well.

When I was in college, I read a book by Elisabeth Kubler-Ross called *On Death and Dying*. Elisabeth described the five stages you went through when dealing with grief and tragedy.

There was denial—trying to imagine it was not true. We didn't want to think it was true. Who really wanted to face reality anyway? Clearly not me.

We got angry with everyone. We were angry with people who'd never experienced the pain and angry with ourselves for having to deal with it.

Then we begged and pleaded, offering up anything we had to not feel the pain, or just have one more day, one more moment.

When that didn't work and anger wasn't worth it, we got depressed until we accepted that we'd done everything we could have done. We let go. But how did you get to that point and go on living? How did you accept the change and become the person you once were?

My anger was what hit me first. It started slow and hung on tight, steady, never letting go.

I couldn't sit still, couldn't eat, couldn't sleep, and couldn't focus on anything but the wave of rage that had taken over.

When the anger finally let go a little, the pain hit.

I wanted to cry, but tears seemed too small, too inconsequential for the void I now had.

I wanted to forget, but forgetting my parents would be like forgetting myself. I didn't want to forget anything. I simply wanted to *remember*.

I struggled to my feet and made my way across the attic, shoving years of memories into boxes and trying to ignore the fact that I felt like this was over. My childhood, my memories of them were trapped inside those boxes.

Moving methodically, removing anything and everything that reminded me of them until there was nothing left. I wanted to run, to scream, to destroy, but I knew that wouldn't help anything. I wanted anything but to feel the pain I felt without them here.

It didn't feel like I just lost Charlie. It felt like I lost my mom all over again once I was in the attic surrounded by her memories.

It'd been years since I'd been up here, and when I was, it was usually during a game of hide-n-seek. I was hardly up here to snoop through boxes then, as hiding was imperative. To say I was serious when playing hide-n-seek was an understatement. I once punched my little friend, Leslie, in the face when she gave my secret location away. Talk about hard-core.

I reached for a photo that was lying to my left. It was of Charlie and me when he first bought Grays Harbor Raceway—I was six. We were standing by the ticket booth, and he was holding the title in his hand. I was on his shoulders, smiling. We looked so happy, so carefree, but the funny thing was that we were.

Did I have regret?

Yes. I wished I had more time with them. My mother was twenty-five when she died and Charlie was forty-two.

How was that fair?

I only wished I had more time with them. I wanted, hell, I had no idea what I wanted. I wanted to say it was enough to whomever it was that was deciding how much I was dealt. I wasn't sure how much more I could handle.

I'd been up here all morning going through old boxes, remembering, avoiding everyone downstairs. Andrea was cooking with Nancy.

Spencer, Aiden, Van, and Jameson were doing God knows what with Lane and the twins, and Alley and Emma were ... actually, I had no clue what they were doing besides annoying me.

The next person who asked how I was would probably get punched.

It seemed everyone downstairs didn't know that if they were in the kitchen, I could hear them through the vents. When I was younger, this worked in my favor on many occasions to know when my dad was coming upstairs. I always had just enough time to hide any discriminating evidence.

Aiden and Spencer were arguing about something, but I couldn't decipher what.

I laughed when I heard Spencer grumble, "Excuse me while I find my balls. I've misplaced them somewhere."

"Get used to it, dude," Aiden said. "Your wife is having a little girl in four months."

I shuffled through the box of Rachel's belongings that had been left up here and noticed an envelope marked with my name. I'd never seen it before, and it remained unopened.

Once I opened it, I'd wished I hadn't.

Again, I was crying abnormally, only now it was amplified by my post-pregnancy emotions and the loss of my father. Shit-storm was the only word I could think of to put those few moments into perspective for you.

The thing with grief was that it looked different on everyone.

I watched everyone once I made my way downstairs, observing how grief looked on them and wondering if that was how I should be acting. Was I responding in the ways Elisabeth Kubler-Ross described I would?

Andrea was standing in the kitchen, baking with Nancy and Alley. When you thought about it, it wasn't only death you were grieving. It was life and the changing of your life that you were grieving.

Our lives would forever be changed by one moment.

I wanted to know why it hurt so bad. Why good things always follow with bad. I just couldn't wrap my mind around this.

I also thought that was how you stayed alive. When it hurts so much you couldn't breathe, that was how you survived. That was how you moved on from that numbing feeling. By remembering that, someday, somehow, you wouldn't feel that way. It wouldn't always hurt this much, and eventually, you'd find solace.

When I walked into the living room later that morning, I found Jameson in Charlie's old chair with Axel, intently watching the NASCAR race.

I smiled, knowing he missed the race for me.

He seemed fine with it, or maybe he was feeling the same as me. Charlie was a father figure to him as well. His expression was blank as he stared at the television like he didn't have any more room for thoughts.

Noticing how everyone around me was acting, I also knew that grief came in its own time for everyone and in its own way.

Don't be surprised if you didn't feel the pain right away. It'd come eventually. Believe me.

The best you could do, the best anyone could do, was to be honest with yourself and don't deny how you feel. Just feel something, anything, because feeling was the first step toward healing.

I couldn't find the twins, but I had an idea as to where they were.

When I opened the door to Charlie's closet, I found them, crying in the corner and holding each other.

So far, since I'd met them, I'd never once felt bad for them ... *until now*.

They may be the Lucifer twins, but they were still only six years old and had just lost their father, the only father they knew. It brought me back to when my mom died, and I was sitting in her closet during the funeral, alone.

Nobody was there to comfort me, but here they had each other ... and they had me.

The *really* shitty thing, the very worst part of the grief that consumed you, was that you couldn't control it. The best you could do was just let yourself feel it when it came and let it go when it passed.

I sat down with the boys, pulling them into my arms.

"S-w-w-way ..." Logan cried against my shoulder. "P-P-P-Pleass-seee not leaveeee u-u-sss," he hiccupped and cried louder.

"Don't worry," I told him. "Who else would annoy me the way you two do?"

"We ... miss him," Lucas cried, throwing his arms around me.

For me, I thought the worst part about feeling this way was the moment I felt among the living again, it started all over again. And every time—every goddamn time—it took my breath away and completely crippled me.

"Can we come live with you?" Logan asked after a few minutes, still crying with an extreme amount of snot coming out of his nose. His arm rose to wipe the snot on the sleeve of his black jacket.

I'd admit they looked adorable in their little suits.

"No," I told him, in the nicest voice I could. "I'm afraid I'd murder one of you ... but I love you guys. So ..." brushing his chocolate hair out of his eyes, he looked up at me. "I think it's best if you stay with your mom, here in this house. And, for Christ's sake, have her cut your hair."

Lucas looked over at me, ignoring my comment about his hair as he, too, pushed his out of his eyes. "We don't have to move?"

"No ... this is your house to stay in."

I stayed in the closet with Logan and Lucas for close to two hours before Jameson came looking for us.

We were in our second game of Go-Fish by the time he found us.

I watched the twins make their way downstairs, thinking of the way grief had looked on them and realizing that even though everyone looked different, and acted, there were still five stages regardless of the appearance.

When the denial slowly moved to anger, we usually wanted to bargain for more time, more of anything. Then came that blinding depression.

But then, just when you think you couldn't take much more, you *finally* reached acceptance. You could try to avoid it as I usually did, but the reality was, sooner or later you had to accept they were not coming back.

Whether it was anger, depression, denial, or blame, none of that would bring them back.

I sat there watching the race on TV with Axel—Justin was racing for me. It sucked missing the race, but there was nowhere else I'd rather be than with my family.

Axel whimpered in my arms, snuggling closer to me after I fed him his bottle. Poor Sway was in no condition to be breastfeeding today. It was comforting to me that just so much as taking care of our son today was helping her through all this.

The announcers on TBS caught my attention when they began speaking as to why I wasn't at the race. It started by them talking with Justin as he stood on the grid next to Bobby before the race.

"Now Justin, you raced for Jameson back in late July last year after his wreck in Pocono ... how do you feel being in these full-sized cars again."

"I'm wondering where the wing is?" Justin teased, glancing over the car like he was inspecting it. "Oh." He pointed at the spoiler. "That must be it."

Bruce, the announcer, laughed. "Yeah, that must be it. Can you handle this beast?"

Justin laughed again.

"You tell me," he pointed at the tree in the infield of Rockingham where it read number nine as the number one starting position.

"Fair enough." Bruce nodded. "Well, good luck today without the wing. Do you think you can pull off a win here for the Riley family?"

"I hope that we can." Justin nodded with a smile. "It would be great to win here today for that team. They deserve that much."

The broadcasting station then cut back to the regular tower announcers where they talked about Charlie and what happened.

Leaning back in the chair, I placed Axel against my shoulder to burp him, hoping he didn't puke on me. I couldn't handle the puke on me—it was repulsive.

"That family has had its fair share of turmoil in the last year," Rocky said, a former Cup driver who was now broadcasting the races for TBS. "Here you have Jameson, involved in that wreck in Pocono last July and in a constant battle with the former driver of the number fourteen Wyle Product Chevy." I found it entertaining that even the news reporting stations wouldn't say his name these days. "Then his wife was involved in a horrific accident in the grandstands in Loudon in September of that same year. Having just given birth to their first son, this was not the kind of heartache the family needed," Rocky explained.

I hated that they were discussing this on national television, but it was what it was. It came with the territory. Everyone wanted to know why I wasn't racing this weekend, and for the fans who supported me every week, they deserved to at least understand why.

"Jimi Riley, owner of Riley Simplex Racing released this statement Wednesday morning: "We appreciate all your support during our family's time of need. Jameson will not be racing this weekend in Rockingham. Justin West, driver of the JAR Racing number nine Simplex/Power Plus Outlaw sprint car, will fill in for the Rockingham race. Jameson will be back in the car for the Las Vegas race."

"With everything this family has been through you only wish that they can get a break from all this heartache at some point," Rocky said, looking to Larry, the other announcer in the booth.

"We haven't talked a lot about this family in the past, but on both sides, Jameson and Sway's families come from a long line of racing blood," Larry said conversationally. "You've got the Riley side where Jameson's grandfather, Casten Riley, who built, from the ground up, one the largest sprint car and stock car engine manufacturers in the Midwest—CST Engines out of Bloomington, Indiana. Jimi, Casten's son, followed in his footsteps into the Outlaw series and then came

Jameson who has made NASCAR history in just one season. Now you look at the Reins' family and Charlie's dad, Luke Reins, who raced sprint cars around the Northwest until he passed away from diabetes in his late forties. In the spring of 1987, soon after the passing of his wife, Charlie bought Grays Harbor Raceway, which happened to be the first track his dad ever raced. Now Jameson owns the track and his wife, Sway, is heavily involved in the day-to-day operations. Racing is a huge part of their family and always will be."

Rocky spoke up again as I moved Axel back to my lap where he sprawled out, stretching after his meal. "You know we haven't talked a lot about this over the years, but we lost Ron Walker last year in Williams Grove, and now the racing community loses another great track promoter, Charlie Reins. When he took over ownership of Grays Harbor, he was quickly drawing in the track sponsors and cars flocked to the shady side."

They went on to talk a great deal about track promoters and how the racing world wouldn't be what it was without these guys selling the sales the way they did.

Ryder showed up after that. I thought he'd be in Ocala, so when he walked in wearing a tie, I choked on my beer.

"What are you doing here?"

Ryder smiled down at Axel. "Nice to see you, too."

"I didn't say it wasn't good to see you, man ... just caught me off guard." He leaned forward and patted my back before removing the blanket over Axel to get a good look at him.

"Sid is driving for me tonight," he said, sitting next to me. "I leave in the morning, but I wanted to stop by."

I knew why he came. Racing, in a sense, was all about who you knew. We got introduced to car owners that way, sponsors ... that was how the sport operated.

Look at what happened to me at the Chili Bowl when I was introduced to Tate.

Ryder knew Charlie from back in the days when he started racing quarter midgets in the late eighties. At the time, Grays Harbor was one of the fastest tracks around, and everyone wanted to race there. It wasn't uncommon for the kids from the east to venture out to Grays Harbor.

So every year Ryder came out at least a few times and got to know Charlie. Charlie then introduced Ryder to Sid Donco who owned Donco Controls.

Donco Controls had been sponsoring Ryder in the USAC divisions since he was fourteen years old. Right there goes to show you it paid to treat *everyone* with respect in this industry. You never knew when you could be working for them at some point.

Ryder and I made small talk for a few moments before I focused on the television again as they started the pre-race activities. Ryder laughed when he saw Justin. "He looks awkward."

"He's looking for the wing."

"I bet he is," Ryder laughed.

Spencer walked into the family room, where we were sitting, holding Lane by the ankles. They sat down in the chair next to Axel and me.

Lane looked over at me as the race began.

"Can I hold him?" his expression was anxious.

It was hard on the kids. I was sure they had no idea why all the grown-ups were crying.

"He just ate," I told him. "Are you sure?"

Lane seemed to contemplate this for a moment before nodding. "I want to."

Spencer helped him, and soon Axel was sound asleep in Lane's arms. I decided it was time to stretch my legs for a moment and then find Sway. I left her in the attic this morning, knowing she needed some time alone. I wasn't really sure what to say to her. She was only twenty-three and both her parents were now gone—nothing I said would be comforting.

When I walked toward the front porch, I heard my name mentioned from a group of women talking amongst themselves. I recognized the one as Mallory and the other looked to be Jen, our new media relations staff member for Grays Harbor.

"How's Jameson holding up?" Jen asked Emma who approached them.

Emma smiled as she always did. "He'd never let on, but I know he's hurting inside."

"He can't stand to see Sway in pain," Mallory added.

I leaned against the wall when I saw Sway sitting on the porch staring at the driveway and listened to the conversations surrounding me.

Everyone asked the same thing: "How's Sway?" followed directly by, "How's Jameson?"

Why did people care how I was? I wondered, but just hearing those brief conversations, I understood. I understood because I wasn't okay. Just like my wife, I was hurting. I'd known Charlie even longer than I'd known Sway.

People filed in and out of their home, paying their respects. It made me sick to my stomach any time I thought how he was actually gone. I kept thinking he'd come down the hall any minute and yell at Logan for something ... but he wasn't. It seemed the hardest part about all of this was acceptance.

No one liked change, and permanent change was even worse.

Jameson stepped onto the porch, his hands buried deep in the pockets of his dark trousers. He leaned against the railing, the sleeves of his gray dress shirt rolled up to his elbows. I watched his slow steady breathing when leisurely he lifted his hand to run it through his hair—his head slumped forward, staring at the ground.

I had snuck out here when everyone started talking about Charlie firing the staff from the track. I was really going to miss the crazy bastard. Nothing would be the same around the track anymore or at home. I already felt difference being here in this house without him.

It felt empty, lifeless, but maybe that was just me.

"What are you doing out here?" Jameson eventually asked.

"Watching Mrs. Taylor's cat lick his balls," I replied imperturbably.

He chuckled and took a seat next to me on the worn wooden steps, bumping my shoulder.

"There's a funeral going on in there."

"Is that so?" I laughed bitterly, watching Mrs. Taylor's cat walk away, flicking his tail with each step. "I couldn't tell with all the black. I thought I was at a Johnny Cash concert."

We sat there and joked for a few moments before I decided it was time to give my speech. I turned to Jameson once we were inside.

"Jameson, I'm warning you ... you leave me alone with Mrs. Taylor for more than five minutes and I'll chop your dick off."

Mrs. Taylor was our crazy neighbor who annoyed the fuck out of me, worse than the Lucifer twins did if that told you anything. When I was nine, she paid me twenty bucks to get her mail for a week and deliver it to her. She talked so goddamn much I quit after two days.

"That's a little harsh, and you really should stop threatening my manhood if you want more children, but ... I wouldn't think of it." He slapped my ass once as we walked toward the backyard where everyone was gathered.

I had no idea what to say during my speech so I reached for the note in my pocket that I found from my mom, feeling the warm tears streaming down my cheeks. I looked over at Jameson who was standing near the fence off to my right—tears glazed his eyes as he held our son close.

He mouthed, "I love you," to me and winked once.

I inhaled a deep breath before I began. "I ... don't really know what to say." I paused, feeling everyone's eyes focus on me. "But I found a note from my mother this morning that really summed everything up for me." Pausing again, I gave Jameson a small smile. "She told me to not look back. She told me that all of this I'm feeling right now, the pain, the anger, the depression, is what I'm supposed to feel, and it's natural. It's normal. She said that everything that happens to you is the pages within the story, and it's your novel. Write the ending you want. She said that what would really define me was when I thought I couldn't go on. How I went on would be my destiny." I finally looked up to find Jameson smiling at me. "I don't know what to say about Charlie except that he did the best he could for me. I never once felt like he didn't love me, nor did I ever feel like I let him down. He supported me in everything I did, and that's exactly the way a father should be."

I couldn't think of anything else to say. I was drawing a blank until I looked over at Axel once again. "Charlie's only wish was to see me walk down the aisle and see his only grandson born, both of which he was able to do. He lived a full life, and he had no regrets. Neither should we. He knew we loved him, and that's all that matters. That's all we can ask is that we tell the ones we love how much we love them and appreciate them for who they are."

I couldn't say any more because at that point, staring at my son, I lost it again and walked away to hide in the closet again.

This time Jameson followed, concerned for his manhood.

So there we sat, Jameson and me in Charlie's closet.

"Where's Axel?" I finally asked after ruining his black dress shirt with snot and tears.

"He's with Andrea," he told me. "I think she needed him to cheer her up."

"He does that for people, doesn't he?"

Jameson leaned over, kissing the top of my head. "Yeah, he does."

"We should probably go back downstairs, huh?"

"Nah ... we can stay up here as long as you need to."

We were quiet for another few moments before I began to pour my heart out to him.

"You know, I thought that if I avoided it, pretended it wasn't happening, that I could bandage the pain once it hit, but that's not the case. It hurts."

"I know, honey," he pulled me to his chest. "I'm sorry I can't take away the pain."

Jameson and I had been through so much since we'd known each other, and I had no doubt this was just another obstacle that would increase our bond with one another.

In some relationships, what happened with Darrin would have destroyed a couple, but not us. If *anything*, Darrin showed me just how much I loved Jameson and how strong we were together.

"When do you need to leave for Las Vegas?"

"I need to be there next Wednesday ... so I have ten days." He smiled with a slow wink. "Can you think of *anything* I can do in ten days?"

"Oh," I sighed dramatically. "I can think of a lot of things."

"Honeymoon?"

"Honeymoon," I agreed.

Time alone was exactly what we needed.

With acceptance came moving on and living the life you'd been given. You owed it to the ones you'd lost to go and do what they no longer got a chance to—remember them in a way that brought you both happiness.

Charlie would have wanted me to continue to be a mother and a wife, and that was what I was going to do. My book was still being written. I may have some torn pages, maybe even dog-eared, but it was one hell of a story.

Restart – The waving of the green flag following a caution period.

"This is a bad idea."

"No, it's not. He'll be fine."

"He needs me though."

"Your husband needs you, too." Alley pushed me toward the door. "Go enjoy yourselves. Next week in Las Vegas you're going to wish you'd taken this time. I'm telling you, this year it's completely different at the track. He can't even walk from his motor coach to the paddock without someone chasing him."

"And he could before?"

"Not really the point," she shoved me into the door. "Leave already."

I handed her everything Axel would need for the next week and then some. Looking over the two suitcases full of clothing, toys, and food for my little spaz, I clearly overpacked.

"Just ... don't leave him alone with Emma and Aiden, I don't trust them."

"I wouldn't either," she laughed. "Last week Aiden asked me if he could take Lane to the bar with him because he was good at pool."

"And one more thing." I turned to face her before I made my way out the door, crying. "If I come back to a son with a mohawk ..." I paused, taking a dramatic deep breath. "I. Will. Kill. Spencer."

"Don't worry, Sway!" Alley laughed, sitting on the floor next to Axel's carseat. "Now go ride your husband's magic stick."

"Okay ... uh, that's ... weird."

"Sorry ... Spencer messed with my playlists this morning." She shrugged and took Axel from his carseat. "Now go, have fun."

"Where are Spencer and Lane?" I noticed how quiet their apartment was. This was also my way of stalling for a little more time.

"They went to play flag football with Van and the twins," she smiled.

Van had taken to the twins these days and made sure they did everything six-year-old boys should be doing.

Being only thirty-one, Van was like a big kid himself. He seemed tough on the outside when he was in protection mode but inside, he was a child just like the rest of the boys in our family.

I left after that because if I didn't, I'd never leave.

I knew Jameson and I needed some alone time and not just at our house. It'd only been three days since Charlie's funeral, and we had yet to actually be alone. Every time we thought we might get a few minutes together, someone was stopping by to see if we needed anything. *We* needed alone time is what *we* needed.

My theories about death and grieving remained the same. Everyone was dealing with the loss in their own way, and it affected everyone in our families, even Jimi who had to leave the next day for Grand Rapids. I'd never seen Jimi cry in all the years I'd known him, but when he watched his longtime friend lowered in the ground, his tears fell, as did everyone else's.

Andrea was keeping busy with the twins, but it was evident everything had taken a toll on her. For someone who usually had a smile on her face, it was hard to see her without one.

Jameson was the quietest. He said little but offered small gestures that meant the world to me, letting me know he was there. I also knew it was hard on him; he loved Charlie just as much as I did. Even though Jameson and I met when we were eleven, Jameson had known Charlie since we bought the track back in 1987. I just failed to realize who Jameson actually was until I was eleven.

I couldn't do anything to bring Charlie or Rachel back. It was out of my control. I still needed to be a mother to my son and I still needed to be a wife to my husband. Slowly, I was entering acceptance.

This was why we were now *finally* going on our honeymoon.

I came to realize through the unfortunate twists in life, that you're seldom offered a second chance at love or life in general. So you should take them when they came. Being married to a NASCAR driver, you're seldom offered alone time ... so take it when it came.

We were sitting there on the plane in comfortable silence. Jameson was looking over schedules for the track while I read a book on parenting. Without paying attention to him, I adjusted my funbags so they weren't popping out of my dress. Then he was practically sitting on my lap, gazing at them.

"Wanna join the mile high club?" he asked, looking a little too cocky.

I smacked his hand away, shaking my head.

"You forgot—we already have," I pointed out, remembering the time on his parent's jet when we went to Savannah.

"It's not the same," he whispered against my ear in his perfected dirty heathen seduction voice. "Come on, honey, it'll be fun. I'll be *quick*. In 'n' out."

In my head, I was imagining being arrested and sent to Guantanamo Bay or some shit like that for even contemplating doing this. How would I explain that one to Axel?

I was all for a little adventure, but really, this had bad idea written all over it. When he broke out the dirty engine talking, I ignored my inner warnings and followed his dirty heathen ass toward the bathrooms located in the back of the plane, overlooking the glances of other passengers.

Once inside the tiny bathroom, Jameson grabbed onto my waist, holding me against him. His lips skimmed across my throat. It didn't take long for him to be shirtless and writhing against me. His lips teased me as my hands explored his flawless body. Over the last few weeks, sex was usually the last thing on our minds. It'd been at least four weeks since we were actually alone, intimately, in *any* sort of way.

Jameson had gotten my dress up and it wasn't long before my fingers skimmed over his sensitive skin of his camshaft for piston stroking, causing his movements to falter.

"Sway," he moaned.

I knew sex wouldn't work in here, but I knew what would.

Touching and teasing took over, our bodies running on emotions

"You feel so good," Jameson groaned against my neck, tightening his grip, and then sinking his teeth into my shoulder. "I've missed you."

I shook my head, arching my body up against his as I moved my hips with his fingers. "Oh, *God* ..." Jameson added another finger, and every coherent thought in my mind was gone. "Jesus Christ!" I yelled entirely too loud for an airplane.

Someone began knocking on the door, but we ignored it, too caught up in our own personal bliss.

Fortunately, for Jameson, when I was in the middle of shaking against him, my hand happened to tighten around him. Jameson groaned and thrust his hips toward me while the knocking turned to pounding and a loud voice came through.

"Dude, I have to go!" More knocking, "Come out already!"

What did my hotheaded dirty heathen do?

He pounded against the door keeping one arm tightly against my waist. "Fuck off!"

"Let go," I panted against his shoulder.

He nodded almost frantically as his lips found mine again. Sucking his bottom lip into my mouth, I tried to enjoy his touches, concentrating on making him feel just as good.

My spastic jerking seemed to work and Jameson was soon swearing and muttering incoherently against my neck before his weight slumped against me, pushing my ass inside the sink.

What if I'm stuck?

I smiled when his lips brushed along my neck and collarbone before he leaned back and reached for the toilet paper. Smirking, he cleaned off my hand and began to pull up his pants.

"Open the door!" the annoying voice yelled again, pounding his fist against the door.

Jameson practically growled and punched the door, leaving a dent in the plastic. "Get lost, asshole!"

I then realized I was stuck, and we really *were* going to Guantanamo Bay.

"I'm stuck," I announced.

Jameson looked between my legs, smirking.

"Don't joke."

"Not joking ..." I wiggled frantically, not smirking, not joking. "I'm stuck. Not joking," I repeated in just as much of a frantic voice one would use while stuck in an airplane sink.

Would they flush me out like waste now?

"Seriously?" he ran his left hand through his hair examining my position in the sink. "You're really stuck?"

"Yes, asshole. I'm stuck!"

"Shit."

The pounding continued, and Jameson spent more time arguing with the douche on the other side of the door than helping me. I was not impressed with his lack of concern for me and my ass.

"What am I going to do?" I asked myself because Jameson was far too engrossed in the shithead on the other side of the door to care about an evacuation plan for my ass.

I tried to suck it in, but really, how does one suck in their ass?

Ass sucking did nothing, and just when I was mentally preparing my speech to my son about how Mommy and Daddy were arrested and deported to Guantanamo Bay, Jameson reached behind me to turn on the water—that was up my ass crack—and started threatening to kick the shit out of the guy outside.

"Wait until I open the door, asshole," Jameson added, hitting the door.

So there I was, stuck in the goddamn airplane sink, my husband pounding against the door and simultaneously tugging on my legs.

It felt strange, water filling in around my ass. I wondered if that's what an enema would feel like. Not that I ever planned on having one, but I could imagine that was how it would feel.

After a good ten minutes of flowing water, it greased me enough that I finally got loose, only to realize Jameson was standing in about an inch of water.

How did we always end up in these situations?

I stood up—well I tried to, but my ass was sore. Straightening my wet dress, I attempted to right my panties but realized very quickly they were destroyed.

"You need to cut this shit out. It's getting old ..."

"I have no idea what you're talking about," he snapped at me, pounding on the door.

"Asshole." I kicked his shin. "Now I have to spend the remainder of the fucking plane ride with no underwear on."

He waggled his eyebrows.

"Lucky me," he leaned forward and kissed along my neck again. "Husband two, wife ... still zero."

"I'm not playing that game with you," despite my bitter tone, I laughed. "You know ... it's not the mile high club unless we have sex," I pointed out with a waggle of my own.

"Pft ... I'm not risking my manhood. If we hit turbulence ..." he cringed, zipping his jeans. "I'm not risking it."

Whoever was on the other side of the door apparently didn't realize my husband had some extreme anger issues and was more than likely going to kick his ass when he opened the door.

"I'm getting security!" he told us.

I wasn't sure if he was a man or child at that point. For all we knew he could be a three-foot-tall little person.

Emma would be sad if that were the case. She loved little people. I thought it was because she felt so comfortable around them, seeing how they were around the same height.

"This is why Wes flies me everywhere," Jameson grumbled and opened the door.

I felt like saying, "Why? Because you are insane and can't play nice with society?"

Security was standing there when we opened the door, and that didn't at all surprise me.

"Can you two please take your seats?" the officer asked.

"No," Jameson objected, crossing his arms over his chest. "I won't take my seat."

A flirty flight attendant made her way over to us.

Completely dismissing me, she looked at Jameson. "Can I help with anything?"

"No," we both glared at her.

"I'm going to have to ask you to calm down." The security guard motioned toward our seats. "Now, please, take your seats."

"I'll take my seat when I fucking feel like it, and I won't calm down," Jameson snapped back at him before turning to me and pulling me out of the bathroom beside him. His fingertips gripped my waist securely.

"Where did all this water come from?" the attendant asked me like I'd done something wrong, which *we* had, but that was beside the point.

I responded with a rude, "How the fuck should I know!"

Jameson's attitude was wearing off on me.

The security guard started threatening Jameson with arrest if he didn't comply and take a seat, at which point I started pushing him to our seats and issuing my own threats in his ear.

He went so far as to kick the seventeen-year-old kid who was bothering us on our way to our seat.

Real fucking mature.

Again, he was like a two-year-old trapped in a twenty-three-year-old body. Lane was more mature than him.

Apparently, I wasn't doing any better though.

When the flight attendant came by to check on Jameson, I gave her a piece of my mind.

"Listen, he's fine," I snapped. "And if he does *need* anything ... I ... as his wife ... will provide it for him." And for good measure, I added a snarky, "Just like I did in the bathroom."

We probably shouldn't even be allowed on an airplane without parental guidance.

Jameson started laughing when she walked away.

"That was hot."

"Oh, you shut up. You're going to get us kicked off the plane with your shitty attitude," I told him, handing him Skittles.

"No, I'm not. That jerk had it *coming*," he exaggerated the word *coming* to specify something lewd and then winked slowly. Leaning back in his seat, he slouched to one side and then turned to look at me in a very cocky way. "This *coming* from someone who just went off on a flight attendant."

"You really need anger management classes and stop saying *coming*!"

"No, I don't," he almost sounded appalled.

"Really?" I challenged, quirking an eyebrow in his direction and then looked at the fuming kid across from us nursing his sore shin. "You don't think so?"

He smirked again. "Nope," he popped a few Skittles in his mouth and chewed slowly. "I don't think so."

When we landed, nothing got better. *In fact*, it got worse.

"You didn't think to check the weather?"

"Well ... I was distracted."

"Apparently," I muttered, pushing my waterlogged hair from my eyes.

This was a disaster. This whole thing had been a complete disaster from the start, and it honestly didn't look like it was going to get any better.

Jameson's plan for our delayed honeymoon was to go away for a few days to Rio de Janeiro before he needed to be in Las Vegas on Wednesday. This left us seven days of pure alone blessedness.

In theory, it was a great plan, but now that we were there, it was not good.

Did I mention we were also in the middle of a hurricane trying to find an island that was supposedly located somewhere in the middle of the south Atlantic Ocean?

First, we missed our plane and had to sit at the airport for two hours waiting for the next flight. Then we got stuck next to this obsessed fan who talked to Jameson the entire flight about how he got started in NASCAR and everything from his favorite color to the brand of underwear he preferred. Then we had the mile high fiasco, which was another disaster.

When we finally landed, Jameson was not in a good mood.

In fact, he was livid.

"I hardly see this as my fault," he added, squinting into the darkness.

"It is your fault," I told him.

His head turned toward me, his eyes hard, hair falling against his damp forehead. We looked like two wet rats.

"How so?" he challenged, water dripping from his nose.

"I don't know," I shrugged indifferently. "Just is."

The wind blew, rocking the boat. We sat next to each other on the floor now, swaying with the waves, our shoulders bumping against each other with each rock of the boat.

I shifted beside him, reaching for my water bottle. It was dark and you couldn't see, so when my hands began searching Jameson tensed.

"Wait a second ... you don't have a fork, do you?"

"No," I said with a giggle. "I was looking for my water."

He sighed dramatically. "This sucks."

"Maybe you should have listened to the guy at the dock who said we should get someone to help us navigate," I suggested.

"I don't need any help," he snapped, throwing his arms up. "You'd think he would have warned us about the weather. What an asshole."

"Did you even have an idea of where we are going, or did you just start driving the boat?"

"Yes."

"Yes, what?"

"Yes, I know where we are going ... I think." He looked over at me. "Listen, I hardly think this is entirely my fault. That douche had a fucking map—he should have given it to us."

"He did!" I pointed to the map on the floor.

"Can you see it?" he goaded. "I sure as shit can't."

We were silent for a good ten minutes before I finally caved.

"Would it help if I showed you my boobs?" I asked, wiping water from my face.

"Maybe, show me and let's see."

Before I could reveal the funbags, the skies opened up and let out the loudest mother-loving crack of thunder I'd ever heard in my entire life. No lie. It actually vibrated my entire body.

Both of us jumped, and my hands went wild searching for Jameson to get as close to him as I could. The storm bubbled up, rocking the boat fiercely. With hands still wild and breathing hard, that's when I found the camshaft.

Jameson chuckled and pulled me onto his lap. "That's not your water bottle, honey."

The rain, warm and sticky, that was just a steady patter before, increased and began pouring what looked like golf ball-sized raindrops onto us, and if the darkness wasn't enough to blind you, the water coming down was. It was like a faucet.

As the storm surged, it was like a scene out of *The Notebook*. The only difference being we weren't in North Carolina, and we weren't famous actors ... okay, well now that I thought about it, this situation had little resemblance to that scene at all—maybe just the rain.

I took a moment to look over this whole scenario. I was horny.

When I went back to the doctor for my six-week check-up, he insisted we wait another three weeks for actual penetration. It sucked, and I was extremely tired of reciprocating motions.

"We shouldn't make so much noise out here. Remember Dayton Peak? We'll attract Moby Dick or something."

I think he was glaring, but I couldn't be sure with all the fucking rain.

"Moby Dick isn't real," he told me. His lips captured mine again, and his tongue swept across my lower lip, tasting me. The water was making our lips—and other things—incredibly slippery. I had the bright idea of wearing a dress, which was now on the floor of the boat because there was no point in having any clothes on with all the rain.

"Moby Dick is too real," I insisted, still kissing him. "He's a whale."

Jameson pulled back. "Sway, Moby Dick is a mythical creature."

"No, he's not, he's a sperm whale. They *do* exist."

"Still, the name Moby Dick, and the story, is fictional."

"Are you trying to shit on my fairytales?"

"Moby Dick is hardly a fairytale."

"Jameson?"

"Yes?"

"Stop talking about Moby Dick and show me your di—"

His lips cut me off as we drifted in the open Atlantic Ocean. It was one of those moments where nothing else mattered—nothing between us but the moist air. The sky rumbled and growled above us as our passion for one another was the only thing we cared about.

With the high waves, a considerable amount of water was flooding the boat, and the taste of salt was prominent to me.

"It tastes like salt," I finally said.

"I didn't come yet."

"I meant the water, jerk," I clarified, grinding my hips against him. "Why do you say that? It's not salty? Where did that saying even come from?"

"It's just a joke between my brother and me. It's funny."

"Yeah, sure it is."

Sitting on his lap, I knew what I wanted, and he was gonna give it up even if I had to rape him.

"Oh," he chuckled and attacked my neck again with nips and bites. "Ow, *fuck*!" he screamed, clutching his leg, or so I thought. I couldn't see a goddamn thing out there to know if he was really clutching his leg. The wind whipped around us, crashing the boat against the waves.

"Fuckkkk!" Jameson moaned. "What the *fuck* happened? It hurts! It burns!"

"What do you mean? What happened?" Frantically scrambling from his lap, I reached for his leg.

"Did you bite me?" he yelled over the sound of the waves and wind. "I'm bleeding ... fuck, it hurts with the salt water!"

"No, how could I have bitten you when my mouth was against yours?"

"Well, I don't know ... something bit me."

I felt something wet and slimy against my foot and practically jumped on Jameson's shoulder because holy shit balls there was a goddamn shark in the boat with us.

It was either that, or that was one hefty salmon.

"OH, MY GOD ... SHARK!" I shrieked in a voice comparable to Michael Jackson in "Thriller."

Jameson went all Steve Irwin of the shark community and kicked it. Yep, kicked it.

As if kicking it was really going to do anything to a fucking shark.

"Are you kidding me?" I punched his shoulder.

I'm not really sure what possessed me to do it, but I picked the shark up and tossed it over the edge. And when I say there was a shark on the boat ... it was a tiny shark, like something you'd have as a pet, but still, it was a shark and teeth that could quite possibly kill you.

Regardless of the size and teeth, Mama Wizard shined and saved the night.

I turned to Jameson who was clutching his calf.

"Wife ten—husband two." I swept my wet hair out of my face dramatically as though I'd just run cross country. "I need a drink."

"How the fuck did you get ten?"

"Because I didn't scream like a little bitch," I told him with poise. "I took care of the problem."

"Okay, first off, you *did* scream and climbed on my shoulders. Second, the goddamn thing bit me. I could have died!"

"You're overreacting." I slumped against the floor beside him, exhausted by my endeavors.

"No ... I'm really not overreacting," Jameson turned, wiping water from his face. "Have you ever been bit by a shark? Or stabbed with a goddamn fork?"

"Well, no ... but that's hardly a shark bite. It's more like a scratch."

He pushed his leg in my face. "That's a scratch?"

Now that I was closer, it was obviously not just a scratch.

"Holy fuck! You need stitches," I told him acerbically. He actually did, but I decided to keep with the sarcasm because this honeymoon was turning out to be a shit storm.

Suddenly, as I was thinking we might die out here, we crashed against something hard and then scraped along it.

The boat jolted forward and then slammed to a stop, throwing us against the seats.

"What if it's Moby Dick? Or another shark?" I asked shyly, covering the funbags that were still playing in the rain.

"It's not ... Moby Dick. And let me tell you something else," he glared. "If it's a shark, I'm feeding you to him." He moved me off him and peeked over the side of the boat. "It's shore!"

The relief I felt was hard to describe. I wondered if that was how the pilgrims felt when they made it to North America. I resisted the urge to say, "Land-ho!" if that's what they said.

I should have paid better attention in history class and then maybe I'd know the correct terms.

"Really?" I peeked over the edge as well to make sure he wasn't joking. I wouldn't want to get my hopes up. I was already picturing this turning into *Castaway* and having to make my water bottle my own personal Wilson.

"Yes, really," Jameson said. "Get your ass out. I'm done with this fucking rain and this boat."

I slapped his wet shoulder. The sound echoed throughout the boat.

Walking forward, his jeans clung to him, but I was more distracted with the fact that he had no shirt on, and the water gliding off his chest was creating a waterfall effect over his abdominal muscles.

With the breaks in the clouds, the moonlight reflected off the white sand glowing against his skin.

"Stop gawking at me and get out of the boat," he clipped, smacking my wet ass as he helped me out. "With our luck, this thing will carry us to China."

I stopped, my feet sinking into the warm, wet sand.

"Where the hell were you in geography class? China is on the other side of the world."

It's not like you're any better dumb shit. You couldn't figure out what they said when they discovered land.

"No, it's not …" without looking back at me he kept walking toward the trees. "It's that way." He pointed at the ocean behind us.

"No, it's not. That's Africa."

Jameson stopped suddenly and spun around to face me, his breath tickling my damp neck. He leaned forward, his lips gliding across my jaw.

"Stop arguing with me, wife," his hands moved to pick me up bridal style. "I'm soaking wet, I'm *extremely* horny, and the last thing I want to be doing right now is arguing about Moby Dick, or where the fuck China is, or talk about what *is* or *isn't* a fucking scratch. I want to have sex with my wife. *Right now.*"

I giggled the entire way to the bungalow he rented.

The secluded house was situated amongst the trees, set back away from the ocean by about a hundred yards or so. It was beautiful—dark, but beautiful. I assumed with the hurricane, the wind had knocked out any power this place might have had. Oh, and did I mention it was still raining and still blowing like a motherfucker outside?

Once we made our way through the dark vegetation and up the few stairs that led to the front door, I heard Jameson groan. "Damn it. It's locked."

"Huh?"

"It's locked, the door ... it's locked."

"Seriously?"

"Do you really think I'd be lying at a time like this?" he challenged.

"Now wha—" before I could even finish my sentence Jameson kicked in the door, the sound deafening as hefty wood splintered, crashing to the ground.

Jameson stood beside me all Hulk-like, staring at the door. He probably couldn't believe he'd gotten it down.

"Was that really necessary?" My eyes focused on him and not his insanely hot body. "I'm sure we could have called someone."

"Apparently it was. Did you see any other boats out there in the ocean?" he asked with a sly grin. "It's the only way onto this island," he then winked and lunged for me.

My head tipped back, giving his lips access to my neck, and when he gently bit, I whore-moaned louder than I think I ever had. "Jesus Christ!"

"Not quite." He pulled my earlobe between his teeth. "But I'm pretty damn good."

Every time I thought about this night, I had envisioned it going slow. A time where we made slow sweet love to each other until the sun came up. That's how a honeymoon was supposed to be, right?

It wasn't going down that way.

At least not this first time, after everything we'd been through in the last day. The need I felt was too great and it was nice to see Sway was in the same frame of mind.

Between the airplane and the boat teasing, it only amplified our need.

Not that I wasn't still upset about being bit by a fucking Great White, but still, I was horny and that took precedence over everything.

Sway ended up on top when we hit the floor once inside the house and immediately snaked one hand behind my neck to pull my face to hers. The other reached down to stroke my camshaft with the heel of her palm.

The beginnings of the erection I had moments ago turned rock hard under her touch.

Gasping when my hand slipped over her, I moaned again and settled my legs between hers, as my right hand now reached for her left knee to draw it up my hip.

Drawing back just long enough to catch her heated gaze, I knew she wanted it too.

There was no more Moby Dick talk, no more China talk, just grunts, moaning, and my bleeding leg.

There was no mistaking the urgency. She wanted this hard and fast, too.

"I love you," I told her, my voice husky.

She moaned against me, wiggling her hips. With that assurance, I pushed inside her.

Sway gasped, her eyes rolling back as I pulled her leg up around my waist.

"Jameson," she sighed, relaxing slightly in my arms.

"Sway," I grunted. "Jesus Christ ..."

That's when our movements turned frantic—arms, hands and legs flailing around, searching for the need. As we rocked against each other, the door creaked with each thrust while the wind howled throughout the house.

Clutching at me, her nails dug into my skin, moaning and tossing her head back and forth against the door.

I bent at the waist, still holding her legs over my shoulders, and continued to push inside her.

Sway moaned and with one last thrust, I was done. The relief and euphoria poured through me in waves as an animalistic growl rang throughout the house. I felt it from the bottom of my feet to the ends of my hair and the pulsing, the overwhelming feelings continued much longer than I recalled experiencing before.

Sex with Sway before the baby had been incredible but it had nothing on this. No way.

Not sure how much time went by but eventually we released each other. When I looked at Sway, her eyes were closed, her hands running through my hair.

"We didn't make it to the bedroom, sorry," I murmured eventually. "And the bedroom is fucking amazing."

"Like that's somehow your fault," she chuckled. "Did you see me rushing in there?"

"True."

We were still in the entryway of the house, on top of the broken door, when I heard a man clear his throat. And it wasn't me.

I turned quickly, looking over my left shoulder, still on top of Sway.

"Me desculpe, sir?" a gruff male voice asked, standing in the doorway.

Sway screamed, arms thrashing around, legs kicking as she tried to cover herself with her shredded clothing.

"Who is that ... who the fuck is that?" she wailed.

I tried desperately to cover her, but it wasn't helping.

I had a couple of thoughts. One, how long had he been watching? And two, who the fuck was he?

"Who is that, Jameson?" Sway asked on the other side of the kitchen, hiding behind the counter.

How she was able to see enough to find the kitchen was amazing to me. I could barely make out my own feet.

"Quem é você?" I asked.

I knew a little Portuguese, which was actually beneficial given these circumstances, but I also wasn't sure if I was making any sense.

I didn't exactly get an A+ in foreign language.

When I was in high school my parents made me take two foreign languages and piano lessons just so I had other interests. Though I became good at them, too, racing always held my attention the longest.

"Eu sou manutenção. Eu esqueci de desbloquear a porta."

"What's he saying?" Sway asked frantically, and I could now see she was holding a fork. "What the fuck is he saying?"

I turned to her, both of us still completely naked. While I tried to comprehend what he had asked, I was more concerned with my wife holding a fork.

"I swear to God, if you stab me with that goddamn thing, I will never have sex with you again."

The man chuckled.

"Gostaria de um sir chave?"

"Yes, I'd like a key." I took the key from him expecting him to leave, but he just stood there, staring at my wife. I lost it. "Are you fucking kidding me? Se perda imbecil!"

"Desculpe sir, desfrute da sua estadia,"

The man, who we never got a good look at, turned and walked away. I wasn't even sure what he said, but Sway's giggling brought me back.

Fearing a return of any more guests, I tried to right the door I tore down. Sway continued to laugh at me trying to get the door back up with the wind blowing. It wasn't exactly easy.

"Why are you laughing?"

She couldn't stop giggling long enough to answer.

"That was like horror movie shit. I thought he was going to murder us."

"And that's funny?"

"Yes," she started giggling again, which in turn caused me to start laughing.

Soon we're both laughing to the point we could hardly breathe.

Tangled together on the floor, our bodies reacted to one another and continued where we left off.

"Should we at least make it to another part of the house?" I whispered.

"I'm partial to the entryway now," she whispered back. "But we should clean your leg up first."

I glanced down at the bloody mess. Now I saw how this all resembled a horror movie. We even had the puddle of blood.

"There's time for that later, honey." I smiled, kissing her lips. "Right now is all about you and me."

Blend Line – There is a line painted on the track near the apron and extending from the pit road exit into the first turn. When leaving the pits, a driver must stay below it to safely "blend" back into traffic.

We were finally in the bedroom. The windows and doors were open as the humid air surrounded us, dampening our burning skin.

The hurricane was losing strength outside, but the power was still out and the palm trees swayed in the steering winds while debris continued to hit the sides of the house.

It was slightly arduous to define the moment we were in, but we were on an island, alone.

Well, the Rain Man could be out there somewhere, but right then, it was just Mama Wizard and Dirty Heathen.

His right hand swept across my sodden upper thigh, hitching it up his hip, and he rolled us over so I was on top of him. I looked down at him, his gaze was intense and I couldn't take it anymore. I leaned forward and captured his lips with mine, molding us together.

Did you ever think about what each kiss *should* feel like? Were they all epic fairytale kisses? Should they be?

I could only say what they felt like with my dirty heathen. When his lips touched mine, every *single* time they touched mine, I felt it everywhere. I felt it from my toes to the tip of my nose. My heart would beat faster, my stomach fluttered with butterflies as though I was falling in love all over again. It was so consuming, so intense, that I never wanted to come up for air. I got lost in the moment and gave myself to him entirely with each kiss.

Twenty years from now that might be different, but for now, I was going to enjoy my butterflies and tingling.

With the storm surging once again, pelting the windows and doors with rain, my mind drifted back to our time in Savannah when our relationship really took a twist.

This was different.

Back then, I didn't know what I was to Jameson. Now, I had no doubt in my mind that he loved me and wanted all of me, even the crazy irrational side that had no sympathy for his shark scratch or his geographical sense.

"You are so beautiful," Jameson murmured against my lips.

For so long Jameson held so much of himself back, afraid of letting anyone, including me, see the real him. But the thing he never realized was that was all I ever saw.

I never saw him as Jimi Riley's son. I never saw the famous Jameson—the Jameson who could rarely go anywhere without being hunted down by pit lizards or garage groupies. I always saw the eleven-year-old shit head who knew what he wanted. I saw the confident, steadfast man that he became.

Now that we were married, he seemed different. He appeared to have let go of the barrier he'd put up around himself and let me love him for who he was knowing that I would never break his heart.

He showed me passion I'd never dreamed of with every touch and every kiss. He let me love him in all the ways I already did.

Even so, it was easy to see the change that occurred in him. He was baring his soul, his heart, to his wife.

Jameson also knew me. He knew what each moan meant. He knew that when I bit down on my lower lip, I was relishing in everything he was giving me. He also knew what it felt like to have my hands caressing his body, as I knew what his felt like. We knew everything there was to know about each other.

Jameson and I were good at the dirty talking and press forging, but this time, it wasn't even close to that.

This time, it was slow. Every movement was slow motion. Our breathing was low, but ragged. Our movements were dawdling, but passionate. Our kisses were deep, but tender.

"Look at me, honey," he whispered and moved so he was hovering over me again. His left hand was behind the nape of my neck, his right resting against my thigh he wrapped around his waist, and then he began to move. Never breaking his steely gaze from mine, my lips moved from his to kiss his shoulders, memorizing how the muscles felt against the sensitive skin of my lips. His warm breath washed over me, overriding any coherent thought I might have had.

It didn't take long before our desire gave way, and our movements were driven. Jameson's hand was still wrapped around the back of my neck, his fingers digging into my skin. His right hand was on my hip, securing me to him as his movements sped. Our tattered breathing filled the air, and when we finally let go, it was just as intense as it had always been, maybe more.

Our foreheads rested against each other, and I listened to his heartbeat slow.

"I love you, Sway," he whispered to me, winded.

"I love you, too."

I felt as if everything I'd been through recently was like this hurricane pulsating outside.

It was almost some sort of metaphor for what our lives had become. A hurricane came to shore destroying everything in its path, leaving you with the devastating aftermath.

I'd learned over the past year that it wasn't about the storm. It was about the aftermath and what you made of it and how you recovered from it. Sure, some storms in your life could be so damaging to you that it was hard to come back. But coming back, rebounding, restarting, that was what really made you who you were. That was what *defined* you and those pages within your story as my mother said.

The more I thought about what my mom's letter meant to me, the more I realized she was exactly right.

I was going to decide how this was written. I was going to write my own happy ending.

Despite creating my own happy ending, one thing held true, you couldn't avoid the storm. Sooner or later, it would find you. But the best part about a storm, in my mind, was relying on the one you loved to pull you through it.

Through everything, Jameson was here to help me navigate this storm. And I let him.

Still naked, laying there for a good hour, we listened to the waves breaking against the shore as the sun began to rise. The lighting in the room had changed from cerulean to a soft but glowing pink with ginger hues.

"I miss Charlie," I whispered against Jameson's bare chest, tracing circles over his scar from where his chest tube was after his accident in Pocono last year.

"I do, too," he murmured, placing a kiss on my forehead. "He was a special man to a lot of people."

"I felt like he came over that morning to say goodbye."

"I know what you mean ... before I left for Daytona he pulled me aside and gave me this long speech about how I needed to take care of you and Axel."

I propped myself up on my elbow. "What did he say?"

His lips twitched into a smile, blinking slowly.

"He told me that you will always be his little girl." His hand brushed my hair away from my face. "He told me that no matter what—put you first, and I'll have no regrets in life. He also said not to work my life away, and he told me ... that he felt like I'd always been a son to him."

Slumping back against his chest, I felt the vibrations of his voice as he continued speaking. "You know ... Andrea and Mallory asked if we wanted to put a memorial race on the schedule for the weekend of Charlie's birthday."

Choking back tears, it took me a moment to actually speak. "I think that's a good idea."

I found that even if you moved on to acceptance, it was hard to let go entirely.

For me, the hardest part was letting go, but it was a necessity. Healing and acceptance couldn't begin until then.

You remembered, though, and that was what you should do. That was the healthy thing to do. Hold on tightly to those memories, as they were all you had left.

They were all *we* had left.

The rest of our days on the island were usually spent indoors and in bed with each other.

We made it to other parts of the house, but spent most of our time enjoying each other. This year was going to be crazy, and I knew that. I intended on taking advantage of the alone time, and he seemed to be on the exact same page.

The disaster of getting here didn't end once we were arrived. It seemed anytime we ventured outside something bad happened.

The one time we took a swim in the ocean, I was stung by a fucking jellyfish.

This wouldn't have been so horrible, but it hurt like a motherfucker, and Jameson spent more time trying to convince me he should piss on my leg than helping with the burning. Again, I wasn't impressed with his lack of concern for my burn. He seemed more concerned with the fact that he needed to pee on me.

"Listen, asshole! This is not the time to be marking your woman. I need serious help!"

He threw his head back in a fit of laughter and then stopped suddenly, glaring. "It's just a scratch."

He was mocking me, and I was not having it.

"That's a scratch." I pointed at his shark scratch. "This ..." I gestured toward my very red-welted calf, and quite possibly the worst jellyfish burn ever handed out. "Is a sting ... and it *burns*!"

"I refuse to have this argument with you again," his fiery stare shut me up for a moment.

I sat there in the hot, white sand, blowing on my burn when he chuckled. "It'd be a lot simpler if you'd just admit for one, it's more than a scratch, and two, let me *relieve* the pain." He winked. Fucking winked.

Resorting back to childlike tendencies when angry, I threw sand in his face. "Jerk."

Our entire trip was like that.

When out-and-about, it was horrible. When alone together in the confines of the house, nothing else mattered but us.

We said fuck it with exploring and just had sex.

A part of me wondered if this would be our marriage. If so, we'd spend a large amount of time inside.

When it was time to leave, I think we were both ready to see Axel.

This was the longest we'd been away from him, and I couldn't wait to see his smiling face. For only being two months old, he smiled more than any baby I'd ever seen.

Why wouldn't he smile?

His parents were awesome. Sure, we were inept as hell but still ... awesome.

I knew the trip home would be just as much of a catastrophe as the trip here, but I was surprised it was actually worse.

It started with the boat ride back to Rio De Janeiro, where Jameson vomited twice over the side of the boat, but refused to admit he was seasick.

Instead, he blamed it on the amount of water he'd swallowed in the waterfall we found on the island.

Yes, he did swallow an abundance of water but it was hardly my fault. He was the one who thought it would be cool to fuck up against the rocks beneath the steady stream of water. We had to stop after a few minutes because we did ingest a great deal of water, but also something slimy was near us, and I really didn't want to hear about another *scratch* from Jameson.

Originally, I envisioned it like *Cocktail* with Tom Cruise, but it was nothing like that at all.

Have you ever tried it? Water splashes you in the face, it's hard to steady your feet, and did I mention that there was something slimy in there with us?

The hilarious part about the entire escapade was me asking Jameson his thoughts on the penis fish. I'd never seen him run so fast.

What sealed the deal and made this quite possibly the worst trip ever was when the guy sitting behind Jameson's seat on the flight kept kicking him.

Utterly annoyed, he rolled his head over to one side, side-eying me. "I'm gonna fucking kill him if he kicks my seat one more time."

"Just relax," I urged in a calm voice I'd perfected since marrying him and becoming a parent. "I'd like to go home, not to jail."

Just as I expected, the asshole kicked Jameson's seat again. What happened next was another experience in my life that was difficult to describe. Jameson and the asshole behind us got in a fight, an actual fistfight brawl over kicking chairs.

"Nice job, asshole. Real fucking mature," I said as we were being escorted to security after landing in Dallas.

Nursing a bloody lip, he said, "He had it coming."

Jameson was placed on a "No Fly" list for threatening a flight attendant and punching a security guard ... security guard being the guy who was kicking his chair. Who knew?

Needless to say, to actually get home, Wes had to come get us because Jameson was not allowed to fly with normal people any longer.

When he returned from security I asked, "How'd that work out for you? Feel good about yourself?"

He had no answer for me. No answer, I was amused with that at least.

When we finally made it home to Elma, it was both a relief and yet another clusterfuck.

We had picked up Axel from Alley and Spencer's apartment on Tuesday night. Jameson had to fly out Wednesday morning for Vegas so I had to hurry and pack everything Axel and I would need for the next week so we could go with him.

I was standing in the garage, getting ready to open the door to go into the kitchen, and I heard noises and a voice coming from inside the house.

Retrieving our bags from the back of the Expedition, Jameson walked up to me holding the bags and smiled down at Axel. "Open the door, honey."

"There's someone in there," I whispered, watchful.

"What?" he asked, his brow furrowing in uncertainty.

We'd been through so much on our honeymoon it was hard to believe anything else could possibly go wrong.

"I hear voices in there," I told him, removing Axel from his car-seat. "What should we do?"

"Uh ... grab the tire iron out of the Expedition," he put on his manly protective face. "I'll call Van."

"Where is he?"

"He's in his apartment, I think."

I went into protective Mama Wizard mode and hunched over Axel.

Jameson slowly moved inside the house, with the tire iron in hand.

Van was there in seconds, holding a gun.

"Where'd that come from?" I asked, eyeing the black handgun.

"I always carry a gun, Ms. Sway." Van offered a nervous smile.

"What if *they* have a gun?"

"Run," Jameson said over his shoulder as if I was stupid for even asking this.

The thought that someone might possibly be inside my home with a gun made my blood run cold. I would kill anyone who would harm my little flailing spaz.

When we made our way inside the laundry room we could hear the voices coming from the family room. Van motioned for Jameson to stay with us as he made his way through the kitchen.

We didn't stay—we followed closely behind our badass Navy Seal.

"What are you two ... *never mind* ... just stay behind me."

All four of us slowly shuffled throughout our gigantic house, room by room, as I carried the flailing spaz with us.

Axel, who usually remained fairly quiet, chose that exact moment to start cooing at his daddy.

We heard glass breaking and then a women's voice said, "Oh, shit ... pick that up."

I knew right then who that was.

Jameson looked over his shoulder at me, glaring. "I'll fucking kill her if she has my underwear!"

Van spun around to face us, his brown eyes dark and contemplating. "Do you know who it is?"

"Dana ... that's Dana's voice."

"You mean *Dana*, the crazy-stalker-next-door-neighbor, *Dana*?"

"Yes," we both said as Jameson took Axel from me.

"I'd better hold him. If I don't, I may possibly kill her."

"What should we do?" I asked, looking between Jameson and Van.

"We need to defend our domain," Jameson proclaimed, handing Axel back to me.

I giggled at his fierce expression.

Van nodded. "Damn straight."

They made their way into the office to look over the security cameras to find out what room she was in.

Sure enough, she was in our bedroom.

After everything that had happened to us lately, I had a feeling we'd be in wheelchairs and this shit would still be occurring. Never a dull moment, that was for sure.

We stepped inside our master bedroom, Van with a gun, Jameson with a tire iron, and me standing behind him with our flailing cooing spaz, who just sneezed.

"Bless you," I whispered, kissing the top of his rusty curls.

Dana froze, standing in front of our dresser with an armful of

Jameson's underwear while Cooper, stood there staring at my underwear drawer.

What a bunch of fucking sickos.

I had this fear they would start asking us to put lotion on our skin.

"What the fuck? Put those back!" Jameson ordered.

"I ... um ... I ... *shit* ..." Dana squeaked out, dropping the underwear, her frantic eyes looked toward our Navy Seal.

"You have five seconds to get out, or I will shoot you," Van warned in a stern voice he used when in his protector mode. It sounded like Christian Bale in *Batman*.

Suddenly, Cooper and Dana made a run for it and were out the door, without our underwear.

"Does this kind of thing happen a lot?" Van asked, putting his gun inside the front of his pants.

"Yes," we both mumbled, spent from everything that had happened in the last few weeks.

An hour later, Van went back to his apartment over the garage, and Jameson and I packed for the Vegas race while Axel played in his bouncy chair beside us.

When we finally had the last of everything packed, the doorbell rang.

"If that's Dana, we're moving," Jameson told me and picked up the tire iron beside his feet.

I really was expecting it to be Dana when I answered the door, but no, it was Spencer.

"I was thinking you could help me with something," he greeted me. "You're—"

"No, I'm not helping." I cut him off and walked into the kitchen to find a much needed drink.

He kept throwing ideas out for ways I could help him get back in Alley's good graces—he'd apparently pissed her off. All of them I quickly dismissed as trite and lackluster. I refused to help anymore. I'd done my good deeds.

"Oh, yeah ... how'd it work out with Dana in your house?" he asked, leaning against the counter.

"What?" I slowly turned my head toward him.

"I forgot to tell you ..." He burst out laughing. "I let her in."

"Get the fuck out!" I yelled, pointing at the door. "Get the fuck out right now!"

"No," he argued.

"Fine." I chugged the beer in my hand before slamming it down on the counter. "Paybacks are a motherfucker, Spencer!"

He threw his head back with one loud, bellowing laugh.

This was war.

The next morning, I put my plan into action

"Wow, no bullshit—do you think it will work?" I asked Van as he explained how this particular taser would work.

Spencer had fucked with the wrong man.

"Yep, it's flawless."

"Really?"

"Yep."

"Is this thing legal?" I held up the taser.

Van adjusted my hand away from the trigger and away from his body with a laugh.

"Well, no ... it's not legal, but it's either that or you could hit him over the head with a hammer."

"I wanna hurt him, not kill him." I took a step toward the door. "C'mon, let's get outta here before the sheriff comes back."

Van and I had snuck into the sheriff's office this morning to snatch a taser. I really thought a taser would come in handy with Dana stalking me and my shitfuck of a brother assisting her.

"Good idea, you're already on a 'No Fly' list."

"Hardly my fault," I mumbled, walking to my car.

It was around six in the morning, and we were all set to fly to Vegas this afternoon when Van turned to me. "Hey, so, Logan and Lucas were asking if they could come with us to Vegas."

"Fuck," I sighed.

I hated to say no after everything they'd been through, but I also did not want any drama in Vegas. I needed to concentrate on racing and not babysitting the Lucifer twins.

I agreed, only because Andrea agreed to come along as well, but I did sit the twins down prior to boarding the plane. "Okay, if you are going to come with us, we have to set a few ground rules. First off, no asking me any questions. Second, if you do anything besides look at Axel, I will strangle both of you. Third, I have duct tape—if you fuck with me—I will use it."

"Got it," they both said, nodding with wide smiles before running toward the plane.

I had a feeling this was not going to be a positive experience.

Van looked over at me and reached for the bags. "You actually sound worried."

"Spend more than five minutes around them and you'll understand," I told him, adjusting my bag on my shoulder.

The plane ride was a complete disaster, as usual. The twins never stopped talking. Sway spent the *entire* time soothing Axel who cried the *entire* two hours, and Emma and Aiden fought the *entire* trip.

I had a feeling they didn't want to tell anyone why they were fighting, but I was beginning to think it might actually be something serious by the way she was crying.

"What the fuck is going on between you two?" I asked Aiden once we got off the plane and loaded our bags into the waiting Expedition.

"You should talk to her about that ... she's made it pretty fucking evident I have no say in any of this," he grumbled, walking away from me.

Besides the time in Eldora last year when another spotter got in Aiden's face from something I did on the track, I'd never seen Aiden worked up or angry. Now he actually resembled me.

I just blew it off. I had way too much on my mind with the race to try and solve other people's problems.

Once we were at the track, the reporters and fans had some sort of obsession with Sway and Axel, wanting pictures of all of us. I didn't mind, but I also didn't want Axel in the spotlight so soon. This newfound fascination left Sway and Axel camping out in the motor coach most of the weekend with Van.

"How's the car today?"

"It's really fast." I smiled. "Yesterday, we had the car in race trim so we'll see. It's not just having a fast car ... it's tires, it's fuel, and, more importantly, position on the track," I told the reporter.

I enjoyed racing in Vegas, as I loved the one-point-five mile tracks. With the asphalt surface and twenty degree banking it made for some exciting racing. I also loved the fact they had a dirt track there.

Who wouldn't?

"Now Justin West drove your car last weekend and pulled off a win for you in Rockingham. Do you think Justin has what it takes to make it in the Cup series full-time?"

"Without a doubt, but that's not what Justin's interested in. He's a sprint car guy. If he wasn't—I know Jimi would be hiring another driver by now. Both Justin and Tyler are incredibly talented drivers."

"Midway through last season everything seemed to take a turn for the worst after your wreck. Was there ever a point where you just said this may not be the season for me?" Neil, a reporter with SPEED, asked me while I stood next to my car before the race.

"Yes and no. I wanted to say it ... I felt it, but everyone was pushing me to continue on, and I'm glad they did. That's why I was able to come back from it and win. We don't give these behind the scenes guys enough credit for everything they do. It was because of them I was able to do it."

I didn't want to come out and say who helped me, only because it was none of the media's business.

"It looks like this season may be a repeat?"

"I don't know about that but I'm sure gonna try," I told him, wrapping my arm around Sway, who stood next to me holding Axel.

Neil turned looked at Sway. "You recently lost your father. Is it hard being around racing so much, knowing the impact he had on the racing community?"

Sway smiled softly looking down at Axel. "No, it is what it is. Charlie will always hold a special spot in a lot of people's lives, but especially mine. He was more than a father to me—he had to be. He raised me by himself," Sway said. "He would have wanted us to continue living our lives. That's all anyone can do."

I glared at Neil for even bringing up Charlie.

"Well, good luck today, Jameson, and congratulations on the baby."

Watching Sway before the race, smiling at Axel, I couldn't believe how well she'd adapted to all this. She just went with the flow of everything. I mean, Christ, she'd just lost her father a few weeks back, but here she was, supporting me and being a mother to our son.

"I can't believe how well you just ... go with the flow," I said to her once Neil left.

"Is that supposed to be dirty?" she asked, adjusting her hold on Axel. His eyes peeked over her shoulder peering out at the line of cars.

"No, silly girl." I laughed, kissing the top of her head. "I just ... thank you."

After the National Anthem, Sway left with Axel to go up to the towers where they'd watch the race, and I got inside the car.

"You copy, Aiden?" I asked when I got my helmet on.

"Ten-four, loud and clear."

Checking switches and adjusting my belts, I asked, "What about you Kyle, you copy?"

"Yep, gotcha."

"You got five laps to green, do you see your pit box when you come around. Spencer's waving at you."

"Yeah, I see him." I laughed. "It's hard to miss his egg head."

"Watch your RPMs as you come by?" Aiden said. "That should be pit road speed."

"3900."

"Okay, so 3900, second gear when you hit pit road, remember that," Kyle reminded me. "We don't need a penalty."

"All right ... let's have a good race here, boys," I said, tugging on my belts.

"Ten-four, just take your time. It's a long race, stay focused."

"Keep me calm."

Once the race was underway, it was hard to think of anything but the race.

I was battling for second place with Colin Shuman and Paul Leighty was right on my ass.

"Is that legal?" I asked when Paul darted below the line to pass me on the inside.

"Three wide ... two wide ... all clear behind," Aiden announced. "Down on the line. Thirty-nine on your bumper."

"Yes, it is," Kyle said with a laugh. It was rare for anyone to pass *me* on the inside. I was known for hugging the line.

"Does that mean ..."

"Yes, it does."

"Thirty-four at your left rear ... two-wide, clear."

"Oh, goddamn it!" I slammed my fists on the steering wheel and for good measure—I tossed my water bottle across the cockpit.

"Pretty much." I knew I couldn't win them all, but that sure as hell didn't stop me from wanting to.

Remember that saying, "Say when?" I didn't know when to say, "Say when."

I'd always want more, but the longer I raced, the more I realized every other driver was exactly like me, always wanting more.

“Stop booing. Everyone is trying very hard,” Emma said, suddenly looking up from her TMZ magazine. Why she was looking at that was beyond me.

“What the hell is wrong with you?” I punched her shoulder and ripped the magazine out of her hand. “Your brother just got his ass handed to him on a pass that should have been illegal. Stop acting like a damn cheerleader.”

“Sportsmanship. Try it,” she replied, taking her magazine back with force.

I went back to listening to the in-car audio.

Next to me, Nancy played with Axel, laughing at every little noise he made.

“The bottom is good ... I just can’t arch it in like I did yesterday,” Jameson said as he battled again with Colin Shuman, the new driver who took Darrin’s place.

I met Colin on Saturday and didn’t think too highly of him. I quickly put him in his place when he winked at me.

“No, no!” I told him, pushing him against the wall of the media center before Jameson saw. “You fuck with me or Jameson and I will rip your balls off.”

I must have been intimidating because he apologized and had been racing Jameson clean today—so far.

“We can do this, just be patient and charge to the front,” Kyle said after they fell back to tenth when a lug nut stuck on the right rear during a pit stop.

“Cautions out, cautions out ... smoker in turn two,” Aiden told him around lap two hundred.

“Who is it?”

“Forty-two, stay high.”

“Pit road is *ooopppeeeen*!” Aiden exclaimed. “Watch the ten car ... he’s taken fuel only.”

I was surprised he was returning to a normal mood. All weekend he and Emma had been fighting, and refused to tell anyone why. I decided to try again.

"What's with you and Aiden?"

"Nothing ... why?" she responded without looking up from her magazine.

"Well, for one, you two have barely spoken these last few days, and two, you haven't stopped crying."

Emma finally looked up from her magazine and glanced over at Axel, then back to me.

"Nothing. I don't want to talk about it."

Emma was the type of girl who cared so much about everyone else she put her own feelings aside. She was crazy, yes, but she was probably the best friend and sister anyone could ask for.

I didn't mind crazy people for two reasons: If not for pure entertainment value, they made you feel slightly better in regards to your own sanity. For this reason, I surrounded myself with them.

"I never did thank you for everything you've done lately ... so thanks," I said, slinging my arm around her tiny shoulders. "With the wedding, the baby shower ... all of it, thank you."

She burst into tears. "You're ... welcome," she wailed, clinging to me.

"Okay, *see* ... something's wrong ... what is it?"

As the race continued, Emma poured her heart out to Nancy and me. She explained that Aiden was feeling neglected by her spending all her time planning the wedding and then Charlie's funeral, and on top of that ... she was pregnant.

The worst part was that Aiden told her they weren't ready for kids, and she should have talked to him about it before she went off her birth control pills. Which she didn't.

Emma was so excited about everyone having babies or getting pregnant, so she stopped taking them—without his knowledge. This wasn't the first time Emma did something without thinking clearly—she had a tattoo on the back of her neck that would make most men blush.

As the race neared the end, so did our conversations. There really wasn't much advice I could offer Emma besides being there for her if she needed to talk. Nancy was too focused on the fact that there would once again be another baby for her to love ... and knit for.

When the caution waved, Jameson came on the radio. "Whew ... it's incredible how fast this thing is now."

"I take it that means no changes?" Kyle laughed.

"You touch anything besides my tires and I'll kick your ass, Kyle," Jameson teased.

"I'd like to see that," Aiden added.

"How many tires did Paul take?" Jameson asked once they were back on the track. Paul must have only taken two because he beat Jameson out of the pits to land himself in first place.

"Two."

"Fuck!"

"We can still catch him."

"Glad you're so positive," Jameson let out a chuckle, the radio cracked.

"You should try it sometime."

"Nah ... I like being real."

Around lap two-fifty Paul did the same move he pulled earlier to pass Jameson for second again.

"Did he just..." You could hear Jameson groan over the radio. "Man ... that sucks."

"Yep."

"Didn't see that one coming."

"Neither did I," Kyle replied.

It seemed as though Jameson had some competition this year between Bobby, Tate, and now Paul.

"Jesus Christ," Jameson yelled. "It feels like I'm doing twenty-five miles an hour compared to him."

Near the end of the race, Colin Shuman had made his way back up to the front and was battling with Tate and Jameson for second and third. There was no way anyone was going to catch Paul now, he had a two-second lead on Jameson with just eight laps to go.

Colin nudged Jameson from behind causing him to fishtail going into turn four. Jameson corrected it and kept the spot, but that didn't stop my hothead from reacting.

"I think he did it on purpose!" he yelled.

"No, he didn't do it on purpose." Colin pushed against him again, Kyle laughed. "Okay, maybe he did."

NASCAR waved the furled black flag at the two of them and Colin backed off, leaving Jameson to finish second.

I kept thinking that this new rivalry might turn into what it did with Darrin, but I also knew that was racing. With Darrin Torres, it was more than just a rivalry between them. It was an obsession to constantly outsmart the other. In the end, I could only guess Darrin got what he deserved.

There would always be someone trying to prove themselves and someone getting in Jameson's face. Like it or not, it came with racing. The difference needed to come from Jameson. He needed to walk away at times, but he also couldn't let other drivers walk all over him. He needed balance and maybe therapy. It was becoming evident there would be no way around not seeking out anger management for him.

After the race and Contender's Conference, we were having dinner in the hotel restaurant when a woman approached us.

She looked familiar, but a lot of people looked familiar when fans constantly surrounded you.

I was exhausted and the last thing I wanted right now was another pit lizard asking me to sign her tits.

"Jameson?" she asked as though she knew me.

All of us turned to look over at her. She was tall with brown hair and green eyes. She looked similar to Sway, and then it dawned on me who she was.

Fuck!

Nervously, I leaned closer to Sway, offering her my hand. I was also silently letting this woman know I was with someone.

"I'm sorry, do I know you?" I asked brusquely, praying she took that as a clue to leave.

No such luck.

"It's me ... Lauren," she said with a smile.

This couldn't be happening.

I felt Sway's hand tense inside of my own and adjusted her hold on Axel. I didn't say anything but looked between Sway and Lauren.

"Remember ... we ..." Her voice faded, and before I could say any more, Sway held up her hand.

"Hello, I'm Jameson's wife, Sway Riley."

Lauren stammered for a moment before finally saying, "Oh ... I'm Lauren Thomas." She glanced at me. "Sorry I ... didn't know he was married."

"No worries," Sway said politely. "We just got married. He wasn't married at the time, I'm sure."

They chatted for a moment, and I sat there dumbfounded that this was even happening.

When she disappeared, Aiden and Spencer broke into a fit of laughter. "That was awesome!"

I reached for Sway's hand again. "Can we *please* go home now?"

"Are you kidding me?" she teased, rolling her eyes. "This is just getting entertaining."

Spencer punched my shoulder. "Nice going, stud," he replied sarcastically. "That had to have been awkward."

If only he knew that I was now in possession of a taser.

I knew this would happen at some point, and I was fairly certain it would happen again. I had no clue who those women were who I slept with when Sway left to finish college, nor did I have any clue how many there were. I threw out a number to Sway before, but I was pretty sure it wasn't anywhere close to that number.

Looking back to that time in my life, it was hard to imagine my life would turn out like this just three years later.

The turning point for me was when Sway came out to Daytona. After that, I realized my feelings were deeper for this woman besides just being friends. I also knew that being friends with benefits would change the entire dynamic of our relationship, and I was glad it did. It made me realize that a friend with benefits wasn't what I wanted. I wanted more. I wanted what I had now.

It was funny how what you thought you didn't need was exactly what you needed all along.

I turned to Sway once we were leaving the restaurant to head home.

"I'm sorry about that."

She smiled and handed Axel to me.

"Don't be ... it was bound to happen sooner or later."

"I know ... I just ... didn't want you to see it."

"Like I said, Jameson ... it's not your fault ... well, it is, but still, you had no way of knowing she'd find you."

I drew her against my side, adjusting my hold on Axel as well. He looked up at me and smiled. "I'm so fucking lucky to have you two."

Sway's arm wrapped around my waist and squeezed. "Yes, you are."

Roll Cage – This is the steel tubing inside the race car's interior. It's designed to protect the driver from impacts or rollovers.

It seemed as though the season was flying by.

We left Las Vegas, flew to Atlanta, then Darlington, Bristol, Texas ... new track each week. Before we knew it, the Coca-Cola 600 rolled around.

That morning Jameson had a meet-and-greet scheduled in the media center. I went with him while Nancy looked after Axel in the motor coach.

Jameson was always good at maintaining crowd control and recognizing when it was getting out of hand. That morning it got out of hand.

Jameson, who rarely looked up during meet-and-greets, watched a group of guys carefully as they pushed forward through the crowd to get closer to the table.

"Hey," Jameson finally said with a sharp warning. "Stop that."

The group of boys who were probably college kids seemed caught off guard by his tone and stopped to stare at him.

That's when they decided to argue that they had waited all day for an autograph and the last time they waited, Jameson declined the autograph.

"Well, when did you ask me?" Jameson asked them.

One of the men, the closest to the table spoke first. "We were in Bristol last March with garage passes, and you wouldn't sign anything for us."

Jameson laughed softly, his left hand with the sharpie in it rose to sweep over his eyebrow before he looked up at them. He pushed a signed poster to his right for the woman beside them. Jameson winked at her when she softly thanked him before he looked back down at the posters being handed to him from different directions.

"Well, there you go," Jameson spoke quietly, but it strangely sounded more of a warning that way. "I was working."

The man to his right started in again, and Jameson focused on him, finally granting eye contact. "I'm not going anywhere. I will sign whatever you want, but you're hurting people when you push forward like that."

"We are not," one had the nerve to reply with as they, once again, shuffled forward.

Van appeared beside me when he noticed the commotion at the table.

That was when Jameson pointed at the guys with a little more warning. "Listen, there are kids and women surrounding ya'll, and you're crushing them against this table when you push. Pay attention." Jameson then shook his head in annoyance and signed their posters.

"What a jerk," one of them mumbled as they walked away.

Was he being a jerk?

No. He was looking out for the people who waited patiently for him, not the ones who thought he owed them something. Those kids gave Jameson shit, and normally it would have rolled right off him as though it didn't mean anything.

But it did.

The rest of the meet-and-greet I could tell it bothered him. Regardless of the fact that Jameson was considered a professional athlete, it didn't mean he owed them anything. They thought so.

Now that he was a father, he cared more about the image he was creating for his son. He didn't want to be known as an asshole.

We snuck back to the motor coach after that for some lunch; Jameson remained quiet, carrying his jug of water when he stopped at the door to his motor coach.

Looking down, I saw the addition Emma had added. There, right before the steps, was a doormat that said: **Beware! Asshole inside.**

He smirked despite the edge of annoyance. "Emma ..."

"Ah, yes." I gave my own smile and laugh. "She has a way about her, doesn't she?"

"Hmm ... yes." He turned and offered me a smile. "She does."

Opening the door, he stepped inside where Cal had made lunch for us and Axel was waiting for his mommy to feed him.

Jameson smiled when he looked at the new hat designs Simplex had sent over. They looked pretty cool, and seeing the word "Champion" sprawled across them was satisfying, knowing how hard it was to earn that title."

It wasn't long before Alley came inside and motioned to Jameson that it was time to get the pre-race activities going so that was where we headed—after Jameson pulled one over on Emma and again replaced her lotion with self-tanner. It was stupid that we found so much humor in something we'd done a dozen times.

Being the race that marked the one-year start of our friends with benefits days, the thoughts swirled of our time together back then.

The tingling feeling in my gut I had that night and the way he whispered "stay" and then finally, coming together intimately for the first time.

Smiling, Jameson approached me as I stood with Axel on the grid, who was slobbering all over me like a Boxer puppy. I couldn't understand where all the salivia was coming from.

"It's different seeing you in this light," he said softly only to me, watching Axel. "I like it."

"Yeah, well all this heat is causing me to sweat like crazy. I feel like I'm wearing a water bra."

"Water bra?" His eyebrow rose.

"I think I have a pool of water in each cup from all this sweat."

Jameson grinned wider. "That's attractive."

"Hey." I shifted, handing Axel to him all the while airing myself out. That kid produced a lot of heat. "I aim to please."

"That you do, honey." Axel bounced in his arms when the race day activities kicked up. A thriving country band, surrounded by screaming fans, played their new single on the stage located in the infield grass. It reminded me of a time when Jameson and I would sit in the infield at the local dirt tracks surrounded by country music, old trucks, and tailgates down sitting on coolers full of beer.

Jameson's arms snuck around my waist swaying to the music as he held our son.

"I wasn't referring to the heat either."

Leaning back against his chest, I whispered, "I know."

I knew he was referring to our time spent in this exact location a year ago. Me feeling like I was about to burst with anxiety, and him, though I didn't know at the time, experiencing that gnawing dread of wanting something you thought was completely out of reach.

But here we were, a year later, after overcoming tragedy, together.

There wasn't a single breeze that day. The heat scorched high in the sky over the Lowe's Motor Speedway grid of forty-three cars waiting for the race to begin.

Though I thought for sure they were lying, the thermometer said it was one hundred and four. It had to be at least two hundred degrees. I was sure of it.

Jameson, to prepare for the heat today, had been carrying around a gallon of water and was well on his way through his second gallon.

"I know in about an hour ..." He shook the half empty gallon jug, "... I'm gonna have to pee."

"And then what?" I asked, laughing at the thought of him asking to stop the race for a bathroom break.

"I just hold it." He looked down to sign an autograph from a pint-sized fan who approached.

"What if you can't?"

"You just go."

I had a feeling this happened before. He'd been awfully quick to change his uniform after the Texas race.

"So you—"

"Stop talking about it." He said, slightly annoyed, but smiling at me.

On days like this when the temperature outside broke a hundred, the heat inside the cars peaked one forty. A driver's biggest concern was the heat. With the safety equipment they wore, gloves, and a complete racing suit, they felt the heat.

The exhaust systems ran underneath the driver's feet, and the heat from the engine and transmission was intense.

With all that heat, they sweat. And when they sweat, it didn't pool in their bra. Their suits absorbed it usually, but it led to dehydration eventually. It was not uncommon for a driver to lose about five pounds during a race just from water weight.

The problem was that dehydration led to more blood flow throughout your body trying to cool you off with less reaching your vital organs. In turn, you dealt with impaired concentration, decreased energy, and fatigue. That was not exactly ideal when inside a car pushing two hundred miles per hour, surrounded by concrete walls.

Jameson had a good ritual on days like this. He'd watch the weather closely, prepare by drinking lots of water and eliminating soda and alcohol—two things that could dehydrate you quickly.

Back in the days when he raced sprint cars on dirt, he'd pack his racing suit with ice packs just prior to the feature events, but now they had cooling systems in their helmets that circulated air and also wore a "cool" shirt. These shirts had about fifty feet of tubing inside of them that had the ability to keep you cool by flipping a temperature switch. They also had something similar built into their seat, and an auxiliary switch on their dash controlled it.

Kyle caught me when Jameson was with the media and asked my thoughts on how Jameson would handle the heat today.

"Are you worried?" I asked. Kyle never showed emotions on race day. He kept his thoughts and remarks focused on the race and winning.

"No, but I want to be sure he's gonna be okay." He fiddled with his headset, adjusting the volume as I'm sure Mason was asking him questions. They used headsets even when Jameson wasn't on the track. It was easier to communicate that way when the team was spread out around the track. "It's hot."

"You're telling me," I laughed, fanning my face with my hand. "I think my bra has a gallon of sweat in it."

Kyle looked around to see who heard me and then chuckled, returning his headset to his ears. "Always a pleasure conversing with you, Sway."

Before Jameson got in the car that afternoon and prepared for six hundred miles, I handed Axel over to Nancy who took him inside the air-conditioned towers. It was too hot for him. Hell, it was too hot for me.

We said our goodbyes, I wished him good luck, and then I headed up to the tower with Emma.

On the way up to the private suites, I ran into Paul Leighty's girlfriend, Elaina. She was new this year and had some things to learn about tact. She flat out asked me if Jameson had signed a pre-nup.

Who asked that?

Up until that moment, the thought of a pre-nup had never even crossed my mind. Jameson never mentioned it. No one in our families ever mentioned it, so why did this girl I'd only met five minutes ago bring it up?

That got me thinking the majority of the race about pre-nups and if Jameson had wanted one. It was a little late now, but he was worth a lot of money these days and had cars, houses, all kinds of stuff I would consider his, but if something happened, I had to mentally stop myself there. I couldn't focus on the race and pre-nups so I instead focused on the race.

"Your fuel window is sixty laps, bud," Kyle told him once he was making the pace laps prior to the start.

"Ten-four," Jameson said and then asked, "I need a couple Gatorades at each stop."

"Will do. Just make sure you try to keep cool and keep drinking fluids."

Being NASCAR's longest night, none of the drivers were thrilled with the heat today. I was worried about him and by lap three hundred, when the sun had finally set, the temperature hadn't dropped, and my fears of him getting dehydrated were starting to grow.

"How do these auxiliary switches work?" Jameson asked. His voice was completely drained.

"If you turn on the one for your seat, you'll have to turn the one for your helmet up."

"Oh," he began to fade in the field, creating a distance between him and Paul Leighty in turn four. "No wonder."

"How are your temps doing?"

It took another lap before he replied to Kyle's question.

"Me? Or the car?"

"Both, I guess." Kyle let out a nervous chuckle that was rare for him. "You hangin' in there, bud?"

He was silent for another lap as he battled with a lap car to stay in his twelfth place running order, and my heart leapt into my throat.

"Yeah, just tired." He let out a whoosh of air and continued with a dull voice. "When I get close to other cars, my temps shoot up."

It didn't help that he was running mid-pack after a pit altercation when Spencer dropped the jack too soon.

On the final stop, water was spewing from the radiator vent on the right side of the hood and got Spencer and Gentry in the face. Whenever the temps in the car went up, the vent on the right side of the car near the windshield spewed hot water.

It seemed every stop, and there were many from the tires shredding about every twenty laps, something went wrong. The guys were dropping air tools, tires were getting away, and Jameson kept getting in the pit at the wrong angle. He had the pit in between Colin and Paul, and every time, Colin got into his pit sideways so that meant Jameson got into his at the wrong angle.

"Damn it, we need to get this together!" Jameson shouted after the last stop. "I need another Gatorade. My feet are burning through the heat shields. Oh, and not the grape one. That was gross."

I laughed beside Nancy who was holding Axel up near the window to see the cars pass by. His wide green eyes fixated on the track below.

Jameson didn't want to make a big deal out of it, but he was, in fact, feeling the heat. That was his way of letting us know without complaining.

"How many more laps?" I asked, mostly to myself, worried about Jameson.

Nancy looked over her shoulder at me shifting Axel to her hip. He latched on to her necklace with his hands and then quickly turned to sucking on it. "I think there's about a hundred."

Those hundred laps were way longer than I, or Jameson, would have liked.

At one point Kyle and Jimi contemplated taking Jameson out of the car and putting in a back-up driver from the Nationwide series.

He managed to hang onto a ninth-place finish, but as soon as he was out of the car and walking away, he collapsed.

The media who were huddled around caught wind of the situation and started in about the drivers doing too much each week and the possible heat exhaustion results.

There was no way you were going to tell Jameson Riley he was doing too much. Yes, he was doing too much between racing sprint cars, the Cup series, running a track, and a three-man sprint car team, but like I said, you couldn't tell him that. He was doing what he loved.

Jameson was forced by the track officials to visit the infield care center along with a handful of other drivers, but his thoughts were once again focused on the race and what he could have done for a better finish, despite his lethargic demeanor.

"Man." He wiped a cold rag across his forehead and over the back of his neck. His matted sweaty hair stood in odd directions. His face, flushed from the hours of exertion portrayed his thoughts clearly to those who knew him well. "I must have slid through that pit box five times onto the air hose." He looked at Spencer who sat beside him being treated for the burns to his hands and forearms when the over-spray from the radiator had scorched him. "Sorry, guys. It just wasn't my night."

They understood, though. Everyone had bad nights. Just look at last year when this very same race was almost lost because of his pit crew.

Later that night when we got to the hotel, the same one we stayed at a year ago, I watched him sleep wondering how I got so lucky to have him.

I couldn't say everything in our lives was easy, but I could say that we worked well through it.

Sometime in the night, Jameson's fingers slid around my neck and then into my hair to cradle the back of my head. I could feel his breath on my face and then his nose at my temple. We exhaled together, and then he moved to rest his forehead against mine.

His body trembled from exhaustion as he smiled. "I can't believe it's been a year."

"Me either," I smiled, knowing despite the complications from the race, he remembered the night and what tonight meant.

That's when the pre-nup ideas came back to me and I voiced my concern.

"Should we have signed a pre-nup?"

I was immediately turned in his arms to face him. "No."

It was a prompt answer. One that you knew he didn't have to think about.

"But what about, I don't know, all the money you had and all your shit. Wouldn't you want your shit protected?"

"What is all this about?" he finally asked, sitting up on his elbow to look down at me.

"Paul's girlfriend asked me if we signed one. I just thought, maybe with the whole Darrin thing, and being pregnant, you may have forgotten about one."

His eyes scowled even in the poorly lit room.

"No, I didn't forget. Phillip asked and I said no. If you were to ever leave me, you might as well take everything I have. To me, I would have nothing left if you were gone. Besides that," he continued, "it's not like you were in it for the money. I knew that." He laughed, leaning back on the bed beside me. His hand moved over the sheets to find mine. "You were in it for the sex."

"Yeah, you're right. I'm in it for the sex."

The topic of the pre-nup was never brought up again. He said his part on it, and I never questioned his intentions. He knew what he wanted.

I'd taken a vow to myself that I'd never hide anything from Axel or Jameson.

If something was wrong, I would tell them.

I understood why people put things off. Fear of the unknown. To me, as I'd said many times, not knowing was worse than the fear of keeping the secret.

What if I hadn't stayed that night in Charlotte with Jameson?

We wouldn't have experienced some of the best times of our lives. In those three weeks I learned more about myself and him than the previous eleven years. I also got knocked up, but I learned a lot.

If I wouldn't have listened to myself that night in Charlotte I wouldn't be looking down on the most beautiful little boy.

Currently stealing flowers from gravesites, he was beautiful and had brought so much joy to our lives. Being a mother to a child where your husband was constantly on the road was difficult at times, but I wouldn't change anything. Well, maybe some of the late night crying sessions or the teething. Those weren't fun.

It had been four months since Charlie passed away, and we were now having our memorial race weekend for him, on what would have been his forty-third birthday.

In those four months, life had changed as it always did with time.

We moved back to Mooresville because of Dana and Cooper.

It never failed. When I was home alone they'd come over, so I made the executive decision to move back to Mooresville.

Along with a pair of restraining orders, it was the best thing for everyone.

By the way, Spencer paid the price for this Dana and Cooper "let in" incident and spent two days in the hospital because Jameson tased him. This wouldn't have ordinarily landed someone in the hospital, but Jameson did it at the worst possible time he could. Spencer was driving.

The conversation between Nancy and Jameson was the most entertaining when he had to tell them who tased Spencer.

"What do you mean you tased your brother?" Nancy gasped. "Jameson, that doesn't sound like a very nice thing to do."

Jameson replied, "It wasn't a nice thing to do, but he let Dana in *my* house while we were on our honeymoon. That wasn't very nice."

She turned to Spencer and his broken arm.

"Spencer," she scolded. "That woman is crazy! Why would you do something like that?"

That went on for an hour, and in the end, Nancy was upset with Spencer and took Jameson's side in the whole situation. No surprise there—Jameson was her baby and could do little wrong in her eyes.

Oh, and Jimi took that taser away after the incident.

Andrea had taken over my position at the track, and Jameson hired a whole array of staff to fill in the voids from us not being there. I flew home every few weeks to make sure everything was running smoothly, but other than that, Axel and I traveled with Jameson, in our home away from home—the motor coach.

This worked well, but if I was being honest with you, raising a kid on the road was not easy. Raising a kid, in general, wasn't easy. There were times Jameson and I got stressed out and took our parenting frustrations out on each other, but looking at our families, we understood that was completely normal. Hell, Alley and Spencer once stopped talking for a week over grounding Lane for sticking toothpaste up his nose.

Alley, the amazing super woman that she was, had just given birth to Alexis Nicole Riley a few weeks back when we were in Daytona. Days after her birth, she was back to working. I couldn't understand how quickly she recovered from childbirth. I still felt out of shape after having Axel. Or maybe that was the ten pounds I still carried around with me.

With everyone starting families, Spencer and Alley decided to have a house built near ours in Mooresville and across the street for Aiden and Emma. Their fifteen hundred square foot apartment in Charlotte was apparently not big enough any longer.

Having the entire family living within walking distance to one another was like living with the cast from *Jackass*. The boys were always thinking of stupid shit to do and usually one of them ended up in the hospital or with a concussion.

In the last four months, Jameson had three concussions, six stitches above his left eyebrow, two broken fingers and three broken ribs. And those injuries were just at home, not racing.

Aiden and Spencer's injuries were often worse because Jameson had a flair for talking them into the dangerous shit. He'd rattle off some ridiculous dare, and every *single* time they took the challenge.

After the third concussion, Simplex, concerned their driver was crazy, forced him to sign a contract that prevented him from engaging in reckless or unsafe behavior that would stop him from living up to his end of his five-year contract with them.

He may have signed the agreement but I think Simplex knew damn well he didn't stop riding his dirt bike or racing sprint cars. Two things he'd rather die over than give up. Asking a guy like Jameson to give up sprint car racing was like asking him to give up sex.

That was clearly not an option.

Emma and Aiden were busy getting everything ready for their little *ones* that were due in November. The shocking revelation really came when they found out they were having twins. Aiden was not at all excited about this but eventually came to terms with it.

Emma was wrong to have decided a *major* life decision without him but they worked everything out after a few weeks and listening to Jimi's words of wisdom.

His exact words after a very public fight at a restaurant outside of Atlanta were, "Listen, you two ... I'm tired of this shit. Act like fucking adults! So you fuck up and get married in Vegas, did you really expect either of you to make responsible decisions when it came to becoming parents?" Neither of them said anything so he continued, "That's what I thought."

I was almost positive Emma learned her lesson when she found out she was having twins, and Aiden's response was, "See ... that's what you get."

Emma had always wanted children, but she also never thought the decision through. She had no idea the impact those tiny humans were about to have on their lives.

When you thought about it, you would assume the driver of the car had the most grueling schedule, but that was not the case.

Take Aiden for example. Monday through Wednesday, Aiden was usually free, until Thursday when he was required to be at the track, spotting for Jameson during practices, qualifying, and the race. He'd stay there with him until Sunday. Monday the process started all over again at a different track, different city. Aiden also spotted for Jameson during any Busch or Truck race, too, and this year, he was scheduled to run thirteen Busch races and seven in the Truck series.

Emma was less constricted because most of her work revolved around Jameson's fan club and charity events she scheduled for him. So now, you add twin boys into that picture, and that wouldn't exactly result in much family time.

Spencer's schedule was similar to Aiden's, but Alley ... poor Alley went everywhere Jameson went. Being his publicist, she had her work cut out for her. Now that she had two little ones, it wasn't unusual to see Alley running around with Lane attached to her back and Lexi snuggled into a Baby Bjorn.

Van made the move to Mooresville with us, though I could tell he was torn by the decision. Every time I flew home to Elma, he came with me. I think over time he'd formed a bond with the Lucifer twins. Van was the only one who could stand to be around the little shits without wanting to kill them.

After Charlie passed away, Logan and Lucas got into a shit load of trouble in school. They were becoming *almost* unbearable for Andrea. I had no idea how Andrea made it through the day with them without medicating them or herself. I would have shipped their asses off to boarding school a long time ago. You'd think turning seven would have at least matured them slightly. Not a chance.

Jameson's season was going great. He was leading the points with Tate and Paul close behind. He'd won three of the last six races and had jumped to a 230-point lead over Tate last week in Charlotte. The tension between him and Colin Shuman was still there, but Jameson had learned a valuable lesson—knowing when to walk away.

I should probably rephrase that: he walked away *most of the time*. In Richmond, after a late race wreck when Jameson blew a tire and collected both him and Colin, he threw his helmet at Jameson and ended up hitting *me* in the back. Jameson did not walk away from that and spent a good amount of time defending his actions to the media and to Simplex who weren't pleased.

Racing in the elite levels of NASCAR, there was no way for him to escape the taunting and retaliation on the track altogether, but he needed to learn to say when, and he had for the most part. He still had his temper tantrums and was still the same hothead who overreacted to the inconsequential things in life, but he was maturing. He could *almost* be classified as an eight-year-old in maturity.

You could say, looking back on the last few months, our lives had changed considerably, that was for sure.

One thing remained the same: we were still Mama Wizard and Dirty Heathen as we'd always been. Some said having a kid changed your sex life. It didn't for us. We made use of any alone time we had.

"Dadadadada," Axel babbled away, crawling around me in the grass and the wild flowers that bordered Charlie and Rachel's graves. I chose to have Charlie buried next to Rachel in our hometown of Aberdeen. I thought that was fitting since they had spent the majority of their lives together in that small Grays Harbor town.

And when I thought about it some more, I would have wanted that for Jameson and me. This way they would be together forever in my mind.

I struggled with losing Charlie—some days were good, some weren't. It was easier being in Mooresville and being around racing again, but still, it was something where I just had to remember what was important and that was being a mother to my son and a wife to my husband.

I intended on being the best damn Mama Wizard I could be.

I gently traced my fingertips over my mother's headstone, reading the script aloud. "Rachel Marie Reins, loving wife and mother."

A few tears fell as I remembered my times with my mom, wondering how different my life may have turned out had she not died. Deciding this would just upset me more than anything, I looked over at Axel as he chewed his second piece of grass.

"Are you ready to go my little goat?" I asked and picked him up. "And you really should start saying Mama. I'm clearly a better choice. I mean look at everything I offer you ... you wouldn't eat if it wasn't for the foodbags!"

Axel grinned at me. It was bizarre to see how much he resembled Jameson at such a young age, but also reassuring. Whenever I missed Jameson, all I had to do was look into Axel's green eyes, and I saw him. The personalities were so similar. He had one hell of a temper, but other than the temper, he was one of the happiest babies I'd ever seen. Just so long as you didn't piss him off, and for God's sake, don't interrupt his feeding time.

Jameson made this mistake once when we were stuck in a rainstorm outside of Bloomington. Needless to say, he never asked me to stop breastfeeding him once I started again.

I sat there at my parent's gravesites for another few minutes telling them everything that happened in the last few months before loading Axel back in the car.

Tonight was the memorial race we'd put together for Charlie so everyone was flying in to attend. We had planned it around the bye week in NASCAR, the Outlaw races, and the USAC schedules.

Only problem was that my dirty heathen was in Grand Forks, North Dakota, with Justin and Tyler at an appearance for their new sponsor on the additional car that he added this year. Not that he needed to add another car to his team, but knowing Jameson, I wasn't surprised he added another one.

So there we were texting all morning, but he had yet to give me a final answer on whether or not he was actually coming.

When I got inside the car and my little goat was buckled in safely, I sent him another text while Van drove to the track.

It was now noon, and we only had six hours until racing started. I needed Jameson for two reasons: one, he pulled the biggest crowd in and we advertised that he'd be there. And two, we hadn't seen each other in close to two weeks and I missed him.

Please tell me you're coming!

It took him about ten minutes to respond, and by the time he did, we were at the track, unloading the t-shirts into the merchandise tents.

Coming, huh, that can be arranged.

I smiled. ***Can we please have a conversation when you're not acting like a twelve-year-old?***

Not likely.

Are you or are you not?

Huh?

Will you be here tonight?

I had to avoid the word coming. It was sad that I couldn't use that word with my twenty-four-year-old husband, but it was true.

Axel started squirming in my arms and babbling about daddy again. Trying to hold a wiggly six-month-old and text at the same time was challenging.

I don't know if I can make it. I'm still in Grand Forks. Sorry.

Damn you, Jameson! These fans are expecting you. What do you want me to do now?

At that point, I was beyond irritated that he led me to believe he'd make it and now he suddenly couldn't. Axel was wiggling so much that I almost dropped him and the boxes I was holding.

"Okay, just stop squirming," I told Axel and set him down on the grass near the ticket booth, knowing he'd just crawl around and pick flowers, which I didn't mind.

Look up.

What? I don't have time for this shit, Jameson.

Look up, honey.

I did and was met with my dirty heathen, smirking, holding a smiling Axel in his arms. I didn't waste any time before I ran to him ... dropped everything and ran to him.

His rich, intoxicating scent overwhelmed my senses, leaving me just as breathless as it always did. He smelled like methanol from the sprint cars, and I wanted to rip all his clothes off with my teeth.

Nancy approached us from behind.

"*Ohhh* ... let me see my grandbaby!" she squealed, as did Axel. He loved Grandma Me-Me. That's what she called herself.

Nancy had been traveling with everyone so she could help take care of Lexi while Alley put out fires Jameson started on and off the track.

"You two go *reunite*," She giggled to herself. "I got Axel." She shooed us away toward Jameson's office with her hands.

We were just making our way up the wooden steps when Mark was, unfortunately, also looking for Jameson, along with a group of fans who had gathered when they realized he was here.

Racing wouldn't start for a while, but the gates had just opened, which meant Jameson wouldn't be able to just wander around.

"Hey, Jameson, I'm glad you're here already." Mark nudged his shoulder. His JAR Racing hat shadowed his eyes, and I smiled that he was promoting Jameson's sprint car team. "Listen, Phil wants to know if you'll be racing tonight? He needs to figure out how many heat races we are going to run."

"It's all right." I could tell he was torn between being with me and his duties as the owner so I made the decision for him. "There will be time later."

Before I could make it a foot away, his tight grasp restrained me.

"Stay in my office. I'll be up in a minute," he whispered in my ear and kissed along my neck before breaking into a smirk. "I missed you."

I giggled, feeling the tickle of his two-week scruff that I absolutely loved. "Show me then."

"Where's Sway?" I asked Spencer and Aiden who were sitting in the announcer's booth going over Justin and Tyler's lap times. "Did she come in here?"

"Look, Justin smoked you on the last lap. Looks like someone may need to stick to cup cars," Spencer snickered. "She's in your office."

He then shoved the remainder of his hotdog in his mouth.

"I hope you choke," I told him and strode past them toward my office. If only I had my taser back.

Once inside, I was thankful I was the one who opened the door and not someone else.

There, my wife was spread out on my desk with absolutely nothing on but a pair of black leather boots that went up to her knees.

"Holy fuck!" I gasped, locking the door. "What if it wasn't me who opened the door?"

"Well, that would have been awkward," she giggled and then a slow, wicked smile spread over her full lips. "Now get over here, champ."

I was across the room before she finished her sentence. My fingers danced across the soft skin of her upper thighs, memorizing the feel of the skin I missed so much. My body knew hers in every way, and it didn't take long before I had discarded my clothes and pressed against her warm delicate body.

"Oh, God, Sway ... I missed you *soooo* much," I moaned when I entered her. I growled in her ear eliciting a shiver of pleasure from her.

"I need some proper bearing alignment," she whimpered and arched her back, pressing her chest into mine. I latched on to her nipples but she quickly pushed me away. We'd been over this before. I had an obsession with them lately, but not the milk that still filled them. The one time that happened was not enjoyable, but I kept forgetting she was still breastfeeding.

Sway threw her head back against my desk, revealing her neck for me. Her legs wrapped around my waist pulling me inside her, both of us gasping at the intense feeling of finally being together again.

Welding her mouth to mine, kissing me so passionately, I almost felt lightheaded with her sweet tongue caressing my own as I slid further inside her welcoming heat. There were no words, just grunts, groans, moans, and the occasional gasp as we moved against each other.

I moved from her mouth and attacked her neck with nips and bites I knew she loved. Her body began to tremble in my arms as she whimpered once again pulling me even closer. I wasn't going to last long like this, not with the noises she was making. My hips began moving on their own, desperate to feel.

Reaching between us I found the spot I knew would send her over the edge in seconds. Her ignition switch was engineered for my hands so it only took one flick and she fired right up.

"*Jesus,* Jameson ..." she sighed, digging her nails into my back, her legs tightened around me.

"How's your compression ratio?" I grunted, my fists tangling in her hair, tugging imperceptibly.

I knew my girl's compression ratio. I knew just how much her combustion chamber could take, and I loved her higher thermal efficiency.

It was sad that all this car talk got me going but it did.

"My compression ratio is increasing its power," she whimpered as her eyes rolled back.

"Good ... we wouldn't want the engine to start knocking from the detonation."

"No, no ... we wouldn't want detonation."

Sway literally screamed out her pleasure as her body convulsed around my camshaft, a camshaft that intended to assure this align boring was done properly. No one wants bad bearings or detonation.

"Fuck, Sway," I gritted between my teeth, all this dirty car talk was sending me into a tumult of need. I kissed her roughly before pulling back to watch her fall apart in my arms.

I moved my hand from her and gripped the edge of the wooden desk, bracing myself. My head fell forward and my eyes clenched tightly shut. I was done for. Panting and moaning her name against the shell of her ear, I was unable to hold back any longer.

I fell against her, exhausted. We lay there for a moment, slowing our breathing before I pulled back, resting my weight on one arm. Her eyes were closed, from exhaustion or embarrassment I couldn't be sure, because the cutest blush I'd ever seen was spreading from her cheeks down to her chest.

I traced the features of her face with my fingertips, rubbing my thumb slowly across her full, pouty lips. Leaning down, I kissed her softly before pulling back to look deep into her eyes. Warm emerald met smoldering green.

"You're amazing,"

"You're not so bad yourself there, *champ*," she reached up, running her hand down my jaw. "I love this."

"I know you do. I did it for you." I ran my fingers up the leather of her boots she'd kept on. "*And,* I like the boots."

She sighed contently, leaning forward to capture my lips once more. "I feel like I haven't seen you in so long ... but then when you're here, it's like you've never left."

We laid there on my desk for what seemed like ages, and I began to wish I could stay right there the rest of the night when Sway's body shuddered and stifled giggles bursts from her mouth.

"What's so funny?"

"Nothing," Sway giggled again.

I leaned back and blinked, raising an eyebrow at her, because clearly it was not nothing by the giggles.

"I was just thinking about compression ratios," she snickered.

I rolled my eyes at her. "Why are you laughing, though?"

"I can't believe some of the shit that turns us on."

"Mmm," I kissed her forehead once. "But that's why we get along so good."

"I was thinking ..." She let out a little snort-laugh as her body shuddered again from repressing her laughter.

"That's never a good thing." I smirked into her hair.

Sway smacked my arm. "I think we should do it in the announcer's booth sometime. I've always wanted to try that." She giggled again. Why this was funny to her I wasn't sure.

"Why is that funny, though?" I asked.

"And we can leave the PA system on ..." she continued in a quiet voice that I had to strain to hear.

"What are you talking about?" I looked at her in confusion.

"While we're doing it ... we can leave the microphones on ... given nobody should be at the track when this occurs ..." Sway's entire body was shaking at that point with pent-up laughter that she couldn't finish her sentence.

I shook my head.

"And that ..." I took her face between my hands and kissed her, "... is why I married you, you crazy, crazy woman," I whispered against her lips, remembering the way they conformed to mine. "We should get back out there. My heat race is in a few minutes." I smiled softly and helped her up.

She acquiesced with a little grunt and pushed herself off the desk, reaching for her jeans. A few more giggles escaped her while she continued to dress.

"You guys oughta install a sound deadener in those walls," Aiden suggested with slightly flushed cheeks when we stepped into the announcer's booth.

Spencer threw his head back with laughter. "Your shirt's on backward, little brother."

Pulling my shirt over my head, I heard Spencer chuckle again and ask Sway, "*Soo* ... car talk, huh?"

She slapped the back of his head as he took a drink of his beer. "I hope you choke."

After fixing my shirt and smacking my brother again, Sway and I went our separate ways for the night.

She was helping Andrea and Mallory in the concession stands tonight until the memorial race, and then she'd be in the flag stand to wave the green and checkered flag.

Emma waddled up to me as I headed toward the pits to get in the car for the heat race.

"Jameson," she waved at me to meet her halfway. "Can you sign these for me? They're for Bucky's grandkids."

"Yeah ... sure ..." I raised my eyebrows at her appearance. She looked exhausted. "Shouldn't you be sitting down there, humpty?" She hated the nickname, which in turn, made me very happy.

She snorted, punching my shoulder. "Don't call me that, asshole."

Humpty left after that, leaving me in my element, the pits surrounded by dirt and sprint cars.

I inhaled a deep breath, my senses overflowing with the sweet smells of methanol exhaust mingling with the sharper burnt smell of the tire siping irons. I listened to the noises as air tools chattered, generators hummed and grinders rasped as crew members roughed up tires. There was the occasional loud "*romp*" of the nearby revving sprint cars and the familiar twang of country music from one hauler to the next.

This was my home.

I looked around at the hundreds of cars that gathered here, remembering *why* they were here. It was essentially Mallory's idea to do the memorial race for Charlie, and it was also something I'd been thinking about for a while.

We got all the cars around the Northwest to come over. Dad, Justin, Tyler, Tate, Bucky Miers, Shey Evans, and Bobby were also here in support. Even a bunch of my old buddies from racing in the USAC series were here along with Ryder and Cody Bowman.

Originally, I wasn't going to race, but I couldn't pass up the opportunity to race sprint cars when I had the chance.

After the first heat race, I noticed my car wasn't handling the way I wanted. Tommy and I ran through the different possibilities of setup changes we could make before Dad approached us, his suit pulled down to his waist where he had it tied.

"Change the springs," my dad leaned into the wing, crossing his arms over his chest. "It'll make a difference."

I didn't respond and stared down at my car.

"Did you hear me?" Dad nudged my shoulder.

"I heard you. I just chose to ignore you," I muttered and began changing the springs like he told me to.

I hated it when he was right, but being a fifteen-time champion in the World of Outlaws, he knew how to run a sprint car.

I caught up with Sway after the trophy dashes and heat races were finished.

She smiled and handed me a hamburger. "You should eat something."

"Thanks, honey." I reached for the cheeseburger in her hand and placed a quick kiss on her cheek.

A group of fans had gathered behind me as I stood there in the doorway to the concession stands eating my hamburger. Sway giggled and motioned for me to turn around, so I did and began signing an abundance of autographs before making my way back to the pits.

"So how is this going to work?" Tate asked, pulling his racing suit over his shoulders. Shrugging, he adjusted the shoulders to fit the way he preferred.

"I'm going to do one lap by myself. Then you guys file in for a 4-wide salute for two laps, but on the front row we are gonna do 3-wide, and then it's a fifty lap main event. After that, my dad and I will say a few words."

Tate smiled and raised his eyebrows. "Just for fun ... right?"

"*Please* ..." I rolled my eyes, reaching for my helmet on the seat inside my sprint car. "Nothing's just for fun on a dirt track."

I heard Justin laugh from behind us with Lily in his arms.

"Don't believe anything he says Tate," he glared my direction. "He caught a race with us in Terre Haute and said it was just for fun."

"It was for fun."

"Yeah," Justin rolled his eyes. "That's why you smoked us. You know," he said contemplatively. "Did you curse our cars that night? Something like only the car owner can win?"

"I have no idea what you're talking about."

I couldn't help a few tears during the memorial laps, not when I knew the reaction Sway was having to all this and wanted to comfort her, hold her, and let her know I was there for her.

I also knew that this was where I belonged, though. I belonged in the car, showing my respect out on the track with the other drivers who made all my dreams come true because of Charlie.

If it weren't for him I would have never become the driver I was today. He allowed me to race out here in the off-seasons and after school. He also gave me the love of my life and pushed us together when we least expected.

On the second lap, I remembered the very last thing he said to me.

"*Jameson ... I'm counting on you to take care of my little girl. She loves you and that's the only thing that matters to me. You've always been like a son to me ... and I'm incredibly proud of the man you've become."*

I promised him I'd take care of Sway, and I intended on keeping that pledge, always.

On the backstretch of the second lap, we all started revving our engines, eager to start racing.

You couldn't see other drivers in the car because of how low you sat in a sprint car, but I could scarcely make out Justin taunting me by revving his engine and edging forward.

I saw Sway perched in the flag stand still, holding the green flag, so when I passed by on the last memorial lap I revved the engine for her, knowing she loved the sound.

My dad, Tate, Justin, and I were on the front row, leading the cars down out of turn three when the fireworks started exploding.

The excitement of being back in the type of cars I loved was pulsating through me. I loved it here.

Once the green flag was dropped, it was racing as usual. Dad and I messed around the entire time, not taking anything too seriously. It had been close to a year since I was last on the track with him. He'd pass me, and then I'd quickly take him on the outside where he usually never went. Justin and Tate got in on the action as well, and by the time there were a few laps left it was clear none of us would be able to catch Justin once he got past Tyler for the lead.

When the race ended, I pulled my car down under the flag stand, as did Dad. We stood there for a moment, smiling as JD, our announcer, made his way down to us.

He handed me the microphone first.

"Jameson ... how does it feel being in a sprint car again? Does it bring you back to your roots?"

"Definitely. I never remember how much I miss racing these until I come home," I laughed. "It's in my blood, I guess."

The fans screamed in response, and even from thirty-feet away the sound was deafening.

"Now, was this your idea to have the memorial race for your father-in-law on his birthday?" JD asked.

Sway and Axel had made their way onto the track, and I took Axel from her, wrapping my arms around the two of them.

"No, it wasn't my idea. Mallory Kelly wanted to have the event for him, which we thought was a great idea. It was Sway's idea to have the race on his birthday."

JD pushed the microphone at Sway, but she shook her head, tears toppling over her flushed cheeks.

Axel, who was staring at the sprint car, said "Dadada," and then squealed, bouncing in my arms.

Dad laughed at how focused he was on the cars and stood next to JD as he asked him a question.

I leaned down and kissed the top of Sway's head softly.

"So Jimi, how's it feel racing with your son again?"

"It feels good," he told him with a smile. "This race was just for fun. I'd known Charlie since he bought the track some sixteen years ago. He was a very good friend of mine, and I'm glad I was able to come out here and show my support for him and our families who were so deeply touched by him." His voice broke near the end, and Sway started crying again, reaching for him.

I took the microphone from JD.

"Sway and I just want to thank everyone for coming out and paying their respects to Charlie." I looked down at Sway wrapped in Dad's arms as I held onto Axel, who was trying to take the microphone away. "I don't know how many more races I can make out here, but thanks for supporting the track, we appreciate it.

The crowd roared to life as I waved and climbed on the back of a four-wheeler Justin had brought onto the track.

I tried to make my way back to the pits, but was quickly encircled by hundreds of screaming fans. Handing Axel over to Van for protection, I began signing autographs once again and attempted to get back to my hauler. It wasn't nearly as bad as being at a NASCAR race, but it was a thick crowd tonight.

I didn't know if I'd ever understand this whole fame thing, but one thing held true: what you gave up to follow your dreams never changed. It was all about the sacrifices you were willing to make.

I knew what I wanted, though. I wanted my son to have someone he could look up to and someone he wouldn't be ashamed to say, "Hey ... that's my dad."

I understood that everything came with a price. But I came to realize that those sacrifices could have some amazing returns.

I was loading the remaining merchandise boxes into the back of my Expedition when a familiar voice came from behind me.

"Hey, Sway ... do you have a second?"

My entire body froze as a chill shuddered through me.

"What are you doing here?"

"I just came to show my respect for Charlie. That's all," Mike told me, holding up his hands in surrender. "I swear that's all." His wide eyes conveyed his nervousness. "I'm sorry for your loss."

"You shouldn't have come here," I whispered, shaking my head. I knew he didn't mean any harm by the way his eyes darted around the parking lot. He was scared shitless. "If Jameson finds you ..." I shook my head not wanting to think of his reaction to this.

"I'm sorry. I had to apologize for everything that happened. I had no idea that's what Darrin was planning. I swear to you, I didn't. I'm not that kind of person."

"I suggest you leave," a snarled voice warned, a body stepping out from the dark cagey shadows of the parking lot.

I wasn't entirely surprised to see Van walking up and was thankful it wasn't Jameson.

Mike held his hands up. "I just came to show my respect for Charlie and tell Sway I'm sorry."

"Well ..." Van's voice faded as he stepped closer to Mike, cornering him next to the beer garden and my truck. "Don't. Ever. Come.

Back. Again ... and I'll *think* about not telling Jameson."

"I'm sorry," Mike trembled. "I don't mean any harm."

"I do, though." Van ran his hand along his jaw. "You don't even want to know how much harm I can cause. And, frankly ... I'm not the one you should be scared of. It's Jameson. If he finds out you're here ..."

Mike didn't waste another moment talking before he was running away, *literally* sprinting away.

Van laughed and slung his arm around my shoulders.

"I can't let you out of my sight for a moment, can I?"

"Apparently not. Did you install some sort of GPS on me?" I teased and loaded the last box.

"No, I just know you by now." I closed the back of the Expedition and Van smiled. "Now come on ... your husband is looking for you."

Before we reached the pit gates, I stopped him. "Van ... don't tell Jameson ... *please*."

"I won't, Ms. Sway," he assured me and motioned to the crowd where Jameson was. "Now get over there. He misses you."

Jameson still wasn't over the whole ordeal with Darrin and Mike for good reason. Hell, I still wasn't over it, and seeing Mike sent me into panic overload, but I couldn't let that break me.

Mama Wizard couldn't be broken damn it.

Watching my husband amongst a crowd of screaming fans, all suppliantly idolizing him, I realized how lucky we were. Against all odds, we had made it. And despite the world trying to tear us apart, we glued ourselves back together with Dirty Heathen and Mama Wizard super glue. The edges may have been blurred and distorted, but they were solid.

While I was standing there, Ami approached me holding Lily in her arms. I smiled at her. "I can't believe how big she's getting."

"I know," Ami laughed. "It feels like I just had her yesterday."

"Well, it wasn't that long ago," I reminded her. Lily was only a month old. "Oh, are you and Justin coming over for the barbeque tomorrow?"

"I think so, then we leave for Knoxville Nationals."

"Right. It's that time of year already, huh?"

Ami and I looked over at Justin and Jameson signing autographs for the fans.

"It never changes, does it?" Ami asked softly, kissing Lily's tiny hands.

I looked down at Axel for a minute and then smiled. "No, it doesn't. But that's the life we live. We're racers' wives."

It was around two in the morning before we finally made it back to the house on Summit Lake. Even though we'd officially moved back to Mooresville, we kept the house on the lake for times like this when we didn't want to fly home right away. We had to leave tomorrow for an appearance in Jacksonville, but it was nice to sleep in my own bed for a night.

As I carried my sleeping son into his bedroom, I understood a lot about my life looking at his innocent face.

I still believed it was better to dream than to not be able to dream at all because who would you be without it?

I knew, for me, that there was no such thing as "say when" because I was always going to want more and most of all, the dreams I thought would never be, were now my reality.

After my first National Quarter Midget Championship, I wanted more. After my first Night Before the 500, I wanted more. After the Hut Hundred, the USAC Triple Crown, Turkey Night, the Chili Bowl ... I wanted more. Say when wasn't an option for me and never would be.

I began to understand that my life was measured in moments. There were moments that tested you, challenged you, and moments that could make you fall to your knees, begging for one more moment, but you see, those moments defined you as a person. You needed to take them as they came because before you knew it, you were out of moments.

Peering down at my sleeping son, I remembered the doubts I had in the beginning. I never thought I was good enough for Sway, and all along she was thinking the same thing.

I remembered a phrase Charlie used to say to us, "It's not the track you race at. It's the high line you chose that takes you to the victory."

We all thought he was crazy toward the end, but that was when he had the most inspirational words of wisdom. More than likely he got them off commercials and cereal boxes, but they were still helpful.

I padded down the hall into our room where Sway was waiting for me. She wasn't sleeping, but wrapped up in the sheets, waiting.

Removing my clothes, I crawled in bed with her and drew her against my bare chest.

"Thank you for coming tonight," her eyes glistened, her breath light and steady. "He would have loved tonight."

"Anything for you, honey," I murmured against her neck.

"Will you sing for me? I miss the singing." She rolled over facing me, the moonlight coming into our room reflected off her glowing ivory skin.

I sang softly to her with just the right amount of drawl and timber she loved that wouldn't make Ray Charles cringe.

These were the moments that I wanted more of. These were the moments that would make me beg for more.

Burn off – Burning fuel during the course of a race. As fuel is burned, the car becomes lighter and its handling characteristics change, challenging the driver and crew to make adjustments to achieve balance.

The hot Florida sun was beating down on me inside the car, blinding me in the apex of turn four, my entire body was sweating from the physical exertion. Kyle and Aiden's raucous voices drowned out the vibrations in the engine that I didn't want to be feeling in the last race of the season.

My arms and hands burned from gripping the wheel so tightly. These last few races of the series were taking its toll on my body.

The season, much like the year before, had its ups and downs. In Talladega, Paul and I were caught up in the "big one."

I flipped my car eight times on the backstretch, earning me a visit to the infield care center and then the hospital. I've had more broken bones in one year than one should receive in their entire lifetime, but still ... I was unstoppable.

I knew what I wanted.

"Don't overdrive the car, Jameson," Kyle said. "I know you want this, but don't push too hard. Just have patience and *feel* the car."

I knew that already. I wanted to reply, "Hey thanks for the advice!" but I kept my mouth shut.

Surprising, huh? I liked to think I'd matured since I turned twenty-four, but that was probably unlikely.

It was the last race of the season, and I was running twelfth. All I needed was a top fifteenth finish to clench the title once again.

Despite a blown motor in Texas, I ran the car for two laps with no power to finish the race. I was like a nasty cold, persistent and unstoppable.

"Maybe try a half round down in wedge," I suggested when the pushing into the corner didn't improve after the last stop. "And I have a vibration. It's not bad, but it's there."

"All right, you heard him boys ... half round down, four tires, and one can. Gentry, pull the hood pins and take a look."

"Pit roads open this time by," Aiden announced.

I slowed my speed coming out of turn three to make our scheduled green flag stop.

When I pulled down on the apron, Kyle came over the radio.

"Bring it down ... second gear 4200 ... three ... two ... one, wheels straight, foot on the break."

Mason instructed the crew while I waited for them to finish.

It was times like this when I really got hasty, because, for one, I had no control and as a race car driver, that was the worst feeling.

I think that went back to my days racing sprint cars when you made the changes to your car based on your driving. If you were tight, it was something you were doing and could adjust. Now, I relied on my crew.

Kyle came over the radio again as the race neared the end.

"Twenty laps to go this time by."

This was about the time in the race where it got intense. It was a part of the race where you laid it all on the line. If you saw an opening, you took it and hoped to hell it was the right move.

So many things went through my head when I was in the car. It was hard to tell you what I focused on most.

"That was 30.75 last time by ... clear by three on the twenty-nine."

I focused on anything from how the car was handling to what my next move might be and how that particular shift of just an inch could change everything about the way my car was handling. You had to always be looking ahead. If not, you'd get boxed in and could forget about your next move.

"Inside on the line ... still inside ... clear," Aiden said. "Fourteen is looking inside. Clear by two."

"Where are we at in the points?" I asked Kyle once I made it through the string of lapped cars.

"If the race ended now you'd finish with a thirty-seven point lead."

That calmed me down a little, but the vibration in the engine flared up again.

Aside from the many thoughts about my car during the race, I also heard voices—strange I knew, but I did.

"Fifteen to go," Kyle told me. "Watch your marks. Take it easy on that engine."

I heard my mother's voice telling me it was all in my actions and make the best of them.

I heard the voice of Grandpa Casten telling me everything in life was only worth what you made it.

I heard the voice of my dad telling me his *any man worth his salt* speech, which I'd yet to figure out.

"What are your temps now?"

The last few laps, my engine and oil temperatures had been slowly climbing along with the vibration.

"218—240," I read off the water and oil pressure to him.

"How's the splitter working?"

On the last stop, Shane, our front tire changer had changed out the splitter for a new one. The splitter was an aerodynamic device fitted to the front of the car that generated down force, creating grip on the track.

"Seems good ... I'm still vibrating on the exit."

"Ten to go ... last lap was a thirty flat, clear by ten," Kyle said. The radio frequency we were on kept breaking up garbling his words. "There's a car slowing—on the—three—"

We ended up changing channels so I could hear him without the interruption.

"I can't run the top anymore. My right rear is sliding on entry," I told him as I passed another lapped car.

"Just do what you can, bud. There's five to go this time by. You're running tenth."

The more I thought about those voices again, my parents weren't the only voices I heard. I heard the voice of my wife telling me to follow my dreams and stand my ground when pushed. I heard her telling me that champions aren't made they're born. And, finally, I heard the voice of my son, saying "Go Daddy!" to me on the phone this morning.

"White flag next time by. *Great* job this season, way to stay focused!"

I drew in a deep breath—thankful the season was finally over.

I loved racing, but I also loved that time with my family.

My dad came over the radio next as I crossed the finish line. "Nice job, kid. You did awesome!"

"Thanks, Dad," I smiled.

It was then I saw this for what it really was. It was all about who wanted it most. I did.

"How does it feel to win your second Cup Championship and the first Nextel Cup Championship?" Neil asked, standing next to me as I wiped away the sweat and the champagne Kyle and Spencer just drenched me in.

"It feels good ... again, I don't even know what to say ... I'm gonna need to work on my speeches," I teased while the crowd around me chuckled. "I need to thank my family ... my wife, Sway. I honestly wouldn't be half the man I am today without you." I bowed my head and looked down at the trophy in my hands. "I don't really deserve this ... my family does. This is for you Charlie," I said and held the trophy up to the sky.

My parents taught me very early on you paid respect where respect was due, and with Charlie, I owed him everything, and I wished like hell he were here to see this.

The last few races of the season Sway was at home with Emma, who was ready to pop any day now. Since Emma had been there every step of the way for Sway and me during her pregnancy, she felt the need to be there for Emma since Aiden couldn't.

I knew when I married Sway that there would be times when she wouldn't be able to follow me around like I wanted. It was part of the life we'd chosen. What I didn't realize was how much it'd hurt to win my second championship without her by my side again. What was best for one of us wouldn't necessarily be best for the other, but that was marriage, right?

After the loads of press and photos, I was finally on a plane home to Mooresville.

When I made it home around one the next morning, the house was dark and quiet. I smiled at the note on the counter from Sway asking me to wake her when I returned. I smiled again once inside the room at the sight of the two halves of my heart sleeping in our bed.

Sway was curled up with Axel in her arms. His pacifier had fallen out beside him, his cheeks flushed from the heat of our fireplace. Sway had dressed him in Jameson Riley pajamas that had my sponsor logo and my number plastered all over them.

I stood there, leaning against the doorframe, watching them sleep for a good fifteen minutes before I made my way inside the room.

Slipping off my shoes and jacket, I crawled into bed beside Sway, kissing her shoulder softly.

I knew she said to wake her, but looking at her now, I couldn't. Instead, I watched them sleep and wondered how I got so lucky to have the dream and the wish.

I was in a deep, peaceful sleep. The kind where you were so relaxed that you were actually smiling in your sleep. It might've had something to do with the fact that my dirty heathen was finally home, and we'd just made slow, passionate love to each other and now, I lay peacefully in my champion's arms.

As soon as my eyes fluttered closed that night, Axel started crying. Knowing Jameson wouldn't wake up, I made my way across the hall to his room.

When I opened the door, his tears said it all. Or maybe it was the quivering lip.

He'd recently been doing this at night. He would do great for the first half of the night and then around three in the morning, he'd wake up crying hysterically.

"Mamama," he babbled and reached his tiny arms up to me, which melted my heart.

I picked him up and sat down in the wooden rocking chair next to his crib. Anyone who said they let them cry it out in bed didn't have a heart.

Jameson and I tried this one weekend in Richmond. I wasn't sure who cried more, Axel, me, or Jameson. After about two hours of this, Bobby, whose motor coach was parked next to us, asked us to either pick the screaming kid up, or to stop crying. He was more disturbed by our crying than by Axel's.

I couldn't blame him on that one.

"Mama's here for you, baby," I whispered against his rusty locks that stuck out. "Mama's here ..."

Axel's hair cracked me up. I tucked a few crazy strands away from his eyes and kissed the top of his head as I settled in the rocking chair with him. He wormed his way closer to the foodbags for comfort and rubbed his fleece blanket against his nose.

Though parenthood wasn't exactly everything I thought it would be, between the temper tantrums, the not wanting to wear clothes, screaming in the middle of the night, and being kicked in the tits any time I changed his diaper, I'd say we were making it through, and hey, he was still alive.

That was a good sign that we at least had *something* under control. Sure, there were the times when I'd forget he couldn't feed himself, but he was quick to remind me of that task. Or the times when I wondered how something so tiny could scream so loud, but we were making it through this.

Within ten minutes, Axel was fast asleep in my arms with his head resting on my shoulder, breathing slow, steady breaths against my neck.

It was times like this that I wanted to stop time.

I wanted to stay in this moment with him, keep him this age and cherish every moment with him, before there were no more moments like this, and he was telling me he hated me.

I wasn't stupid. I knew once he became a teenager, he'd hate me, and I was already mentally preparing myself and contemplating how I'd deal with it.

I wondered if everyone felt like this, as if your life was passing you by and you were only left with the moments you couldn't describe?

There were moments in my life that I wanted to remember as though I was living in them. I wanted to record my life, if that were possible.

I'd always felt like there were days when I wanted to go back to a certain moment and remember the exact emotion I was feeling. I wanted to go back to sitting with my mother on Sunday mornings when we gave ourselves pedicures and remember the way her infectious laughter sounded or what her smile looked like. I wanted to go back to the days at the track on Saturday mornings where my dad and I would prep and water the track together.

I wanted to go back to the exact moment I fell in love with Jameson during our summer together. I remembered the feeling, both comforting and harrowing, that washed over me knowing I loved him. Jameson was sitting inside his car after a race in Knoxville. His helmet was off, but he hadn't gotten out of the car yet.

In that particular moment, with sweat and dirt smeared over his face, the distinct smells of burnt rubber and methanol floating around us, I knew that I loved him. I didn't know why, but looking at that smirk of his that night, having just won the Triple Crown Nationals at eighteen, and how his green eyes glowed in the dark summer night, I just knew. I remembered feeling anxious and excited all at the same time and wanting time to stand still so I could stay in that moment.

I wanted to go back to the moment I felt Axel kick for the first time, standing in the flag stand watching his daddy race. I wanted to go back to the moment I heard his first scream and the look on Jameson's face when he held him.

These were all moments that you took for granted in life when they were happening, but they mean the most to you. And you didn't realize when they were happening that later you'd wish like hell you could get those moments back. The comforting thing about it was that even a smell could bring you back.

Every time I smelled nail polish ... I remembered my mom. Every time I smelled rain ... I thought of being with Charlie at the track. Every time I smelled racing fuel ... I thought of Jameson and the moment I fell in love with him.

Axel was starting to snore by now, so I gently carried him back over to his crib and laid him down. He curled around his piggy that Jameson had gotten for him, sighing contently.

There were also times when your memories brought you back to horrible moments in your life that you wanted to forget, but couldn't. Just the same, even a smell could bring the moment crashing back to you as though you were once again living in that painful experience.

I still remembered the day my mother died. Valentine's Day would also be a day I associated with the death of my mother. I'd always associate the Daytona 500 with the day my father died, and I'd always associate a dark stairwell with Darrin.

I hadn't forgotten about what Darrin did to us, but I'd moved on and focused on the positive side of it. Darrin showed Jameson and me how unbreakable our bond with each other really was. He showed me what a beautiful love story we had. Sure, it was different, but that was what made it so goddamn perfect in my mind. We were writing it to our perfection.

It wasn't something that everyone else had. It was us. Crazy but exciting, irrational but stable, and I felt pretty fucking lucky to have found the other half of my heart's missing piece. So instead of focusing on the dark haunting moments, I focused on the ones that took my breath away—the ones that made me feel like this life I was living was epic.

I focused on the magic. I focused on the magic between a man and a woman, the sparks, the fluttering hearts, the fairytale, and the Mama Wizard, her Dirty Heathen, and their flailing spaz.

The next morning I got up early intending on making my champion and our adorable spaz pancakes. I tried, I really did. Jameson didn't let me get more than an inch out of bed before his arms of steel were wrapped around me, pulling me toward him. After being apart for so long, I didn't mind. Pancakes could wait.

In the middle of our morning dyno-testing, Axel had other plans. By ten, he was screaming his adorably chubby little face off and crying profusely that we hadn't come and rescued him from his crib yet. I usually would have freed him by now, and we'd be eating breakfast, only now I was enjoying dirty heathen for breakfast.

Eventually I managed to get Jameson to focus, and we made our way into his room. Not prepared was an understatement. He was not in his crib but was instead standing next to his dresser, smiling, removing all the clothing from each drawer.

Perfect. I'd just put those away.

"Does he always do this?" Jameson asked, leaning against the doorframe, scratching his mess of hair.

"No … I've never seen him get out of his crib before. I didn't know he could get out."

Axel looked up at us and handed Jameson Mr. Piggy and his pajamas he'd taken off, leaving him in just his diaper. How he managed to get his clothes off was beyond me too.

Looking down, Axel watched his own tiny arms swinging back and forth as though he never knew they could do that. Then, with a smirk, he looked up at us.

"I think he knows something we don't," I told Jameson.

"He does. He knows we have no clue what we're doing. He can smell the fear."

I grinned. "Like a cougar?"

Jameson smacked my ass. "Not funny."

"Can you change him?"

"Yeah ... sure," he agreed with a wary expression.

I made my way downstairs to make breakfast thinking they'd come down soon. An hour later, he finally came down stairs with Axel walking behind him holding Mr. Piggy.

They were both wearing different clothes, and Axel's hair was wet.

"What took so long?" I asked, placing the pancakes on the table. "Your breakfast is getting cold."

Jameson reached down and picked Axel up.

"He peed on me ... and him ..."

Axel giggled in his arms and reached for me.

"Did you pee on Daddy?" I cooed at him, giving him a high-five.

"Yayaya..." he babbled, nodding his head. I personally found this new nodding thing adorable. Every time you asked him a question, he nodded as though he was so proud he could nod his head.

The offseason was passing quickly, and before we knew it, Thanksgiving had arrived.

"You'd be surprised where your life can take you, Andrea. Hell, Jameson and I got drunk on Purple Rain drinks and slept together. Look where that landed us." I motioned to Axel sitting beside Mr. Jangles on the floor while he took a few handfuls of his fur from him.

Andrea and I were discussing her recent involvement with Van. I kind of thought something was up between them when they left together after our Fourth of July party, but I didn't want to assume anything.

Turns out, Andrea needed a woman to talk to.

"Is that supposed to make me feel better?" Andrea asked, peeling potatoes for dinner.

"Yes, did it?" I stuffed a cookie in my mouth.

We were waiting for everyone to show up for Thanksgiving dinner at Emma and Aiden's house. Andrea and the twins flew in last night, and when Van's eyes lit up, I knew something was up.

"Well … I think you just told me to get drunk and sleep with Van." Avoiding eye contact, her eyes focused on the beer I was holding. I knew that look. I'd perfected it in my pit lizard days.

I angled my beer toward her. "Pretty much."

She smiled.

"You whore!" I giggle snorted.

"You're one to talk!"

She had me there. I shrugged once. "True, what did he say afterward?" I asked, wondering what it was like for others that this happened to.

"Umm … it happened after the Fourth of July party." Her eyes did that please-don't-judge-me sideways glance. "I freaked out afterward because of the whole Charlie thing and being too soon, and that he would think it was a mistake … anyway …" she shook her head, reaching for another potato in the bag. "He said one thing that I'll always remember. He said, I just want to feel … feel anything. For so long I've hidden myself away, but I want to feel something. I don't want to be like this forever."

When she looked up, I was emotional eating and stuffing cookie after cookie in my mouth. "Oh, my God … poor Van! I had no idea he felt like that." Another cookie. "He just seemed so … *together*."

"That's what you see. When he's not working or … he's *just* different."

"I guess so."

Our conversation soon drifted as everyone made their way into the kitchen to check on the food we were cooking.

I should clarify. Nancy was cooking, and Andrea and I were catching up and peeling potatoes. I hadn't seen them since the Fourth of July party. I couldn't believe how much the Lucifer twins had grown.

Logan was finally as tall as Lucas, and they seemed to have been acting more mature. The other thing I noticed was how much they were starting to resemble Charlie.

Emma waddled into the kitchen, holding her side. "Is there anything to eat in here? I'm starving."

Spencer walked in, too, looking for food. "Careful sis, if your ass gets any bigger you'll need a beeper when you back up," he snickered, popping a couple deviled eggs in his mouth and sat down on the stool next to me.

"You're such an asshole, Spencer," I told him, shaking my head in disapproval when Emma burst into tears that someone called her fat.

"Hey ... I'm honest." Spencer crammed another egg in his mouth. Jameson walked in and leaned against me. "You're just lucky you didn't have twins with all the ice cream you ate."

Jameson stuck up for me and smacked the back of Spencer's head.

"What the fuck are you talking about? Sway was never fat when she was pregnant."

"Ow, fuck!" Emma screamed and clutched her stomach.

Aiden ran into the kitchen to grab her, but slipped on the water she had spilled.

Only problem was, that wasn't water from the sink. Emma was in labor.

It's just like the women in our family to go into labor on a holiday or a major event. All the Riley children were born after a race Jimi won. Lane was born in the pits at a dirt track. Axel was born on Christmas. Lexi was born after the Daytona July race, and now the twins on Thanksgiving.

What could I say? We specialized in excitement.

The next few hours were spent calming Emma and Aiden down.

They were freaking the fuck out, worse than Jameson and I when we went into labor. At least she didn't need to get dressed and spend hours just getting her husband to wear his own clothes.

Once they were at the hospital, Emma delivered the twins within two minutes of getting there. Jameson drove them because he insisted that he was the only qualified driver. Smartass.

Everyone stayed out in the waiting room until Aiden came out with a huge grin.

"Emma is doing great ... *after* being sedated ... but she's great." He waited for a moment, as though he practiced saying that in the mirror or something before his eyes went wide. Clearly, we wanted to know more. "Oh ... the babies are great, too."

I don't think you could have wiped that grin off his face.

For someone who didn't want kids, he sure seemed happy that his boys had arrived safely.

Alley and I jumped to our feet at the chance to see the twins. Nancy stayed at the house with Jimi to watch the Lucifer twins, Lane, Axel, and Lexi so we could assist Aiden with Emma.

Emma was in a bit of a frenzy once the doctors told her there was no time for pain medication. Couldn't say I blamed her on that one.

"What are their names?" I asked when I peered down at the one in my arms. Alley was holding the other.

Emma and Aiden exchanged a loaded glance, as did Jameson.

"What?" I looked back and forth between the three of them. Spencer and Alley were too caught up in staring at the other baby.

Jameson, who had been standing against the door, just watching me, smiled and made his way over to pull me against his chest gently.

"The one you're holding ... is Charles James," he whispered softly, kissing the side of my head.

Jameson even had to take baby Charlie from me. That's how hard I was crying.

"Shhh ... shhh ... it's okay, honey," he soothed against me.

"I know ... it's just that—" I gave up trying to answer and cried into his hooded sweatshirt.

Once I finally calmed down—took me a good twenty minutes—I was able to hold Charlie again and learned that the baby Alley wouldn't let go of was named Noah David.

Two new little Gomez babies arrived on Thanksgiving.

Giving birth seemed intense and maybe even magical, but the act itself was disgusting to me. Even though it was disgusting it still held something incredible, which was new life.

Adding Spoiler – This is a term used to describe the changing of the direction of a spoiler or wing on a race car. Usually adjusting the angle of the spoiler creates down force and gives the car more grip on the track.

It wasn't long after the birth of Emma and Aiden's boys that we found ourselves heading to New York for the championship banquet.

Watching my husband give his second championship speech was probably right up there with the day our son was born. I was so proud of him. He worked so hard for everything. He deserved this.

I sat there in my cream stupidest-idea-ever-with-a-baby-in-your-lap evening gown with Axel, elated. He was wearing a tiny tuxedo that resembled Jameson's, and I didn't think I had stopped smiling since I put it on him.

He was adorable.

My smile widened when they announced my husband. My eyes locked with Jameson standing in the shadows of the stage, his head bent forward displaying the nervous energy he fought so hard to disguise.

"What this young man has done in the last two years most spend their entire careers trying to accomplish, and this twenty-four-year-old kid has done it with poise and reverence. Ladies and gentlemen, please welcome your Nextel Cup Series Champion, Driver of the Ford number nine Simplex Shocks and Springs, Jameson Riley!"

When Axel heard his daddy's name, his head shot toward the stage.

Jameson made his way to the podium and stopped. His head remained bent forward staring at his hands before he smiled and slowly met the gaze of the audience as they cheered.

He then laughed and shook his head as the cheering continued longer than it had last year. In the background, they played a video montage of his season highlighting each win and then a few of the disappointing finishes he'd had. I watched closely as Jameson turned and watched the video until the screen stayed on the image of him holding the championship trophy beside his dad in Homestead.

With a smirk, he faced the podium again. He nodded again and took a deep breath, a nervous energy radiated from him.

"There are so many people I need to thank this year, and I know I can't think of all of them, so if I forget you, I'm truly sorry." He smiled and looked over at Axel and me sitting on the side of the stage and winked.

He went on to thank his crew, sponsors, family, and a handful of drivers. I knew I was crying when he started thanking his family and naming each one and the strength they brought to the team. I could feel the tears tickling my cheeks as they ran down my face. Axel, who was still seated on my lap, looked up at me when he sensed my hysteria. I thought maybe I should control myself, but all I could do was sit and watch my best friend, my husband, and the father of my son, thanking everyone he thought deserved this title more than him.

Kyle looked at me with wide eyes at one point. I waved him off and continued my girly-emotional-breakdown.

As I couldn't stop crying, Axel had wiggled loose and all but ran over to Jameson. My dress wasn't exactly the dress to wear if you needed to chase a kid around, but before I could make a fool of myself, Jameson waved me off.

When Axel reached him, the crowd *aww-ed* in response.

Jameson bent down and picked him up. "This is my son, Axel."

Everyone, including me, *aww-ed* again at the look they exchanged with each other, and Axel gave him that big cheesy grin he was so good at.

"This little man and that *absolutely* beautiful woman sitting right there ..." he pointed at me, keeping his eyes locked with mine. "They are my inspiration. They never let me down, and late at night when everything else fades away, they are there for me ... *no matter what*." He winked at me again. "I never thought I'd win another championship this soon. Hell, I never thought I'd win the first one, but everyone I thanked ... they deserve this just as much as I do, if not more."

The proud Mama Wizard I was lost it completely and cried against Jimi's shoulder.

After the championship banquet we planned a birthday celebration for our little spaz. It seemed, like it did every year, no matter what I did to slow the off-season, time flew by.

Emma really did outdo herself on it once again. It looked like a winter wonderland, complete with an ice-skating rink, which I found dumb seeing as he was one and could barely walk, let alone skate.

What really annoyed me was the fake snow everywhere. Somehow, the shit kept ending up in my mouth.

How did someone put up with all those flakes?

It got everywhere and it was impossible to get rid of. It was so grainy and obtrusive and no matter how much I tried to brush the shit off, it stuck to my skin and clothes like tar. How was I supposed to enjoy myself when miniature microbes were attacking me?

Van approached me as I tried to put together Axel's go-kart Justin and I built for him.

"It looks like a goddamn snow globe exploded in here," Van huffed, brushing the white flakes from his JAR Racing sweatshirt.

"It's annoying," I agreed, brushing more away.

"Have you seen Lucas?" he asked, handing me a wrench I needed but couldn't reach.

"No ... why?"

"He ate a quarter."

"Kids eat quarters all the time," Spencer said when he walked up. "I wouldn't worry about it. *Now* ... if he shits two dimes and a nickel, then you should worry."

The guys stood joking around with me as I finished putting together the kart.

Over the last year, Van became part of the family. He still served as our bodyguard, but most of the time he was hanging out with us like he was our brother and it suited all of us just fine.

Sway was busy with the kids since we had a shit load here. Just a year ago, it was only Lane and the Lucifer twins around. Now, we had Axel who turned one a week ago, Alexis, who was just shy of five months, and then Aiden and Emma's twins, Noah and Charlie, who were a little over four weeks old.

I repeat—we had a shit load of kids.

Lane jumped on my back before I could make it over to Sway who was chasing Axel across the yard.

"Uncle Jameson!"

"Hey, buddy!" I reached around and pulled him into a headlock, his legs dangled around me as he fought to get loose. Alley approached us carrying Lexi in her arms.

"You guys all packed?" she asked, looking between Aiden and me.

"Where are we going?"

"Tulsa. I've been telling you this for three goddamn weeks," Alley said, handing Lexi to Spencer. "The Chili Bowl, remember?"

"I wasn't listening," I told her while Sway again chased after Axel who was heading toward the cars.

"Neither was I," Aiden added when he found out he was supposed to come with me.

"When do we leave?" we both asked.

"Tomorrow morning at eight."

Damn it.

Justin, Tyler, Tate, Bobby, and me all planned to go to the Chili Bowl this year, but I hated leaving so soon after I just arrived home. Mostly because I knew that after the Chili Bowl, I started testing in Rockingham and then Daytona.

Being a champion was great, but it was wearing on my sanity.

Later in the day, the boys and I challenged each other to a game of hockey on the ice-skating rink Emma had put in our backyard. Sway felt the need to remind me of my contract with Simplex.

"Don't do anything stupid!" her eyes did that judging once over. She was getting really good at that look.

"I wasn't planning on it!" I yelled over my shoulder and pointed toward my makeshift pads made of toilet paper rolls and maxi pads.

Sway looked down at Axel.

"He never plans on it," she told him and he nodded.

We stood there as Gentry, Kyle's brother, explained the rules to us since he used to play in high school. None of us paid a goddamn bit of attention to him. We just intended on fucking each other up anyway.

The game, which wasn't a game at all, was on delay soon after it started so Van could help Ethan and his broken arm off the ice.

"I'm freezing here!" Spencer grumbled, rubbing his hands together.

"Here's some matches," I told him and tossed the matches in his direction. "Set yourself on fire."

Eventually the ass beating continued until Tyler knocked Spencer's front tooth out with a slap shot. Alley was not pleased, but Lane thought it was pretty awesome.

In the end, Dad broke up the game mumbling something about this being a horrible idea, and if I got hurt, Simplex would have a shit fit.

"Is that all you do is bitch?" I glared at him, tearing away the remaining toilet paper rolls from my shins.

"I bitch because look who my children are," he countered with the same glare.

He had me there.

Sway managed to get everyone gathered up to sing happy birthday to Axel. I'd never paid much attention at a kid's birthday party, but watching my son sitting in his go-kart the way I did when I was his age was something I would never forget. His toothless smile said it all as he jerked the steering wheel back and forth.

Sway sighed softly, leaning her head against my chest.

"Thank you," she whispered, looking up at me with her adoring green eyes.

"No, honey, thank you." I dipped my head down to kiss her forehead.

It was hard to imagine life getting much better than this, but I also knew my time here with my family was about to end. But for now, for tonight, we were a family once again.

Watching Axel blow out his birthday candles, I realized that this wasn't what I would have dreamed about a few years ago, but it was so much more than I ever expected.

After Axel was sound asleep in his bed and our home was free from our family, I made my way into our room where Jameson was packing for the Chili Bowl. One look and he was no longer packing but tending to his Mama Wizard.

Two hours later, I was standing in our bedroom getting ready for bed after our shower when I glanced down at the picture on my dresser. It was one of Jameson and Axel right after his birth, the look on Axel's face was contentment, as though he knew his daddy's hands would never falter.

Distracted, I dropped my pill, yes, *the* pill.

Oh, shit!

I reached down on the floor to grab it, but unfortunately, it wasn't there.

"Oh, goddamn you, Mr. Jangles!" I pushed him away. "You suck!"

Pit Stand – Sometimes referred to as the "war wagon." This stand, on the inside of the wall adjacent to the pit stall, is where key team personnel, most notably the crew chief, car chief, and often the team owner, sit during the race and communicate strategy. It is outfitted with satellite television screens, timing and scoring information, radio controls, and other communication relevant to race operations.

I bit my nails nervously while Alley and I sat on my toilet. Well, I sat on the toilet; she sat on the edge of our tile tub, biting her own nails.

Last night Mr. Jangles ate my birth control pill. This wouldn't have been so bad except this was the fourth pill in my cycle he'd eaten this month. When I took a closer look at the dates on the box, I should have started my period by now. I was now a week late, which would have led to only one weekend I could have possibly gotten pregnant, the weekend Jameson flew home before the last race of the season. That was the night we spent the majority of our time in bed.

"This can't be happening," I muttered incoherently to myself.

Even though I was talking to myself, Alley replied, "*You*? How the hell am I going to keep track of your shithead of a husband with three kids? Did you know that in Phoenix I had to separate him and Colin three times in the matter of an hour after the first practice session?"

"You're the one who got knocked up," I replied defensively. "That's hardly my fault or Jameson's."

"I didn't say it was your fault," she sighed and slumped down, holding the pregnancy test in her hand. "I blame these Riley men."

"I agree." I finished peeing on the stick and then sat next to her. "Axel just turned one. How the hell am I going to manage another one?"

"You better not turn pink, you asshole stick!" Alley shouted at the innocent pregnancy test. Then she started crying in a very melodramatic way. "Why does this keep happening to me?"

"I think I remember this conversation we had, or at least I think I do." I turned toward her. "I asked what the best birth control was ... and you said: No sex."

She held up the sticks in my face, both sporting the pink lines. "You clearly didn't listen to me."

"Neither did you, *hypocrite*." I held her positive stick up in her face.

We stared at each other for a moment, started crying, and then resorted to lying in my bed all morning after Emma came by. We did nothing but watch reality TV until Nancy arrived with the kids.

Nancy had been watching them so we could take the boys to the Lake Norman Air Park to meet Wes so they could leave for Tulsa and the Chili Bowl.

On the way back to our house in Mooresville, I told Alley I thought I might be pregnant.

Alley, the hard ass bitch that she could be, broke and started bawling because she was three weeks late herself and hadn't told anyone. So we stopped off at Wal-Mart on Norman Station Boulevard and picked up a few pregnancy tests and a box of donuts.

Nancy let herself in and came upstairs to my room with all the kids. I'm not sure how she could handle them all, but she had Lane carrying Noah, who looked like he was carrying a bomb that was about to explode.

Axel was on her shoulders with a very large grin and a chocolate donut in his chubby little hands. Most of the chocolate had been licked from the donut and was either on his face or in Nancy's hair. In her arms she had Lexi, who was sound asleep, and she was pushing Charlie in the stroller.

I wondered for a moment why she didn't have Noah in the stroller, as well, but it appeared she had too many bags in there to actually fit kids in it.

Axel started squirming when he spotted me in the bed.

"Mama, Mama!" he practically flung himself off Nancy's shoulders to get to me.

She had to set Lexi down before this could happen, which irritated Axel. As I'd said before: when he wanted something, he wanted it right away.

Pushing myself up from the bed, I went to him in fear for Nancy's hair that he was pulling on to get down.

"Calm down, buddy. Mommy's right here."

He smiled wide. "Mama."

There was nothing better than a hug, but a hug given by a child is by far the greatest feeling. They gave everything to you unconditionally because that was what they felt.

Somewhere along the way of life we lost that—the ability to do as we feel rather than what we think.

Not my baby, though, he loved me.

"Did you have a good time with Me-Ma?" I sat down on the edge of the bed with him.

That was when Nancy, just as Emma did after she went shopping, showed us everything she bought for the kids.

Axel nodded with a chocolate smile and curled up on my lap to eat the rest of his donut.

Emma reached over to take Noah from Lane when he found the donuts we had on the bed. Lane had a habit of forgetting he was holding something when chocolate or sugar of any kind was involved.

"It appears you've already had a donut, Lane," Alley deduced after seeing his chocolate smile.

Lane shrugged carelessly and continued the selection process. Once he had his *specific* donut selected, he crawled up next to his sleeping sister on the bed and patted her head.

"Mommy," Lane began, "I was thinking today ..." He paused, took a large bite from his donut, and looked up at Alley as she looked over at him, pulling her long hair into a bun. "I wanna get a taboo like Daddy has."

Emma, clearly not thinking, piped up, "It's called a tramp stamp, Lane."

Alley tossed a pillow from my bed at her head. "It's not a tramp stamp. Yours is worse!"

Emma had recently let her hair grow out to cover her trasher token she'd gotten over a year ago.

"Yeah, well, I covered mine up."

"So did Spencer," Alley pointed out.

Emma pointed at Lane, who was watching this debate curiously. "Then how does your four-year-old son know about it?"

Lane raised his hand but didn't look up from this donut. "I'll be five soon."

Alley and Emma were too caught up in their argument to notice.

"It doesn't matter, he still knows, and now he wants to be just like his dad," Emma said matter-of-factly. "Let's hope that *never* happens." She placed Noah in the stroller beside Charlie to contain the little squirming peanut.

"You know what, Emma?" Alley pushed her knocked up theatrical self from the bed and stood in front of Emma. Her five-foot-nine stance hovered over Emma's barely five-foot height. Once she was standing there, ready to pounce, her emotional pregnant side took over. "What the hell am I going to do?"

"About what?" Nancy asked curiously, looking at me and then Emma and Alley.

"She's knocked up again," Emma announced.

Alley was under a great deal of stress these days. That was the only answer for what she did next. The only answer I could come up with at least. I thought she'd been hanging out with Jameson too much, and that was precisely why she was so stressed.

Alley attacked Emma, Emma attacked Alley, and there the kids, Nancy, and I sat, watching.

"Take it back!" Alley screamed at her, pulling at Emma's waves of black hair.

"No, you take it back!" Emma countered, pulling Alley's hair.

This went on for a few minutes. It wasn't like they were really doing any sort of damage to one another, just wrestling and yelling.

Lane, who was sitting next to me, leaned over and nudged my shoulder with his. "I think Mommy give soon.

"I don't know, Lane, your mom is tough. She has Emma on size, too."

Lane rolled his eyes. "I mean with the taboo, Auntie."

"It's a *tattoo*, Lane, not taboo. If you tell the tattoo artist you want a taboo, you'll end up like Emma and have to grow your hair out."

"I said tattoo," he sighed.

"I'm curious ..."

I let out a giggle when Alley spanked Emma's ass and said, *"I'm only doing what your tattoo says."*

Glancing down at Lane and his donut, I continued, "So what will your tattoo say?"

"Not sure." He licked his donut. Axel, who was still sitting on my lap, took Lane's donut from him and handed him his "already licked" donut as a peace offering. "It be manly, though." He looked up at me. "Why he always still my food?"

"*Steal* your food?"

"That's what I said."

"Okay, that's enough, girls," Nancy said, separating them. Emma was panting heavily as was Alley. They both slumped back on the floor on their backs, exhausted. "What's going on?"

"Alley's pregnant and being an emotional bitch," Emma told her breathlessly.

Alley swung her arm up and smacked Emma in the throat.

"There are children present, Emma," Nancy told her.

Lane hopped down from the bed, went over to Emma, and held out his hand out.

Axel followed suit and did the same thing.

"Since when does he do that?" she asked, pointing toward Axel after handing Lane a dollar bill.

"I'm not sure. Last week he pooped a dime so I'm assuming someone is giving him money."

Axel and Lane were satisfied with their money and sat down on the bed again.

"So you're really pregnant?" Nancy asked, helping Alley off the floor.

"Yes," Alley spit out. "Your son and his super seed knocked me up."

"That's what the taboo should say!" Lane announced happily, jumping up and down on the bed. "Suber seed!"

We all looked at one another. I started laughing hysterically. Nancy couldn't help it and gave way to her snorts and giggles.

"Sway's pregnant, too," Alley said in between her own laughs.

"Sell out."

"Wait." Nancy waved her arms around. "So you're both pregnant?"

You could literally see the excitement building. Nancy would adopt an entire country of children if she could. The only reason she and Jimi stopped having kids was because Nancy had too many problems having Emma so soon after Jameson, so her doctor advised them not to have any more.

"Try to control your enthusiasm," I told her. "You already have five grandkids, seven if you count the Lucifer twins—which you do for some reason."

"That doesn't matter. I love all my grandchildren, even the ones that are not technically mine."

Just as she said this, Charlie, who she had picked up from the stroller, puked all down the front of her. She held him close, puke and all. "Regardless of what they do."

The next few days passed quickly, and I found myself keeping busy with Axel to avoid the truth. I was pregnant again. I made it to the doctor in town to confirm, and sure enough, another positive result.

And then the day finally came when Jameson was set to arrive home. I did the only thing I could to avoid reality. I made cookies, and that turned into a full on feast.

"Do I tell him now, or do I wait?" that was the question I'd been repeating to myself for the last three hours.

Any minute now, Jameson would be home from the Chili Bowl that he won. I wasn't sure whether or not to tell him tonight or later. I didn't want to take away any excitement he had from his win. Not that it wasn't exciting to have another child, because it was, but I hated for anything to get in the way of the thrill of an earned victory at the Chili Bowl.

And, oh, did the thrill shine? Jameson could hardly control himself that night. Once the guys got back around five on Sunday night, everyone gathered over at our house.

Already drunk, Jameson of course attacked me the moment he walked through the door.

I went with it, and then there I was, watching my very drunk husband recount his victory.

"What I want to know is, since Tommy set up both our cars ... how the hell did you win?" Justin asked, picking up Lily, who came running to him when Axel pushed her down and stole his Mr. Piggy back from her.

"Maybe the same reason why you always win Turkey Night and I don't," Jameson replied, leaning back in the chair. His eyes took on an amused look when he thought of all the times Justin had taken

Turkey Night from him. "I swear Irwindale hates me. I've never run good there."

"You won a few years back," Justin reminded, Jameson taking a seat next to him.

Jameson chuckled. "Still ... I haven't won since. I've been every year since I was what ..." He looked over at Spencer. "Seven?"

Spencer nodded.

"See, that track hates me. Loves you, hates me."

Making my way back into the kitchen to check on the food and make sure everything was kept stocked, I realized our house was full. Most of Jameson's pit crew was there, along with the sprint car teams, and most of our family, as well.

Even with all this excitement around, I was still nervous that I was once again pregnant. I thought back to when I got pregnant with Axel during our "friends with benefits" days.

This was different in so many ways, but it didn't stop me from being nervous.

What if he didn't want another kid?

We had finally adjusted to Axel and traveling with him—how would one more fit into that?

So there I was, milling this over in the kitchen and eating cookies when Jameson approached me from behind.

"Here," his drink in hand swung around the front of me as he placed his chin on my shoulder. "Ami made it. It's good."

"What is it?" I sniffed the cup. "Christ Almighty, is there anything besides alcohol in there?"

He chuckled and took a drink. "It's root beer and rum. Mostly rum." He pushed it toward me again. "It's good."

"I'll take your word for it." I turned in his arms to face him.

"You're not drinking?" His eyebrow arched in question as one hand rubbed down his jaw.

"No ... not tonight."

"But I won the Chili Bowl," he pouted. "We're celebrating."

"I know that." I sighed and hugged him. "I just ... well, I ..."

Sensing my hesitation as I fumbled over my words, he pulled back to look at me. A long moment passed before he smiled. "Are you …?"

I didn't know what to say so I nodded.

"Say it," he demanded with a smirk.

"What?"

"Say it," he repeated, the smirk growing into a full-fledged grin.

I slapped his shoulder and stuck another cookie in my mouth. "Why?"

Jameson stood quiet for a moment before he tipped his head to the side. "I just want to hear you say it."

Our eyes locked, that silent bond between each other spoken. He wanted me to say it because when I found out with Axel, I never actually told him—he guessed it, which he did again. He wanted to hear the words this time.

I leaned forward, motioning for him to come closer before I smiled; he trapped me between the counter and the island with his arms, hovering over me.

"I'm pregnant," I whispered in his ear. His arms that were wrapped around my waist tightened. "Are you happy?" You couldn't miss the apprehension in my tone.

"Yes, of course I am," he pulled back to look at me, his fingers curled under my chin, forcing me to look up at him. "Did you think I'd be mad?"

"Well, no." I paused and looked around as Ryder walked into the kitchen to get food and drinks. "I just … I worried that adding another kid would complicate this more for you."

"Nothing is complicated about us expanding our family."

"So you're okay with it?"

"Yes," he nodded eagerly. His grin widened as he took another drink of his mostly rum. "Couldn't be happier right now." He started walking toward the family room before he spun back around and stood in front of me. "Are you happy?"

"Yes," I answered immediately.

And I was. I wanted more kids; I just didn't think it'd be this soon.

Jameson left to party with his boys in the family room while Alley made her way back into the kitchen. She'd just put the kids to bed upstairs and looked exhausted.

"I remembered why I hated being pregnant," she huffed and stuffed a cookie in her mouth.

"Why's that?" I asked, leaning against the counter.

Nancy walked by with Axel sleeping in her arms and motioned toward the stairs. I assumed she was putting him to bed for me. He had this ability to fall asleep anywhere and at the most random times—like in the middle of dinner or in the bathtub. The bath was a problem, and well, so was dinner after he inhaled mashed potatoes up his nose one night.

"I hate all the hormones and the cravings, *oh*, and the exhaustion."

"Me too."

"Did you tell Spencer?"

"Yeah, he noticed how big my boobs were," she looked down. "I had to buy a double-D size bra."

I laughed once. "Was he happy?"

"Yes and no. He's nervous about how much he's away from the kids already, and now we're adding another when Lexi isn't even one yet."

It was tough on everyone involved in racing, not just the drivers. The crews, spotters ... they all sacrificed any sense of normalcy.

Alley laughed and looked over at me. "Let's just hope we don't have them on the same day."

I finally convinced Jameson to come to bed around three in the morning. He grabbed Axel out of his room and brought him to our king-sized bed.

Axel curled up against his chest and fell back asleep almost immediately.

"Why did—"

Jameson's index finger silenced me and then moved to his lips where he whispered, "Shhhh …" and then he pointed down to Axel. Moving closer, he rested his hand on my belly.

After a few moments, he spoke. "Do you think it'll be a girl?"

"Hmm … I kind of hope so," I said softly, trying not to wake Axel.

The good thing about him was he slept like me. Jameson could start a sprint car in his room, and he wouldn't wake once he was asleep.

Lying there with my expanding family, my anxiety over our lifestyle got to me.

"Do you think … I mean … it's soon to be having another baby, isn't it?"

"Yeah, I guess so. But I wouldn't change anything about it," he turned over, propping himself up on his elbow to look over at me. The sun was starting to rise over the lake, the light filtering in through the sheer drapery. "I know I'm not around much, honey, but this," he motioned to us lying in bed. "I live for moments like this. Having another baby only sweetens that for me."

"Sweetens?" I giggled softly.

He laughed as well before kissing my forehead. "I just feel bad that I'm living my dream, and you are taking care of our family. You're my pit stand."

"Is that what you think? That you don't help?"

"I don't really," he shrugged. "Even when you're at the track with me, I feel like you're the one having to keep track of him, and now another baby, I just worry about your sanity in all of it."

"Just like you … I wouldn't change anything. I love being Mama Wizard. Being at the track is where I'd rather be anyway, with you, as your pit stand."

His eyes focused on mine and then fell closed.

"I love you," he whispered, intertwining our hands together.

The next morning, I heard quite possibly the cutest thing ever—Jameson and Axel talking.

"Good morning, little man," I heard Jameson say as he opened the door to his bedroom. Axel was never fun to sleep with so we ended up putting him back in his bedroom this morning so we could get some sleep.

"Daddy!" Axel chirped like he hadn't seen him in days. Snuggling into the bed, I laid there and listened to them on the monitor.

Jameson must have sat down with him on the floor because I heard him say, "Here."

He usually did this when you sat down in his room, and he began handing you toys he thought you needed.

"Did you miss Daddy when he was at the Chili Bowl? I won by the way."

"No," Axel answered. I knew he missed him, but being one, he hardly understood what you were asking. Unless you asked if he wanted ice cream ... the answer to that was always, "Yeah!" complete with a head nod.

"Well, that doesn't make me feel any better, little man. I missed you guys."

They seemed to play for a while before Jameson spoke again.

"Did you know Mommy is having a baby?"

"No."

"She is. You're going to be a big brother."

"No."

"I think you'll make a good big brother. We need to work on your sharing, oh, and potty training."

I could hear the rustling of Axel's diaper as Jameson got him changed and then the ordeal of dressing. Axel loved to take his clothes off, but refused to put any back on.

"Come on, little man. Let's go get Mama some decaf coffee."

"Yeah!" Axel chirped with enthusiasm.

"So I mention Mama and you finally say yeah?"

"Yeah."

"We need to work on that, too."

"No."

I think Axel understood more than we gave him credit.

When I heard the Expedition start up in the garage, I turned the monitor off. My hands moved from behind my head to my stomach where new life was forming. It was crazy to think something was growing inside me again—part of me and part of him, together.

Moments like this, I understood why people chose to be alone in life and the fear of getting hurt. Losing someone to death was easier than losing them to heartache.

If what I had with Jameson simply vanished, the heartache would never die.

Regardless of the happiness I felt having my family together, the family *we* created was worth any risk of ever being hurt. Just like the racing family we were, we stacked our pit stand with equipment to get us through this crazy life, oh, and added kids along the way.

In-Lap – This is considered a lap where a driver makes a pre-arranged pit stop during the race or practice. Drivers push hard to drive fast in order to gain time during the pit stop.

On September 9, 2005, thirty-four weeks and four days later ... what we *hoped* wouldn't happen, happened—Alley and I went into labor at the same time.

Aside from Aiden, Spencer, and Jameson, most of us were up in Alger, Washington, at the Skagit World of Outlaws race. It was a two-night feature—hot as hell—and we'd finally made it to the final night.

Jameson and his Cup team were in Richmond for the NASCAR race. Managing a sprint car team, a track, and racing full-time in the cup series was wearing on Jameson this year.

We hadn't seen each other in about two weeks and frankly, I missed my dirty heathen, as did Axel. He had this way about him that if he hadn't seen him for a few days, he started to become unruly. Kind of like tonight.

"Give me that!"

"No!" Axel yelled at me.

My adorable little spaz was actually yelling at me. It never failed that any time we were at the track Axel stole parts from the hauler. Here I was, nine months pregnant, extremely uncomfortable, hot, and running around after my almost two-year-old son. If you never waddled your way around the pits of a dirt track chasing a toddler, you weren't missing much.

"Axel, please give that wrench to Mommy."

He shook his head. "No—mine." He hugged it to his chest tightly. "Mine!"

I wasn't sure where he learned the word *mine*, but I hated it. Everything was either "no" or "mine."

I'd been cramping all day, which wasn't unusual for this late in my pregnancy, but when I had to stop and steady myself against Justin's sprint car, I began to wonder if this was going to progress to labor here shortly. Thinking this, I panicked.

Alley found me after the heat races, holding her swollen stomach. "Christ, this hurts."

"Walking?"

"No, these cramps,"

"You're cramping, too?"

"What?" Jimi asked as he walked past, his steps halting. His eyes did a once over on the two of us. "Did you just say you're both cramping?" he didn't wait for us to answer. "Listen, you can't have these babies tonight. You *just* can't."

"That's not really within our control, Jimi," Alley replied and sat down in a chair Emma had gotten for her.

Just then, Lane came running past with a corn dog and Axel running after him.

He stopped in front of us. "I don't understand, why he always take my food?"

"He likes you," I told him, ruffling his mess of honey hair and then clutching my side.

"I like him, too, but I not steal him food."

"His food," I corrected him. "You don't steal *his* food."

Lane sighed, rolling his eyes and handed his corn dog over to Axel. "That's what I said."

Axel, bright-eyed now that he had food, sat down in the dirt to eat his battered lips and assholes as Jameson called it.

Alley and I wondered if tonight another set of Riley kids would be added to our family. This went on through most of the heat races. Alley found out she was having another boy, and well, our little one refused to let us in on the sex. Every time we tried to see on the ultrasound, the baby covered up. We had a mystery baby.

After the feature events, everyone was loading up when I really started to feel like I was in labor, and on top of that, my water broke.

At that point, I was calm. It was short-lived...

I waddled my fat ass inside Jimi's hauler while he talked with Cody Bowman about next week's race in Cottage Grove.

Cursing to myself when a contraction hit, I stumbled in pain and slammed my knee into a spare torsion bar lying on the floor.

"Sway." Jimi's eyes shot into the distance when he heard my scream. "Is that you?"

"Yes, it's me. Who else would it be?"

"I don't know," Jimi replied with a shrug. Cody excused himself and walked out the side door. "What's wrong with you?"

"I'm in labor," I blurted out, steadying myself against the car.

"You're what?" Jimi shot up from his chair so quickly he smacked his head on the rear end hanging on the sidewall of his hauler. "You can't be serious! Alley and Emma just left with the car. She's in labor."

Where in the hell was I when that happened?

Oh yeah, I was in the bathroom feeling like shit.

When I went into labor with Axel, it wasn't quick by any means, but I was also early. With this child, the kid took its sweet time. I was a week late, which was why Jameson wasn't with me. We thought for sure the baby would hold off another week since my last exam showed no movement. Having hovered like a Queen Bee my entire pregnancy, it was rare that he wasn't with me. But as luck would have it, this was the last race before the Nextel Cup Chase began, and he couldn't be with me and needed me to be with his sprint car team.

All that being said, my labor moved quickly. So quickly, I couldn't make it to the hospital. In turn, I was stuck here at a dirt track with Jimi, Justin, Tommy, Tyler, and Ami. Emma and Alley were at the hospital.

"Oh my God!" Tommy covered his eyes. "I can't watch this."

He jetted out of the hauler when a few track safety officials made their way inside the hauler.

"Men are so stupid," Ami rolled her eyes. "Just breathe, Sway, everything will be fine." She looked over her shoulder at Justin. "Did you call Jameson?"

"Yeah," he held the phone up. He too looked a little nervous and ready to jet any second. "He's on the phone."

I quickly grabbed it from him.

"Jameson?"

Ami motioned to Axel, who was walking around collecting wrenches and shocks for his collection. "I'll take care of him," she mouthed and picked him up.

"Yeah, honey, it's me," Jameson breathed. "Are you okay?"

"No, fuck no!" I yelled. "I'm in labor at a goddamn dirt track. What about that is okay?"

"I'm on a plane right now. I'll be there as soon as I can."

I sighed, knowing he was coming from Richmond. There was no way he'd make it, not with these cramps. "How long?"

"How long what?"

"How long before you're here?"

"A few hours."

I screamed out in pain as another contraction hit me hard. "You're not going to make it in time."

Jameson groaned. "Put my fucking dad on the phone!"

I handed the phone to Jimi, who by now was looking a little green. I went back to my pain.

"Listen," I could hear Jameson's voice yelling at his dad. "No looking. I mean it, *no* looking."

Jimi looked offended. "It's not like I would want to check out my daughter-in-law's track layout, okay?" he sighed. "I have no desire to even see this shit. You should be here, not me. I'm not all right with this, Jameson. I'm just not. Get your ass here, right now!"

Track layout? I started giggling.

I heard Jameson again. "Well good. Keep it that way," he let out a frustrated sigh. "Now keep her calm. I'm on my way."

Ten minutes passed and I wasn't sure why they couldn't just transport me to the hospital. This seemed ridiculous, but it might have had something to do with the fact that every time they tried to move me from my spot on the floor of Jimi's hauler, I screamed at them and told them to leave me alone. I kicked everyone out except for Jimi.

Jimi looked incredibly nervous and completely uncomfortable with the entire situation.

"This is horrible," he voiced, completely uncomfortable with this entire situation.

I was almost positive Jimi felt the same as me in regards to how disgusting childbirth was.

Jameson, in not so many words told his dad he'd kill him if anything happened to me. Scaring Jimi, the only one here to help me, just didn't seem like a good idea to me. I could've been wrong.

So there I was, legs spread, a tarp covering my crankcase, a Hans device supporting my neck (it was all we had in the hauler), with each one of my legs propped up on the rear tires of Jimi's car while two safety officials assessed the situation.

"Mrs. Riley, we need to transport you, but it seems it's progressing quickly. I think it's best that we just stay here."

I held up my hand. "Two things you need to know," I told the man and woman safety officials. "I do not want the word *crowning* said. And, second ... well, I don't know what the second thing will be ..." I pointed at them. "Do you know what you're doing?"

"Yes ma'am, we do."

"This sucks," Jimi said, pacing the hauler and biting his fingernails. "Why do I have to be in here? Why can't Ami?"

"She's taking care of Axel."

"I can do that, why can't I do that?"

"The last time you were alone with Axel ... you fed him dog biscuits."

"So ... those things were delicious," he sat down next to me, running his hands through his black hair and tugging. "I can't do this. I really *can't*. You don't seem to understand that."

"You'll be fine. Just calm down," I told him. He was really starting to freak even me out. "You have to stop stressing me out."

"I might not make it." He shoved a wet rag at me haphazardly, only partially paying attention.

"Sit down and stop being a pussy," I ordered.

"If I see blood, I may pass out. Where's that no-good husband of yours?" He once again glanced out the hauler to where Justin and Tyler were standing guard to ensure no one could come inside. "I can't do this."

The track official checked me one last time and said I needed to push because I was completely effaced. As it was, I had my legs clamped again in hopes Jameson magically made it across the United States in the last few minutes.

"Where the fuck is Ami?" Jimi asked again when they moved to get everything ready for me to push. "She needs to get her ass in here."

Tuning him out, I didn't like the way they said effacing or dilating. Along with the word crowning, those words alone were enough to send me into a panic attack.

Nothing changed from the time I progressed from a seven to a ten. Jimi was still freaking out and asking the medical staff if he could have an epidural.

"We don't have the equipment for that sort of thing."

"Well, that's stupid," Jimi balked. "What the fuck are you guys good for anyway?"

"Sir," the female official looked up at him. "We are track safety officials, not a hospital or even an obstetrician."

"Do you even know what you're doing then?"

The male official looked up at Jimi. "I think we know more than you do."

"I highly doubt that. If you did, you'd have an epidural on hand or even adrenaline."

Jimi and the official continued to argue as I tried to push this kid out in the race car hauler surrounded by nothing sanitary. It wasn't lost on any of us that we should have gone to the hospital, but no, I'd decided to stay put.

I screamed, as did Jimi and Tommy, who had accidentally walked in when the baby started to come out.

"Looks like it's a girl!" the official said with a smile.

When she came out, the official handed her to him as she looked up at Jimi, his panicked expression melting to adoration.

There, in the midst of the dirt and methanol filling the crisp fall night, another Riley was added to the family.

"She's beautiful," Jimi said, handing her to me. I laughed that she was wrapped in his driving suit.

"Jimi," I refused to look at him, knowing damn well what he did. "Please tell me you at least have underwear on."

"Yeah," he chuckled looking, toward the baby. "I decided since I didn't want to see your track layout, you wouldn't want to see my gear shift."

"There's no doubt in my mind Jameson and Spencer are your sons."

I took one look at my daughter and started bawling. She looked identical to me, but I saw so much of my mom and Charlie, as well as Jameson, in her. She had his exact lips and hair color.

"What's her name?" Jimi asked. With eyes rimmed with tears, I smiled.

"Jameson wanted to name her Arie Marie."

"What?"

"Arie. Pronounced like R-E."

"What's with you two and naming your kids strange names?"

"You're one to talk there, smartass. You named Jameson after whiskey."

"I have two with normal names," he defended, still staring at Arie.

"Yeah, I always wondered how that happened."

He laughed, handing Arie to me.

"Nancy was sleeping when they came around with the birth certificate. I wrote the first name that came to mind."

"Whiskey, huh?"

"Hey, it got me through the birth of him."

"So you saw him born?"

"No, hell no ... I've never seen a kid born ... *until* today."

"So this was your first?"

"Yep," his hand rose to wipe the sweat from his forehead. "And I can't say I want to see it again. That was horrible. I just may have nightmares. All that blood and screaming and blood," he shivered. "I need some air."

Everything moved quickly once she was born, and we needed to get to the hospital so Jimi, of course, drove.

Arie was tiny, but had a lot of attitude. She already had the Riley scowl down when we made it to the hospital and the nurses tried to bathe her. I couldn't stop smiling that I had a daughter now. The only thing that marred my happiness was the fact that her father wasn't there to see her birth, or even right now, while she was being cleaned, measured, and weighed.

Ami, who had kindly kept an eye on Axel during the labor and birth, came in holding him on her hip. When Axel came in, he looked at me with wide, happy eyes, but then he spotted the baby—who wasn't him—in my arms ... and he wasn't thrilled.

Neither was Jameson when he finally arrived.

He rushed through the door to the room. "Did I miss it?" his eyes, just like his son's, caught sight of the baby in my arms. "Is that ...?" he rushed to my side, peeking down at her.

"Daddy, meet your daughter ... Arie."

Jameson didn't say anything more. With a smirk I knew well, he climbed in the bed with his family and wrapped his arms around all three of us.

After a few minutes of gazing at her, he whispered against my forehead, "She's beautiful, honey ... just like her mother."

Once again, we were lost in our tiny bubble of perfection. For a few hours at least. That was, until Spencer and Jimi came walking in, holding the other little Riley who was added to the family tonight. Alley was lucky enough to have him, with drugs, in the hospital. Although she did have Lane at a dirt track in the back of Jameson's hauler so I assumed she understood the stress I felt.

Cole Jacob Riley, very different from Lane, was a spitting image of Spencer with his black hair and big blue eyes. He looked almost identical to him when he was a baby, so Nancy said.

"Where the hell are your clothes?" Jameson asked Jimi, who was still in his underwear, when he walked in to check on us.

"I had to wrap her up in something," he motioned to Arie. "Now, if you'll excuse me, I need to go talk to my sponsor about a new hauler. This is just not going to work for me any longer."

I let the boys argue amongst themselves and got lost in my little wonders, my son and daughter. Axel seemed curious, and he kept peeking at Arie as if she wasn't real.

"Baby?" he asked, pointing at her with his chubby little index finger.

"Yes, this is your sister, Arie."

Axel smiled, his eyes focused on her. "Baby," he repeated.

My fairytale just got better. Just when I thought my life was everything I wanted, Arie was brought into the world, adding to the unbelievable happiness I felt. The thing about fairytales was having faith in things that didn't come true, and appreciating them when they did.

A tiny hand freed from the blanket and her delicate fingers curled around my pinky. I smiled down at her, so pure and innocent. I was too overcome by the child in my arms to speak. My daughter.

I was the father of a daughter now.

For months, I prepared myself for the idea of having a daughter, and my gut instinct told me Sway was carrying a girl even though the ultrasounds revealed nothing. I had no idea how to act around a girl. Even with Lexi, my niece, I never knew how to be around her. With Axel and Lane, it was easy for me. I related to them. With Arie, would I know what to do? And what happened when she got older? And dating?

Oh God, talk about fears.

I placed a soft kiss on her forehead, rocking her gently when Spencer came in holding his newborn son. "Hey," he said softly, peering down at Arie. "She's beautiful."

"She is." I glanced up at the baby in his arms. "How's Cole?"

He smiled. "Good, he looks like me."

We talked quietly for a little while before my fears of fathering a little girl emerged.

"Is it different with Lexi than with Lane?"

Spencer seemed to contemplate this for a moment before answering. My gaze focused on Arie when he spoke. "Having a daughter is different. I find myself easier on Lexi than Lane. Just ... be prepared to give in ... *a lot*."

I chuckled softly, trying not to wake the babies. If this was anything like the way Sway owned my heart, as well as Axel now, I was so screwed.

Even though I was supposed to be leaving for Atlanta right now, I couldn't force myself from this angel in my arms. Just her tiny presence relaxed me.

Thankfully, Alley was in a hospital bed and couldn't boss me around, although she had her phone with her.

Jameson, you're supposed to be in Atlanta right now. Tell Spencer to get his ass back in here.

"Your wife is looking for you," I told Spencer as he reached to trade babies.

"She'll get over it," he cooed down at Arie. "You sure are pretty, sweetheart."

"Look at you, big guy," I spoke softly, cradling Cole to my chest. He was big compared to Arie. He had at least two pounds on her. Cole looked identical to Spencer when he was younger, as Lane and Lexi looked more like Alley.

Sway woke up about an hour later when Spencer choked on a fry he'd shoved in his mouth after Mom brought us food.

My phone began vibrating with calls from Kyle and Dad wondering where I was.

Sway knew I needed to leave and always knew the anxiety I felt toward this. She also knew that I didn't want to leave.

"You *have* to, Jameson. It's your job."

"I just want to be with you guys," I told her, looking down at our kids in her arms. "Nothing else matters right now."

She smiled and kissed my hand that was wrapped around her cheek.

"You know I don't hold it against you ... and neither do they," she gestured toward Axel and Arie who were both asleep. "We love you no matter what. We love you even though you have to leave when our baby girl is only hours old. We *love you*, Jameson."

Kneeling next to the bed, I nodded and reached for Axel's tiny hand. His fingers instinctively wrapped around mine as he slept. There was no doubt in my mind they loved me ... but it didn't change the fact that it hurt to leave.

An hour later, I was on the jet back to Atlanta with Spencer.

"This feels wrong," I told Spencer, who sat next to me.

"I know what you mean," he sighed. "We missed the birth of our children today, and now we're leaving when they're not even a day old."

"You know you don't have to do this," I offered. "I can easily find someone to fill your place for a few weeks. You can stay with your family."

He didn't hesitate before looking up from his phone at me.

"I know that. But you're my family, too. I don't do this just because it's a job, Jameson. I never have. I love what I do, and I love that we're a family doing it together. Alley understands that because it's the same reason she does it. It's more than a job to us. It's our way of life."

Racing could control every aspect of your life if you let it. But the thing was, it was my life. There was no controlling it. It owned all of us. Sway understood why I needed to be in Atlanta Saturday night; it marked the end of the regular season and the chance to make it into the chase. The points between the top four were so close. I couldn't afford to risk a back-up driver. It needed to be me in the car.

So I went to Atlanta and left my wife, my son, and my infant baby girl back home.

The sacrifices ... they never got easier.

Catch Can – A smaller can with a spout held at the overfill port to catch the gas spilled over. This can also allow the air trapped in the tank to vent faster than normal, critical for faster pit stops.

“I want owc cleam!” the tiny vein in my soon-to-be four-year-old son’s neck was popping out as he said this.

“You want what?”

“Owc cleam!”

Laughing, I contemplated what that meant. “I’m guessing you mean ice cream?”

“That’s what I said.”

Oh, geez, now he sounded like Lane.

“No, you said owc cleam. I don’t even know what that is, and it doesn’t sound edible. It sounds like a kitchen cleaner or something.”

“Mama ... I just *need* it,” Axel told me, his intense vibrant green eyes focused on the bowl I was holding full of his favorite peanut butter ice cream with chocolate syrup.

Apparently, all the Ben and Jerry ice cream I’d eaten while pregnant with him had rubbed off, and he was just as enthusiastic toward the fluffy, wonderful creation as me.

I remembered the first time we gave him ice cream. It was during a rain delay in Atlanta.

Atlanta, Georgia, during the summer was miserable, regardless if it was raining or not, so during that particular rain break we fed our six-month-old son ice cream. From that point on, every time someone had ice cream, it was like Axel knew and would do just about anything to get some of it, much like his mother.

Axel was similar to me in many ways, but he resembled Jameson. He had the same expressions, same attitude, and same quirky skin phobia (he barely let me put soap on him.). But what got most people was how much he looked like him in the face.

I once took him grocery shopping with me and this older woman, clearly a fan of NASCAR with her Tate Harris memorabilia plastered all over her, stopped us near the checkout counter.

"Wow," she gasped, staring at a three-year-old Axel. "He looks just like Jameson Riley, the NASCAR driver."

I smile politely at her.

"Yeah, well," I began, "If you see him around the track, tell him his wife said hello."

Because of her reaction, that was the last time I ever told someone I was married to the Jameson Riley. It was like I told her I was married to Brad Pitt for crying out loud. Took us forty-five minutes to get away from her and from that point on, Emma did my shopping for me.

This had its own drawbacks, but it was worth it not to run into fans at the grocery store.

"Mama?" Axel called out with a mouth full of ice cream. "Re-Re stole Mr. Wiggles." Ice cream trickled down his chin and onto his gray JAR Racing t-shirt.

"Well get him back from her," I replied, closing the dishwasher door and starting the final load of dishes from last night's dinner. I should have done them last night, but Jameson got home around nine, and well, we got distracted once the kids were in bed.

"She not giving back. I need back!"

This was my life these days. My kids fought all the time, and if they weren't fighting with each other ... they were fighting us. The bad part of this was—they won. Most of the time, their arguments were worse in public or at the track. I always sensed when Jameson was getting stressed as they fed off him and then everyone was upset. To be fair, Jameson was working most of the time he was at the track and having the kids there shot his anxiety levels through the roof. Now he not only had himself to worry about, but what he said and did directly affected a family. A family that was there at the track with him and was subjected to the judging media.

In turn, there were times when Jameson had the occasional outburst at Axel's tendency to run away at the most inopportune times. Like when cars were driving past in the paddock or garage area. The kids threw fits at the worst possible times, and when we were in a hurry, they decided at that moment to slow down.

"Mama!" Axel screamed, throwing himself on the floor. "Give it back!"

"Arie, give Axel back his Mr. Wiggles," I told her, taking Mr. Wiggles from her chubby little hands.

Her response: "No!"

That was her standard answer for everything and was usually followed by a tremendous amount of wailing and tears.

Arie had just turned two in September, and if I thought Axel worked us over at times, Arie put him to shame. She could get absolutely anything from Jameson with just a flutter of her beautifully thick black lashes.

When she was born, Jameson was in awe at how much she resembled me, but I saw Jameson in her features as well as her attitude. She had his smirk for one, his lips, and, of course, his exact hair color with my emerald eyes. Axel had the lighter, grass green that Jameson had.

Life was changing as it always did. We were still living in Mooresville, but we kept the house on Summit Lake for the weekends we visited Elma. Another baby was on the way, yeah, quick I know. Imagine my surprise. Arie was only eighteen months old when I got pregnant with this new little spaz. I cried for nearly a month.

Jameson was on top of his career. He'd won four back-to-back championships and finished second this year.

As always, time brought changes to our hectic lifestyles.

Trying to raise two kids on the road was hell. Arie thought the motor coach was home for the first year of her life. When we were home, she cried. When in the motor coach, she was happy.

Axel wasn't happy unless he was at the track with his dad. When he was at home, he was asking when he could go back to the track and when Daddy would be home—it was sometimes as though I didn't exist to him.

Arie loved me, though. Or at least she pretended well.

All this led to one thing—the crazy irrational kids and I traveled with Jameson. There were times when we stayed home, depending on what track he was racing at, but most of the time, Thursday through Sunday, we were at the track.

One bad thing about staying in a motor coach with Jameson, me, Axel, and Arie ... the kids were always around, which left little alone time for the Mama Wizard and her Dirty Heathen. We had to think of new inventive ways of getting alone time.

We made use of times like going out to dinner, and cars worked well for the occasional dyno testing. Leaving the kids with Tate and his wife Eva was also an option on race weekends. They loved the kids as though they were their own, and Axel thought Tate was pretty cool. Alley and Spencer were also options, but this always left the question of where to do it at, along with the harassment from Spencer.

Once, and I was ashamed to admit this, we made use of a bathroom in the pits. Embarrassing as hell, because Bobby picked that exact moment to walk into the men's restroom when I was screaming like a hyena. It took me a while to realize why he kept smiling the rest of the weekend until Jameson confessed that Bobby felt bad for walking in and told him. I still can't look at Bobby without my face turning a shade similar to the devil's ass.

After I ruled out bathrooms, cars always seemed to be where we got it on. This was why I *always* requested an SUV when renting cars. I wasn't stupid. All this dyno testing might have something to do with the fact that I was, once again, pregnant with a flailing spaz. I also put

Mr. Jangles up for adoption. Damn thief.

Axel was now in school on Monday through Wednesday so this meant most of the time I had to fly out a day later with the kids. That was only if Axel didn't get into trouble. Parent teacher conferences were my least favorite thing to do. Honestly, I'd rather set myself on fire than attend a parent teacher conference where the teacher went into detail about the time she met my husband or Axel's lack of concern for anything that didn't relate to racing.

We were hiring a private teacher for him next year.

"Sway, are you in here?" Emma called out as I heard her come in the front door. Then I heard a loud crash followed by, "Oh, shit."

"You're paying for that!" I yelled out to her, making my way into the living room to see her frantically cleaning up the glass from a picture frame she'd knocked over with her suitcase she carried around as a diaper bag for the twins.

Noah and Charlie began running around the house looking for Arie. They were turning three next week and their temperaments showed it. That was not to say my two didn't throw fits because, Christ Almighty, at times it was as though the devil replaced my beautiful rusty-haired babies.

"I'm sorry ... I'm running late," Emma told me.

"For what?"

"Swim lessons—remember? We talked about this a few weeks ago."

"Right." I nodded. "I just don't see why we should put them in swim lessons. I mean, they're not salmon. Why do they need to learn to swim anyway?"

"Sway, what happens if they fall into the water? You live on a lake."

"That's what floaties are for. Besides, they're too young for swim lessons. Arie wants nothing to do with the water. I have to bribe her to get her to take baths. And Axel, well if it doesn't involve a race car—good luck getting him into the water."

Emma sighed, knowing damn well she'd never get my kids to agree to this. Yet another trait they inherited from their father—extreme stubbornness.

JAMESON

For the first time in almost a year, the family and I were on our way to Elma for Macy, Andrea and Van's little girl's first birthday party.

Returning to the Northwest always made me laugh. I was offered a key to the City of Elma this last summer. Anyone who knew me found this entertaining. The sheriff was constantly sending me to traffic court for various speeding or reckless driving infractions when I lived here. I was hardly a model citizen.

Not long after this, while I was driving home to Elma, as I entered the city I saw a sign on the side of Highway 8 that read: *Home of NASCAR Champion, Jameson Riley*.

Laughing at the irony of it all, I snapped a picture and sent it to Sway with a text that read: ***We used to steal this sign back in high school.***

Her response: ***You better bring that shit home so we can hang it on the wall!***

Every time we stole the sign, they replaced it with another and added the last date I stole it. Eventually we lost interest in stealing the sign, but it was still entertaining that my hometown cared enough about me to have a sign made.

When we entered the city today, the sign was still there. Sway chuckled beside me when she saw it had been replaced yet again.

"Pretty soon they'll have to add Axel's name to it."

I laughed. "Probably."

I had just started Axel in the USAC quarter midget Division. He turned four last week and was granted his USAC license, so naturally he got a brand new quarter midget all ready to go for his birthday. Justin and Tyler helped me get everything set up in time for him to race in the "Duel in the Desert" in Phoenix this coming March.

To say he was excited was an understatement. Axel had been showing interest in racing since birth, but now it was similar to the way I felt about racing. We started him out with a go-kart at one, and now he'd outgrown it. I should rephrase that—the yard outgrew him.

Just like when I was younger, he had a track in our backyard at the Mooresville house—quarter-mile clay oval track. And just like me, he threw a fit when it was time to come in at night. I made a point every Tuesday morning, to go out there with him and race. It became hard once winter came around so what did I do? I installed a covered roof over the track. I couldn't have a crying little boy, could I?

Once we arrived at the house on Summit Lake, I snuck over to the track to test out the car we got for him. Sway knew it was only a matter of time before I took him to the track. I had to make sure everything turned out, right?

So Axel, Van, Tommy, and I made our way over to the track before heading out to the birthday party. Van and Tommy wouldn't have missed this either. Over the past few years, Axel had become like a son to Van and for good reason. He spent more time around my kids than I got to these days, but I also knew they were protected.

I would never regret the decisions and sacrifices I'd made, because financially it had secured our future, but those decisions and sacrifices had drawbacks. I had missed Arie's birth, which was extremely hard on me, and I'd missed Sway's birthday twice now.

It was strange, but something happened when you became a NASCAR Champion and people stopped seeing you for you, and instead as some sort of a rock star who wasn't bothered by fame. That wasn't entirely true. I hated fame, and more importantly, I hated that fame for my family. Growing up, Axel would constantly be considered Jameson Riley's son, just as I was always Jimi Riley's son. It was an endless cycle in the racing community. Knowing all this, I shouldn't have been surprised to see fans waiting outside the gates at Grays Harbor

Raceway when we pulled in.

I had no problem with fans. They were the reason my career had really taken off, but when I was with my family, I wanted to be with them and give them the attention they deserved. Yeah, that one fan only wanted a few seconds of my time, but what happened when I gave just that one fan a few seconds? Well, then the next fan wanted a few seconds, and then the next, before you knew it, you'd spent the last thirty minutes giving each fan just a few seconds while my four-year-old son patiently waited inside his race car for his dad to show him how to drive it.

"I'm sorry, but my son is waiting for me," I told the last fan who wanted an autograph.

"Just one second of your time," he pleaded, handing me the die cast car.

"I really am sorry, but I need to get going." I began to walk away when I heard the guy lean over to his friend and mutter, *"What a jerk."*

That type of snide comment irritated me to no end. I wanted to turn around and say, "Fuck you!" I had just stood signing autograph after autograph for these fans, and when I finally needed to draw a line to the madness, they acted as though I blew them off. You couldn't win, and I began to realize I shouldn't care.

These fans blew us up to be these heroes. We were people, racers where nothing else mattered but the noise, and I thought at times, they forgot we were actual people with lives outside of the tracks, too. Some fell victim to the fame and became the image created for them, no longer knowing themselves, because, God forbid, they should be disappointingly normal.

"Daddy, what I do?" Axel asked me, putting his helmet over his untidy mess of rusty curls.

I smiled, watching his excited eyes.

I still remembered the first time I sat in one of those cars and my first race, which was at this very track. I was so amped up I hardly listened to my dad's advice, but thought I should give Axel the same.

"All right, this is similar to what you see Grandpa and Daddy do in sprint cars. Tommy is going to push start you, okay?"

Axel nodded with enthusiasm, his helmet visor flipping shut. He knew race talk.

I had to chuckle. "Get comfortable with the speed before you go throwing it into the corners, okay?" He nodded again. It wasn't that these cars exceeded twenty, but still, he was four. "This weighs slightly more than the go-kart you had so get used to that first. Once you're in that spinning drift, that's not the time to second-guess the speed. You drive it in too hard and you'll end up in the wall. What happens then?"

"Momma yells at you," he grinned.

"Exactly." I patted his helmet and pulled on his belts before Tommy pushed him off. As I expected, he knew exactly what do to, and the little red Honda fired to life.

"It's hard to believe he's big enough to be doing this," Van said, linking his fingers in the chain link fence we leaned against.

"I know. It's seems like just yesterday Sway gave birth to him."

Van laughed when Axel, who'd been pushing up the track with each lap, bounced the right rear off the outside cushions like I always did, as did my dad. It's a feeling every dirt-tracker knows and is comfortable with, but once that right rear hits the outside cushions, it jolts your car forward, giving you that added boost needed to pass when slower cars get bunched down on the rails.

Axel made another five laps before I walked back down onto the front stretch where he stopped when he saw me. Like I told him, he pulled it out of gear before flipping his visor up. I watched him rub his eyes like I always did. I was still amazed at how much he picked up from me just by watching.

"I do good?" his eyes held hesitation.

"You did great, little man," I told him. "That last lap was faster than mine when I was your age.

The hesitation vanished. "Mama will be proud of me."

He tried so hard to make everyone proud of him, when really, just having him around was enough for us. I didn't know where he ever got that he needed to make us proud of him, but it didn't stop him from trying.

"Can I go again?"

"Sure, buddy. This is for you. Let me know when you're done." I leaned in closer. "Do you want me to track your lap times?"

He nodded. "Yeah."

I kept track of everything I could for him—from lap times to tire pressure and technique. It wasn't like I needed to do that with a quarter midget, but it made him feel special and that was what today was about.

Growing up around the track, Axel already knew the basics in dirt track racing. He spent countless hours asking questions of me, Justin, Tyler, and my dad on how to race on dirt.

I managed to get him buckled in the car on the way to the birthday party before he started with his questions.

"How come ..." This was how all his questions began. "When I hit toes holey things ... I not steer very good." His adorable voice had me smiling. He reminded me of Lane at this age when he frequently missed words.

"Those are called ruts, buddy." I started telling him more about the ruts and didn't leave anything out. I also talked to him like I would another adult. My dad always did that to me, and I knew it helped my career more than the opportunities he provided me. "The ruts are caused from wheelspin. You'd think the track would be nice and smooth, but it's rough, huh?" he nodded, listening closely as we pulled out of the pits. "Tracks with a lot of moisture, like Elma, can form ruts, and if your car isn't set up to roll over the ruts, the consequence is often a crash. Normally, when your car hits the ruts you want it to ride over it, but if the tire catches the rut, all the car's weight is then transferred to the right rear causing the car to roll over. It's worse in sprint cars because of the staggered tires."

"Why are they stammered?"

"Staggered," I corrected him. "They're staggered for a number of reasons. For one, it helps the car turn left. Essentially, this will work in your favor, but sometimes it won't. The rear tires are the only ones staggered, meaning the left rear is smaller than the right rear."

"Why?"

He never waited for your answer before he dove into the next question, much like me. "Sprint cars have a one-piece rear axle connecting the left and right rear wheels and don't have differentials. So if you have both tires, the same size, and with the high compression ratios, the car would end up in the fence as soon as you hit turn one." He seemed to understand so I continued. "Do you remember when we went to Knoxville Nationals this last summer and Grandpa Jimi was adjusting the stagger on his car?"

"Yeah," his brow furrowed together while he listened intently. His head tipped to one side, slightly contemplating everything I'd just told him.

"At Knoxville they're known for a drier slick track, meaning you don't need as much stagger as you'd need at Elma or Cottage Grove where the clay is thicker with an almost mud consistency."

Once we made it back to the house for the birthday party, Axel had asked every question he could think of when it came to stagger and ruts.

I remembered being the exact same way. At his age, I dreamed of racing non-stop so I understood.

"How'd it go?" Sway asked once she found me in the family room of our Summit Lake home.

We offered to hold the party here since Charlie's old house that Andrea and Van were living in was nowhere near big enough for our expanding families.

Wrapping my arms around her swollen belly, I breathed in a deep breath. I enjoyed the time away from racing during the winter months for moments just like this, knowing I'd be able to wake up beside my wife and not have to leave for another track. Instead, tomorrow we'd be going on a small vacation, just the two of us.

"It went good," I finally answered when she slapped my hand

away, which I had placed on her ass.

"Behave," she told me, tapping her index finger to my nose. "We have kids *and* people everywhere."

"There are kids and people everywhere," I had to remind her before pulling her into the bathroom just off our kitchen. "That's never stopped us before."

"At some point, I'd like to have my body back from having your kids."

Smirking, I took a firm grasp on her ass. "You're really to blame for that."

Her right hand rose quickly and punched my left shoulder, the one I'd just had surgery on a few weeks back when I separated it in a crash at Talladega early in the year.

My brutal glare stopped her before she gave in and muttered a "Sorry." It was still very sore.

"You were saying?"

"Nothing ... I wasn't saying anything. What did you want?"

"You." I tipped my head toward her.

"No, not happening." Her eyes widened when I cornered her against the wall. "We have a party going on out there."

"Like I give a shit about that." I kissed along her jaw before I slowly swept my tongue along her bare collarbone. Her arms tightened around my neck, and I knew I'd won.

Having sex while your wife was eight months pregnant was difficult, but in a tiny bathroom it was damn near impossible, and Sway was not helping by moaning wildly.

I was just about to start moaning when Aiden knocked on the door.

"Hey, Jameson, are you in there?"

Shit, do I lie?

"Uh, yeah dude." Sway's horrified eyes met mine frantically. "I'll be out in just a minute."

He laughed. I'm sure he knew exactly what was going down in here.

"We need to stop this." Her attempts at pushing me away ended when my fingers grazed her ignition switch.

"You were saying?" I leaned in to capture her lips with my own.

Her whimper when my tongue entered her mouth confirmed she didn't want this to end.

"Shut up," she told me with a scowl. "I was telling you to shut up."

I reached down to widen her stance against the countertop she had hunched over so I had room to maneuver around the engine I knew so well. My lips moved from hers to graze across her shoulder blades and the nape of her neck where I gently bit. It worked.

"Oh God, Jameson!" she screamed.

Hearing the chuckles outside the door from Spencer and Aiden was the last thing I cared about when I let out a groan that could have shaken the entire goddamn house.

"Holy shit," Sway gasped, bracing against the edge of the sink.

"That's right," I nodded haughtily, pulling my jeans up.

"Such a jackass."

"You weren't saying that a moment ago," I reached forward, drawing her against my chest. "It was something along the lines of *'Oh Jameson, you fuck so good!'* Yeah, that was exactly what you said."

"Jesus," she shook her head, one eyebrow quirked at me. "I didn't think your head could get any bigger. I was wrong."

Once outside the bathroom, I had some explaining to do.

"Where'd you go, Daddy?" Axel asked, dragging his little friend, Lily, around with him.

Lily West was Justin's daughter who was just a few months shy of Axel. Those two were just like Sway and me growing up—pretty much inseparable.

Still buttoning my jeans since Sway left the goddamn door open before I was fully dressed, I answered him, "I had to shower."

"There no shower in there."

Shit.

"I just splashed some water over my face."

He glared in my direction before looking over at Sway. He was more perceptive than I give him credit for.

"Sure, Dad."

Dumbfounded that my four-year-old son realized what his mom and I were doing in the bathroom, I slipped back into the kitchen to give Sway shit for leaving the door open to find her crying in the kitchen.

"Honey, what's wrong."

She turned to face me, smashing her face in my chest. Her hands grasped at my shirt.

"I'm sorry ... I don't want this baby to be born yet."

"It won't." We still didn't know the sex of the baby. Just as Arie had done, this new little one refused to cooperate during ultrasounds so it was a mystery as to what the addition to the brood would be. "You still have another month to go."

The baby wasn't due until the beginning of February. We had time to get Sway used to the idea of giving birth again. It was then that I noticed what I was standing in. Her water had broken.

Sway looked down and started crying harder.

"I can't! I don't want to do this again."

She hated giving birth, but once it was over, she was ready for more.

"It's all right, honey. We've done this two other times," I soothed gently, stroking her back. "You'll do fine."

"No, I won't," she shook her head. "That's easy for you to say. You're not shooting kids out your crankcase!"

"Well, I should hope not."

Her expression turned furious. "Jameson?"

"Yes." I smiled, trying to coax her into laughing.

"Shut the fuck up and take me to the hospital!"

A few things happened in the matter of four hours. Sway screamed loud enough that I was sure my eardrum had ruptured. Axel and Arie were awarded Blizzards for helping me control their hysterical mother, *and* I got a speeding ticket.

Much to Sway's surprise, and the cop who tried to pull me over,

I didn't stop and now had three local police cars and a county sheriff following me to Saint Peter's Hospital in Olympia.

"Daddy tobble," Arie giggled when I pulled her out of her seat to give the kids to my mom before I was arrested for resisting arrest.

Another four hours later, and I was heading back to the hospital when Aiden caught me in the hall.

"Dude, get in there," he motioned toward the door to Sway's room. "She's having the baby *right now*!"

When I entered the room, Sway was doubled-over, screaming in pain.

"What's wrong? Should she be in this much pain?" I panicked when I looked into her eyes and saw fear. This was beyond the normal childbirth pain—something else was wrong with her.

Dr. Sears stepped in front of me before I could reach her. His hands came up in capitulation when he took in my impious glare.

"Everything is fine, Jameson," his voice was urgent. "We just need to take Sway for a caesarean. The cord is wrapped around the baby, and I can't get it out naturally."

I nodded and reached for Sway, who was limp against the bed, exhausted by hours of pushing.

"Honey, are you okay?"

"The baby ..." was all she managed to say before crying out again. I felt the punch to my gut hearing her cry out in pain—pain I couldn't take away.

The doctors worked quickly—not as quickly as I would have liked them to, but eventually she was wheeled into an operating room where I was forced to stand in the hall until I barreled through the doors with two security guards on either side of me.

Dr. Sears shook his head. "I'm amazed you stayed out this long."

Disregarding his comment, I headed straight for Sway. "Jameson?" She looked over toward the door and our eyes met. Hers were laced with tears, confusion, and concern, as were mine. "Is he okay?"

My eyes darted around the room looking for the baby. They focused on the small infant struggling to breathe on his own while doctors assisted him. He was blue and motionless.

Immediately I was beside Sway, reassuring her everything was fine and praying I was right.

"He'll be fine, honey," I choked out when I didn't hear any sounds coming from him.

"Jameson, don't lie to me ... I don't' hear anything."

Tears streamed down my cheeks. It was the longest moments of my life. "I don't know. I don't know if he's okay," I finally told her.

How could I tell my wife, who had carried our child for the last nine months that he wasn't breathing and might not make it?

I couldn't.

It was only another few seconds before we heard the scream.

"Oh, thank God," Sway breathed into my cheek I had resting against hers. "Go check on him. Please ... tell me if he's okay."

I could still hear his faint cries when the nurse appeared beside me.

"See for yourself, Sway," she said, showing him to Sway.

Looking at him, it was as though we were looking at a newborn version of Axel again.

"He looks just like Axel did," Sway said, peeking over at him in amazement.

"He does," I agreed, taking him gently from the nurse. "He's beautiful." My eyes focused on Sway. I smiled when she smiled at me. "We made some cute kids."

"I was wrong. Your head can get bigger."

Later that evening, the kids returned to see the new addition.

"What his name?" Axel asked, holding his newborn brother. "He cute."

Sway and I exchanged a quick glance before I nodded and winked at her. "What should we name him, buddy? Mom and I thought you and Arie could help us."

Arie, who'd been squirming around in my arms, finally relaxed enough that she'd fallen asleep. I shifted her weight to adjust my hold on her prone sleeping position.

"Re-re sleeping," he told me. "How we name him then?"

"How about you name him?" Sway suggested. "Arie would call him *no* if she got to name him."

It was true. My little rusty-haired angel replied to most everything with "no" or "Daddy." She thought I was the best thing in the world, besides apple juice, of course.

Axel, still holding his baby brother, stared at him for a good three minutes before looking up at us.

"How about Stagger?"

Sway looked over at me for assistance. She has a hard time telling the kids no. She once brought home a monkey from the zoo because the kids pressured her enough that she caved and purchased it. I didn't even know you could purchase a monkey from the zoo, but apparently with enough persuasion from a four-year-old and a frantic mother, they offered up the monkey.

The monkey Axel named "Mr. Pooter" was adopted by Spencer and Alley a week later when he felt the need to wear Sway's underwear around our house.

"I don't think Stagger would be a good one. What about something a little more modern?"

"Modern?" He looked down at the baby again. "How 'bout Casten?"

I smiled, and so did Sway.

My grandpa Casten had passed away this past summer from a stroke. It was hard on our entire family, which I knew didn't go unnoticed by Axel.

"I think Casten is a great name for him," Sway said, reaching for the baby Axel handed her. The baby whimpered the way Axel and Arie both did when they were newborns. "Casten Anthony?" Sway smiled over at me.

Nodding in approval, I laid Arie beside Sway and then picked up

Axel.

"Why don't we go get Mama some ice cream?"

"You read my mind," he said, nodding readily. "I was just thinking that she need owc cleam."

Once in the cafeteria, he confessed what I expected he would.

"Daddy," he began with the serious intense stare he had when he wanted to get his point across. I had the same look so I knew this was important to him. "Are you ... I still your little buddy?"

I stopped walking.

"Of course you are," I knelt down to his level, forcing him to look at me. "What would make you think you're not?"

He was silent for a moment before his nervous expression met mine. "You have another boy now."

Instantly, I scooped him into my arms.

"You're always going to be my little buddy, no matter what. Even if Mama and I had another ten boys ... *you*," I pointed to him, "are always going to be *my* little buddy. Do you know why?"

"Because I race?" he offered.

"No," I smiled softly. "You and I share something, just us. We understand each other." I tapped the side of my head. "And we have a special bond, buddy." I wasn't sure what else to say to him to convince him that I had a special bond with *him*. I loved all my kids the same, but you had different bonds with each one. Axel and I, well we thought the same, acted the same, and looked identical. I'd always relate better to him for those reasons. Axel also held a special place in my heart that reminded me of Sway and how we got together in the first place. Something that was complicated as hell resulted in something beautiful—Axel Charles.

Eventually we made our way back to Sway's room where Axel climbed into the hospital bed with Sway. She wrapped her arms around all three of our kids.

Later that night, after Aiden and Emma had taken Arie and Axel, Sway and I laid in bed with our newest addition.

"I can't believe how much he resembles Axel," Sway said softly, her head rested against my chest.

"I know, it's really weird."

It was weird. They could have been twins. Arie looked a lot like Axel and now Casten, as well, but she resembled Sway more with her wide green eyes and heart-shaped face, whereas the boys were a mirror image of me.

"I love you," I told her, pulling her closer to my chest without hurting her.

"You better, but I think I'm done popping out your kids for a while."

"I think three is enough."

She was quiet for another few moments before she said the words I expected to hear.

"I wish Charlie could have been here."

"I know, honey, I'm very sorry," I murmured, kissing her forehead and then Casten's.

Losing Charlie never got easier for Sway, and it was part of the reason we now lived in North Carolina. Being in Elma reminded her of Charlie too much. But the thing about Elma was, it always brought us back to where we truly felt like a family.

Pit Board – A board used by the crew to inform drivers of lap times, lap until pit, and other information.

Taking care of Axel and Arie for a few weeks after Sway's C-section was a lot of fucking work. I never realized how much energy those two had until I was alone with them. It wasn't so bad when I just had one, but both of them together—I couldn't understand how in the hell Sway did this every day.

It was exhausting, and I could completely understand why some animals ate their young.

Arie was a handful. I could handle Axel because we thought the same way. I knew what I wanted and, in turn, I understood him.

Arie was something else entirely.

One particular trip to the grocery store after we arrived home from the hospital guaranteed I'd never take her again. Hating grocery stores in general, this didn't help matters.

There I was, picking out some fruit when a sales associate tapped me on the shoulder.

"Um, sir?"

I turned around to see a woman pointing at Arie, who was stark naked and looking up at us with curiosity. Emerald green eyes outlined by thick black lashes blinked as though she had no idea there was anything wrong with this situation.

Seeing as she was only two, this could have been worse, but what made me laugh was the way her diaper had been tossed in the apple bin and her clothes were strategically and neatly hung on the bananas.

"Can you please keep your daughter clothed?" she asked and then fished the diaper out of the apples for me.

I just laughed. What else was I supposed to do?

It wasn't like she knew any better.

I laughed, mostly because I had no idea what else to do. Sway had left me lists. An actual fucking list on what it was that I was supposed to do, but taking clothes off in a grocery store wasn't on the list.

When I got home Arie was clothed again and I asked Sway if she did this often.

Sway laughed as she burped Casten. "Yeah, all the time," she told me like it was no big thing. "I once had to duct tape her diaper on."

"Thanks for the warning." I stood there as Arie once again stripped.

"No problem," she giggled. "What's with all the apples?"

"They made me buy them."

Tommy, who frequently stayed at our house, came into the kitchen and grabbed an apple from the counter. The apples I intended on throwing away.

He took a seat at the kitchen island and ate the apple. "Your kid's naked again," he said, commenting on the obvious as Arie streaked through the kitchen on her way to the backyard.

After a moment, he noticed us staring at him and trying like hell to contain our giggles.

Sway leaned into my shoulder. "Should we tell him?"

Tipping my head toward hers, I chuckled. "I don't think it would even make a difference to him."

"What is your problem?" Tommy asked, finishing his apple.

"Nothing," we both replied, snickering.

"You guys are so strange," he said, walking into the family room to play a video game with Axel.

Sway got up and headed for the apples. She opened the door to the trash bin, and I sprung up to stop her.

"Don't do that. We have to at least make a pie for Spencer with them."

"Oh, good point," she grinned and put them into a large bowl away from the rest of the fruit on the counter.

Later that night, I decided to take my family out to eat since Sway was still recovering and most of my energy was spent on the kids that afternoon and neither of us felt like cooking.

So, there we were at the local Outback and Arie tossed her juice cup on the floor. Naturally, Sway bent under the table to get it.

Axel was busy playing with his food, and Arie thought she'd help Sway out by saying "There, look there!" at the top of her lungs every few seconds. As if Sway didn't know it was under there.

I hated going to restaurants with the kids because it was like we spent more time making sure they weren't being annoying to others, begging them to eat, picking up shit they threw, telling them to stop staring at people, and then trying to actually eat our own meals. It was a nightmare.

Tonight wasn't any different.

While Sway was down there I looked around the room when a group of frat boys started cheering at what they thought was my wife giving me a little micro polishing under the table.

I would have never allowed this with kids present, but I decided, against my better judgment, to pretend a little.

I nodded a little arrogantly, provoking them.

"Oh, there it is," Sway said, reaching for the cup that was now by my foot.

Trying to keep this up a little longer, I threw my head forward as though I really was enjoying it and kicked the cup away.

"Don't kick it, asshole."

I grinned again and the group of guys high-fived each other.

Sway eventually got the cup, got back in her chair, and glared at me. "Jerk."

Axel snorted and looked at me with a smile. "You made Mama mad."

"Nothin' new, little man," I said, taking a big bite of my steak and then chewing slowly before I winked at Sway.

She shook her head and then excused herself to feed Casten in the bathroom. She returned at the worst time when the group of frat boys came by.

"Man, you are our hero!"

I smiled and nodded but gestured toward Axel and Arie looking up at them curiously.

"Shh," I gestured to my little spaz kids and their curious eyes. "My kids are here."

Clearly what I did wasn't appropriate, but it was funny.

A few other guests had looked in our direction at the commotion the guys were making.

"What was that about?" Sway kicked me under the table when a woman muttered something about what I did being completely inappropriate.

"I have no idea," I said and finished eating my steak that Axel had spilled his milk on. I wouldn't have eaten it at that point, but I couldn't let on to Sway what I had done.

My wife was not stupid by any means and picked up on it.

"Why, you dirty man," her head cocked to the side with suspicion. "With our kids present!" She smiled despite her bitter tone.

I looked around, ashamed and amused, and then leaned forward and motioned for her to come closer with my finger. She did and I winked.

"So many judging looks coming your way."

Her mouth twitched into a smile, one she didn't want to reveal.

She kicked me again, but I did get some micro polishing that night after the kids went to bed. She loved me and couldn't stay mad.

I was out on the balcony outside our master bedroom lying in a lounge chair when Sway came out after putting Casten down for the night.

Slipping outside, she stubbed her toe on the edge of the railing just as she always did when she came out here. "Son of a bitch!" she cursed. "We need to move this."

"We can't. It's a railing."

She knelt beside me and then lowered herself on my lap, her legs falling to the sides leaving her crankcase directly in line with my camshaft that was very eager to have some attention.

Removing my shirt, her hands lingered over the ridge of each muscle as though she wanted to remember the feeling and texture. Looking down at me, her left hand rose to cup my face, bringing my lips to hers. With a need I couldn't explain, I gasped at the feeling of being covered in her skin.

Taking in a deep breath, I folded my arms behind my head.

"That was not a very nice thing you did at the restaurant ..." she whispered, moving down my body as she removed my jeans enough to get to what she needed.

I couldn't speak when she drew me into her mouth. So warm. So soft. I missed it so much.

"Jesus, Sway, I want to fuck you so bad," I breathed into the night air.

The subtle waves of the lake created a light slapping at the dock. The clouds from the day had rolled apart, highlighting the lake with glistening silver streaks.

My focus wasn't on the lake. It couldn't be with this beauty sliding down my body; giving me pleasure in ways I'd never imagined feeling for the rest of my life. Thoroughly determined, her hands reached around my hips to draw me deeper into her mouth, her movements speeding as though she couldn't get enough of me. It was just the opposite. I couldn't get enough of her.

My hands shot to her hair trying to tug her up when I felt the familiar stir in the pit of my stomach.

"Honey, you should move if—"

Just as she always did, she pushed my hands away, but she did slow her motions. She wasn't done with me, and that just excited me even more.

"It's like you know exactly what to do," I stroked the side of her face tenderly.

She looked up but kept me inside her mouth, her eyes soft, and I watched carefully as I slid in and out of her full lips, hypnotized by her unreserved love for me.

My breathing turned erratic as I tried to fight the feeling. Regardless that she slowed her moves, the way she was looking at me, and the way I was sliding in and out of her mouth, I was giving in to the hold she had on me. Flashes of our past passionate lovemaking, on this very deck, fluttered behind my closed eyelids when my head fell back, my body clenched, and I knew I couldn't hold off.

Sway crawled back up my body, and her lips found mine as my head lulled to the side.

"I hope it was good as you pretended it to be in the restaurant."

Rolling my eyes, I laughed. "I know it was wrong, but I couldn't help myself. It was funny."

She removed herself from the lounge chair, grabbing her midsection as she did so in.

"You okay?"

Sway winced and righted herself into a standing position. "Yeah, just sore." I stood beside her, buttoning my jeans when she poked at my chest. "You shouldn't do that with the kids present. What if someone would have made a big deal out of it? You wouldn't want your sponsor finding out your wife was micro polishing with kids present, would you?"

Now that she put that spin on it, no, I wouldn't. It was in good fun and just a joke to rouse a few teenagers, but in turn, I didn't think of how that looked to the outside. Here I was, a NASCAR driver, and I'd pretended my wife was on her knees under the table with my three kids present. Not smart.

I kissed her forehead. "You always know what to do."

Sway laughed, slipping into our bed. She patted my side. "I should know what to do. I write the pit board."

I laughed. "You write the pit board, eh?"

"Yep. I know when you need your next pit stop." I laid down next to her after removing my clothes. "I know what adjustments you need on your next stop. I know how much fuel to give you and the right air pressure adjustments. I know you." Her index finger touched my nose.

Smiling that she was right, my eyes closed. "That you do, honey."

Glancing around at the overflowing shopping cart, I knew who was to blame for this. Having only come for coals for the barbeque, I had a feeling I wouldn't be leaving with *just* coals.

"Axel Riley, get your ass over here right now."

The mother next to me gasped at my crudeness.

"Sorry."

I was thankful all the kids weren't with me at the moment. It never failed. When I had them all together the little shits liked to scurry in different directions as I would try to get them in line or try to keep from dropping everything in my hands. It was like they knew I wasn't an octopus and could sense the fear any time I picked something up and had no free hands.

Axel came tearing around the corner with an arm full of chips and marshmallows. Somehow, though I'm not sure how, he found room in the cart. "I got what I need. We can go now."

"Smartass," he snorted and smiled. "Why do you need all this?"

He held out his hand with the same smirk Jameson gives. Without thinking, I pulled out a dollar and gave it to him. This no cursing thing was making my kids' millionaires.

"Thanks, Mama," his eyes focused on the marshmallows. "Lane and me ... we gonna have a s'more."

Anything Lane wanted to do, Axel wanted to do. Anything Lane and Axel did, Noah, Charlie, and Cole copied. It was an endless cycle, and soon Casten would be involved.

"S'mores, eh?"

"Yes, that's what I said."

A few hours later, we were heading back to the campground with our s'mores, chips, and whatever else Axel stuck in that damn cart.

Jameson laughed when he walked up to the Expedition as Axel and I tried to carry the bags. "I thought you were getting coals?"

"I did." I slapped the bag with my free hand, trying to conceal my own smile. He'd taken Axel to the store before and knew the drill very well.

He grinned and leaned against the back of the car, his arms crossed over his chest.

"I see that," he gestured toward the bags. "I was referring to all that."

"Um ..."

He pulled me firmly against his chest. "Admit it, honey, they own you."

"If I avoid it ... it doesn't exist," untangling myself from him, I glared.

Still leaning against the side of the car, his head tilted to the side as his hand ran down his jaw.

He winked. "So ... you wearing a bikini under that dress?"

"Wouldn't you like to know," I snarked as I strode past. "Don't forget the bags."

"Tease!" he yelled after me.

Walking toward the lake, I heard the laughter of the kids playing in the water, the crackle of campfires nearby and the crisp pop of beer opening. It was the sound of camping.

Why did it always feel like life was passing you by in a blur?

Before you knew it, you were a mother of three, your husband was worshiped by women, and maybe even men, all of the world, and you didn't know where all the time went.

All I really knew was that when we had the opportunity to be a family, we were.

After the July 2008 race in Chicago, Jameson had a bye week before the race in Indy. Against our better judgment, we took all the kids camping—tent camping to be exact.

Aiden convinced all of us to go camping at Lake Guntersville State Park where he spent most of his time growing up. We had so many people with us that we had to rent out most of the park.

Let me give you an idea of how *many* people we had. So starting with us was me, Jameson, Axel, Arie, and Casten.

Six-month-old Casten wasn't exactly running around. He was constantly attached to the foodbags or eyeing his older brother and laughing.

Spencer and Alley were here with Lane, who had just turned eight. Lexi and Cole were also here, but instead of running around after the motorized vehicles like the older boys were, they were playing in the shallow parts of the water.

Then we had the terrible toddlers, Aiden and Emma's hellions, Charlie and Noah. Not as bad as the Lucifer twins but were definitely giving them a run for the title of the worst children ever. It must be something with twin boys. I could only assume that with age, they'd be even worse.

Being only three-and-a-half, they still had time.

Speaking of the Lucifer twins, they were here, too, but seemingly well-behaved for the most part. They'd just turned eleven, and it appeared Van kept them in line.

Justin, Ami, their daughter, Lily, and their new little one-year-old boy, Kale, were with us, as well.

Then we had the adults without kids: Tommy and his girlfriend, Melissa, (and yes, the Melissa who represents Simplex), Tyler, and Cody. Ryder showed up with a new girl on his arm and Tate, his wife, Eva, and their son, Jake, came out. Bobby, Paul, Andy, and even Colin Shuman came out for a night.

With Jimi and Nancy, too, it seemed we had everyone here.

With this many people, it made for some interesting times.

I didn't know why we went camping. It wasn't like we have ever had a good time doing it. Most of our time camping was spent running around after the kids and remembering all the past bad times we'd had camping.

Unlike our brush of death before, there were no cougars in the area, but there were seven little boys under ten years old and two who had just turned eleven to annoy us.

I couldn't count the number of times we told those boys, "Stop throwing rocks and put that goddamn stick down!" or "Get the goddamn stick out of the fire!" and "Give me the goddamn stick!"

Then there were the moments after cooking the s'mores that we said, "The marshmallow is on fire, get it out of the fire, don't throw the marshmallow at your sister, and give me the goddamn marshmallows!"

It was hell. I couldn't understand why parents would willingly put themselves through this regularly. I sure as hell wasn't going to. I loved my kids dearly even if they threw rocks at me, spit on me, or punched me in the throat when they were throwing a fit, but when we were outdoors, it was worse.

Axel, my beautiful little four-year-old son, was being a little shit. He was upset that we didn't bring his go-kart or his quarter midget so he was on his worst behavior.

Jameson had to tell him on more than one occasion that he'd never race again if he didn't straighten up, but he insisted on being a complete turd. We'd only been there five minutes when Jameson had to discipline him for throwing rocks at Logan. Not that I blamed him, but still, Logan and Axel needed to learn they couldn't just do whatever they wanted.

Jameson and I wanted him to have some balance and time away from racing from time-to-time, but just like Jameson, he wasn't having it.

Instead, he was buzzing around on Lane's dirt bike.

Lane headed in the opposite direction of the Riley boys and racing, preferring two wheels to four.

Jameson may have had something to do with this as he was constantly riding his dirt bikes around our property in Mooresville. Lane soon picked up on it. Right after he turned six, Spencer bought him one for his birthday, and he's been riding ever since.

So the kids stuck sticks in the fire, rode dirt bikes, swam in the lake, and were just kids.

The adults drank. It was the only way to remain sane.

Even though there didn't appear to be any cougars or bears, the bugs were another story. They were obnoxious. There were small ones, big ones, colorful ones, some the size of fucking birds, noisy ones … I feared for my skin and soon for my sanity when the itching began. I felt sorry for addicts who went through withdrawals and wondered how in the world they didn't take a grinder to their skin.

If I could have found one, I would have.

I must have lathered up with an entire bottle of calamine lotion while Jameson washed his skin obsessively like he would actually wash away the bites. It didn't work, and in the end, we itched.

"I don't like this," Jameson said conversationally, slapping away a bird-sized mosquito.

"Me either." I took a drink of my beer, peering down at my speckled, itchy skin. "There are so many bugs."

"It's Alabama. What did you expect?"

"So?"

"That's all this state has, besides peaches, is bugs."

"Peaches are from Georgia."

"Sway," his eyebrow arched. "They have peaches everywhere."

"I know that. I'm just saying that the term *peaches* goes with Georgia." I scratched my forehead. "Not Alabama. Just like apples go with Washington and oranges go with Florida."

"Does it really fucking matter?"

"Yes."

He snorted and stood up. With a stretch, his back arched, and he yawned, running his hand through his hair and then down his jaw. Eyeing the lake, he motioned with his head toward the direction of the lake. "I'm going for a swim."

Alley started laughing beside me while lathering up Lexi with sun block.

"I can't believe Aiden thought this would be fun," she said only to me.

Emma was all about camping and couldn't stop organizing and making our campsite homey, so God forbid we bad mouth the trip in front of her.

I never got up from my little throne next to the campfire. Hoping maybe the bugs would leave me alone, I realized by not moving, I attracted them like a fluorescent light.

Later that night, after dinner, Spencer and Aiden took all the kids to go watch fireworks and that left Jameson and I *alone*.

You can imagine how we made use of the time.

"You wanna get naked?" he asked, wiggling his eyebrows at me.

"You know ... sometimes women like romance."

"Oh—sorry," he moved to sit next to me, the rusty highlights in his hair sparkling from the light of the fire. It was a sweet gesture when his hand rose to cup my cheek and leaned in to kiss my forehead. "Honey, please get naked with me?"

"You're such a knob."

A few minutes later, we were both naked inside our tent.

"Can you scratch my ankle?"

"Yeah—sure." I scratched his ankle.

"Thanks," he grunted, pushing me forward to grasp my ass with his hand. I liked it, a lot.

To me, there's nothing better than camping in the middle of nowhere and having hot, dirty sex with your dirty heathen while the kids are occupied.

Speaking of dirty, dirt was everywhere in the tent. And, in Alabama, the dirt was more like clay and it stuck to you. I was itchy, and the dirt kind of felt nice chafing against my skin.

"Can you scratch my back since you're back there?"

"Yeah—where?"

"By my ass … *oh, yeah* … right there." His movements didn't stop either, and I wasn't really sure what felt better, the scratching or his movements, so I moaned. "Oh, yes!"

"You like that?" he asked with a hint of arrogance. "Fuck yeah, you do."

"Yes!"

Suddenly he stopped. "Wait, what are you liking more—the scratching or the sex?"

How the fuck did I answer this one? They both felt good, but the combination of the two was what was *really* good.

"Both," I squeaked.

I heard him sigh and fall back on the ground.

"This isn't working," he started itching his arms like a junkie.

I scrambled on top of him to straddle his hips. "Yes, it is working."

"No, it's not. We itch, and we look like we have chickenpox. You know how much I hate stuff on my skin and look at it!" His eyes closed. "I want to go home."

"So you don't want to …" I swiveled my hips once, his back arched as his hands stopped itching and flew to my hips.

No more words were spoken as the dirty heathen took over. It was one of those times when you didn't say anything because you just had a mission: getting done before the kids came back.

By the time we were done, we were sweating, covered in red clay and a few more bug bites.

"Ow!" Jameson yelled, rubbing his leg. "Something bit me!"

I grinned.

"Was it a cougar?" I started laughing uncontrollably. "Or maybe it was a shark."

Holding his calf, he scowled. "No!"

"Come here." I motioned for him to lie against my chest, still laughing. "Let the mama wizard see."

He was hesitant, but any chance at cuddling the funbags was appealing to the dirty heathen, so he did. Examining his calf, above his shark bite, there was a raised blotchy patch.

"Oh, you poor thing," I cooed, running my fingers through his hair. "Are you going to be okay?" Despite my calmed tone, I was still laughing.

"Stop laughing." He pulled back to glare. "This is *not* funny. What if I was bit by a deadly spider?"

"Well, then—I will apologize when you die."

He side-eyed me. "Nice."

It wasn't long and the kids returned, all of them popping off their rev limiters as Jameson would put it.

After that, it was the battle of getting the little shits to bed and to stay in bed. It was almost like they smelled the fresh air, and once it hit their lungs, they acted like fucking brats.

It took Jameson, me, and Spencer just to get Axel into bed, and finally Nancy had to step in.

Arie was easy. She went out like a light when Jimi captured her in his arms.

Casten stayed awake for a while, eyeing everyone curiously, but it seemed okay since he was a baby and couldn't tell anyone how ridiculous his parents acted when the kids went to bed.

He did, however, pass out about the time Tommy, who was suffering from allergies and took to drinking Benadryl, plopped down in a camping chair next to Jameson and started telling him about how he thought he needed a raise.

Tommy was joking because Jameson gave willingly to everyone on his team, whether it was the Cup team or sprint cars.

Every year, Ford handed Jameson a brand new truck of his choice. And every year, he then handed that truck over to one of his boys. He always went all out on Christmas and birthdays for anyone on his teams. Most thought he was an asshole, but he knew everyone's birthday on his team and surprised them every year with something most could never dream of affording.

Why did he do that? Because to him, he wouldn't have any of the luxuries he had now if it wasn't for them.

Jameson, concerned that his only mechanic on his sprint car team was drinking Benadryl as though it was a juice box, looked at Jimi, who was still holding Arie, for help.

Jimi shrugged when Jameson tried to take the bottle from him and gave us the same look he'd given Nancy when she made him sit through the *Sex in the City* movie.

"He's drinking Benadryl through a straw," Jimi reminded us. "I guarantee you that's the least of your problems tonight."

And, my God, was he right. That night was similar to the old pit lizard days. Thank God there wasn't a tattoo parlor nearby, although we did have a branding torch courtesy of Spencer.

It started when Spencer said, "I bet you can't swim across this lake."

You never said that to these boys and expected them not to react. Ever.

Jimi stood, shifting Arie to his other arm and motioned around. "The shit is about to hit the fan, and I'm tired. No one kill themselves tonight. It's supposed to be relaxing and the nearest hospital is miles away." He looked at Tommy and Spencer. "You two stay away from my fucking tent tonight."

Jimi and Nancy put Arie in our tent and then snuck off to theirs.

So what did happen when the parents went to bed?

Oh God. Where did I even begin?

Spencer started in with the 'I bet you can't do that' shit and that resulted in Jameson, Justin, Tommy, and Aiden swimming across the lake. About one minute into it, Justin confessed he couldn't swim very well and ended up coming back when he couldn't touch anymore.

That left Jameson, Tommy, and Aiden battling it out in their own version of aquatic survivor. I was amazed someone didn't drown out there with the way they were dunking each other.

Halfway across the lake, they gave up and decided drinking beer was more entertaining than drowning. It also had something to do with Justin reminding them there were snakes in the lake.

Spencer—convinced they had no balls for not completing his stupid 'I bet you can't do that' task—threw insults at them all night.

Tommy, wanting to one-up Spencer, decided he was going to fill water balloons with piss.

The worst part, my twenty-eight-year-old husband joined him.

Here was the thing, though, and what these dumb shits never considered—Spencer had pulled off more pranks than all of them put together. He knew when he was about to be pranked and usually knew how.

So there Jameson and Tommy were drinking one beer right after another and peeing in the balloons. Around one that morning they had enough for their war against Spencer.

Only problem was Spencer caught onto them and decided he was going to one up them and sprayed them with WD-40. If you'd never seen what this did to balloons, it was entertaining. The chemicals ate through the balloon in about five seconds.

Spencer, his intelligence soaring that night, enlisted Logan, who refused to go to sleep, into sitting behind Jameson and Tommy and spraying the balloons with WD-40 before they launched them at Spencer. Needless to say they exploded mid-air all over them.

"Abort mission!" Tommy hollered in complete horror, soaked with his own urine. He looked at Jameson. "I'd be okay if it was my own piss. I do that at least once a month, but yours ..." He shivered. "I can't handle that. I can't."

Jameson, who was hiding behind me for cover, looked around, tipped his baseball cap up and grinned. "Oh, Tommy, it's just my urine. I'm clean."

Tommy, who had dodged under a canvas camping chair, glared and ran after him.

"C'mere asshole, I'm gonna piss on you and see how you like it!"

Jameson shot out into the woods to avoid him with Tommy following.

After making sure the kids were still sleeping, I sat down next to Ami.

"I have bets that one of them ends the night with a broken bone or stitches."

"For sure," Ami cracked another beer and handed me one. I took it since I'd pumped enough for Casten the last few days, and I figured I could have one free night.

We could hear the boys in the distance all yelling obscenities at each other; Jameson's laughter, Spencer's laughter, and then, finally, Justin and Tommy squealing like little girls quickly followed by Jameson and Spencer screaming.

Once I started drinking that night, I couldn't tell you with accuracy what actually happened, but it was one of those nights I didn't care. It was nice to just be a kid again.

Any time once of us thought we'd woken up the kids, we started giggling like a bunch of girls at a slumber party and saying "shhhh" on repeat.

Around four, we were still going strong when we heard movement near the tents. Jameson practically jumped onto my lap.

"Do you think it's a cougar?" he asked, pulling his baseball cap down to hide his panicked expression from the others.

"No," I pushed him off. "And, if it was, I'd feed you to him."

He laughed, remembering those words from our honeymoon. Everyone else looked at us curiously. Apparently, to Jameson and me, it was the funniest thing we'd ever said to each other, and we both laughed uncontrollably. It was probably the alcohol.

All our laughing woke up Jimi.

Emerging with a grunt from his tent, Jimi looked around the campsite and shook his head with a smirk. His hand rose to scratch the top of his head. "I don't even want to know how this happened."

Tommy, who'd passed out by the fire, groaned and sat up. After looking around for a moment, he lay back down and asked, "Is the room still spinning?"

Jimi kicked a few bottles out of the way and made his way back to his tent muttering something about his grandkids being more mature than their parents.

Ryder stood, brushing aside the crumbs of the two bags of chips he'd eaten and walked over to Tommy and looked closer at his face.

He stared at him for a moment before turning to all of us. "His eyebrows are gone!"

"No shit?" Justin perked up. "They just grew back from the incident at Dog Hollow."

"Yep," Ryder looked closer. "They're gone."

"Fuck yeah," Jameson pumped his fists in there air. "He deserves that."

Ami felt the need to remind Jameson that Tommy was the one who was peed on tonight.

"That's not really the point," Jameson, said reaching for another beer and a bag of barbeque chips.

"Not the point, my ass. She made a perfectly good point," I reminded him, only to have Jameson glare.

He stopped when I took his hand and rested it on my bare knee.

"Now, let's go see about a tree I saw out there," I winked at him just to get *my* point across.

"A tree? Why in the world would you want to see a tree?" Spencer asked and then caught on. "Oh, right."

Alley quirked an eyebrow at her husband. "Sometimes I wonder how you get through the day."

"That's rude," Spencer actually looked offended. "I'm perfectly capable of getting through the day."

"Yeah." Alley rolled her eyes when Jameson and I stood, she added, "Sure."

On the way into the woods, I asked him if he thought we were getting too old for this sort of thing.

When he didn't respond, I turned to see him leaning against a tree, his arms crossed over his chest.

I was drunk, but despite this, I took a moment to look over my husband. His hair was crazy, gray t-shirt soaked with the beer Ryder dumped on him earlier, and his brown cargo shorts were weathered and worn from being his favorite pair for the last two years.

My eyes went lower to see that he wasn't wearing any shoes.

I laughed. "Where are your shoes?"

He shrugged and offered that smirk I loved so much.

Slowly, he pushed himself from the tree and came to stand within inches of me. His eyes traveled south again and landed on my shorts as he fumbled for a moment with the button. He was trying to remain sexy about this, but he was so drunk that every time he tried to keep a sexy mysterious look to him he'd smile and we'd both start laughing.

Holding back his laughter, he began to drag my panties slowly down my legs.

Pinned against the tree by his hips, I was determined to make this last longer than I knew it would. Pushing back against him, my hands found his shorts. My fingers got the button undone when I felt his stare again. He watched each movement as I slowly let the camshaft out.

He smiled. I smiled.

"He's missed you," he breathed, bringing my lips back to his.

Kissing Jameson was like ice cream for me on a hot summer day, hell, any day. I couldn't get enough of him ... or ice cream.

Jameson seemed frustrated he couldn't get my shirt off fast enough so I, once again, pushed him back to assist with the pit stop.

Helping him out, I pulled my shirt over my head, instantly regretting the cool night air as it provided quite the reaction to the funbags. It had been a while since they'd been out to play after having kids. So many times I had to keep my bra on just because it wasn't worth the effort of having to constantly tell Jameson to stop trying to get his mouth around them.

I looked up at Jameson watching. He only stared, his laughter suppressed, with silent words, and it only made me want to scream. I wanted to know what he was thinking and to hear him say dirty engine words to me, but no, he just stared with that smirk and warm eyes that spoke for him.

All laughter aside, he wanted me.

He reached out tentatively and touched the side of my face, holding my jaw in the palm of his hand. Moving closer, his lips rested behind my ear and he whispered, "Are you gonna fuck me or just stand there and stare?"

I attacked him like a cougar, and he couldn't stop laughing at me. We ended up somewhere against a tree and then the ground and then back to the tree. We were both laughing, clinging to each other, and making the best of our time alone even though our friends and family were making animal sounds not more than thirty feet away.

My legs wrapped around his waist using his shoulders as leverage. He moved me the way he wanted.

While I enjoyed this, the only problem was that, as with Dayton Peak and the pit lizard days, my ass was scraping against the grain of the bark and giving me splinters. I wasn't sure if my cries of pleasure were from the bark scratching all my bug bites or from Jameson. Either way, it was kind of nice.

"Fuck, honey," Jameson growled and pushed me harder against the tree.

His movements sped, as did his hips, and we were lost in a world of scratching bug bites, sweaty bodies, breathy words, hurried touches, and laughs.

Any time I was with Jameson, it was a flurry of emotions both emotional and physical swirling inside me. He had the power to stir up and turn wild those very same feelings whenever he felt like it. I hated that he could do that to me, but I took pride that I could do that same to him if needed.

Believe me, not every time you had sex with your husband was it going to be this way. Sometimes it was quick and dirty, other times it was slow and sensual, and then there were the times when you just didn't mix. Something felt off, maybe it was you, maybe it was him, but guess what? That was marriage.

But this time, against the tree, I briefly thought to myself, "Well, this is the second time in your life you've been fucked against a tree," and then I thought, "Hot damn, this is the second time I'm being fucked against a tree."

Focusing on the moment, my dirty heathen pressed his forehead to mine, one hand wrapped around my right thigh and the other holding onto a branch above my head. My eyes darted to his arm beside my head watching the way the thick muscles flexed as his hips moved. My eyes traveled over his shoulder and then to his face and the way his brow knitted together in concentration, the way his lips parted slightly as he let out soft grunts of pleasure. His eyes were closed, but when I breathed his name, he opened them for me just about the time we fell.

I don't mean fell into our rev limit either. I mean actually fell.

"Son of a bitch!" Jameson shouted, trying to break our fall as his knee slammed into a log.

"Get over here." Jameson roughly grabbed me by my hips and placed me on all fours.

On the ground.

In the woods.

Hot fucking damn.

I completely lost it and found my rev limit and then some.

I wasn't sure what it was that made it so hot and sent my temps rising, but I'd like to think it was because of the way he manhandled me and shoved me on all fours to satisfy his need.

"That's right," Jameson said in a rush of winded words and a cocky nod when I finished moaning and turned to look at him.

He looked so hot with chips of wood in his hair, polished body from the humidity and working up fast time.

Removing myself from him, I threw his shirt at him. "Someday you'll need your own country to house that head of yours."

I left him sitting there in the woods and began to make my way back to camp when I heard Tommy yell, "Hey look, it's a cougar."

I knew he was joking, but I'd never seen Jameson run so fast. He flew past me and was standing by the fire before I'd barely taken two steps.

"Hey, asshole, thanks for caring about your wife!" I shouted at him and then tripped over a log and face planted.

When I made it back to the fire Jameson was wrestling with Tommy and a bottle of pink hair dye.

Apparently, Tommy was trying to replace Jameson's shampoo with pink hair dye when Jameson caught him.

I, for one, could have cared less about the hair dye or who got their hair dyed when I returned. I had so many cuts, bruises, splinters, and abrasions that I needed a first aid kit and a few words with Jameson and Tommy.

Tommy ran from Jameson when he kicked him in the shin and realized he shouldn't have, but instead slipped and smacked the back of his head on a log.

Tommy laid there for a moment before he panicked.

"Oh, God, *please* tell me I don't have blood coming out of my ears! Please tell me!" he groaned, pushing his hands through his orange hair and down his face roughly.

"No," Jameson kicked him in the side, still without shoes on. "You don't have blood coming from your ears, dumb shit."

Pushing Jameson aside, I knelt next to Tommy, pretending to check for blood. "Nope, no blood. But you do smell like piss and tequila, and you're missing your eyebrows." And then I smacked his forehead. "Don't ever do that to me again!"

"Do what?"

"Threaten a cougar sighting. We take that shit seriously in this family."

"Oh, please, it was a joke." Tommy curled into a ball with his log. The sun peeking over the trees revealed his pale face. "If I never see tequila again, it will be too soon."

Justin laughed, hanging on Ami, his own face just as pale. "He said that last week."

Still sitting next to Tommy in the dirt, he looked at me, with wide blood shot eyes. "I sometimes think that my pranks will work on Jameson."

"Fire crotch," I shook my head, rubbing his back softly. "I sometimes think that I could have been a professional dancer, and then reality sinks in, and I say to myself, that's a pipe dream."

He looked concerned. "Are you saying I'll never get him back?"

"No. I just don't want you to get your hopes up."

Tommy moaned and fell back into the dirt. "Did they really brand my chest?"

I nodded with a smile. "Yes, that really happened."

"Are my eyebrows missing?"

"Yes, that really happened, too."

Before heading back to our tent, I looked at the campsite and cringed at what ten adults were able to do in one evening.

We had no beer left, no hard alcohol, and most of our food was now gone. Not to mention we almost set the picnic table on fire, successfully discovered how to make a bomb with Pepsi and Mentos, made a beer bong with Ami's breast bump, gave Tommy a tattoo on his chest that said, "I'm your bitch," with a branding iron Aiden had made, and lost Ryder. Like actually lost him.

It was time for bed.

Jameson, who used the kids as a defense device when I found him in the tent, had nothing to say for himself until I showed him the cuts on my back from the tree.

"I'm sorry?" he offered, playing with Arie's curls as she slept on his chest.

"Sorry, he says," I repeated, shaking my head before zipping myself up to my nose in my sleeping bag.

"Daddy, Daddy!"

I groaned, opening my eyes to the blinding light coming in through our tent. I got very little sleep with all the bugs and everything that happened last night. Oh, and when I finally did reach the tent, Arie wormed her way in between us.

I tried numerous times to put her on the other side of Sway, but no, every time she found her way back to me and my sore back.

After about the tenth time of Arie saying, "You awake?" that morning, I opened my eyes to find her staring at me.

"Finally." Arie sighed. Her big emerald eyes gleamed with brightness. "Get up," she ordered, pointing her tiny finger at me.

For being nearly three, she was demanding. I blamed Emma and Alley for that.

"Flowers."

Oh, right. I promised her we'd pick flowers today. How we were going to find flowers here was beyond me. So far, all I'd seen was red clay mud, water, and bugs.

"Daddy!" she yelled, jumping on me. "Up."

"I'm up, sweetie, I'm up!" I turned over to see Sway was still sleeping. "Just let me make some coffee first. And don't wake up Mommy. She's mad at me."

She seemed to contemplate this for a moment. "One mimmut."

"You are so adorable," I grabbed her chubby cheeks in between my hands kissing her nose. "So adorable."

"No me not," she said sternly, frowning as she pushed against my chest.

"Oh, yes, you *are*." I tickled her ribs as she cackled, continuing until she was screeching loud enough to wake Spencer and Aiden.

I let her up after that so she could catch her breath. For the first time I noticed what she was wearing, and I had to bite my lip to keep from laughing. She obviously dressed herself this morning. The outfit started-off normal enough—a t-shirt and jeans, the jeans were tucked into bright yellow boots. Along with those, she was wearing a pink ballet costume over the shirt and a tiara that was slightly askew from our tickling war, on top of her head.

Chuckling the words out, I muttered, "Ten minutes. Yes, ma'am."

Even though my little angel couldn't tell time, I knew by the way she stomped from the tent, she'd be back in less than two minutes.

Sure enough, Arie came stomping back, this time with a life jacket around her and a bucket in hand.

"What's with the life jacket?" I knelt down to adjust the straps to fit her snugly.

She glanced over her shoulder at the boys having an early morning water fight by the lake.

"Aunnie Amee."

I saw Ami wave at me. After last night, she must have known the boys got a little crazy at times because she strapped life vests on Arie, Alexis, and Lily for their safety.

Sway woke up from Spencer's screaming when Aiden threw a snake he found in the lake at him just before Arie and I left to pick flowers.

I heard her grumbling about the bugs and her cuts when she yelped as she unzipped the tent.

"Oh, son of a—"

"Say good morning to Mommy, Arie!" I said loud enough for her to hear.

I did this for two reasons. One, I didn't have any money on me to hand over to Arie for Sway's cussing, and two, Arie was like a goddamn sponge. Anything you said, she repeated and at the most inconvenient times.

"Good morning, sweetheart," Sway smiled at Arie who lunged for her and looked at me with a glare and then smiled. Her smile was somewhat concerning, though. It was one that had me wondering what I was missing. "Did you sleep good?"

"Yeah."

Sway looked over her outfit. "Did Daddy dress you again?"

"No, me." Arie pointed to herself.

Sway kissed her chubby cheeks.

"You did good. You look beautiful!"

They spoke for a few minutes until it was time for Casten to eat, and he didn't like to wait.

"C'mon, sweetie, let's go get Mommy's present," Arie popped up from Sway's arms and followed me. I smiled back at my wife, but she glared.

Being out in the backwoods of Alabama, we didn't find any flowers—found a few snakes, and quite possibly the largest spider I'd ever seen in my entire life, but no flowers. That depressed my little girl to the point of tears. You could imagine how this made *me* feel. I didn't like Sway crying, let alone our adorable little spaz children.

I didn't deal well with the crying, so in turn, I was now making a s'more at eight in the morning to keep the tears at bay.

On the way back, Arie looked up at me and grinned. "Daddy, why your hair pink?"

I shook my head remembering Sway's smile. "Oh, because Daddy has assholes for friends."

"Assholes?"

"Never mind."

Sway came walking up to the fire seeing me making s'mores. "Sucker."

"You're one to talk." Slowly, I turned the marshmallow to keep from burning. "You went to get coals yesterday and bought half the goddamn store."

"Whatever." She sat down beside me with Casten in her lap. "Nice hair."

"Yeah, I think the color goes nicely with my skin." I gestured to all the bug bites.

"That it does, sweet cheeks." She kicked my ass and almost landed me in the fire headfirst.

"Nice," I said, brushing ashes from my shirt. "I'm not sure I would have saved you."

"Asshole."

"Stop it," I looked over at Arie was now staring at us. "You're setting a bad example for our kids." I couldn't even say it with a straight face. I think all our kids knew we weren't exactly model parents.

Arie came bouncing over to me with chocolate all over her face. "Where's my massmello?"

"Marshmallow?"

"Yeah."

"Here you go, princess." I handed over the marshmallow and smiled at Sway.

It never failed. We gave into the adorable spaz children, no matter what. But when your kids became part of your pit board, you'd do anything to keep them happy and running just as smoothly as you were.

Sway and I also knew this would backfire someday. Some might even call them spoiled. Spoiled *maybe*, but not with possessions, with love. That was a bit cheesy I knew, but it was the truth. I strongly believed we couldn't worry about the future right now. We had to live for each pit stop and discover who they really were within the race. Even if that meant bribing them at times and making s'mores at eight in the morning.

Crush Panels – Metal panels that are inserted around the bottom of the driver's compartment and wheel wells to keep fumes and intense heat away from the driver.

It was early, too early for my liking, to be leaving for the airport, but I was. It took me a good hour to actually get out of bed this morning because Sway was giving me pouty lips and showing me her boobs, which is why I was running late to pick up Justin in Martinsville. Wes, on my time clock, was late as well when we landed to pick him up.

Justin and I were racing in the World of Outlaws race at Skagit Speedway on Friday night, and then I would fly back to Richmond in the morning for the Cup race. Tyler and my other driver, Cody Bowman, were already in Washington.

"Jameson, I need to drop you off here," Wes told me when we landed in Martinsville Indiana, where I met Justin. "I need to get to Jacksonville to get Jimi. He needs to be in Alger tonight, as well."

I gave him my best "What the fuck!" expression, without voicing it.

Instead, I said, "You mean I have to fly with other people?"

"Yes, your no fly order was lifted," Wes chuckled. "I think you can handle it."

"So Jimi is more important?" I scoffed, annoyed. I was already late because of Sway and her magic crankcase.

“He pays the fuel for this thing. So, yeah, I think he’s more important, kid.”

“That’s bullshit, Wes.” I slammed my bag down and pointed at him. “If I get arrested, I’m blaming this entirely on you!”

My threat just washed right off him, as I’m sure he laughed all the way to Jacksonville.

An hour later, I missed the flight Alley booked for Justin and me.

“What took you so long this morning—we could have been there by now?” Justin asked as we walked through the airport.

I smiled and went to say something when he shook his head and held his hand up. “Never mind—I don’t want to know.”

We finally found the ticket booth and got new tickets for the next flight only to discover it was departing right now. In our mad rush back to the gate, Justin dropped his ticket so we had to back track. Once we found the ticket, we made it to the gate to see the door closing on us.

“Fix this, asshole,” Justin said virtuously.

Once again, I hardly thought this was *entirely* my fault. “You lost your goddamn ticket.”

He pushed me toward the ticket booth in front of the closed door. “And *you* were late this morning.”

Looking from an angry Justin to the woman at the counter, I knew my option.

It was time to unleash some charm. Taking in a deep breath, I stepped forward.

“Excuse me, Miss ...” she immediately turned to face me, her cheeks flushed. She was young—nineteen or twenty maybe.

That’s right, you still got it.

“I’m Jameson Riley and my friend ...” I motioned behind me to Justin—he flashed a charming smile of his own. “Well, we *really* need on that plane.”

“Oh, sir ... I’m sorry I can’t. They are securing the cabin,” she said hesitantly.

Her eyes glanced furtively around the airport, avoiding mine.

C'mon, just look at me. I knew if she looked at me, it was over. I knew that sounded cocky, but I was well aware of the effect I had on women these days and knew the ways to get them going.

I smiled my most seductive smile and leaned against the counter. My forearm gently brushed against her fingers clinging to a clipboard. At the contact, she inhaled sharply.

"The problem with that is ..." My eyes met hers. "I need to be in Alger later this afternoon for a race."

She looked confused for a moment and then comprehension flashed across her face when her eyes *finally* met mine. "Are you Jameson Riley, the NASCAR driver?"

I winked for good measure. "That would be me."

She then laughed and started rambling on about racing and getting the doors to the plane open. Justin and I both gave her autographs and took a couple pictures with her before they finally allowed us to board the plane.

Yet another reason I preferred to fly with Wes. I didn't have to flirt with him.

"You're lucky your charm worked."

"It always does."

Maintaining eye contact, Justin shook his head and stared at me as I took a drink of his coffee.

"Sway was right," he said sourly, "your head *can* get bigger."

We made it to Skagit without any more problems. That was until we got inside the cars.

It was hard to believe that three years ago my little girl was brought into the world at this very track. Those thoughts made me think of my family who was at home this weekend.

With the Cup schedule, I could only make one night of the racing, and then it was on to Richmond Saturday morning for the race and then back to Mooresville to celebrate Arie's third birthday on Tuesday with our family.

It was one destructive night of racing, and by the time the main events rolled around, I was wondering why in the hell I even came up here. All I could think about was how much money this was going to cost me this week to get these three cars ready for Cottage Grove Monday night.

I never went very long without racing on dirt. If I did, I went through withdrawals, which was exactly why I was out here for one day.

So there we were, sometime after the hot laps looking over our cars lined up beside each other in the pits.

Justin leaned back on his rear tire, pushing his fingers against the rubber. With the lower psi the rubber flexed under his touch. "It's crazy out there tonight."

And it was. The track was slick with only one groove, making it hard to pass anyone. Tyler's car was flying, but Justin and me were far from flying.

We were hanging on for dear life, hoping like hell we didn't wad it up in each turn. I loved racing Skagit, a relatively flat track made for the good slide jobs in the corners, but with only one groove working tonight, it was pretty much impossible unless you hung it out there and prayed to fucking God you didn't end up in the wall. With a wife and three kids now, that wasn't an option for me any longer.

As it turned out, none of us had a good night, including Tyler, who broke the track record during qualifying.

"How'd ya do?" I asked Justin, pulling my suit to my waist.

Justin frowned. "Broke a lower control arm."

"Hell, my right front tire could be in Seattle by now." I flipped the car six times on the backstretch when I got tangled with a local guy halfway through the A-feature.

"I broke a torsion bar, too." He kicked it. "Actually, make that two …" Justin got on his hands and knees and scraped a few large chunks of mud from the front right wheel. "And an axle."

I laughed.

"My rear end is in turn four ... well, kind of. Most of it is in turn four, my shock mount is in turn one. My rear axle is ..." I glanced over my shoulder toward the track. "In turn two."

Hell, together we broke every piece on the cars. It was carnage out there.

Tyler came rolling by on the back of my dad's four-wheeler holding a shock mount in one hand and his helmet in the other. He held it up when he walked past. "This was the only salvageable part on the car."

I really didn't want to see this parts bill tomorrow. With these cars leaving Sunday morning for Cottage Grove, we used the back-up cars brought with each team, but it didn't matter, I still had to pay to have these three fixed.

That was racing. You could easily dump a hundred thousand in a motor alone, just to have it blow up on you in hot laps.

Speaking of engines, they seemed to be our biggest problem this year. With Grandpa Casten passing away last year, the future of CST Engines was unknown. CST Engines was what almost every team on the Outlaw Tour used for engines, along with most of the national sprint tours.

When Grandpa died, his partner, Rick Denton, had no clue what to do and neither did we. Grandpa built the engines while Rick merely acted as the sales associate. Old Casten had no business conversing with the public.

Uncle Randy and my dad ended up taking over ownership of the business, but had to hire Harry, my engine specialist on the Cup team to build the engines until they found someone. Harry tried, he really did, but Grandpa knew sprint cars. They were his specialty. In turn, he could build us an engine that would usually last the entire season.

After a few months, Dad and Randy ended up having to hire another engine specialist, Kerry Andrews, and let Harry just concentrate on the Cup cars. I think it was more that Harry actually told him he'd quit if they didn't.

Eventually things got better, and the engines were close to what Grandpa was providing, but it took nearly a year of trial and error before we found a design that worked best for us. As you could see, this put a lot of stress upon every team.

It was always something in racing, no matter what form. If you weren't fighting with the engine, the shock package needed attention.

But, hey, that was racing.

On Saturday night, I found myself in Richmond for the last race before the chase.

"You have about four more laps until we stop," Kyle told me around lap one eighty of the Chevy Rock & Roll 400 race.

I loved Richmond, but not tonight.

It seemed like my luck for breaking cars wasn't going any better than it had Friday night at Skagit.

"We have to get this packer out of the right front," I told him, knowing he'd make the adjustments.

Instead of relying solely on the spring rubbers to adjust the suspension and handling of the car, we added shock packers, which allowed the shock to absorb a fair amount. Instead of a shock compressing, let's say, seventy-five percent of its potential—we would put in a packer to decrease the shock travels. This allowed it to only half-way. Shock packers, combined with spring rubbers could make the car react differently and give us more room to experiment with setups. We either used one or the other, or together, depending on how the car was handling and the track we were at.

With Richmond, you started in the daylight and finished under the lights. Those races were always tricky because of how temperature sensitive it became. One minute you were loose and about to kiss the wall and then next you were so tight the car wouldn't turn.

"What's your water temp?"

"210 - 215."

"We'll put a piece of tape on it this next stop. Three laps."

"Pit road is open," Aiden told us when it was time to pit. "Four thousand second gear. The six will pit in front of you, you'll need to come around him to get into your pit."

We made our green flag stop along with most of the field, which took us from our sixth place spot to fourth. It wasn't good enough—I needed to win tonight.

Currently, Paul, Colin, and I were right on the bubble to make the chase. For the first time in my five-year Cup career, I might've not made the chase. I'd spare you my thoughts on the chase format; I was *not* a fan of it. Other sports could keep their playoff format. I didn't like it. I didn't like it because if I was running strong all season and running in the top five with a comfortable lead and did shitty those last few races, I still had a chance. In the chase, that wasn't always the case.

"Where am I at in points?"

The format had been modified from the previous years and now included the top twelve in points. Even though I hated this whole "chase" shit, this new rule was in my favor this weekend.

"You're eleventh if the race ended right now. Paul is struggling mid-pack right now, something about a vibration."

This helped my chances tremendously.

After another fifty laps, nothing improved. The car still felt like it was lifting when I entered the corner, not something I enjoyed.

"It's not helping. What did you change, anything?"

"What's it feel like now?" Kyle asked.

"Forty-two at your door ... clear." Aiden guided me through a pack of lapped cars.

"The same. It feels like it's dragging, and my right front is way too high."

"On entry, middle, or exit?"

"Entry and exit."

"Your last lap time was a 32.30. Bobby is running a fifty in front of you."

Another twenty laps went by, and the car got worse, if that was possible at this point. "I've never felt anything like this before," I complained.

"Just hang in there, bud, we'll put some air in the right front."

"That's not the problem. The right rear actually feels like it's coming off the ground. We have to get the front end down more."

Kyle was quiet for a few moments, probably contemplating what the hell that meant and what would fix it. The hardest part of his job, aside from my frequent mood swings, was trying to decipher my explanations of the way my car was handling.

"Let's go with a thirty-second round out of the right front and a sixteenth out of the left. Do you think we should change the splitter?"

"I wouldn't just yet."

Before we had the chance to make the changes, Colin tried to make a pass on Bobby for the lead and pegged the outside wall hard, sending debris flying everywhere, bringing out the caution.

"Cautions out—stay high."

The twenty-four of Andy Crocket checked up and sent the rest of the field fishtailing to avoid hitting him, and the debris slung out over the backstretch. This would have worked in my favor having Colin out of the mix. Only problem was that when Andy checked up, the seventeen of Nathan Weise was not paying attention and clipped the back of my car sending me into Andy's bumper.

"Damage to the front end," Aiden announced.

Assessing the *steaming* situation, it was apparent the radiator was shot, along with my hopes of the chase this year. This was not good. I was never satisfied with anything other than a win and neither were my sponsors.

"Son of a bitch!" I yelled, flashing a hand gesture at Nathan. He flashed the same gesture combined with a few words that I couldn't hear. Whatever they were, it pissed me off even more.

"It blew the radiator out," I told the crew. "Where's the garage?"

Pulling the car past the pit wall I realized that I had no idea where to turn.

"You can get there from where you're at," Aiden told me from his position on top of the tower in turn one.

"Tell me where to go. I can't see shit, and there are no signs pointing toward the garage."

"Down the hill. Turn right after the gate."

"Was that so hard?"

"Listen!" Aiden snapped. "I'm up here with God knows what kind of bugs crawling on me. I'm sweating like a fucking pig and you want directions to the garage. Don't be an—"

I had no choice but to laugh when Aiden started coughing, apparently from swallowing bugs.

My crew did what they did best and got me back on the track, but the damage to the points was already done. I missed the chase by twelve points, yes, twelve fucking points.

I was unbelievably dejected. Since I started racing, I had never finished outside of the top ten in points for any series I ran in, ever.

After the race, I made my way toward the motor coaches to change and get my bag before heading home to Mooresville. Colin and Nathan were walking the same direction. Colin Shuman and I tolerated each other. I wouldn't, by any means, say we were friends, but it was easier than fighting with him. On occasion, we would have a beer. Hell, he even came camping with us once.

So there I was, walking behind them when Nathan, a rookie driver this year and the same guy who cost me that chase, popped off, "Did you see Riley out there? He was driving like an asshole."

"Yeah, I saw," Colin mumbled. "That's what he does best."

My anger for the night soared.

"You know," I said darkly. They both spun on their heels to face me. We were in between the motor coaches now, out of sight of everyone. "If you two want to question my reasoning on the track ... ask me. Don't smart off behind my back."

"It was nothing, Riley, just relax." Colin snorted and leaned against the side of my motor coach.

Ignoring Nathan's wide eyes, I stepped closer to Colin. "I race you the same as I race any other guy out there. You don't like it, tell me to my face."

Colin smiled. "I don't like the way you race."

I laughed one hard laugh. "And I don't like the way you race. You don't think out there."

Colin knew this was a battle he wasn't going to win. We didn't agree on the track, never had, and probably never would. But we both knew that was as far as it went. Off the track, I could tolerate him. At times he reminded me of Darrin, but Colin was just a hotheaded kid.

Neither one of them said any more, but just gaped at me in silence.

As you could imagine, my mood when I arrived home that night was not good. Colin and Nathan had pissed me off. I missed the chase, I knew Simplex wouldn't be happy, and, on top of that, I missed my family.

Sway had stayed home with the kids because Casten was sick with a cold.

Around two in the morning when I walked in the house, I was greeted with Sway and all three of the kids sleeping in the living room in a makeshift fort of blankets, chairs, and pillows from all over the house.

My mood improved significantly as I sat down on the floor next to Arie and watched them sleep. My sleeping little girl looked nearly identical to Sway.

Axel had stirred slightly when I set my bag down and eventually opened his eyes, rubbing them once he realized I was sitting there. Placing my index finger to my lips for him to be quiet, he grabbed his blanket and came to sit on my lap next to the couch I had leaned against.

"I missed you, Daddy," he whispered, snuggling into my arms.

"Mmm ... I missed you, too, little buddy."

"Sorry you didn't win."

"It's all right. You can't win them all." Axel had seen me win a lot, but I wanted him to understand it wasn't always like that, not with the competition these days.

I spent the rest of the night out there in the fort they had made and woke up to eight-month-old Casten drooling on my face and giggling. The kid never stopped laughing.

Rolling over, I began tickling his chubby little rolls. He belly laughed, squirming for me to stop. Arie got in on the tickle-fest as did Axel.

Soon we woke up Sway.

"You're home," she said, blinking as though I wasn't real.

"Yes, I am." I winked as our little flailing spaz children bounced around the room.

Sway crawled over to me from her place inside the fort, her crawling distracting me.

"Don't do that," I groaned, averting my eyes.

"Do what?"

"Crawl. I miss you, and *crawling* is not helping."

"Oh—sorry." She wasn't sorry. She knew damn well what she was doing.

The rest of the morning was spent making blueberry waffles and playing with the kids in the fort. Arie's birthday was Tuesday with the party planned for that night. Today, we planned to do whatever she wanted.

"What would you like to do today, sweetie?" I asked her as she climbed down from my lap at the breakfast island to steal her Barbie from Casten who was using it as a chew toy.

Axel laughed at him. "He's like a dog."

I laughed as Sway picked him up. "Come here, you little puppy."

Casten loved Sway—thought she was the greatest thing ever. He was still breastfeeding at eight-months old and Sway did not like this, by the way. She was never a fan of breastfeeding to begin with, but we both knew it was better for them so she did it anyway.

"We can do anything you want today," Sway told Arie.

Arie always looked to Axel for advice and now was no different.

After what appeared to be an intense conversation with Arie, they turned back to us.

"Can we go to the zoo?" Axel asked.

"I need to discuss this with your dad," Sway said, teasingly, as she pulled me aside. "We can go to the zoo, if they want," she whispered. "Just make sure they don't talk me into anything. The last thing we need to do is come home with a pet cougar or something."

I rolled my eyes. "Very funny."

"I thought it was."

"Arie, honey, will you please tell your brother that if he succeeds in catching that fish, I'm taking the fish home and leaving him here."

"Okay," she said before running over to say something to Axel. I saw him turn toward me and smile sheepishly.

Jameson came walking up after staring at the tank of sharks for the last ten minutes, paying no mind to the fact that his almost five-year-old son was trying to catch one. "This is lame. I've always hated the zoo."

I replied, "Why, because you belong in one?"

His only answer was to arch his eyebrow at me as his phone rang for the hundredth time this morning. The entire hour and a half drive to Asheboro was spent with him on the phone talking with Marcus and his dad about their plans for the rest of the season. I felt bad for him, and for the first time in his career he would finish outside the top ten in points. For a man like Jameson, that was a hard pill to swallow.

"Let's go get me a pet," Axel said with bright eyes, pushing Casten in his stroller.

I ruffled his hair and smiled. "Nice try, kid, but no."

I had to let him down easy, but I hated to tell him that I was not buying a pet. I was lucky that I was able to keep three kids alive as long as I had. There was no way I could take care of another pet, too. I needed to stand my ground on this one. Mr. Jangles did not need a friend as far as I was concerned.

Most of the day Arie wanted to watch the lions and cougars. Jameson did not, for obvious reasons, and took the boys to see more manly animals, which he said were the apes. How they were manlier was beyond me, but I had a feeling it was only because the apes hadn't tried to eat him yet.

We were walking toward them when Arie looked up at me. "Mama?" she asked.

"Yes?" I knelt down to her level.

"Daddy mad?"

Arie was very perceptive to Jameson's mood swings and sensed his attitude this morning. "No, sweetheart. Daddy is just a little stressed out from the race last night."

She seemed to consider this for a moment before asking, "He need ice cream!"

"You know ..." I picked her up. "I think that is *exactly* what Daddy needs."

I hated to think our kids ever thought their dad's temperamental personality had anything to do with them, but it wasn't something I could change. Jameson needed to. There were times when his temper got the best of him, but he always guarded it around the kids.

While the kids ate their ice cream, Jameson was once again on his cell phone with Jimi. Axel watched him carefully, the concern present in his features. He worried about Jameson all the time and constantly tried to make him proud.

Slightly irritated that this day was supposed to be for Arie, and Jameson had spent the majority of the day on the phone, I sent him a text knowing he'd read it.

Look at your kids right now. Get off the goddamn phone.

As I expected, when his phone beeped at him, he looked over at them staring at him.

Jameson hung his head dejectedly. He knew. "I gotta go, Dad. I'll call you later tonight." He hung up quickly, turning toward Axel and Arie. "So what's next on the agenda today?"

Once again, they talked amongst themselves before Arie nodded and Axel spoke. "Water park—definitely the water park."

Jameson looked toward me slowly. "Oh, great, honey ... the *water park*," he repeated sarcastically with an upbeat twist he knew the kids wouldn't pick up on. Jameson didn't like water parks for a number of reasons. The biggest one: people.

Today wasn't bad at the zoo, but usually anytime we went anywhere, people followed us. Jameson Riley was a household name around these parts. Anytime someone mentioned NASCAR, they associated that with Jameson Riley. All this resulted in Van tagging along everywhere. He kept his distance, though, never letting on we had security around.

"Who thought water parks were a good idea?" Jameson asked as Casten took a nap on his chest while Axel and Arie waded around the sandbar.

"Disney."

"That's Disneyland, not water parks."

"So, I'm sure they had something to do with it."

Jameson shook his head and glanced down at his vibrating phone. "I'm not going to answer it," he assured me.

"I didn't say anything."

I laughed when a small wave from the wave pool knocked Arie over and Axel helped her up.

"I know, but you were thinking it."

"I just want you to see how they look at you. Axel hangs on your every word."

"I know he does," he nodded, watching them play. "He wants to race the Dirt Nationals at the end of the month."

So far, Axel had raced in all the USAC Quarter Midget races and was running third in their championship point battle. I knew my little boy was ready, but it was still nerve-wracking. He was so tiny and to see him racing around with other kids scared me sometimes.

"I know ... do you think he's ready?"

Jameson seemed to contemplate this for a moment before replying, "Yeah, I do." He glanced over at me. "Are you nervous?"

"Yes and no. I've watched him at home ... he seems confident enough." I shrugged, sipping my water. "I worry about the other kids wrecking him."

"That's part of racing, honey. We can't control it."

I knew we couldn't. Hell, if we could, none of what happened with Darrin would have happened. Not a day went by that I didn't think about what happened in Loudon. It was hard not to.

I looked at what I gained in return. Life. I pulled through. Axel pulled through. Jameson pulled through, not completely, but he did move on.

Together, we all pulled through. You couldn't control everything. All you could do was go with the flow and hope like hell you caught a break every now and then.

Preparing for Arie's party left me a little on edge. I felt the need to drink at any kid's party because I couldn't handle all the commotion and children in one place. I loved my kids, but when people were over at our house and sugar was involved, I no longer liked them. So I drank.

Shortly before I had finished the cupcakes, Axel came in with blood pouring out of his nose.

"Mama, I did somethin' bad."

I looked at him and knew exactly what he'd done. "How far up there is it?"

"A little." He shrugged and looked at his feet.

"Jameson?"

Axel bolted the other direction afraid to let his dad see him in such a compromising situation. I mean, he very nearly shoved the fucking thing into his brain. It wasn't coming out without some help. Help I was in no condition to provide after my second long island iced tea that I'd been pretending was regular iced tea.

"What do you mean he stuck a Lego in his nose?" Jameson asked when I explained.

"That's exactly what I mean." I giggled, feeling the alcohol in my system a little more. "He's four and a half, nothing they do makes sense. Now go, he needs help."

Jameson groaned and walked toward Axel huddled in the corner of our kitchen holding his hand to his bloody nose.

"Why did you stick it up there?" I heard Jameson ask him.

Axel didn't answer, just shrugged as a tear slipped down his cheek. Poor kid.

Jameson went to work retrieving the Lego from his nose. I had to laugh when Lane, who did this when he was three, and remembered this well because it had to be surgically removed, patted him on the back and said, "It happens to the best of us."

Arie's third birthday was already turning into a clusterfuck, and we hadn't even served the cake. I, for one, couldn't wait to eat cake. Emma had whipped it up and frankly, it looked like heaven with frosting that could give even the healthiest of us a heart attack.

Jameson had to leave tomorrow for Loudon, New Hampshire, so me getting drunk and bathing myself in frosting wasn't exactly a good idea. Besides, it was my daughter's birthday.

I put down the long island iced tea and stuck to water after that.

Arie, who was still going through her terrible twos and progressing nicely into the horrible threes, was running around telling everyone she was a princess and her Daddy was her prince.

Axel never went through this phase and the temper tantrums. Sure, he had his moments, but with Arie, wow, I wasn't prepared for her. That wasn't to say she was as bad as the Lucifer twins or the Gomez boys, but she was ... wicked at times, and Jameson refused to admit this. He thought she was perfect. So perfect that for her third birthday, he had her bedroom in our home in Mooresville transformed into a Disney fairytale, complete with a carriage for her bed.

"So she's not spoiled or anything," Alley piped in when I showed them the room prior to cutting the cake.

"You're telling me." I sighed. "It's getting out of hand."

Jameson really was creating a problem. Anything she ever asked for, he got for her. So far, we'd kept Arie from seeing it. This wasn't very hard because she still insisted on sleeping in Axel's room with him at night. He didn't enjoy this, by the way.

"What are you going to do when the boys start to realize how spoiled she is by him?"

"Axel knows, but he could care less; he's too into racing to care about that. And Casten ..." I looked down at him laughing at Cole, who was punching himself in the face and then falling down laughing. "I don't think anything could make him upset."

It was true. My little one was all smiles, all the time.

Casten was a very active little boy. He wouldn't sit still for anything, but at nearly a year old, it was to be expected. Unlike Axel, Casten was spontaneous and up for anything. You could literally wake him up from a nap, and he was ready to go do whatever you wanted and smiling while doing so. He smiled in the morning and never stopped until he fell asleep.

Jameson came up to me with wide, excited eyes and Arie latched on to his back in her princess dress she insisted on wearing while Emma constantly fretted with her crown.

"Is it time to show her?"

He showed way more enthusiasm than Arie. "Yeah, go ahead."

"Show me what?" Arie peeked her head up.

"Your birthday present," Jameson said, climbing the stairs toward her room.

"Maybe she sleep in her room now," Axel grumbled as we all climbed the steps.

He knew what we were doing and was more than willing to help, even at four, to get her out of his room.

It took a lot to surprise Arie. I blamed Jameson and all his extravagant gestures toward her. So when we opened the door to her new, ornately magical fairytale room, I was surprised by the squeal of delight she let out. It made me a tad jealous I never had a room like that.

"Oh wow, Daddy!" Her eyes squinted as they always did when she was so excited she couldn't control herself. It was the same face Emma often made. "It so *pretty*."

She danced around the room from one thing to the next, squealing louder than Emma, who was just as taken by the room. I was sure she was already planning a sleepover for her and Lexi. Emma had boys, and when Aiden put his foot down about them playing with dolls, she turned to her two nieces.

We didn't see the girls the rest of the night, and for the first time in months, Arie slept in her own room ... with Axel on the floor. He refused to sleep in the carriage.

Jameson and I watched our two little sleeping monsters with their cousins, who slept over that night as well.

"It's hard to believe she's three already," Jameson whispered, placing a kiss on my forehead.

"Mmm ..." I smiled, hugging him tighter. I laughed when Arie sat up in bed and made sure her princess crown was intact and then laid back down, snuggling closer to Lexi.

After a few moments, we made our way down the hall to our room. Jameson had me pressed against our king sized bed within seconds and was working on removing my clothes.

"I've waited all fucking day to do this to you."

"Shame on you, Mr. Riley, it was our child's birthday." I giggled, pulling at his jeans.

He got them past his hips before he smiled wickedly and looked down at me, naked and spread across our bed. "That doesn't stop me from *wanting* my wife."

I never grew tired of hearing him say the words, "my wife." It sounded territorial in a sense, but I didn't care; I loved it. It made me feel like I belonged to him, and that was all I'd ever wanted.

"Now, honey, I only have tonight with you before I head to Loudon. We need some align boring done. These bearings ..." His strong hand slipped in between us, his fingers dancing over my ignition switch. "They need to be properly aligned."

It didn't matter that we only had one night. We made the best of any amount of time we had with each other, remembering. Before he positioned himself between my legs, he glanced around the room.

"Where's that goddamn cat of yours?"

I giggled. "I had his tubes tied. Don't worry."

Jameson's brow furrowed. "Was he a she after all?"

"No, he was a *he*."

He seemed to contemplate this for a moment. "So how did he have—"

"Jameson," my lips silenced his words. "I think my compression ratio is about to explode."

His eyes darkened as he spread my legs apart with his knees.

"Well then, we wouldn't want that, would we?"

"No, we wouldn't." I giggled.

We tested out some align boring, piston stroking, reciprocating motions, deburring, porting of the heads, and micro polishing. The dirty heathen and the mama wizard were back and setting fast time for the night.

It didn't matter that we now had three little adorable spaz children. We still knew how to revert back to those pornographic days we once had. Now we were just polished and knew all the dyno testing results. We had it down.

The problem with being apart for the last few weeks was that our testing was over fairly quickly. As soon as I arched into him, he threw his head back and groaned this loud, growling, needy sound. And though I didn't reach my rev limit, seeing him like that was enough for me.

"I'm sorry," he mumbled, panting above me. "Jesus, I'm really sorry."

I giggled. "Don't worry, it was fun to watch."

"You always amaze me," he chuckled, rolling to the side. "I can't last more than a few minutes, and you say it was fun."

"It was."

Later that night before we went to bed, we checked on the kids.

"It's hard to believe how much they've grown," Jameson spoke into my hair. His arms wrapped around my waist, pulling me against his chest. "They're little people now."

My eyes caught the papers scattered across the bedroom floor from where the kids had been coloring earlier in the night.

"Someone is their hero," I whispered in his ear and pointed to the dozens of pictures of Jameson and his race car.

Jameson chuckled softly.

"They're young. They don't know any better."

Turning in his arms, I pulled back to look at him, running my hand down his jaw and saw the same worry I always saw when it came to our children. He was constantly afraid he wouldn't live up to the image they had of him. But he already had. They didn't care if he didn't win the championship every year. All they cared about was that he was there for them. And he was.

"You mean everything to them. All they want in return is your love."

As your children grew, you did, too ... in a sense. We wanted to see what they would become, but in the same sense, they were looking to us to see how we grew. You couldn't tell them to be the best they could be, all you could do is try to be that yourself.

"Is that all *you* want from me?"

"That's all I've ever wanted," pulling his lips to mine, I whispered, "What you are to the world means nothing to me. What you are to *me* means everything."

He leaned against the wall motioning with a nod of his head toward our sleeping children. “I just don’t want them to know. I want them to stay innocent in all this.”

I knew exactly what he was implying. He didn’t want the weight of our world on them. They needed protection from it. Eventually, we wouldn’t be able to do that, but for now, while they were young, we *wanted* that.

Yellow Line – A painted yellow line that is used to mark the separation of the racetrack from the apron. In restrictor plate races, NASCAR has decided if a car goes below the yellow line to make a pass the position will not be granted and you will be penalized.

As with any year, the off-season flew by, and before I knew it, Speedweek was starting.

For the 2008 season, I finished thirteenth in points. It was the lowest I had ever finished in any division I ever raced.

You can imagine what this did to my mentality.

When we left Homestead, I was depressed. Yeah, I won the most races that season but still, I hadn't won the championship. I understood I couldn't win them all, but I still tried. If I ever got to the point where I didn't try, I was retiring.

The off-season was hardly an off-season. From the hauler drivers to the mechanics and engineers testing our cars, racing was a way of life. Just because it was the off-season didn't mean we were on vacation.

I usually took the week of Thanksgiving with my family and two weeks around Christmas. Outside of those times, I was either testing, racing sprint cars, or working with our sprint car team. With three cars running in the Outlaw series, I had my work cut out for me.

Thank God for Tommy and Spencer, or I would have pulled my hair out by now.

Back at the shop in Mooresville, my Cup team was working on the cars for the next season. Whether it was a new paint scheme or manufacturer changes, it was busy. In the offices, new merchandise was designed and schedules were being finalized. I was paraded in front of sponsors and appearances all around the county. So despite the NASCAR season only running from February to November, it never truly ended for us.

Then we had all the dealings with Grays Harbor. Luckily for me, Jen, Andrea, and Mallory were wonderful and able to get the schedule done, sponsors lined up for promoting the events, and the annual memorial race for Charlie scheduled. Without them, Sway and I wouldn't know what to do. With three kids and our busy schedules we hardly had time to run a track, but we would never get rid of it. That track brought everything about our lives together. It would always stay in our family.

By the time I left for Daytona the first week in February, I wasn't even sure of the day. The arrival of Sway and the kids the day of the Budweiser Shootout improved my mood considerably. It didn't improve my aggression, though.

With the new season, new drivers came into the series.

The talk that season was Nadia Henley, a woman driver. I wasn't sure you could even call an eighteen-year-old a woman.

She'd apparently gone through a driver development program from the same team Darrin came from. As you could imagine, I was weary of her from the start.

This year she had a full sponsorship with Leddy Motorsports and Lazer Energy.

I didn't have anything against women drivers and raced them just the same, for the most part. Now where I might rough up a seasoned vet, I wouldn't do that to a rookie, let alone a kid/woman rookie.

Nadia, with her spitfire attitude and red hair to match had one hell of a chip on her shoulder when Daytona rolled around. I wasn't sure what to make of her so I kept my distance.

"Is that her?" Spencer asked when we stood on the grid prior to the duals.

I glanced over my shoulder uninterested in the commotion surrounding her. "I guess so."

Spencer watched her for a moment, curious as to how someone so tiny could handle these cars. He assumed she was sleeping her way to the top.

Mostly he was joking because there was no way she could get million dollar sponsorships without of some sort of wheel talent.

Another driver who wasn't sitting well with me was Shelby Clausen, another smartass eighteen-year-old kid trying to prove his own determination.

If you asked any other driver out there ... veterans ... rookies ... anyone, they would tell you that each year it got harder and harder to win these races. The level of competition was so high that even some of the top drivers went years without a win. Hell, even Steve Vander, one of the sport's most renowned race car drivers, hadn't won a race in one hundred and three starts. That was a long time without feeling the pure bliss of pulling into victory lane.

Having won the last race of the season, I felt confident going into Daytona. All that being said, Shelby didn't make this easy. Drafting in Daytona is an art—I think I'd stressed that before. Rookies, well they didn't have that great of a feel for it so it was harder to find another driver that would draft with them. Often enough, they found themselves tailing in the back just trying to make it to the finish. Understanding this, I gave Shelby a push or two. We had tested in Dover together over the winter so I thought, "Hey, let's give this kid a break."

I was fucking wrong.

So there we were coming out of turn two when Shelby shot out of the draft behind me and tried to pull some kind of kamikaze move on the outside.

It backfired on him almost immediately, and he was left high and dry. He came back twenty laps later and did the same exact thing, ending up last once again. He had a strong car, that was for sure, maybe even strong enough to win, but he had all balls and no brains.

Clausen must have pulled this move another five times before he tried drafting in behind me. I didn't have a problem with this because Bobby, who I preferred to draft with, had just pitted, and I knew we'd be pitting in just a few more laps. Clausen latched on to my bumper and pushed me around the track, but when we made it to turn four, I slowed. He didn't pick up on Aiden telling his spotter I was pulling off, and he bumped. Bump drafting in turns was not a good idea. Not for me at least. This bump sent me flying into the inside barrier of the pit road entrance.

"Coming hard into the pit road," Aiden warned the guys to have them back away from the wall. Sure enough, I slammed hard into the pit wall just as the guys scrambled away.

Well, at least now I was already in my pit box.

"Hey, look, you're in your pit already," Kyle chuckled despite his frustration.

"Heavy damage to the left side," Mason said and then began directing orders to the crew.

I didn't say anything more. I could have blown up, showing my aggression toward this Clausen kid, but I didn't. I kept my head together and managed to pull through with a top ten finish.

Even after the race, when he noticed me walking toward the hauler, I kept my cool. I didn't say any single word to him—only a head nod.

When Phoenix rolled around in April, I couldn't say the same thing.

Night races always left everyone fired up, and goddamn was I fired up after that race from both Shelby and Nadia.

I had qualified for the pole, my entire family was there, and I wanted to win the race. Having come off a win in Texas the week before, I had a taste of victory.

Clausen was driving like a fucking jerk and making all sorts of spastic moves on his hunt to the front—he had a strong car and was running second with twenty laps to go. Since Daytona, he'd yet to even finish a fucking race so when he came charging to the front, I figured he'd just wreck. He didn't, though; he stayed with me, and with ten laps to go, he challenged me for the lead with Nadia right behind me, too.

"Clausen is at your rear ... at your door ... still there," Aiden told me. "Henley looking to the inside. Keep your line."

"Keep your cool, bud," Kyle warned.

He knew me too well.

"Still out there ..."

"How many more laps, and what are my lap times?" I asked, trying to hold my line as Clausen stayed with me through turns two and three, and Nadia was contemplating making her move. I just knew she was going to do something stupid.

"Three laps to go. You're running at a 27 flat—Clausen is a 27:20."

I felt slightly better—but not as confident as I wanted to be.

Three more laps! I chanted to myself.

We stayed side-by-side, bumping and banging, putting on a good show for the fans when Clausen came down hard on me in the last turn. He basically cut me off. I had no choice but to lift. He was leaning on me so hard when I lifted, he shot down in front of me, and I ended up smashing into the back of him, destroying both our cars and Nadia when she smashed into me. Tate, who was running fourth, won.

I was happy to see Tate win, since he hadn't won since mid-season last year, but I was fucking pissed.

And that was putting it lightly.

I was ready to kill that shady five-foot tall bastard when I got out of the car. Once again, my temper flared in front of hundreds of thousands of fans. I pushed him, he pushed me, and before you knew it, we had an all-out pushing match not unlike the ones Darrin and I got into back in the day. Only difference here was this Shelby kid was a lot smaller.

He didn't understand who I really was, but he was about to find out.

"What the fuck was that?" I asked, not calmly.

"What? I had position on you," he answered, shrugging.

"Position, really?" I shoved him again. He fell back against his car, scurrying to find his footing as I stepped forward. "You call one inch position?"

We didn't get to finish the debate before NASCAR officials were separating us.

I clearly didn't think about NASCAR, and all too soon Kyle gave me the word as I trudged toward my hauler. "They want to see us in the hauler."

They wanted to see me, along with Shelby and his crew chief, who'd apparently been having some physical words with Aiden.

This was when Nadia Henley got in my face. "What the fuck was that?"

"What?" I spat in disbelief.

Alley, who was standing beside me, pulled on my arm. "Jameson, let's go."

I think she knew there was temptation on my part to shove this chick.

That was when Nadia reached out and grabbed my arm, too.

"You think just because you win championships you can do whatever you want on the track, don't you?"

I laughed bitterly and flung my arms out of their grasps.

"Yeah, well ..." I winked at Nadia. "Welcome to the big leagues, sweetheart."

Alley snickered to herself, but kept step with me as I headed to the hauler.

"Nice. Two fights in one night," Alley added, brushing past a horde of reporters.

"I'm on a roll."

When I stepped inside the hauler, Kyle and Clausen's crew chief, Matt, looked up at me. I made sure I slammed the door.

"Do you ever think about what you have at home when you pull shit like that?" Kyle greeted me when I threw myself in the chair next to him.

I wasn't sure what the fuck he was even referring to. Surely, he didn't see everything out there—he must have missed the part where Clausen *caused* the wreck.

"I know *exactly* what I have at home." My tone was harsh, but hushed, given the various people in the hauler. "You act like this isn't personal to me, and I should just treat it like a job. It *is* personal. This is my fucking life, Kyle!"

"I know that," he shot back just as forcefully. "All I'm saying ... is that I *do not* want to spend this season in this fucking chair!"

We both needed to calm down so I walked away. Kyle was heated, because once again, our team had to repair a damaged car. We had to answer to the sponsors, and worst of all, Jimi Riley.

Lisa told both Shelby and me this was our warning. I knew the next time we got tangled together we'd be paying for it, but it didn't stop the anger.

I steered clear of Clausen once we left the NASCAR hauler. I had a feeling if *I* was alone with the little fucker I'd show him just how pissed I really was about his supposed "position" on me.

The media caught up with me as I left, and I wasn't level-headed. Was I ever after something like this?

No.

"Jameson, can you tell us what happened there? Is this rivalry with Shelby Clausen escalating into what happened with Darrin Torres?"

That did it for me. I lost it. Only problem was, my wife and son were nearby.

I turned to the reporter and stepped forward. "Every goddamn time I get tangled with someone, you guys make it out to be way more than it really is. And every year, it's the same bullshit! It doesn't matter what I say to you to defend my actions on the track. They are, and always will be, irrelevant and twisted to your advantage."

I then proceeded to forcefully push his microphone out of my face, causing him to drop it. Now it wasn't my most graceful moment, but then again, I'd said and done worse. My choice of words wasn't perfect, but I was mad. At least I was honest.

Sway caught up with me with Axel close to her side.

"Jameson, calm down," she whispered softly, her eyes darting to Axel.

We were beside my hauler by now so I ducked inside with them to avoid any more media interactions and to calm myself down.

Axel eyed me carefully before smiling.

"You almost won," he offered in his adorably timid voice he had when he was trying to calm me.

It took me a moment, but I eventually smiled and reached down to pull him into a hug.

"I know little buddy."

You had to understand where I was coming from before you thought, "Jesus, pull yourself together in front of your kids."

In my mind, between Darrin, Colin, and now Shelby and Nadia, it was the same shit every year, and it got old really fast. I kept waiting for a year when they would forget. But just like me, they couldn't.

In that interview when they compared this to a rival they knew I harbored ill feelings for, that pissed me off and hurt. Yeah, it'd been nearly six years since the incident with Darrin, but it was still very real to me and still hurt. I was simply expressing my pain. I never wanted all of this; I only wanted to race. But with that came rivalry with other drivers, and that rivalry was fed by the media—whether I liked it or not.

You see, in our sport, you were allowed one angle, one image, and everything you said and did on or off the track had to fit into that angle.

The following weekend in Talladega, Shelby had apparently learned a lesson about drafting and dealing with me. Never saw him the entire race. That might have been because my car was awesome, and it was difficult for anyone to pass me, let alone a rookie who had no clue how to cut through the draft.

For now, Shelby and I agreed to disagree, much like Colin and me. But the difference came when after the Talladega race Shelby stopped by my motor coach to apologize for Phoenix. I thought that was pretty cool considering he was an eighteen-year-old kid. Either way, he scored points with me that day.

The thing with Nadia simmered down, but she made it known we didn't exactly get along and tried to paint the picture that I was some sort of biased driver and felt threatened by a female driver.

That couldn't have been further from the truth than the words spoken by that reporter who said the rival between me and Shelby was just the same as Darrin and me.

Sway and I were adamant that we wouldn't go more than a few weeks without seeing each other. Physically, I got extremely cranky as you could imagine, and emotionally, my little spaz family kept me grounded. After Loudon in late June, it had been nearly two weeks since I'd seen Sway. Though Axel had traveled with me much of the time, Sway had stayed home with Arie and Casten.

I stayed in Loudon Sunday night and finished press interviews from the win followed by an appearance in Charlotte Monday morning, and then I was on my way home that afternoon.

The sight before me when I got home made me miss being here everyday.

Sway had all three of the kids outside, spraying them down with water.

"What are you doing?" I asked with a chuckle.

"Mama's hosing us," said Arie, her bright emerald green eyes wide with excitement.

"Well, that just sounds ... weird. Don't say it like that," Sway told her.

I chuckled at them and leaned against the sliding glass doorframe.

"No child should ever go through life without showering outside," Sway said, looking back at me. "It's inconceivable."

"Why are they red?" They had spots of red and black paint covering their entire bodies.

She shrugged, pouring soap on Arie's head. "We painted the movie room. Help me out, they're a mess."

While laughing at my ridiculous wife, I rolled my sleeves up and got to work washing the boys. Axel thought it was funny when I scrubbed their heads like dogs, and Casten soon thought it was funny, as well. Anything Axel liked, Casten liked.

After a while and a water fight later, I looked around the backyard for Casten and couldn't find him. Next thing I knew, he was over in one of the flowerbeds making mud pies. He didn't have any water to make them so he used his only resource: urine.

"Are you serious?" Sway asked when she realized what he was doing.

I pointed at him and shook my head, leaning against the side of the back deck. "What do you think?" she laughed along with me. "I'm not sure whether to be proud or disgusted."

We eventually got our little mud pie maker in the house and cleaned up and on our way to dinner with Spencer and Alley to celebrate Lexi's fifth birthday.

I don't mind the occasional birthday party and acting like a kid again, but I did *not* like Chuck E. Cheese's.

Axel agreed with me.

On the other hand, eighteen-month-old Casten was crazy. The kid laughed all the time, had more energy than Emma, and never stopped laughing. Did I mention that already?

The kid was constantly bouncing off the rev limiter and was a tornado of destruction with a blinding smile who drew you in and relaxed you at the same time. He was the perfect combination of both Sway and me, but he did remind me more of Sway.

"Is he for real?" Axel nudged my arm while we sat and watched Casten toss the balls from the ball pit at unsuspecting people and then duck and hide in the balls as if no one tossed them. How an eighteen-month-old kid could figure out to do this should have been surprising, but not for Casten.

I shrugged indifferently.

There were so many people and kids around—screaming and having a good time—it was hard to actually talk with anyone, but I eventually made my way over to Spencer and Aiden at a table drinking beer with my dad.

"What's with the little one?" Dad asked. "Does he ever stop laughing?"

"Not that I've seen."

I took a slow drink of my beer, watching Casten closely as he tossed one at Cole, Spencer's youngest, who walked past. Cole didn't like being fucked with by anyone so he jumped head first into the balls and roughed the little guy up a bit, well as much as a three-year-old kid could.

"What's the plan for Axel and Indy next week?" Spencer asked, keeping one eye on Lexi and Arie climbing on a rock wall.

"Well, we leave for Daytona tomorrow afternoon. The race is on Saturday so then we leave for Indy on Monday. I need both of his cars ready by then." Tommy plopped beside me with Casten on his shoulders. Casten immediately crawled onto my lap and looked up at me.

"Bite?" he asked.

He did this any time he wanted a bite or drink of something.

"No, monkey, this is mine." Sway and I called him monkey because he climbed *everything.*

Casten eventually lost interest in my beer when he noticed there was pizza at the table.

"I'll have both cars ready by then. The Honda 160 isn't ready, though. We still need to change out the tie rod in it—he broke it last week."

"Doesn't matter," I told him with a shrug as Axel sat down with us. He looked completely bored. "USAC won't allow him to race it in a sanctioned race until he turns eight."

"All right." Tommy nodded, and Axel frowned. "I have both 120 cars ready."

Spencer laughed. "Did you know they moved him from the Red to the Blue Honda 120/Animal class?"

"When did that happen?" I knew the USAC rules these days just as well as I knew NASCAR or the Outlaw rules being the owner of yet another team. "You have to run three events before they move you up." Trying to calculate the races he'd run this year, my brow furrowed as I looked over at Axel. "I thought you missed a few?"

"I did. I missed the Mason Dixon Shootout and the Milwaukee Mile." He counted on his fingers. "I ran Dual in the Desert, Western District Qualifier, Midwest District Qualifier and the High Desert Classic. That's four." He held his tiny hand in my face displaying four fingers to me.

"Oh, yeah," I nodded, ruffling his hair. He smiled up at me. "I forgot about the High Desert Classic."

It's not that I meant to forget about it, but April was a busy month for me between the Cup schedule and the Outlaws. I never had a chance to make it out there for that one, and usually I made it out to at least one night of his racing.

USAC quarter midgets usually ran twice a month, and the events started on Wednesday and ended on Saturday nights. When my Cup schedule allowed, Wes was busy shuttling me back and forth between tracks. No matter what, though, Sway or I was there with him.

We decided from the first sanctioned race he ran in Phoenix last year that we would always be present, at least one of us. My parents were, until I got old enough that Spencer and I could haul the cars around ourselves, and I wanted us to be part of his career just like my family was.

"I still need to get him registered for the Dirt Nationals," I told Tommy as Axel's eyes lit up. Last year, he wasn't able to run due to his age. He had to be five by August, and his birthday was in December, so they denied the entry, even with my persuasion.

"I get to race Dirt Nationals?" He was practically bouncing in his seat.

I nodded with a smile of my own and tipped my head in Tommy's direction.

"I can't be there for the last night, but Mama and Tommy will be with you."

Axel seemed to contemplate this for a moment but smiled anyway.

I hated that I'd miss it, but this was the life I led, whether I liked it or not. It made it easier that Sway was so willing to follow Axel around, just as my mom did, but I also felt comfortable having Tommy with him. Usually Tommy was the mechanic for Justin's sprint car, but as Axel started racing, Tommy found himself engrossed in his career.

You couldn't help but want to. He was so curious and determined to learn everything he could about racing, even more so on dirt. He never really cared as much about the stock cars I ran, and that didn't bother me at all. I knew he was my kid that way. Sure, I loved racing NASCAR, but for myself, dirt was what I loved. Naturally, so did my carbon copy.

Lexi's birthday party finally ended around nine that night, and the kids had been so amped up on sugar they all fell asleep on the way home.

With a five-year-old, a three-year-old, and an eighteen-month-old ... this was ideal for a number of reasons—you could guess why.

After the entire family got back from Daytona for the race and Fourth of July, it was Monday morning, and we had two quarter midgets to get loaded and on their way to Indy. Tommy called on Sunday and told me when he went to the shop all the oil had drained from the primary car we had for Axel, so we had to get back and prepare another car. This was difficult when Sway and Emma showed up later that afternoon.

I was always amazed at the chemical reaction in children when they ingested sugar. It was insane. I didn't ever remember acting this way, but I was sure my mom and dad would disagree with me.

Sway frowned at our sweet little girl throwing herself onto the floor of my race shop when I took her sucker away. I only did this when I found she was letting our yellow lab, Rev, lick it.

"We really should stop having kids," Sway said. "They're out of control."

Even though we now had three, we still had no fucking clue how to parent them. That was evident just by looking at them.

"You're telling me." I ran my hand through my hair, searching around the shop for Casten; he was a quick little bugger. "Last week I left Casten in the car when I came inside. I keep forgetting how many we have."

Looking closer, I spotted him inside of a used sprint car tire, sleeping.

Trying to get both the cars ready and loaded was not working with everyone here. Tommy was absolutely no help when he showed up with Corbin, our mechanic for Tyler's sprint car. Everyone with JAR Racing was always willing to help me out with Axel's cars; I guess maybe because I paid them to. Either way, it was nice to have their help.

When four o'clock rolled around and the cars still weren't loaded, I began to lose my temper.

Which was also about the time Noah and Charlie felt the need to try and spray paint the walls of the shop. I lost it completely.

"Sway?" I snapped, pulling her inside the office, the door slammed shut behind me.

"I'll get them to leave," she said when she took in my jittery demeanor. "Are you okay?"

"Okay?" I snorted. "Those little shits are worse than Logan and Lucas. Get them out of here! I *need* to get Axel's car ready, and if I have to explain to him that he can't race because his cousins destroyed his car, I won't be happy and neither will your son."

"I know ... I know. We're leaving."

Instantly I felt bad about everyone leaving, but this was important to Axel. He'd been talking about the Battle at the Brickyard for months now. Last month, in Milwaukee, he flipped his car and thought for sure he was done for his season until I got him two more cars. I knew this was not the way to teach him about responsibility, but I also understood the frustration he felt having wrecked. Axel never once acted spoiled and never expected to be able to race. If anything, he felt guilty for doing so.

I wasn't sure why, but I knew my little guy enough to know he felt that way.

Before I could get started, I still had to get the twins out of the shop.

"I don't see what the big deal is ... so they spray painted the wall. Paint over it," Emma snapped back at me, gathering up her hellions.

"Spray painted the wall?" I choked. "Those little shits set my car on *fire* last week!"

Aiden was snipped when the boys turned two, and he realized that reproducing with Emma was essentially a bad idea. The decision also could have had something to do with the fact that at two years old, they cut the brake line to his truck. They were dangerously mechanically-inclined assholes, and you could never, ever turn your back on them.

Axel and Noah never got along. You could barely have those two in a room together without one of them trying to start a fight. They were complete opposites in every way.

I'd never met kids like Noah and Charlie, and I'd been around some horrendous kids growing up at dirt tracks. I wasn't lying when I said the Lucifer twins didn't even compare to them. These kids put them to shame, although the Lucifer twins were hardly considered animals any longer.

At eleven years old and engrossed heavily in baseball, they'd straightened up and behaved like civilized humans. More than likely, this had something to do with Van being an ex-Navy seal, who wouldn't put up with their bullshit.

"Dad?" Axel called out, coming around the side of his car. It was just him and I in the shop now. "Where does this go?" he asked, holding up the shock Tommy brought by this morning after having them re-valved.

I showed him how to put his shocks on, impressed at how much attention he paid to detail when it came to racing. I also had a feeling he'd follow in my dad's footsteps and stay on the dirt side of the sport. He hated when the USAC series went to asphalt tracks, but I encouraged him to work on both. And he did. Well into his first season now, he'd won four of the five events he'd raced in.

Regardless of how well he did on the asphalt tracks, he loved dirt.

Whenever we got Axel around the track and the other kids his age, the confidence he possessed in racing excelled. He was determined, confident, agile, and everything I'd raised him to be when it came to racing. He knew what he wanted and that was to win the Battle at the Brickyard. I'd won this event back when I raced USAC when I was twelve. Axel just turned five, but I wanted him to understand how competitive this sport was, and as a parent, I worried about him. When I saw him wreck for the first time I nearly had a heart attack and instantly felt bad for Sway and my parents for anything they might have felt when I'd wrecked.

"He's just like you were at that age," my dad said, standing beside me while we watched Axel make his qualifying run. Dad was set to leave this afternoon with Justin and Tyler for Terre Haute, but we all came out to watch the qualifiers and heat races.

"I know." I laughed, kicking some dirt around beneath my feet when the announcer came on.

"Ladies and gentlemen," the announcer yelled enthusiastically. I smiled instantly, knowing exactly what had occurred by the roar of fans in the bleachers looking up at the leader board. "Axel Riley in his first time here in Indy just broke the quarter midget record with that last lap. The record, held by his father, Jameson Riley, who won this event six times, had remained untouched for the last seventeen years. Who would have ever thought his son would be the one to break it?"

My dad and I started laughing. *Irony*. I wasn't sure what was more entertaining to me, the fact that my quarter midget record had remained untouched for the last seventeen years or that my son broke it.

When Axel made his way back into the pits, he was all smiles having heard he broke the record.

"You did it, little buddy!" I said, smiling down at him.

He was in my arms the second he got untangled from his belts. "Did I do good?" he asked sincerely, pulling back to look at me.

"You did amazing!" Holding him at arm's length, I smiled. "You did everything I showed you to do in qualifying. Great job."

I only had today to be here, and then I had to leave for Chicago for the NASCAR race, so this meant I wouldn't see Axel race in the main events on Saturday night if he made it to them.

Axel knew how I felt about that.

"It's okay, Dad," he told me, eating his hotdog after his heat race. "I don't care that you have to leave. Us racers understand," he added a wink on the end. He sat there munching on his hotdog with his arm slung around Lily.

"Is that right?" I asked, signing an autograph for a fan who stopped by Axel's pit.

Sway, who was holding Casten on her hip beside me, laughed.

"Yeah," he shifted his weight, leaning against Lily more. "We do what we need to do to race."

It was true. It was in our blood. We raced because we needed to. Anyone who told you differently was lying. Like Sway always said, the people who asked you why you did what you did—leaving your family behind to race—didn't understand why you were doing it in the first place.

Our family understood.

Axel and I said our goodbyes. "You keep him in check," I told Lily as she smiled at my son. “Don’t let his confidence get too high.”

“I won’t,” she replied, grinning. Her bright, lively blue eyes lit up as she looked over at Axel signing autographs for some nearby girls.

My mind wandered back to the days when Sway sat in my pit, watching me. And looking down at Lily, I realized how Sway felt all those times. I made a mental note to have a talk with Axel before he took her friendship for granted as I did to Sway.

I chuckled, pulling Lily into a hug. “Don’t *worry*, sweetie,” I told her reassuringly as she took in the other ten little girls surrounding Axel. For one, I’d never allow Axel to be with anyone other than Lily, given he was still very young and didn’t need to have a girlfriend, but I was too attached to Lily to have it any other way. I also knew my son and could sense he was just like his father—eyes for only one woman.

“I know,” Lily said with a smile. She seemed to understand already, even at five.

Sway walked me to the car with Casten on her hip. Arie stayed behind with Ami and Lily in Axel’s pit.

“You don’t look so good,” Sway deduced, taking in my appearance, as we got closer to the SUV waiting to take me to the airport.

“I’m not. I shouldn’t be missing this.” My eyes stayed on the concrete, successfully avoiding hers. Casten squirmed, reaching for me so I took him in my arms, holding him tightly.

“Truck,” he said, pointing to the car with a laugh.

“Yes, monkey. That’s a truck.” My eyes finally focused on Sway. “I just don’t want him to think I’m never going to be there for him.”

“He doesn’t think that, Jameson. He’s very perceptive and knows what your schedule is like.”

I knew that, but it never stopped the anxiety I felt when I missed something one our kids did.

We said our goodbyes, and she promised to keep me informed of his heat races throughout the day.

Once Spencer, Aiden, Alley and I arrived in Chicago, I hardly had time to check on updates, but Alley and her altruistic side emerged. She kept me up to speed. So far Axel had qualified fastest and won his heat for his class and moved into the events for Thursday.

When Thursday rolled around, I was swamped with appearances, press interviews, and then practice. My car wasn't exactly where I wanted it, so once again we found ourselves searching for the best setup. Even though I'd won eight races with twenty races into the season, we struggled at tracks like Michigan, Sonoma, and Pocono.

Before I got in the car for qualifying on Friday, I caught a glimpse of Alley's blonde hair in the sunlight.

My heart started pounding, hoping she had good news from Indy.

"He's in the A-Main tomorrow night!" Alley announced, as she entered the garage.

I smiled widely as did Spencer. "Really?"

"Yeah, he won the B-Main and transferred up. Sway is so excited, I could barely understand her." She laughed. "You want to go?"

"What, I thought I had an appearance in Joliet?"

"We moved it to tonight."

Against my better judgment, I pulled Alley into a hug. "I fucking love you!"

"Hey," Spencer slapped my shoulder, pulling us apart. "That's my wife."

"I don't care, she just made my day."

Spencer winked at Alley who was now wrapped around him. "How about we go make use of some *alone time* in Jameson's motor coach?"

"I swear to God, Spencer, if I find ass prints on my mirror again ... I will kick your ass." Hoisting myself into the car, I could hear them laughing. I had no problem with them hanging out in there when they needed to be alone, but sex was strictly off limits.

With the news that I'd get to see my little guy's first Battle at the Brickyard, qualifying went well. Aside from my car running like shit, I had a *great* attitude and ended up getting a third place starting position for Sunday's race.

"Mama, do you think Daddy is mad he not here?"

Lane nudged Axel as he ate his French fries. "*He's* not here," Lane corrected him.

"That's what I said," Axel said, throwing a fry at him.

Lane laughed and ate the fry he threw. "No, you didn't."

"Shut up," Axel groaned and looked up at me. "*He's* not mad, is he?" He tossed another fry at Lane.

"No, buddy, he's not mad," I told him, feeding Casten a couple fries from my plate in front of me. "Daddy just wants to be here with us."

After applying another coat of sunblock to my little rusty-haired babies, Axel expressed his concern for Jameson again.

"Do you think Daddy might see me race tomorrow if I make the main?"

"Honey, he has an appearance to do so I don't know that he can make it here on Saturday."

He nodded and walked back to his pit with his head hung. I never worried about how demanding Jameson's schedule was until Axel began racing. Jameson said he'd try, knowing it was only a thirty-minute flight to Indianapolis from Joliet ... but his appearance was at the same time as the main events. The chance of him sneaking away was slim.

I sent him a text Friday afternoon before Axel started the B-Main.

I miss you ... but I think your little buddy misses you more.

I then clicked a picture of Axel sitting in his car and sent it to him.

It took Jameson two hours before he replied. ***What about the other two? They don't miss me? And what about Mama, she don't miss her dirty heathen. He misses her!***

I laughed and responded while watching Emma try to find Charlie inside Axel's trailer, used to haul his midget.

I think they miss you, but Arie is entertained with your mom and making signs for the fan club they created for him. I don't think Casten even knows you're gone. Sorry. He's more entertained by all the dirt and the people.

I see how I rate. How's Axel doing?

Good. They're getting ready to start the B-Main. He's starting tenth with the inversion.

They're inverting them?

That's what I said, but yes, Jeff decided to invert them when Axel won the C-Main by an entire lap.

Let me guess ... they pulled the engine for inspection after that?

Jameson knew USAC all too well.

Yep.

Tell him good luck for me. I'm heading out for qualifying now.

Good luck to you, too, then, and yes ... I miss you!

Miss you, too, honey.

"Sway?" Emma called out on her hands and knees inside the trailer. I tucked my phone inside my purse and peeked through the double doors. "Have you see Charlie. Noah is over ..." She sighed and threw her hands up. "He was right there. What the fuck!"

"Emma." I giggled and pointed inside Axel's back-up car. Both Charlie and Noah were curled up in the seat, sleeping.

"Awww," Emma cooed and snapped a picture with her phone to send to Aiden. "They are so cute."

"*When* they are sleeping," I added with a smile.

I had to admit, with their black wavy hair and bright blue signature Riley eyes, they were adorable, but they were shit heads. Having just turned four in November last year, they were slightly more behaved, but still assholes if you asked me. I had a feeling most would agree with me, especially Aiden, who currently had a broken arm because of them.

The horn sounded in the pits letting us know if was time for the kids to line up for the main. I made my way over to Tommy and Axel as they lined up on the grid. My little boy was fumbling with his helmet while his head rested on the wheel. Nancy, who had followed me over there with the kids, motioned toward the stands and herded the rest of the kids into the bleachers while I tended to Axel.

I crouched down beside him, rubbing his back. “Are you okay, little buddy?”

When he looked up at me, his eyes said it all. Axel was very confident when he was on the track, but his nerves got to him before each race, something Jameson never had to deal with. I’m sure there were times when Jameson had nerves, but not like Axel. Sometimes he would become physically sick before a race.

“I’m scared,” he told me softly.

I nearly cried when I saw him on the verge of tears as well. With over 270 kids racing, the fact that he even made it to the B-Main should have showed him he shouldn’t be scared. But with 270 other kids, that was what scared him the most.

Where was Jameson for this sort of thing? Or Justin, yes, Justin would be good, too.

Only another racer could have reasoned with Axel when he was like this. I’d tried before, but it was always Jameson who had calmed our little guy down. His fears broke through, and he admitted, “I want Daddy here.”

I wasn’t exactly Axel’s favorite; I knew where I stood with him. Jameson first, me second.

By the grace of God, I think, Lily came hopping around the corner of his car and kissed his helmet. “Good luck, Axel, I’ll be cheering!” she said with her excited blue eyes glowing.

Axel perked up. “Really?”

“Yep, I made this.” She pointed to the sign in her hand that said:

Go Axel Riley #9!

Awww, to be five again.

“See buddy,” I encouraged, rubbing his back again. “We will all be cheering with you. I’m gonna videotape it, too, so Daddy will see it.”

"You mean he get to watch me later?" His anxiety washed away as he spoke.

"I will show him as soon as I see him," I promised and kissed him good luck, leaving him alone with Lily for a minute. At five, they hardly had much of a girlfriend/boyfriend relationship, but they kissed on the cheeks.

Ami walked up, holding Kale on her hip. "How's he doing?"

Shaking my head as Lily reached in and hugged him, I leaned into Ami's shoulder. "How come she can comfort him, but his mommy can't?"

"Oh, sweetie," Ami cooed, rubbing my shoulder with her one free arm. "I feel the same way. Lily fell off the monkey bars last week and told me that she wanted Axel."

"How'd Justin take that?"

"He wasn't there, but when I told him later he wasn't thrilled that Axel rates higher than we do."

We both watched as Lily skipped away to sit in the stands with the rest of the kids and wave her sign as the cars rolled onto the track.

Tommy pushed his car off and then sat down beside me with a huff. "That kid is pickier than his father."

I just giggled as he wiped sweat from his brow.

"Poor fire crotch." I reached over to ruffle his orange curls.

"Cut it out, people are looking at us." He pushed my hands away.

"What are you talking about?"

"People ... they're looking."

I glanced around; no one was paying any mind to us. "No one is looking at us."

His eyes glanced toward a woman off to the left sitting with her son. "Someone is looking."

Oh, I get it. Fire crotch had the hots for the mama in front of us. Ami, sitting beside me, started laughing. I took every opportunity I could to embarrass him, and now wasn't any different.

When I went to stand, his arm caught mine and roughly pulled me back down. "Don't you even think about it, shit head."

"I'm thirsty," I told him, smacking my lips together. Ami was now laughing so hard she was crying and snorting. I turned toward her. "You're not helping. Stop it."

This did nothing for her attempts and made her laugh harder. Our kids noticed from two rows in front of us and looked back at us like we'd lost our minds. If only they knew we never had them in the first place.

"Do not move," Tommy warned and clicked his stopwatch. I lost interest in embarrassing fire crotch when the four pace laps the kids ran were completed, and the green flag was dropped. At this particular event, they allowed for a one-way receiver in the cars attached to the helmets that helped with safety for the kids.

"Green flag," Tommy told Axel as the cars all raced toward the line.

If you have never been to a quarter midget race, you're missing out for two reasons—one, the crazed parents and two, the little racers who couldn't keep their cars on the track. They never could complete more than a lap or two without spinning themselves or someone else.

Not my little guy, though; he kept his car straight, paid attention to the flags and other cars with the help of Tommy, and even passed others. Their B-Main event was 20 laps—by lap 7, Axel was leading.

His fan club in front of us started cheering like crazy, even jumping up and down. I made sure I got them on the video for Jameson.

"I think he's gonna pull this off." Tommy nodded with a smile when Axel took the white flag.

I could hardly control my excitement, handed the camera to Ami and started cheering for him just as loudly as the kids.

"Go, buddy, go!" I yelled, acting like a complete idiot.

Everyone cheered. "Ladies and gentlemen, the winner of the Junior Animal 120-class, Axel Riley!"

Quickly, I sent a text to Jameson and Alley letting them know he'd be in the A-Main tomorrow. I knew Jameson was in the car right now, so I figured Alley would tell him.

Later that night, Emma, Nancy, Ami, and me, along with Tommy took all the kids out for pizza. I took some time to step out and call Jameson to see if he'd be able to make it tomorrow since he didn't reply to my text.

"Hey, honey," he answered in a low voice. I could hear the faint sounds of engines revving in the background and assumed they were making some changes to the car.

"How'd qualifying go?" I already knew he got third, based on ESPN playing in the restaurant, but I always asked.

"Got third … we're changing out the gears, though, so hopefully that will make it better," he told me. "How's Axel?"

"He's missing you. He keeps asking when you will see the video of him in the B-Main."

"How about tomorrow?"

"What?"

"Tomorrow … what time does the main start?"

"The Junior Animal 120 Main starts at ten."

Jameson was silent for a moment before he covered the phone with his hand and yelled for Alley. "Can Wes get me there by ten?"

"Yes, he will have you there anytime you need."

"Really?" I asked. Not only would Axel be pumped, but so was I.

Jameson thanked her and then asked, "What hotel are you in?"

"Radisson Garden Inn," I told him. "Are you coming tonight?"

"I think I will. That way I can spend more time with you guys and then be back in time for happy hour Saturday afternoon."

We ended our call soon after that when it got too loud for me to hear him. He asked me not to tell the kids he was coming—he wanted to surprise them.

When Axel saw all the kids who raced with him today with their dads, it took all I had not to tell him.

You didn't really see the strain our lifestyles put on everyone until you saw it in the eyes of our children. They didn't deserve it, but they took the brunt of it.

Later that night, most of us were back in the suite getting ready for bed when Arie was telling Axel a very detailed description of her encounter with a spider earlier in the day. He wasn't nearly as into it as she was, but Casten thought it was funny—he thought everyone was funny.

"It was really big!" Arie motioned with her hand in a circle that I was sure a whale could stick his head through. There was no way the spider was that big, and if it was, I would never return.

Axel, who was brushing his teeth, spit in the sink and wiped his mouth with his hand. "I'm sure," he replied with a roll of his eyes.

For being five, he had quite the attitude, much like his father.

Casten walked up to me and handed me his diaper he had removed. "Ucky."

"Monkey, you need to keep this on. I don't want you ..." I didn't finish the words before I felt the little trickle of pee down my bare calf.

"I'm not a fire hydrant, kid!" I told him, picking up my laughing little monkey. He'd be two in January so I knew potty training was nowhere close to the light, but I still hoped, since he wouldn't keep his damn diaper on. He just liked to have fun and taking off his diaper and peeing on people was funny to him.

Right before I put the kids to bed, there was a knock on the door. I smiled and looked over at Axel, who was pulling his blankets up over his chest. Lily crawled into bed beside him. "Hey, where did you come from?" I didn't remember Lily coming into our room.

"My mommy said I could sleep here."

"Oh, did she?"

What a traitor. She knew I already had three in this suite with me, and now she was adding to the madness. Ami thought it was funny watching me parent. A lot of people did. I couldn't understand what they found so entertaining about it—probably because I had no idea what I was doing.

The person at the door knocked again. I figured it was Jameson so

I looked over at Axel. "Why don't you go get the door, buddy?"

He didn't hesitate before he bolted out of bed with Lily behind him.

"Who are you?" Axel asked when the door opened.

Who are you? Surely, that wasn't Jameson. Nervous about who was knocking on our door, I walked over.

Before I could make it around the corner, the man answered, "I'm Gab, is your mommy in here?"

"Gab who?" Axel asked. I giggled when I came around the corner to see Axel with one hand securely around Lily and the other holding the door from opening any farther. My strong little boy.

"Gab Kinney."

"We don't know a Gab Kinney."

The man sighed and looked in our room. "Is your mommy here or not?"

I didn't like his tone, not at all. It was demanding, and no one was demanding with my kids unless I said so. I did not say so to this *Gab*, who I'd never met before. I quickly dialed Van and then hung up when he answered. This was our silent way of letting him know we needed him. Like I said, Van was never far from me and the kids—he had the room next to us.

"I'm his mommy ... who are you?" I saw Van appear behind him in the doorway.

This Gab fellow looked relieved to see an adult, but hadn't noticed Van watching behind him. He looked around the same age as me, maybe a few years older—dark hair, tan, brown eyes, almost appeared to be Mexican or at least someone in his family was Mexican.

Gab smiled. "I'm Gab Kinney—a representative with A-Tech. I'd like to speak with you about maybe sponsoring your son here."

Axel smiled and looked back at Gab. "Well then come in."

I stopped him. "I'm sorry ... I'd rather you speak with my husband about anything to do with his sponsorship. JAR Racing is the primary sponsor, but I'm sure they would be willing to explore others."

Van came into the room behind Gab. "Oh." Gab looked between

Van and me. "Is this your husband?"

"No," I told him. "My husband is Jameson Riley, I'm sure you've heard of him."

Gab looked confused. "No, actually I haven't."

He was either lying about knowing Jameson or lying about being a representative with A-Tech, a company that designed titanium engine parts. Surely, being in racing, or at least representing a company that was so heavily involved in USAC, he should know who Jameson Riley was.

Van seemed to sense the same confusion I felt and stepped closer to Axel and Lily standing by the door. Axel had been in enough of these situations with us in the past, and he knew to stay next to Van.

"What's going on in here?" Jameson asked, peeking his head inside the door. His eyes scanned the room cautiously.

"Daddy!" Axel yelled and ran toward him. Jameson caught him in his arms with a smile, his brow furrowed as he looked over at this Gab guy standing next to me. "Who are you?"

Gab looked nervous and reached out to offer his hand to Jameson. "I'm *uh* ... Gab with ... A ... Tech."

They shook hands, and Jameson held on to Axel as he moved closer to me.

Van picked up Lily. I was thankful our other two had already fallen asleep and weren't running out here to see what was happening.

"Gab, huh ... what happened to Wayne?"

"Wayne?"

Jameson handed Axel to me. "Yeah." He stepped closer to Gab. "A-Tech has been an associate sponsor of my Cup team and sprint car team for the last two years." He let out a chuckle. "Wayne Matson is their representative who I've dealt with. So my question is ... who are you, and what are you doing in my hotel room?" Jameson's voice was hard and demanding.

Van simply stood aside—holding Lily—with a smirk on his face. Van may be the bodyguard for us, but if I would be afraid of anyone in any situation, it would be Jameson, hands-down.

Surely Van had Jameson in size. Hell, he even had Spencer and Jimi in size. What most failed to realize with Jameson was his brash temperament that left you wondering when and how he'd react.

"I don't know Wayne, but I am a representative with A-Tech. They asked me to see about sponsoring him." Gab pointed toward Axel.

Jameson simply nodded, his eyes focused on Van's for a brief moment before he placed his hand on Gab's back. "Let's talk outside."

Gab agreed and looked over to me. "It was nice meeting you, Sway."

I smiled politely as a chill ran down my spine. I never once told him my name.

Van handed Lily over to me just as I heard Jameson's voice raise slightly.

"If you know what's good for you ... you'll walk away right now?" Van warned Gab as I pushed the kids toward the bedroom.

"Mama ... who was that man?" Axel asked. His eyes were nervous.

"Nobody, buddy ... Daddy will be back in a minute."

Sure enough, Jameson came back inside not more than two minutes later.

"Hey, buddy," he whispered toward him, trying not to wake Arie and Casten. "Let's watch that heat race."

Two hours later, it was close to midnight and poor Axel had fallen asleep on the couch with Jameson. Lily was on the floor with me as we watched Axel's race on replay.

As quietly as I could, I took Axel and Lily back into the bedroom with Arie and Casten. Amazingly, they stayed asleep, even when I nearly dropped Axel on top of Lily.

When I made my way back into the living room of the suite, Jameson wasn't there.

"Jameson?" I whispered and then heard him laugh quietly.

"In here, honey.

Turning around, I saw him lying in the bed already. Smiling like a fool, I was out of my clothes and closing the door all in under a minute. "What happened with that guy?"

His eyes seemed guarded. “How often does that sort of thing happen?”

“You mean random people wanting to sponsor our son?”

“No ...” His hand moved from my hip to touch my cheek, his eyes focused intently on mine. “How often do people get past security in the lobby to your room?”

“Security in the lobby? I wasn’t aware there was any?”

He chuckled softly and let his hand fall from my cheek as he pulled me closer. “There is always security in the lobby of any hotel you or our kids stay at.”

“Oh,”

“This hotel, however ... we won’t be staying here again for that reason. He shouldn’t have been up here.”

“Who was he?”

“Van’s going to look into it, but he definitely doesn’t work for A-Tech. I called them, and they’d never heard of him.”

“Jesus,” I panicked. “I let Axel answer the door, thinking it was you!”

He nodded. “We do need to be more careful. Axel is getting a following now, and whether we like it or not, he’s a target. If someone doesn’t like me as a driver, well, they might take it out on him.”

I knew that already. We experienced that when Axel raced in the Western District Qualifier in March. When Axel outran a kid on the track, the kid’s dad took his frustrations by screaming at Axel about Jameson and his temper. It was something all of our kids would be facing having Jameson Riley as their father.

My mood for sex was ruined with the thought that my little spaz children were in danger.

Jameson sighed, the guarded expression returned, and kissed my forehead before pulling back to look at me. “He was looking for you.”

“Why though.”

“We don’t know yet, but Van caught onto it when he only said goodbye to you.”

“Yeah ... I never told him my name.”

"That's not why." Jameson blinked slowly. "Just like our kids, you're a target, too. You're very attractive and in the public eye. They see you, and they see ... opportunity."

He didn't need to say anymore; I knew what he was insinuating. This wasn't the first time I'd been cornered by men, even after Darrin. There had been a handful of various men over the years who had come on to me or saw that I was Jameson's wife and made a move. I didn't know what it was, but when men found out I was married to Jameson, they tested their luck. Maybe it was for some kind of bragging rights, if I paid interest to them—I don't know—but it was all part of this lifestyle we had. Paying no mind, I ignored them, and the fact that it was even happening for the simple reason that it didn't bother me. I knew from the very beginning, when I committed myself to Jameson and his career choice, this was a possibility. To have him, I'd endure anything.

"What's the air pressure in the right rear?" I asked Tommy, handing him the gauge.

"Jameson, can my son get your autograph?"

Keep your cool, I told myself. I had to say this a lot this morning. All I wanted to do was help get my son's car ready to go, but the fans here had another idea when they saw me in the pits this morning. I signed autographs, took pictures, talked to reporters ... I had done everything this morning but what I came for, which was to see family and to see my son race.

The right rear of Axel's car kept losing psi as it sat on the grid so Tommy changed it out while I signed yet another autograph.

"Daddy?" Axel called out as the horn sounded for the kids to report to their cars. "Can you push me off?" Tommy usually pushed him off on the starts and re-starts, if needed, but when I was around, I made sure I was the one to do this for him. Another fan approached us and I shook my head. "I'm sorry, not right now. My son is about to start his main event. Catch me after the main, and I'll sign anything you want."

The woman who had approached us simply smiled and walked away.

"Of course I will, buddy." I knelt beside Axel's car as he adjusted all his straps and pulled his helmet on. "Now remember, stay focused. One car at a time."

They inverted the field again, since Axel had transferred up through the mains, he was starting fourth. "I will be talking to you through the radio in your ear. I'm just going to tell you when a caution comes out and when it's green again, okay?"

He nodded; the fear in his eyes was evident. "Do you get nervous?" he asked.

I had to think for a moment, because no, I didn't really get nervous anymore. There were times when I would say I was anxious to race, but nervous, no. But I knew the feeling, and I remembered when I was his age and even older during the time I traveled around. Sure, I was nervous back then.

"When I was your age ... yes," I finally told him when I saw Lily skipping over. "But you know what my dad told me?"

"What?" I saw what Sway was referring to when she told me Axel hung on my every word. Here he was, holding on to any piece of advice I could offer him in this moment.

"Take one lap at a time, one car at a time."

Axel smiled up at me and then looked at Lily. His bright green eyes sparkled as she sported a t-shirt that said: Axel Riley's Fan Club. She then spun around to show him the back had his number, and underneath it said #1 Fan.

"Are you good, buddy?" I finally asked after chuckling at Lily's enthusiasm.

"Yeah, I'm good, Daddy." He smiled at me and then Lily again.

I made my way to the infield, standing with the other fathers, all of them giving me the look that said, "We know who you are," but also telling me, "That's why your kid places so well—money and Daddy."

That had absolutely nothing to do with it. Yeah, if Axel destroyed a car, he had another one the next night or week, but that had nothing to do with his talent in the sport. I didn't care how good your equipment was or how many sponsors you had funding you. In the end, this sport came down to talent and patience. Some might not believe that, but I did.

Look at when I started in USAC on the East Coast. Sure, I had money but my money did nothing for me when I came head-to-head with the fire-breathing beasts from the East. Talent got me where I was today, and talent had gotten Axel where he was, currently in first place with one lap to go.

He'd been battling hard, swapping the lead with a kid named Shane Jennings, when Shane's front right tire caught Axel's left rear. Axel wobbled slightly while Shane smashed into the tire barriers, leaving Axel to take the win.

I had seen him win before, but the Battle at the Brickyard would be comparable to me winning the Daytona 500—something I had yet to do.

His fan club was jumping up and down, my mom included. Sway was crying, which was nothing new. When it came to our children, she was a little basket case.

When the cars pulled off the track Axel came back around to be presented the trophy.

"Is Shane okay?" was his first question.

"Yeah, buddy, he's fine. See, he's right there." I pointed to Shane, who gave Axel a thumbs-up and walked back to his car with his dad.

The next thing he asked, "Are you proud of me?"

I couldn't for the life of me figure out why he always asked this. "What would ever make you think I wasn't proud of you?" I asked, hugging him once he untangled himself from his belts.

He seemed to contemplate this for a moment, not immediately answering. When he did his voice was small and quiet. "You and Grandpa ... you are ... legends." He shrugged as his eyes fell. "I just wanna make you proud of me. I wanna be like you." He avoided my eyes, looking at his shoes.

Placing my hand gently under his chin, I forced him to look me in the eye. "You are, buddy. Everything about you is just like me. I don't know if you should be proud or worried." We both chuckled and before we could have any longer in our father-son moment, the announcer was wanting to interview him.

"Did you have a good time?" he asked Axel, who stood strong beside me.

"Yep."

"Did your dad give you any advice here?" He motioned to me.

Axel looked up at me and winked. "Yep. He told me, be patient."

"Well, considering your dad is a NASCAR Cup series champion ... you should listen to him, huh?"

"I did."

"Yes, you did, because this monster trophy is bigger than you!" He handed Axel the trophy that was no doubt bigger than my pint-sized son. "Ladies and gentlemen ..." The crowd whistled and screamed, most of which came from our family. "The winner of the Junior Animal 120-class ... Axel Riley!"

My dad was right when he told me nothing compares to seeing your kid's dreams come true. I just hoped that this was *his dream* and not something he felt he had to live up to like some unspoken expectation. Knowing he wanted to race was comforting. I never forced him to do this, but in the back of my mind I wondered if all that pressure I put upon myself to be great somehow imparted him to do the same.

Either way, I needed to be careful of the yellow lines. They blurred so easily when it came to parenting. It was easy to let yourself push your dreams, but the line needed to be drawn. They were their own people and they had every right to live their dreams and not yours.

Before we left that night, I found that woman I turned down the autograph for and made sure she got the autograph she was looking for. To me, that was me showing my appreciation for her respecting my privacy.

Stop-and-Go Penalty – A penalty that requires a driver to stop at their team's pit for a timed penalty before re-entering the race.

"We *need* a night out, Sway. We just do!" Emma stressed, pulling at her hair as she watched Noah smack his brother in the thigh with a plastic knife. "Noah," she scolded. "Put down the fucking knife!"

A handful of guests gawked at us.

"If they were my kids, I would agree you need a night out," I told her, taking another drink of my mocha.

I couldn't get enough coffee these days. It seemed, like with everything else, our lifestyle was catching up with me, and I turned to coffee. I had this deal with myself that for every cup I had, I had to drink a full glass of water. This just meant I was drinking all the time, and when I wasn't drinking something, I was peeing.

I was now down to two cups a day because I couldn't spend my life in the bathroom.

All my habits aside, we did need a break. It was the middle of the season, and the battle for the chase was in full swing. Jameson was riding in the wild card spot and just as hungry for the spot as the other four drivers in line.

With a string of three top twenty finishes, he had dropped from his fifth place position to eleventh in the points and was feeling the pressure. In turn, we all felt the pressure building. Jameson was good about controlling it, but there were the times when he would lash out at his crew or the guys back at the shop for simple mistakes. He couldn't blame them for everything, as he was struggling on the track. It happened to every driver out there, and they all took it just as personally as Jameson did.

"So, about going out ..." Emma caught my stare at the wall. "I was thinking we could sneak out when the guys are in Atlanta."

"You know Richmond follows that. With the chase—"

"Sway," Emma silenced me. "We. Need. A. Night!"

"*You* need a night. My kids are good."

Emma looked over at Casten gathering all the sugar packets on the table at Starbucks and then stuffing them in his pocket for later. It explained his sudden bursts of energy late at night.

"You don't have angels either," Emma remarked, gesturing to Arie who'd been staring intently at a group of teenagers before she rolled her eyes. It was slightly amusing every time I saw her roll her eyes. Come on, at nearly four years old, wouldn't any child be cute rolling their eyes?

"Emma, Jameson will never let me go out in Atlanta. It's out of the question."

"Okay." She turned to me. "Just don't tell him. Say we're going out to the movies."

"Yeah, that's not happening. I don't lie to Jameson about things like that. He just worries we will get into trouble, and you know us Emma, we get into trouble."

"We do not."

"Really? What about the time in Los Angeles when we went shopping and those fans attacked us?"

"They didn't attack us, Sway."

"What about the time in Richmond when we went to that restaurant and had to sneak out the back because our kids trashed the place?"

"Our kids won't be there."

She had an answer for everything so I pulled quick time and went for the pole.

“What about the time we went to Jacksonville, and we ended up—”

“All right. I get the fucking point,” she glared, leaning back in the seat to drink her iced tea.

Emma didn’t like to be reminded of our trip to Jacksonville last winter when we got so shit faced that Jameson had to carry us back to the hotel, and Emma ended up naked on her balcony singing “Take My Breath Away” to a hobo on the street. After that night, she wasn’t allowed out without adult supervision, and Alley wasn’t enough. You get Alley drinking enough, and all her common sense turned into bullshit.

The sun coming in through the window next to her sparkled her long black waves of hair. I reached out to touch her hair as I always did. It was mesmerizing.

She slapped my hand away. “Stop that.”

“It’s just so pretty.”

“Yeah, well, touch your husband’s hair, not mine.”

Casten, with a bright smile, sensing some opportunity, moved from the chair next to me, having collected enough sugar packets, and joined Arie at the table next to us. With the same curiosity as Arie, Casten and Noah sat quietly watching the teenagers.

“Sway, please. I *need* to go out, and Andrea is flying in, and Ami said she’d come.”

“Wait a second,” I waved my hand around before grabbing her face between my palms, seeing through her wicked ways. “You’ve already planned this fucking trip, haven’t you?”

Emma nodded.

“This is peer pressure, you know.” I flipped the lid to my mocha and handed it to the barista for a refill. She knew me well and understood when I was here with Emma refills were imperative. Fuck my water theory.

“It is not,” Emma argued, handing the girl her iced tea for a refill. “Peer pressure is for high schoolers.”

Sam—the barista at our local Starbucks—laughed at our argument and our kids destroying the small café.

"No, it's not," I told Emma. "Peer pressure is for everyone."

"Bullshit," she sighed, reaching for her lotion to lather up. "Just go out with us."

"One of these days your brother is going to kill you. You know that, right?"

"Whatever. He'd miss me too much."

"He wouldn't just forget about you or anything. I think there'd be a grieving period."

"God," she huffed and stood to gather her brats. "You two act as though there's something wrong with me and my kids."

I watched as Charlie smacked the barista on the ass as they left.

Nothing was wrong with them, my ass.

Mine weren't any better when Arie sat down beside one of those teenagers and started asking her questions about her piercings. I was surprised the girl didn't leak when she drank her coffee.

Against my better judgment and sanity, I convinced Jameson to let me go out with the girls Friday night when we were in Atlanta. With the race being on Saturday night, and a few days before Arie's fourth birthday, we only had Friday night and hoped none of us got into trouble.

Jameson wasn't pleased and voiced his concern many times. I wasn't sure what was worse—me going out with the girls, or him keeping an eye on all three of our kids. Even more, Aiden and Spencer thought it'd be cool if they all got together and watched the kids as a team. Somehow they thought with all of them together they could manage eight kids under the age of ten.

I tried to point out they were outnumbered, but it was almost like they took that as some sort of challenge, and it became a mission to make it through the night.

If only Emma shared the mission to make it through the night.

It started soon after the Nationwide race on Friday night when we left our husbands at the suite in downtown Atlanta. We did have a chaperone—Van.

Emma, Alley, Nancy, Andrea, and even Ami joined me on our night out. I couldn't tell you what bars we stopped at, just that there were so many I couldn't keep track. I was one drink away from shit-faced most of the night and just kept it up.

Nancy and Andrea, who rarely went out and it was even more rare that they drank, could barely walk—very close to alcohol poisoning—by the third bar. But, no, they kept step and drank us drink-for-drink despite that.

Nancy found entertainment in Jameson's favorite drink these days, Monster energy drinks mixed with vanilla vodka. I thought that was what kept her going so strong.

Around midnight, we were all going strong, when I got a text from Jameson that said: ***I found Casten's diaper and shirt in the bathroom, and he's missing. Does he have any secret hiding places I should know about? When should I panic?***

I replied: ***Well, when I can't find him at home I have Axel look for him. For some reason he comes out of hiding when Axel barks like a dog and pretends to run around on all fours. Just do anything that causes a commotion and he'll come running for the entertainment. He's just bored so he hides. And, no, don't panic unless he doesn't come out.***

I didn't get a reply right away so I tucked my phone inside my purse and went about the night.

"I think I'm done for the night," I told Emma by the fourth bar, swaying slightly as I held onto the table we were gathered at.

"No," she said adamantly. "This isn't a one drink night. This is the type of night that we should drink a fifth of whatever and show up at the bar to see what happens. I'm expecting one of us to get arrested."

"Emma," Nancy scolded. "That would not be good."

"Mom," she began, setting her lemon drop down on the table, looking like she was about to give a presidential debate.

For some reason, Alley, who'd been pounding beers all night, thought her expression was the funniest thing she'd ever seen and let out a string of laughs followed by snorts and some tears. It wasn't pretty.

"Listen to me," Emma started in again when Alley gained control. "For the three times I've been arrested in my life, I've enjoyed every experience."

I tried multiple times throughout the night to convince Emma to call it a night—all with no success.

Tommy showed up about one. Emma was pissed that he showed up because this was apparently a girl's night, but I held some comfort that Tommy was around. Usually I didn't do stupid shit when he was around. Tommy did.

I'd like to think I'd matured since my days of getting rip-roaring drunk and tattooing myself, but that night turned into stupidity after Tommy arrived. It was a part of the night that I referred to as the point-of-no-return.

Jameson had been sending me all kinds of weird text messages throughout the night, asking how to do simple tasks with the kids I knew he already knew, but I also understood this was his way of silently making sure I was okay.

Found Casten. Spencer lit the toaster on fire and Casten came out of the pantry eating graham crackers. By the way, does Arie usually take off her clothes and run around naked? That's not normal, right? Do our kids ever run around fully clothed? By the way, she's nearly 4. We should get clothes on her.

And then after I replied, assuring him that was normal, he sent another text an hour later that said: ***Got Spencer and Aiden to bed, but the kids won't stop! How do you get Arie to sleep without her binkie? She's nearly four. That thing has to go at some point! I'm sure they don't allow them in kindergarten.***

It was something like three, and the bars were closing so I told him I'd be back in a little while to help him out. Boy, was I wrong.

That was when Tommy fucked us all. Not literally, but he did cause a blown tire or two.

We'd lost people before. Actually, we'd lost someone every time we went out, but I had no idea it'd be Nancy. We were walking down the street to the last open bar when we lost her.

Alley freaked out and was about ready to call the police when Tommy piped up with a confession that shocked us all.

"I kind of told her ... it'd be cool if she got a tattoo." All five of us slapped him on the back of the head after his horrifying confession.

We found her about forty-five minutes later with a tramp stamp that read *Hit This* in bold calligraphy with a red lips at the end.

"I can honestly say I don't have the tackiest tattoo in the family now," Emma said between giggles.

It was horrible. I was sure Jimi wouldn't be pleased, and Tommy would need to join the witness protection program when Spencer and Jameson found out what he convinced their mother to do.

After that, we made it to the last open bar and stayed there until we got kicked out. Alley got a lap dance from a girl wearing barely anything except thigh high red hooker boots. Andrea threw up on the bartender, only to ask for another drink. Ami found that she was a champ at darts—only she wasn't throwing them at a dartboard and had to explain to the owner of the bar why she broke all their windows.

Alley caught her hair in a fan and chunks had to be sacrificed.

Van had to leave to take Andrea to the hospital when she got in the way of Ami throwing darts. Turned out when they got lodged in your ass it bled a lot when pulled out. She looked like she had hemorrhoids and wasn't pleased.

Tommy, completely intoxicated, decided he was in charge now and that just resulted in an even worse plan when he convinced Nancy to steal a cop's horse.

I couldn't understand where Nancy's sense of direction went and why she was following Tommy and his shitty advice tonight.

Nancy made the cop pinky swear not to arrest her when she failed the breathalyzer, but as it turned out, walking around in public was considered frowned upon, too. That landed Tommy, Nancy, Emma, and me in jail when we went to her aid with the cop who couldn't understand that she was a fifty-year-old woman who'd drank too much and branded her lower back.

She clearly wasn't rational, and he needed to consider that before arresting us. But no, that cop was not friendly.

As we sat in jail, I looked over the string of text messages from Jameson, which I hadn't noticed while attempting to gain control over my mother in-law. Each one cracked me up. Most were just messages, but there was a few of Spencer and Aiden wearing make-up—no doubt a product of Lexi and Arie. Those two put make-up on everything, including Casten, which was the next picture. My little baby, not so little, was all dolled up in a princess dress, wearing a crown and plastic earring. He looked pretty good as a girl ... as did Aiden.

"How do you still have your phone?" Tommy whispered in my ear, glaring at Alley, who'd been giving him the stink eye since we landed ourselves in this shit hole in Atlanta.

By the way, if you'd never been arrested in downtown Atlanta, keep it that way.

What a nightmare.

"I smuggled it in through my bra."

"Oh, cool. I usually shove mine down my pants."

"That's ... disgusting, Tommy."

He shrugged, undeterred by my remark, and made friends with the guy next to us before flirting with the woman next to Emma. I had to remind him where we were, and clearly picking someone up in jail wasn't the smartest decision he'd ever made. I could have been wrong, though.

"Hey, she's a step up," he winked at the girl, and if I was being honest, I wasn't entirely sure she was a woman, but I wasn't telling Tommy that. "In college, I once fucked a female body builder. Not cute, and it was like fucking Vin Diesel with a twat. Beastly even."

I laughed until I nearly pissed myself before he looked at me with a straight face. "I was so disgusted with myself that I only lasted fifteen seconds, and then she proceeded to bench press me. Talk about emasculating."

"Oh, fire crotch." I leaned against him, using him as support. "What would I do without you?"

"Probably laugh a lot less."

"So, what ... did you date her after that?"

"Hey, I didn't say it was a relationship. We fucked, and occasionally I took her to Subway."

"Some would classify that as a relationship. Not me, but some." I smiled when he glared. "But it was nice of you ... to take her to Subway and all."

Another half hour passed after Alley called Van to have him come get us, but apparently he couldn't so he sent Jameson. I was a little worried.

"So, Emma." I kicked her shin when she fell asleep beside me. "Was this your idea of a good time?"

"Actually," she burst into tears. "No."

Oh, Emma. She was just Emma—wanted the best and ended in disaster every time. Look at her kids. Perfect example right there.

Tommy perked up. "Hey look, it's Jameson."

We all looked over to my husband, leaning against the cell with a smirk. I burst out laughing at his appearance. The girls had gotten a hold of him—braided his hair, put eye shadow and lipstick on him, and managed to paint his eyelashes and fingernails. He belonged in here with us.

He smiled at me. I frowned.

He laughed. I stuck my tongue out. It became a game until the officer came to release us.

It took a pretty penny to get us out, and Tommy said he'd pay Jameson back.

"Goddamn right you're paying me back. And you can help explain this to reporters when they ask why my wife *and* mother were arrested," Jameson, though amused, wasn't pleased by this.

Tommy agreed, and Nancy looked at me and Alley standing against the wall outside the jail looking like we'd been gang raped.

"You mean to tell me I got a tattoo?" Nancy's face was somewhere between complete mortification and humiliation that her son knew what happened.

Tommy put his arm around Nancy. "We oughta party more often."

"No," Jameson shoved Tommy away from his mom. "Keep it up, and you'll be finding yourself another job."

That shut Tommy up.

On the way up to the suite, Jameson and I stood in the elevator in silence when an older couple on their way to breakfast stepped inside. Though I still looked very gang raped, my husband's appearance was far more laughable.

Through snorts and gasping, they barely contained themselves and exited a few floors before ours, but what really set me into fit of giggles were the group of college girls who stared Jameson down as we passed on the way to our suite.

"So many judging looks coming your way," I whispered in his direction, only to have him trip me.

The group of girls snickered at me.

"Now who's judging who?"

I glared, picking myself up from the floor. It was my only redeemable response. I had nothing left in me after that night.

Air Wrench – This tool uses compressed air to quickly remove wheel nuts on contact. A crew member proficient with the air wrench can save a team valuable seconds on a pit stop. It might also be called an air gun or impact gun.

After being arrested, we kept things low as the season was getting intense, but so was the interest in my relationship with Jameson. I wasn't sure why, but everyone wanted to challenge the connection we had. It was like nowadays people didn't believe in a lasting relationship that had stress and obstacles in its way. Well, I did, and I damn sure wasn't about to let anyone threaten it.

One night after the race in Bristol, I was walking back to the motor coach to meet up with Jameson, and we were heading to Elma for a couple days. I got halfway there and realized I'd forgotten Casten's stuffed monkey in the hauler so Van ran back to get it for me. I stood waiting for him when Rusty, a Nationwide driver, approached me.

Rusty was about twenty-three or so and had a knack with the ladies. He thought, and I would argue this, he was God's gift to women. He had no idea the man I had in my bed every night was by far the best.

So standing there in the darkness of the paddock waiting on Van, Rusty came up.

"What are you doing out here all alone?" he asked, stepping from his golf cart.

"Oh, well I forgot something in the hauler, and Van went to get it."

"So Van, he's like your bodyguard?"

I rolled my eyes. "Yeah, something like that."

He smiled, brown golden eyes trying to work their magic. "I can see why a girl like you needs a bodyguard."

He stepped closer, blocking me against the side of Paul's hauler.

I felt the nervous goose bumps and the sudden urge to run. Since the incident with Darrin so many years ago, I didn't like to be cornered by anyone.

"So, Sway, how about you say we, oh, you know," he let his voice drop lower to a whisper, "We go back to my motor coach?"

Was he fucking serious?

I must have given him that look because he replied, "You can't tell me Riley gives you everything you need. He's so focused on racing he barely sees you for what you are."

Again, was he fucking serious?

He stepped even closer, his breath blowing across my face.

That was when the shit hit the fan.

"What's going on here?" Jameson asked barely controlled.

I knew then, one wrong move, one wrong word and this Rusty guy would regret ever stepping my direction.

Even submerged in the shadows and harsh lighting, his temper was thick. Like a race at a superspeedway with twenty cars running in a pack on the last lap, I knew what was coming.

Rusty stepped back, distancing himself from me.

"Nothing, just talking to your wife here," Rusty said casually with a hint of arrogance. "Nice run tonight."

Jameson looked to me for an answer, avoiding Rusty. He knew by looking at me it wasn't that and reacted exactly the way I expected.

"Sway," Jameson's voice had that tone, and I knew then Rusty was about to see the big one. "Meet me at the motor coach."

My gaze upon my husband shifted over his shoulder to see Van standing there. I joined Van and never looked back.

Van sighed and continued to walk with me.

"How is it that I can't leave you for a second?" he handed me Casten's stuffed monkey.

"I don't know, Van."

I hoped Jameson didn't get into trouble, and frankly, I was getting tired of this crap. Why wasn't it that anyone could have a marriage without people trying to test their luck?

It was something I'd never understand.

Jameson returned with Spencer beside and motioned for me to get inside the Expedition waiting for us. I loaded the kids, and we took off to airport without another word.

When we got home and inside our room, he looked at me and leaned against the wall as I got ready for bed. "Did he hurt you?"

"No. Did you hurt him?"

"No," his eyes dropped to the floor. "I just had a few words with him."

I knew what that meant, and when I saw Rusty the next week, he wouldn't even look at me and had the faint yellow markings of a black eye that was healing.

Riley was still very much Rowdy Riley.

Toward the end of the 2009 season, I had made it into the chase and was well on the way to my fifth championship when we got caught up in the big one in Talladega. A lot of chase contenders were involved, as well, so that was good, but not where I wanted to be heading into the final three races of the season.

Everything was busy right now. Sway was in Mooresville with the kids helping Tommy and the boys with the sprint car team. The World Finals started on Wednesday, and here I was on a Sunday night, after the Talladega race, drinking with Tate and Bobby.

We all just needed a break. Sadly, I didn't get one.

I was standing there next to the bar, waiting for another round of beers when a man approached me for my autograph. I gave him one and expected him to leave me alone, but he decided to invade my personal life by asking how my son was doing. Now, I don't really have a problem with that—he was in the public eye now, and there wasn't anything I could do about that. What I had a problem with was those who asked about Sway. Given our history and the year we'd been having, I took that shit personally.

When his attempts got him nowhere, he went a step further.

"You're wife sure is pretty," the man said conversationally, though I didn't take it that way by his dark tone. I didn't like this guy. One, he was standing too close to me, and second, I just didn't like him.

I was well aware my wife was attractive and understood other men coming on to her. Who wouldn't?

What I didn't appreciate were the ones who felt the need to come on to her in front of me. To me, marriage was sacred. It held a bond like none other. I valued it greatly and to have men disregard me as though my wife wasn't my wife wasn't something I was okay with. Actually, it pissed me off to no end. Just like the time in Bristol with Rusty, I lost my cool.

"Don't." I shook my head slowly as I reached for the three beers the bartender handed me.

"Don't what?"

"Threaten me," I growled, turning to look at him. "Do you honestly think you're the first person to threaten my family?"

"I only said she was pretty," his words didn't match his expression, though. "Why are you so defensive about that?"

"Come on dude!" Bobby yelled from the table. "I could have gotten them faster than you."

I nodded toward Bobby that I had the beers and was heading back to the table when the man followed me.

"I only said she was pretty. What's the harm in that?"

Bobby and Tate caught on fairly quickly that I was moments away from showing this guy what the harm was. "You're in very dangerous territory," I told him as threateningly as I could. Now that I had the man backed up against the wall, it dawned on me who he was. He was the same guy from Indy—Gab. But as Van had found out, his name wasn't Gab Kinney. It was actually Garrett Kinney, wanted for arrest in Atlanta, Houston, and El Paso on possession of narcotics and burglary in Seattle.

"You're awfully protective," he chuckled. "Has she cheated on you or something?"

"You are lucky I'm even letting you say that to me right now."

"Oh, so that's a yes?"

"Listen to me, Garrett!" His eyes widened in surprise that I knew his *real* name. I snapped, slamming my beer on the table as both Bobby and Tate stood from their place at the table. "*My* wife and *my* family are none of your fucking business, is that clear?"

His hands rose defensively. "I was only pointing out a fact."

"A fact that is none of your concern."

Keeping his hands securely in his jacket, he struggled against me.

"Jameson, let him go," Tate warned stepping closer.

"You should listen to your friend."

I had half a mind not to let him go. Flashes of Darrin surged through my blood, leaving me boiling. This wasn't Darrin, just some smartass looking to piss me off, but it didn't change the feeling. Throughout the year, it seemed everyone was testing me.

Knowing this came with fame, I tried not to read too much into it. But still, it was there, haunting me.

Bobby ushered the guy away from me while Tate sat me down at the table again. "Relax man."

"Relax?" I balked. "That guy just told me my wife was pretty. How do you think that makes me feel?"

Tate seemed to contemplate this for a moment but didn't answer.

"Let me ask you something, Tate ... how would you feel if someone threatened Anna or Jake?"

"I would have reacted the same way, but he didn't threaten you. He said she was pretty ... there's a difference, Jameson."

"Really? There is?"

"Yes, there is."

"Could have fooled me because that's the first thing Darrin said to me."

"What?"

"That Sway was pretty."

Tate hung his head and then slowly shook it. "You have to stop comparing every man to Darrin. Yeah, he was crazy, but Sway is pretty. You're not going to get away from men thinking she's attractive."

"That's not the fucking point." I slammed my beer down on the table and walked out. Bobby was coming back inside as I was leaving, and I blew past him with just a head nod.

Instead of catching a flight home, I decided to drive that night. Once you were on I-85, it was only a six-hour drive and after the race and then the bar, I needed the time alone. Throughout the season, it was hard to find any sort of alone time. No matter how in love you were with your significant other or family, you needed alone time.

Once I was driving home, I was able to calm down enough that I called Sway to let her know I'd be there some time in the early morning.

"What do you mean you're driving?"

"That's exactly what I mean."

She sighed. "Why didn't you just have Wes pick you up?" I could hear at least two of the kids screaming in the background.

"I just ..." Letting out my own sigh, I ran my hand through my hair. The freight trucks passing by hummed beside me. "I needed some alone time."

"Oh, okay. Well drive carefully."

"I will," I told her. "I love you."

Sway told me she loved me too and then hung up after that. She called back an hour later and had me sing Arie to sleep. Lately she insisted I sing her to sleep every night so how could I deny my princess that?

When I finally arrived home, I felt better, but I was so tired I hardly had any sense to think. Just not hearing everyone tell me what I should be doing, or should be feeling was enough for me. It was a constant stream of advice these days from sponsors, drivers, my team, everyone, but my family had an opinion of me and wanted to cast their thoughts upon me. I could give a shit what everyone else thought, but it was them that stressed me out the most. While I didn't care what they thought, it still weighed on me, almost as if it was a burden.

Being at home always made me restless when I had racing on my mind, but all that seemed to be the least of my worries the next day when I was watching the kids so Sway could go to the store.

Sway's cell phone kept ringing so eventually it annoyed me to the point I answered it.

"Hello?"

I waited, but no one answered—just breathing.

"Hello?" I repeated, riled from last night and then with the kids this morning.

Axel and Arie spent the morning arguing over what cartoon they wanted to watch while Casten decided it was a good idea to pee on our living room floor—all this while Sway was gone. I wasn't sure how in the hell she handled all three of the little spaz monsters without drugging them. It definitely crossed my mind, but I quickly ruled that out as child abuse and something most would frown upon.

No one answered and eventually I got sick of the silent line and hung up. Two minutes later, the same goddamn thing happened. So when Sway finally walked through the door, grocery bags in hand, I was *not* happy.

"What's wrong with you?" she asked, setting the bags on the center island of the counter and then swinging the door to the garage shut so Casten couldn't sneak out. Any time the kid saw an open door it was like a bunch of prisoners trying to escape Alcatraz.

"How long has this been going on?" I held up her phone.

"A while, I guess," the fact that she knew what I was referring to made me that much more irritated with the entire situation at the bar last night and now these fucking phone calls.

"How long, Sway?"

"A month maybe?"

"Goddamn it, you should have told me," I snapped as she flinched at my harsh tone. Casten looked up at me, glared, and kicked my shin.

"No yelwing!" he told me and scurried to Sway where he usually hid.

"What is with him?" I asked, rubbing my shin, confused why my youngest kid was kicking me. Casten was a funny kid. He never paid much attention to me and usually when I'd get home he'd give me this slow once over gaze as if he was saying to himself, "So, you're my dad?"

Talk about feeling inadequate. It was like he thought I wasn't anything special.

Ignoring me, she picked him up and held on to him as she continued to put the food away like nothing happened. Something did happen, and damn well wasn't going to again. I spent the next two hours lining up more security guards and a new cell phone for Sway, along with more security cameras at our house and the one in Washington.

"Jameson, this is uncalled for," Sway told me when I handed her the new phone later that night. "We don't need to be hounded by security. Van is enough."

"You leave me no choice in the matter, Sway. You and *our* children will be protected from this bullshit!" I snapped harshly. "You should have told me this was happening."

"You have been acting strange since that guy in our hotel room in Indy, what's your deal?"

The fact that she didn't understand why this was important wasn't lost on me. She, of all people, should understand why. I walked away before I once again lost my temper, but as we laid in bed that night going over the schedule for the next week before we left for Charlotte,

I confessed my fears.

I gazed at him; his strong hands ran through his hair as he watched the flames from the fireplace. Letting out a sigh, I wondered what he was keeping to himself when he turned to me, his face radiant in the glow from the dancing light.

He smiled softly when I entered the room, returning the smile.

Snuggling against his chest, his hands cradled around me securely.

"All of this with Rusty and Garrett makes me remember," he whispered into my hair before softly kissing the side of my neck.

"Remember what?" I asked curiously, though I had an idea of what he meant.

His fingertips ran up my shoulder into my hair, trailing across the scar that remained on the back of my head. "What should never be forgotten."

In a sense, it shouldn't be forgotten. Darrin taught us a vital lesson about protecting ourselves. It had been five years since the accident, and we couldn't forget. Every time I washed my hair, I felt the scar left on my scalp. Even so much as the smell of blood, a dark stairwell or hospitals would remind me of that time in our lives. There were even times when I looked at Axel and thought of it. But it wasn't a bad thing as we used it as a reminder of how quickly everything could be taken away from us.

What Jameson was telling me was that he was reminded, too, and that when he overreacted, it was his way of surviving it.

So because this Garrett fellow called me about twenty times a day to breathe in my ear, he amped up our security. Axel was in pre-school now, and since we were on the road so much, we ended up getting a tutor instead of public or private school.

Lane, who just turned nine, was pulled out of fourth grade at Park

View Elementary School in Mooresville because he got into a fist-fight with another kid over Jameson. It wasn't just our kids who were affected by this. All the Riley kids were. This left us hiring our own teachers. And it wasn't that we didn't want them having interactions like this—it was just getting dangerous given the following Jameson now had. I wouldn't say that he was as famous as Brad Pitt, but almost everywhere we went, he was noticed. In turn, our kids were noticed.

At the completion of the Outlaw World Finals, the series announced Jimi would be inducted into the National Sprint Car Hall of Fame in Knoxville, Ohio. He'd won over eight hundred career wins and won his twentieth championship this year. Greatness, that was for sure.

Jameson had always been in awe of his father's raw talent in a sprint car, but when he was inducted into the Hall of Fame, that awe was replaced with reverence.

Similarly, already looking up to Jimi, Axel was in heaven when we took him to Knoxville with us.

Between Jimi being inducted into the Hall of Fame, Jameson winning the championship this year, and changes being made at Grays Harbor, we had a busy off-season.

Thanksgiving flew by since we were in Irwindale with the kids for Turkey Night. Jameson won, while Justin, the usual winner of the event, finally took second to him.

After the awards banquet, we spent Christmas in New York. The kids enjoyed the city so much we decided to stay. Once New Year's had come and gone, it was back to preparing for racing.

We had the three drivers on the Outlaw team, Axel racing the USAC quarter midget Junior Animal division, and then the dealings with the track.

For a long time Grays Harbor had needed attention, so Jameson and I poured some money into the facility by adding grandstands, more concessions stands, and made the entire facility a place where children were welcomed, complete with a playground in the pits.

With the addition of another bodyguard, Clint, the stalkers seemed to be lying low. We still had the occasional crazed fan, obsessed pit lizards, and strange packages delivered to the house, but having security around helped. The nice thing about Van, and now Clint, was that it wasn't like they were security. Van was part of the family now, and Clint loved to play jokes on everyone when he wasn't on guard. Put him in a room with Jameson, Spencer, and Aiden, and they were trying to figure out the best way to embarrass each other. I didn't mind that as much as it made me feel safe and provided entertainment at the same time.

Our lives were moving forward. Axel was six now and racing as much as he could. With the roof on the track at our home in Mooresville, I was lucky to get him to come inside—especially once Jameson installed lights.

I never worried much about his safety out there because, for one, we had cameras installed in the house so that I could see him on the track. On top of that, he wasn't allowed on the track without a parent or someone with enough sense to come get us if he wrecked.

Behind the track was a motocross track so it was rare if any of us saw our children during the day. Lane was competing in races around North and South Carolina and racking up some nice wins so Jameson put in a track for him, as well. Our property became the local hangout.

Arie was, without a doubt, in love with her father. She was absolutely nothing like me. I wondered at times if she was even mine. Arie loved clothes, painting her nails, doing her hair—girly things. I was convinced she was conceived for Emma. Having two little asshole children of her own, who were only into dirt and destroying things, she had nobody to govern the girly world with, so that's where my sweet little Arie and Lexi came in. They adored Aunt Emma.

Then there was Casten, Mama's boy. He'd just turned two, and while he acted like your typical two-year-old, Casten wasn't a fit thrower. He laughed all the time. It was actually kind of strange, but the kid thought *everything* was funny and had the most infectious laugh.

Last year, Jameson had won the championship and Turkey Night, Chili Bowl, and was well on his way to winning the Daytona 500 this year when he got caught up in a wreck on the last lap. His career was taking off, which left him with no time for anything.

On top of that, he turned thirty in June. He wasn't wild about turning thirty, especially in a sport like racing. It meant that he was no longer the kid in the series. He was now looked at as being a wise driver, so to speak, who did not throw fits. Now if you knew Jameson, you knew this was basically out of the question. He still threw stuff after races; got in the faces of other drivers; was fined for aggressive driving; and received a suspension for one race when he punched a NASCAR official for telling him he was setting a bad example for his son.

I was going about life as I always did, just going with the flow. Our kids were growing, Jameson was happy, I was happy, our family was happy. What more could we ask for, right?

I would ask not to get old.

Did you ever wake up in the morning, look in the mirror and wonder how the fuck you got so goddamn old? I did. Every day I spotted another reminder that I was no longer twenty-three, but instead, turning thirty.

Now I was pulling out gray hairs, yelling at my kids more often from lack of patience, waxing in areas I never expected hair to grow, let alone be gray, and finding the need to exercise daily to keep my ass under control.

Getting old sucked. Much like pregnancy, I couldn't find a single thing I enjoyed, well, physically that is. Emotionally, I was extremely happy. I just thought I was wearing this body out. I wonder if they offered replacements.

In late August, my fears of getting old finally got the best of me.

Jameson had a bye week before heading into the race in Atlanta and was once again at the shop with Tommy making changes to the sprint cars before Knoxville Nationals.

Once Arie and Casten were down for naps, and Axel was speeding around the track out back, I finally had a moment to rest and clean up the paint Arie spilled in the kitchen before Jameson saw it. I could only imagine what he'd say when he saw the mess. If you thought he was obsessive about anything touching his skin, he had the same reactions to cleanliness around the house. Now if only he could manage to clean up after himself.

When he finally got home around ten that night, I was exhausted.

With the extreme events those kids had put me through today, sex was not on my agenda. My dirty heathen had other ideas, and as soon as Casten fell asleep, he was attacking me.

I tried to get into the mood for him because we seldom were alone these days, but I was exhausted. Could you honestly blame me with three of Jameson Riley's children around to annoy me all day? In one day they spilled an entire can of paint in the kitchen, and Axel jumped his quarter midget over the pool, followed by Lane jumping his dirt bike (they'd been watching Jameson and Spencer too much these days). Arie and Lexi put make-up on Casten and Cole. Casten decided to try out Mr. Jangles's litter box, and Mr. Jangles went missing, only to later find him taking a dip in the pool, missing more fur. Noah and Charlie came over with Emma. That right there should sum up the rest of my day for you. I was tired. That was all there was to it.

All that being said, Jameson knew my body; he knew it well. So when I wasn't really into it that night, he knew.

Some people told you they had the greatest sex life ever. Others told you they never had sex, and that it was horrible when they did. I guess it depended on who you talked to. Luck of the draw? Or luck of the Irish?

In reality, everyone had different obstacles in their relationship that set them apart from their friend's relationship.

Maybe you fought about money, kids, work, or even having sex.

The thing was, it wasn't always going to be mind-blowing sex. Even with Jameson and me, two people who were sexually attracted to each other from the beginning and have always had a strong sexual chemistry, there were times when it didn't work, when we started and didn't finish, or times when I didn't get off and he did. It was marriage—leg cramps, sore, tired, kids screaming all day, bills to pay, with all those daily obstacles running through your head. It wasn't always easy to shut out the rest of the world and just be in the moment with your other half. I got it.

Jameson, thought, he didn't always understand that.

He stilled above me, searching my eyes. "What's wrong?"

"What do you mean?" I replied innocently.

Jameson seemed to sense the lies in my facial features and rolled off me.

"Sway, you're faking it," he said, offended.

"No I'm not." I also tried to sound offended, but I wasn't sure that worked. After all, he knew I was faking it, and I was pretty sure he knew I was lying.

"Don't lie to me." He got off the bed and pulled his shorts on. "I can't believe this."

"You're overreacting."

"I'm overreacting? How many times have you faked it?"

This was turning out badly. "I haven't been faking it," I repeated, trying to buy some more time to think of a better lie.

"Did I do something wrong? Is it me?"

"You didn't do anything wrong," I said, pulling up the sheets. "I just ... have a headache."

Nice one, Sway. Real fucking original.

He didn't acknowledge that poor excuse.

"I've always been able to please you," he mused. "At least I thought I was," he started to mutter. "Maybe I've lost my touch. *Oh, my God ...* I've lost it. I turned thirty, and I've lost it!"

"Jameson, it wasn't you," I climbed off the bed and moved to sit next to him on the floor now. "Let's try again."

He looked at me with a shocked expression and pointed toward his now soft camshaft. "Do you honestly think I'm ready to go again?

I think I need Viagra?" he said the last part in question though I was sure it wasn't meant to be one.

"This is getting ridiculous," I grabbed his face between my hands. "It. Wasn't. You."

He was about to say something else when his phone rang. He sat there glaring at me, actually glaring at me, before getting up to answer the phone.

"Yeah ... no ... because I don't want to ... no, you do it ... leave me alone ... all right, fine, bye," he slammed his phone shut. "Fucking Spencer," he grumbled.

"Who was that?"

"Spencer," he replied, pulling his shirt over his shoulders without looking at me. He made his way toward the door. "I'll be back later."

"Where are you going?" I asked timidly.

"To the shop."

"It's nearly midnight."

"They're loading the cars for Knoxville and noticed Cody's was leaking oil. We must have cracked the cover when we changed gears."

"Oh ..."

He was about to walk out the door, but slammed his fist into the wall and came back over to me. He bent down close to my face and kissed me. "We'll talk about this when I get back."

"About what?"

"My performance," he shook his head. "I can't believe I lost it."

"I'm going to tell you again, asshole, that wasn't your fault."

"We'll still talk."

Shaking my head at my crazy husband, I curled up and was asleep a few moments later. It was late by the time he returned, but in the morning, at breakfast, he felt the need to discuss it further.

"About last night," he looked up at me as he ate a slice of bacon. "That's never happened to me before."

"Daddy, can you put the head back on my Barbie?" Arie asked him, shoving her Barbie next to his pancakes. He did, and she skipped off to the living room where the boys were watching cartoons.

"We don't have to talk about this."

I couldn't think of any more lies to tell him, and I really didn't want to tell him the truth. It was stupid. I was just tired, felt old, and I found a stretch mark yesterday. It was so dumb that I figured he'd just laugh, but *clearly*, he was overthinking it.

"Oh, yes we do," he insisted, setting his bacon down. "You say it wasn't me, so what the fuck was it?"

"It was me …" I sighed.

"Well …" he sighed, too. "I think I should see a urologist or something."

"I think you need a therapist, not a urologist," I stood up. "You're being ridiculous."

He did that thing that he did when he knew I was lying. I cracked under the pressure.

"Fine." I threw my arms up in the hair. "I found a gray hair and a stretch mark yesterday," I wailed. "The kids are driving me insane, and I might add, I think the little one has decided against toilets and uses a litter box. That's weird, right?" His brow rose curiously, and I slumped back in the chair. "Please, say something."

He did the opposite of what I thought he would—he laughed so hard he fell out of his chair.

Stupid husband.

I kicked him on the way to the bathroom to look for more gray hairs and stretch marks. The older I got, the more I got. It was an endless cycle as time passed, and it did pass quickly.

I couldn't understand why Jameson didn't find this a matter of importance, but then again, I didn't think him seeing a camshaft doctor was important.

Over the years I'd gained weight. Gravity, the fucking bitch, wasn't helping.

With Axel, I gained around thirty pounds of which ten never left.

With Arie, I gained twenty-five, and again five stayed. Now with Casten, I only gained twenty, but then again five became a permanent fixture.

As a result, I'd packed on a good twenty pounds that refused to leave, but placed in a way that I could get away with it. I didn't look bad either. For someone who was always fairly small, I looked healthy and still kept good muscle tone. The only problem was that most of my weight gain took up residence in my ass, and I became a five-foot-two version of Jennifer Lopez without the tan.

Jameson never complained. Hell no, he loved curves. After a while, I stopped trying to lose the weight and just loved my ass. After all, it was softer to sit on. And who didn't love a nice soft place to sit?

Not everyone adopted my theories on a softer place to sit.

Emma tried relentlessly to lose the weight she'd gained with the twins, but she still carried a few extra pounds. She took weight-training classes, jogged with Jameson, and then when he pushed her into oncoming traffic as she didn't understand that jogging was his attempt at relaxing, she was forced to just accept the fact that she had a few extra pounds.

"I just don't see why he won't run with me," Emma would say to me.

"It might have something to do with the fact that you never shut up," I would tell her.

"That's a lie. I was quiet for the first mile and after that, well, that's just unheard of for me."

Emma just didn't get it.

"I feel bad for her," I said to Jameson later that night when I accepted my cushion.

"Why?" Jameson didn't look up from the laptop. More than likely he was checking the points standing and not interested in Emma.

"She thinks she has to be a certain weight," I came to stand behind him. My hands ran up his arms to his shoulders.

"Well, that's stupid," he looked up at me, eyes sparkling as they always did. "She looks great the way she is."

I smiled running my fingers through his hair. "You're a good brother despite trying to kill her."

"Uh, she tried first when she stabbed me."

"Are you ever going to let her live that down?"

He looked back down at the laptop. "No, probably not."

Later that night, Jameson showed me just how much he loved those curves I had when he attacked me in the kitchen after the kids had gone to bed. He also showed me that he had no problems with his camshaft and matching me stroke for stroke.

"Fuck, honey."his eyes darkened, and I knew it was over. "Get those sexy fucking legs up here."

I did. He was on his knees on the kitchen floor with me spread out before him like the pit lizard days. Watching his muscles flex, he positioned my legs on each one of his broad shoulders. His hands slipped to my ass and squeezed.

"Don't ever lose this," he growled, squeezing harder. It was a good thing my ass cheeks were real or they would have popped.

"Oh, I've tried. It's not going anywhere."

"Good."

And those were the last words spoken before I was trying to control my screams on our tile floor. It seemed inappropriate to be align boring on the kitchen floor, but then again, why did we put in heated floors if not to hump on them occasionally?

I never really thought about how I would feel heading into my tenth season in the NASCAR Sprint Cup series. The one thing that remained all these years was my support system.

My team was pretty much the same as it was when I started, aside from a few crew-members who shuffled back and forth between teams.

Our family still traveled with us. On any given weekend, you'd find my wife, my kids, my parents, and my siblings somewhere at the track. We were all part of this. I think that was why I was still in this sport. Without my family, I honestly didn't think I could do this each week.

My sponsor remained the same, and over the winter we signed another five-year contract.

When I signed with Simplex, I had no idea they'd support me throughout my entire career. Let's face it, sponsors came and went, but I had a relationship with Marcus and Melissa now. We understood each other, and they trusted our team.

What didn't change were the obsessed fans and pit lizards.

It never failed—the women were everywhere at a NASCAR race. So many times, I wished this wasn't part of it, but it was. Never wanting Sway to get hurt, I never told her how many times I had to kick them out of my motor coach or how many times they found my hotel room and showed up naked.

She didn't need to hear that shit. Hell, I didn't want to hear it, but it was reality for me.

Dana Sloan finally moved on from stalking me to stalking Shelby. Shelby seemed to enjoy it.

These days, there were new pit lizards stalking me, and a few of the old—Ashley being one of them.

When we were back in Daytona, just before the Budweiser Shootout, she took it too far when she asked when she could go for a ride again, in front of my daughter.

That was not okay with me.

Arie looked up at me with wide, curious eyes clearly wondering why another woman was flirting with her daddy. She may have only been seven, but she was fairly perceptive to this sort of thing. It happened that often.

"Don't you *ever* say that to me again," I warned and tightened my grip on her arm, pulling her away from Arie. "I don't remember a goddamn thing from that night. I was drunk. I woke up in a Safeway parking lot. You need to get over the fact that it will *never* happen."

I watched her expression carefully, my glare never wavering. She needed to understand how serious I was about this.

"You'll give in eventually Jameson, they all do," she stepped closer, her breath blowing across my face. "Just ask Bobby."

Was she fucking serious?

I'd known Bobby since I started in Cup ten years ago, and I never once thought he'd give in to Ashley. Not to mention, he was married and had been for the last three years.

"I don't give a shit what Bobby does; he's not me, Ashley," I told her firmly.

"Whatever, Jameson," she rolled her eyes.

"No, not whatever. You need to understand right now that it will never happen. Stop coming on to me. Stop calling my wife, stopping talking to my kids. Stop." My voice continued to rise until I was nearly yelling at her in the middle of the paddock with other team and media personnel walking around.

"Fine," she huffed, stepping back. "I'll leave you alone. Just admit you had a good time."

"I don't even remember it. That should tell you how good it was," I knew I was hitting low, but at this point, it was the only option.

Tears pooled in her eyes, and for a moment I thought she was joking until her cheeks flushed with embarrassment.

"You're an asshole," she mumbled and walked away—*finally* walked away.

You're an asshole meant nothing these days. I heard it so often it barely fazed me anymore.

The following weekend, I caught up with Bobby just before we began driver introductions for the Daytona 500 and asked about his interactions with Ashley.

"Ashley caught up with me last week ..." my voice trailed off, hoping he'd understand.

"Let me guess ... she told you."

I groaned. "Bobby, why would you do that?"

Bobby leaned closer for privacy as we filed through the gates to the stage. "I don't know why. It just sorta happened one night."

"Were you married then?"

He didn't say anything, and that pretty much answered my question. I knew this happened with other drivers. The temptation was there and was readily available for us if we wanted it. Not once had I ever acted, or been tempted to act on it. Sway was everything to me. It just wasn't an option for me. The fact that Bobby had cheated on Kelly sickened me.

I always thought that eventually the nerves of standing on the grid of the Daytona 500 would fade, but no. I was fine all morning, but when I stepped on pit road the morning of my tenth career Daytona 500, the nerves hit me.

"Jameson, how are you feeling this morning?" a reporter with ESPN asked while I talked with Tate and Bobby by my car.

"Oh ... I'm feeling good," I replied, laughing at the joke Tate has just told.

"I hear both your boys couldn't be here today, racing, huh?"

"Yeah," I hated talking to the media about my kids. It was none of their fucking business, but it was part of the game. "They raced in the Duel in the Desert yesterday and won their divisions." I smiled. "Casten is just getting started, but he's taken really well to it. Axel helps him along."

"Speaking of Axel, he's really tearing it up in the quarter midget series. Heard he's won two district championships and a handful of regional and track championships."

I laughed, leaning back against my car. "He did," I agreed. "He's nine now and chomping at the bit to get into the full-sized midgets, but you have to be twelve these days."

Back when I started, age wasn't enforced as much, but after a few kids were killed in the series, the age restrictions were strictly enforced. Hell, I was racing a full-sized sprint car by the time I was twelve, but looking at Axel's size compared to a full-sized sprint car—I had no problem with the age enforcements now.

"Hothead in the making, I hear. Didn't he throw his helmet at a

USAC official last weekend?"

Another laugh escaped. "Yeah, he's worse than me at times. Doesn't like to finish second." I shrugged. I was considered calm on the track compared to Axel. After he threw the helmet at the official, he was suspended for a race. It took him being suspended to realize he had to control the temper or they wouldn't let him race.

Sounded familiar, right?

I'd cooled my jets these days, being a father humbled you, and when you saw your kids' reaction to a fit you'd thrown on or off the track, it really made you think about that image you were creating for them. Not only did you face the ramifications, but your kids had to, as well.

Colin Shuman, Shelby Clausen, and I had spent enough time in "the big red hauler" last season that we had assigned seats. Even with all the arguments and wrecks we got into, we usually ended up throwing back a few beers afterward. That was when I felt I grew up.

"Well, good luck today," the announcer said and left me to get ready.

Once I was inside my car, the pre-race jitters were wearing off, and I finally began to relax when I realized why I'd been so amped up this morning. Sway wasn't here.

She'd only missed three of my ten starts here, and those were from having my babies, but now she was with our babies.

Arie decided to come with me to Speedweeks and stayed for the 500 race. My little angel was standing beside my car handing me a good luck charm she made me.

"Here, Daddy, I made this for you," Arie beamed, handing me a beaded bracelet.

"You did?" I looked down at her wide and excited emerald green eyes and thought of Sway. "I'm sure I'll win now."

"You will." That was one trait my little angel possessed. She believed in her daddy, and if anyone told her differently, well, she told her big brother, and when that happened it was over.

Axel would do just about anything to prove you wrong, and his determination never wavered when it came to protecting his family's name. Arie was the same way. But with Axel, he seemed to be a mixture of Sway and me. He could be cocky, arrogant, and indomitable, but he could also be relaxed, amiable, and blasé. The kid was wise beyond his years and a force to be reckoned with. By the time he was four, it was apparent Sway and I were in over our heads.

Now Casten, he was in it for fun. If he wasn't having fun, he didn't do it. He was blithely carefree and loved everyone—just like Sway. You rarely saw that kid without a huge smile. Even when he was sleeping, he was smiling, and he had the negotiation skills of a politician, no lie.

Arie listened to my in-car audio on the pit box and provided her own commentary on the race and her thoughts. Much to my surprise, but not hers, I did win. After ten years of trying, I finally won the Daytona 500.

Arie was there to greet me in victory lane, along with her brothers and my wife, who must have shown up sometime during the race.

I smirked when I saw Sway jumping up and down with the same excitement our kids showed, knowing that their father was a Daytona 500 winner.

"I knew you could do it," Sway whispered in my ear when I pulled her hard against my chest. With our schedules, it'd been weeks since I last seen her. "You behave, dirty heathen."

I winked. "I love you, honey," I whispered back before our kids were climbing on us.

All those times away—the late nights, the early rises, and the sacrifices—were worth it at times like this.

The only thing I ever hoped for out of all this was that those who helped me along the way understood they were a part of what I did and always would be. When I won a race or a championship, it wasn't just for me, or my dad as the car owner, or even Simplex as my sponsor. It was for *everyone*, and I hoped they felt the same excitement I felt in winning. I was sure no one exactly felt like I did, but I sure hoped they realized what it meant to me to have that support. Yeah, I was a six-time NASCAR Sprint Cup Champion and had won 113 Cup races, but I owed a lot to everyone else.

My tenth season in the Cup series was by far my best year yet. Not only did I win the Daytona 500, but I also won the All-Star Race and managed to pull off my seventh Cup championship.

It was a good year.

One of the most closely guarded secrets in NASCAR, besides the rulebook, is how much each driver is paid. You see it with the NFL, NBA, NBL; most nationally recognized sports flaunt what a particular athlete is paid each year, but not NASCAR.

Word got out on occasion, but you'd never hear a driver say, 'I made *this* amount.' Not only did we receive a base salary from our owner/sponsor, but we also got outside money from prize money, contingency awards, and endorsement contracts. It wasn't uncommon to see a veteran driver raking in around $15 - $25 million in a season.

Without a doubt, this seemed to be one of the best years of my career with a record number of poles and wins and the championship title once again. Financially, I was also on top of the sport. Along with my $900,000 salary from Riley Simplex Racing, I received forty percent of my winnings, and then my endorsement deals from clothing companies, safety gear, shock companies—the list went on and on. Then you accounted for my owner profit in JAR Racing, and the twenty percent I took home from each time Justin, Cody, or Tyler pulled into victory lane, and I really wasn't hurting for money.

But all that didn't matter. Sure, it was nice, but I wasn't in it for the money. I was in it to race, and you know what happened because of that?

I became the best driver in the series.

Back Out – When a driver takes his foot off the gas pedal (all the way or part way) he "backs out" or "lifts" the throttle.

Despite my sanity, I agreed to let Logan and Lucas come out for Fourth of July 2013. Why they wanted to come out here was beyond me. They were sixteen. Didn't they have more appealing things to do?

I just knew having sixteen-year-old half-brothers around my spaz children was a bad idea.

Their plane got in the night before we were set to leave for Daytona's night race.

When Spencer went to get them from the airport, I was relieved that Lucas had stayed home. I could handle one of them.

"We're here!" Spencer announced, slamming the door behind him. Jameson wasn't home yet from the shop, as they were apparently making some changes to Justin's sprint car before it headed to Dodge City, Kansas, tomorrow morning.

"Sway ... you in here?" Spencer's booming voice echoed throughout the downstairs.

"Yeah," I sighed, removing the cookies from the oven. I couldn't figure out for the life of me why I decided to make cookies. It wasn't like I wanted Logan to feel welcome, and, God forbid, want to stay. "I'm in the kitchen."

Spencer and Logan came around the corner, standing next to the island. Logan laughed. "Since when do you bake?"

"I bake a lot, asshole," I shot back, throwing a cookie at him.

"Really, judging by the number of kids in the movie room fighting over a movie ... I'd say you do *other* things in your free time."

I noticed the kids came into the kitchen to see what all the commotion was about.

"Where the hell is Jameson?" Logan asked, looking around.

"He's at the shop. He'll be home later."

Logan shrugged, eating the cookie. "Well, aren't you happy to see me or are you pissed Luke didn't come?"

"Although he's the normal one, no, I'm not pissed. And, yes, I guess I'm happy to see you," Logan stood and wrapped his long arms around me. I laughed at how tall he was. "Jeez, you're tall these days."

Spencer plopped down on a stool. "He's barely five-six, Sway."

"Hey, I'm five-seven now."

"Is pissed a bad word?" Casten asked Axel. I didn't even know they had come into the room yet. "If it is, I'm up to ten bucks now."

I grabbed Casten and headed for the island, setting him on the stool. He held his hands up in defense. "I was only kidding."

I hugged him tightly.

"I'm warning you two now," I looked over at Axel, and I would have told Arie, but she wasn't in earshot. "Don't listen to Logan. He's riding the crazy train and collecting passengers."

"We don't want to be passengers?" Casten asked innocently.

"No, you don't."

"Geez, Sway," Logan sighed, "you act like I'm some kind of delinquent."

"You are."

He ignored me completely and went in for the kill. "Hey, Axel, how's it going, little man?"

Axel just stared at him, probably wondering how in the hell he was related to something like Logan.

Logan had the power of persuasion down to a fine art—just like my kids. This was going to be tough, and I knew my kids were in danger of corruption. They were like sponges.

Logan looked up at me. "What's for dinner?"

"I have to feed you, too?" I asked in horror. I didn't remember Andrea telling me anything about feeding him. "And what the hell is up with your hair?" What used to be brown was now black and had red streaks in it.

"I let my girlfriend do my hair," he shrugged. "She's is beauty school."

"Looks like she's doing *well*."

"So what is for dinner?"

"Jameson is bringing pizza home," all the kids, Logan, and Spencer included lit up with excitement. I decided now was time to tell Logan my rules. "Listen dude, I have rules."

"Great," Logan moaned, leaning back in the chair. "Let's hear these so-called rules. They may be deal breakers."

"No smoking, no drinking, and no cursing in front of the kids, unless you want to lose all your money. If you get arrested for any of your bright ideas, you're on your own. I'm not bailing you out."

Logan looked confused, clearly not paying attention to anything I said to him. "Did you pop out another kid?"

"They're not all mine," I pointed to each kid. "Those three are mine. That one is Lane. You've met him before, dumbass. And in the other room is Lily, Justin's daughter, and I think Lexi, Cole, and Noah are in the movie room somewhere. Charlie is with Aiden getting some groceries for tonight."

"Tonight?" Logan looked more confused. "What's tonight?"

"We're having a little get-together since Lexi's birthday is on Wednesday, and we'll be at the track. You're just in time for an eleven-year-old's birthday party."

He rolled his eyes and ate yet another cookie.

"Where's Luke, I thought he was coming, too?" Lane asked, grabbing a few cookies from the plate, as well.

"He's got a game this weekend in Seattle," Logan answered, before following Lane outside toward the track where Axel disappeared.

Axel wasn't one for crowds or birthday parties so I couldn't blame him. If only I could have joined him. At least Lucas wasn't here, too. This way they wouldn't gang up on me.

Logan and Lucas were heavily involved in baseball, and both were well on their way to receiving scholarships for college. At least this was better than the alternative for the little hoodlums—prison.

Once Jameson arrived home, and the rest of the family showed up to celebrate Lexi's birthday, the night thankfully passed in a blur.

The next day, we were on our way to Daytona for the race with Logan in tow.

Taking Logan to a track like Daytona was a bad idea. Not only was he sixteen and into girls, but Daytona was notorious for their pit lizards. This was very exciting for Logan. In turn, he wanted to spend all his time around Jameson, as that was where the pit lizards were.

The infield in Daytona was out of control at times. Once, and only once, I took the kids through there on my way out. What took two minutes to get through took two hours of explaining when girls flashed their funbags at my innocent little boys.

Jameson qualified for the pole, but then blew up the engine in practice so he was not the nicest person to be around. Every time I turned around he was yelling at someone, and we got to the point that weekend that if we saw him coming, everyone fled.

While Jameson was getting a feel for the back-up car in happy hour I went to check on the kids at the playground where Emma was watching them.

"Don't be mad," Emma said when I saw Casten holding a bloody towel to his mouth and nose.

"What happened to him?" glancing down at my little boy, I knew. He looked distraught.

You wouldn't believe the shit my kids could get into at a race track. Daytona was by far the worst, so I knew something was coming.

"Hi, Mama," he mumbled, holding the towel against his face, his tiny shoulder slumped forward.

Kneeling down, I brushed his mess of hair out of his eyes to get a better view. Having a mischievous nine-year-old already, I knew exactly what happened when I saw the purple blob lodged in his nose.

Play-doh.

"What made you do that?"

"I'm sorry," he offered, looking at his hands.

"Don't be sorry, monkey ... just, uh ... don't push it up there any farther."

I actually wasn't sure it could go any farther without lodging in his brain, but I could be wrong.

Emma collected the rest of the kids and followed me to the infield care center.

While they cleaned up his nose and attempted to get the blob out, I ran back to the motor coach to get his monkey, which he said he needed to make it through the rest of the day. He may be my brave, happy five-year-old, but he still needed his stuffed monkey just like Axel still needed his Mr. Piggy.

"Where's Casten?" Jameson asked once back at his motor coach. I kept one eye on Logan and one eye on Jameson, clutching the stuffed monkey to my side.

"He's detained," was my answer.

Jameson quirked his head to the side before climbing back inside the golf cart when Alley gestured toward the media center.

Both Noah and Charlie quickly darted in the other direction and hid behind Aiden.

"He stuck Play-doh in his nose," Logan told him, swinging his arm around my shoulder. "He's in the infield care center with Emma."

"Why would he do that?"

Noah and Charlie chuckled, and I pushed Logan away. He thankfully tripped over his own feet.

"You couldn't keep your mouth shut, could you?"

"What?" Logan asked. "It's not *that* big of a deal."

"It is a big deal. He doesn't want everyone knowing his shit head cousins coaxed him into sticking Play-doh up his nose."

Logan shrugged indifferently. "It happens to the best of us."

Just as Jameson got back out of the golf cart, knowing he had some father duties to tend to, Emma sent me a text message stating Casten broke down and was crying.

Turning toward Jameson, I yanked him by his racing suit with me. "Come talk to him, he's crying."

Jameson groaned but followed. "Why is he crying?"

"Probably because he tried to stick Play-doh into his brain."

In every infield on the circuit was an infield care center. Drivers and their families were treated there for sprained ankles, cuts, scrapes, sore throats, and the flu ... pretty much everything.

This wasn't the first time one of my kids visited the infield care emergency room. Axel had frequent visits at Bristol, Charlotte, and Daytona. Arie had stumbled over a tire in the garage area at Fontana and received her first set of stitches when she was two. And now Casten, who had an issue with sticking things in his nose. Let's just hope that issue didn't expand to chemicals when he got older.

Later that night, after getting Casten ice cream to make him feel better, he spent the rest of the night curled up in Jameson's lap, playing Xbox with Logan. Usually he was a Mama's boy, but at the first sign of illness or injury, he wanted his daddy, much like all my children.

Due to a nasty infection, Casten needed a hefty dose of antibiotics so I took him with me to fill the prescription when we went back to Elma for the Outlaw tour. It felt good to be back home for a few weeks, and hanging out with Andrea and Macy was my favorite part. A not-so-favorite part was running into Chelsea for the first time since before the accident—especially since Casten was with me.

I never wanted her to see the kids. We tried to keep them out of the public eye as much as possible, but times like this I never thought I needed to. Everywhere in Elma we went, people never bothered us. The same went for Mooresville. These were two places where we truly felt at home. I should have known I'd run into her in Elma, though.

"Sway ... is that you?" I knew her voice, how could I not? It haunted me for years in high school. Casten gripped my hand tighter when he felt me tense, looking up at me.

Turning back to look at her, I had to bite back a laugh that she had gained about fifty pounds.

"Chelsea?" My arms instinctively picked up my youngest spaz, holding him close to me.

"Wow, it's good to see you," she said, her blue eyes appearing honest for once.

Casten looked from me to her. "Who is that?"

"This is Chelsea Adams," I told him.

She held her hand out to him. "You look just like your daddy, sweetheart."

"Well, I should, he's my dad," Casten responded.

"Oh, I can tell with that remark," she laughed. "You must be the youngest one ... Casten, right?"

We both nodded as I gave her a confused look. "The internet ... it's not hard to find out."

"Back to stalking these days?"

Her eyes widened in surprise. "No, I'm not. Listen, Sway, I'm sorry for what happened."

"Sorry doesn't really take it back, Chelsea," I whispered. Our kids didn't know the troubles we'd had prior to them. I didn't want them to, knowing eventually there would be no way around that.

Chelsea sighed, knowing this wasn't the time for this sort of thing, when my eyes glanced toward Casten, who was curiously watching our interaction. "I wanted his heart back then Sway, but it wasn't his to give. It never was."

I could have told her she was wrong, but she wasn't. We didn't know it then, but our hearts were taken that night beside that black sprint car when we were eleven. Neither one of us ever had a chance alone.

JAMESON

"How does it feel on the straight stretches?"

I shrugged. Flipping open my visor, Kyle leaned inside the car. "Good, but not great. It still feels like it's bottoming out on me."

"We could try an air pressure and a spring wedge to see if that helps."

"It couldn't hurt."

"All right," he nodded. "Do you need water or Gatorade?"

"Nah, I'm good." Kyle put my window net up again and then moved back so the crew could make some adjustments. We were currently testing at Texas, in probably the hottest temperatures of the year. In the two-hour test session we did, I drank six bottles of water and had no urge to use the bathroom—I'd say I was a little dehydrated.

I ended up making another hundred laps or so before parking beside the hauler in the infield where Kyle, Bobby, and Mason were waiting.

Everyone was sound asleep by the time I got back to Mooresville. Quietly, I crawled in bed, hoping not to wake Sway, who was curled up on my pillow.

My eyes were just about closed when I felt a tiny hand against my shoulder. "Daddy?"

I could hear a soft melodic whisper that pulled me out of the almost-sleep. My baby girl's breath blew across my face as she nudged my shoulder again. "Daddy?"

"What's the matter, princess?" I whispered back, blinking into the darkness.

Arie sighed. "I had a bad dream. Can I sleep with you?"

Opening my eyes just enough to make out her tiny frame, I lifted her in between Sway and me. She curled up next to me, her head resting on my pillow. Arie was a snuggler with me, not so much with Sway, but she loved a good cuddle in the arms of her daddy.

Every time she slept with us, she had to be touching me, and usually with several body parts.

"I hate bad dreams," she said with another sigh.

"Do you want to tell me about it?" I asked, throwing an arm around her and rubbing her back.

"You wrecked and didn't come home to us," she wiggled and snuggled closer. "It made me sad."

"Don't worry, baby, nothing is going to happen to me," I whispered, kissing her forehead.

Within a few minutes she was sleeping in my arms. This was always a fear of theirs. At least Arie's. I never heard Axel or Casten talk about it, but Arie was different. Even though I promised her, I couldn't. I never knew what would happen from week to week on the track. All I could hope for was the chance to let my family know I loved them.

I'd mentioned this before, but other women were relentless. And it wasn't even the pit lizards. It could be anyone. Any time they found out who I was, it was like they thought if I gave into them, they won something. It wasn't happening, though. I was happy with Sway.

We were comfortable with each other. Just like my favorite dirt track, on any given night I knew how to get fast time, I knew where the ruts were, and I knew just how much speed I could carry through the corners. I knew how to throttle through the turns to glide over the ruts. Just like any bullring track, I knew her as she knew me.

I also knew even good marriages failed at times. But it started with one simple miracle—two people fell in love. That was what I valued. Sway and I fought sometimes over everything from time with each other, to me leaving my underwear lying around the house. I'd never say it was perfect, but it was pretty fucking good. All that being said, that was why these women throwing themselves at me were *never* an option, or even so much as a thought.

One particular woman, Kristy, worked for me as a scorer for our team and was rather flirty. Spencer warned me countless times that there was something more to her, as though she took the job to get closer to me. For a while I thought he was right until she began dating Colin. But then Kristy and I had to spend a few afternoons together when she stepped in for Alley as my publicist for an event. Kristy really wasn't any different from any other girl.

One night while we were in Chicago for the race, she knocked on the door to my motor coach fairly late as I was just getting ready for bed. Sway and the kids were in Eldora at the Little Dirt Nationals for Axel and Casten. I was flying out tomorrow to catch a few heat races, but this left me alone.

Thinking it was Spencer again I answered the door in just jeans, without a shirt.

"Oh ... hey, Kristy." I reached for my shirt on the back of the chair near the door. "What's up?"

She was crying. That much was evident by her reddened eyes. I invited her in, she told me that she and Colin had gotten in a fight, and she was feeling upset about it. She thought she wasn't good enough for him being a NASCAR driver. After a while, when I told her I needed to get some sleep, she hugged me and confessed her real motive.

"I came in here hoping that you and I could ... you know."

Well, shit, Spencer was right.

"Kristy," I let out a deep sigh. I knew where this was going with that look on her face. I'd seen it on countless women. "You're beautiful. I'm married, not blind, so when I tell you that you are, please believe me. But I love my wife more than anything in the world so *this*," I motioned between us, "is not an option. *Ever*."

"I know," she mumbled, tears streaming down her reddened cheeks. Her expression brought me back to when Sway left me in Sonoma all those years ago.

Kristy was pretty and resembled Sway in a lot of ways, there was no denying that, but I also knew it really didn't matter. No one would ever fill the aching void I felt when Sway wasn't with me.

"You know ..." I began handing Kristy a tissue. "My wife, Sway, and I went through something like this."

"*I know*," she nodded. "I read that somewhere."

"What I meant was that even though you think you can't have Colin, you can. He loves you."

"You don't know that."

"You're right," I offered. "I don't know if he loves you, but I can tell you from a man's perspective, he appears to."

She was silent and then turned to hug me. Carefully, trying not to lead her on any more than I already had, I wrapped my arms around her, returning the hug, and then pulled her away to arms' length.

"Go get him," I told her with a wink.

There were times where I got lonely and I missed Sway, but the thought never crossed my mind to turn to another woman. Like I said, it wasn't an option for me, never would be.

Another woman to frequently try her luck was Nadia.

Now Sway never came out and said it, but I knew her feelings toward Nadia. It was the same as every other wife whose husband raced in the series. They didn't trust her.

I also never appreciated how Nadia thought she was better than our wives.

Well, to me, our wives had done more.

Nadia also thought the wives were gold diggers and never took the time to think otherwise. What she didn't know was that, Sway, for example, ran Grays Harbor Raceway most days, made sure everyone with JAR Racing got their flight schedules, drivers were paid, raised our kids, and kept me grounded.

To me, she had the hardest job out of all of us.

She was there when the spotlight wasn't.

Something I knew a girl like Nadia wouldn't be. She reminded me so much of Ashley and Chelsea, it was revolting.

But, I was still pleasant to her when needed.

Sometime after the summer race in Charlotte, I was at a bar with Tyler having a drink when Nadia showed up. He'd yet to meet her, so I introduced them and that was that. We parted ways for the night.

Only problem was when Tyler went to the bathroom, Nadia found me at the bar.

"So what, you're gonna ignore me?" she asked when she stood there for a good few minutes, and I had yet to say anything to her. The paper wrapping on my beer was more interesting than conversation with her.

"I was trying to," I told her, finally looking her direction. "And you're making it hard."

Her eyes, focused on mine, gave her intensions away. And being away from my wife, sure, if I was like any other guy, I could give in. It'd be easy. But that's not me and never would be me.

"You're always an asshole, aren't you? Why are you—"

I cut her off immediately. "How would you know?" I laughed. "You made your mind up about me a long time ago."

"No, you made it for me," she replied and motioned for the bartender to get her a beer and one for me. "You never give people a chance to prove otherwise."

"Just like everyone else, you have one image of me and it's not the right one," I said, looking at her again. And, honestly, I started to get a little upset. "Everyone has this perception of what I'm like because of my driving style. It's far from how I am as a person."

She smiled, relaxing. "I know. I was just giving you a hard time. How 'bout a drink?"

I'm not exactly sure if I was thinking, I probably wasn't, but, Tyler and I had a drink with her. When Tyler left around midnight, I got up to leave, and Nadia reached for my hand.

"Oh, come on, stay for one more?"

"Nadia," I stood, putting some space between us. "You got the wrong impression here. I'm not that kind of guy and never will be."

She looked a little confused, then hurt, then maybe a little angry. "Jameson ... you're seriously going to pass this up?"

I turned and looked at her over my shoulder. "Have a good night, Nadia."

I then tossed a fifty at the bar and left without another glance.

Like I said, these women were never an option. Did I tell Sway about the encounter?

No.

I wasn't trying to keep something from my wife, but then again, I didn't want her worrying about something she didn't need to.

In my mind, I was doing the right thing.

Once September rolled around, it was time for Dirt Nationals in Eldora. Fortunately for me, the Cup schedule opened up, and I was able to attend. Sway was with Arie at her dance recital. I'd been to a dance recital, and though I loved watching my little girl and niece dance around like the angels they were, I could only handle so much pink and screaming girls.

So here I was, with my boys. Only problem was, my little guy was extremely temperamental tonight.

After hot laps when the USAC official told me Axel needed to cool it or he'd be suspended, I felt the need to talk to him.

When he pulled the car beside me, slammed his helmet against the side of his car and kicked the left rear tire, I intervened.

"What's with you?"

"Nothing," he snorted. "Nothing is wrong."

"Bullshit."

My little guy was a typical eleven-year-old these days, hormonal and aggressive, just like his dad. Laughing, I pulled him with me toward the concession stands.

"C'mon buddy, let's get you a beer or something."

Axel ended up calming down after inhaling about three hotdogs and begging for that beer (which he never received). Sway made it before the feature events began and then ended up having to leave when Arie puked all over her. This left me alone with Axel, Casten, and, of course, Lily who refused to go anywhere if Axel wasn't with her.

"Keep an eye on him," Sway told me as I carried Arie to the car, who had apparently been sick all day but wanted to see Axel race. "He seems … like his dad tonight."

"I know," I grinned and kissed her and Arie goodbye. "We should be home sometime after midnight, I assume."

When I got back to Axel's pit, two USAC officials had separated him and Payton, another quarter midget driver.

"What the hell happened?"

Casten laughed. "Axel punched Payton."

I turned toward Axel, who was sitting next to his race car, nursing a bloody lip. "Why would you do that?"

He shrugged and leaned his head against his arms resting on his knees. "I just … did."

On the way back home that night I got out of him what I feared would someday happen. He was defending me. "Payton said you didn't deserve to win all those championships."

"Don't pay any mind to Payton," I told him. I knew it wasn't Payton Raymond saying that. It was his dad. No twelve-year-old knew who deserved a championship and who didn't.

"It's not easy, is it?" he asked when we pulled down our long driveway.

"What's not easy?"

His mirror-like green eyes focused on mine. That same determination, that same fire I had flashed through him. "Being the son of a legend."

"I suppose it isn't." I never thought that Axel would feel the same way I did growing up, and I wasn't prepared for that. But there was no way for him to avoid it. Now he not only had to face the same pressures I did, but his were amplified by the fact that both his father and grandfather had revolutionized the sport. Here he was, just a kid, trying to step into the shoes. It wasn't easy for any driver, let alone the son of two of the greatest racers of our time.

I thought for sure Sway would have freaked out looking at his black eye, but no, she just smiled and looked down at him. "How'd that work out for you? Did it go as planned?"

Axel being the smartass he responded, "Actually, yes. Thanks for asking."

At some point in your career you'd ask yourself if you were happy. Up until now, I hadn't had to even question it. I was happy with my career. I was doing what I loved, and my family was still a part of that. My boys were tearing it up in the USAC divisions, and my sprint car team was a force to be reckoned with.

The question came for me when the off-season hit and our eleven-year anniversary came around. Last year, for our ten-year, we were in New York for the championship ceremonies, and though it was nice, New York wasn't us. Sway and I needed *alone* time. With the way my schedule was for the off-season, I wasn't sure where that alone time could come in because, once again, the championship week was the same week as our anniversary. Having come in fourth this year, I had certain obligations for the season.

It wasn't even the day that we were trying to celebrate; neither of us minded celebrating another day, but it was just the fact that there wasn't *any* free time. So this left us with the week after Christmas. The only problem was I was again scheduled to be in Grand Rapids for my sprint car team. I was working on a few new sponsors and needed to tie up a few loose ends with them.

The morning I left, Sway encouraged me as she always did.

"Good luck," she said enthusiastically to me. Her face was hidden by the dark curtain of her mahogany hair as she tried to sew a button back on one of Casten's shirts. "I don't know why I try. I can't even thread the goddamn needle."

Chuckling, I leaned down to kiss the side of her neck. "I'm sure my mom can help you. She used to do that sort of thing all the time."

"Yeah, I'll ask her. She's coming over tonight anyway to drop off some new merchandise for you to approve."

"Right. I forgot about that."

"Make sure you update that Twitter thing, too."

"What?"

"Twitter. Emma set you up with a Twitter page."

I must have had a complete "What the fuck?" look because she just continued to stare at me as I stared at her.

"I think it's something like Facebook, only not as personal ... or something. Ask Axel, he has one," she looked up at me. "But I closely monitor that. I don't want any creepos following my baby around."

"He just turned twelve. He's hardly a baby anymore," I sighed, looking at my phone again. I didn't like the sound of this new stalker site. "When did he get this Twatter thing?"

"Twitter, Jameson, and he's had it for a few years. He has a huge following. It helps with his fans."

I knew Axel had fans. Little girls screaming his name like they were at a boy band concert, constantly surrounded his pit; the younger USAC drivers wanted to be friends with him. Whereas I was an asshole at his age, Axel was friendly to his fans and loved the attention he got.

"So what do I do with it?"

Sway took my phone and opened the Twitter application Emma had apparently installed. "There." She handed it back to me. Looking down at my phone, I looked at what she wrote.

@JamesonRiley Heading to Grand Rapids with my team

"Why in the world would you write that?" I was outraged she would go against my privacy. "Now these assholes are going to stalk me."

"Like they don't already ... it's a way for your fans to get a more *personal* experience."

"What about my *personal* experience?"

This just seemed like some invasion of privacy, and my wife had something to do with it. Traitor.

Clicking on the profile button, I noticed I had close to one hundred thousand followers. "How did all these people know I had this thing?"

"It was announced on your website. Do you pay attention in any of the meetings we've had regarding the public relations side of Simplex Racing or JAR Racing?"

"I do. I just didn't understand what Twatter was. I thought maybe ... let's say I was completely off base."

Sway smirked and stood up to walk into the kitchen. "It's Twitter, not Twatter. You're going to be late."

Right, I was supposed to leave. "I should be home in a few days."

"All right," she turned and wrapped her arms tightly around my neck. "I'll miss you."

I breathed in deeply, trying to hold on to her scent, making the few moments of alone time we had last before my lifestyle interrupted it. "I'll miss you, too, honey."

I said goodbye to the kids after that. They were all out back on the track. Lexi and Arie were the flaggers, and the boys were all racing. It took a great deal of effort to get Axel to actually get out of the car, but eventually I did and was on my way to Grand Rapids.

That's when it hit me. In between the moments where Tommy had nothing to say, I thought of Sway. I was questioning how happy I was with this entire situation.

I was thirty-four years old now. How long would this be okay with me? Or her? Would she really want this lifestyle forever?

Sway supported me through everything. Even when I wouldn't have agreed with myself, she supported me.

"Hey, Tommy," turning toward him, he looked over at me.

"What?"

"Would you be able to handle the meeting with QT?"

"Yeah—why?"

"I need to ... I *want* to spend some time with Sway."

When we landed in Grand Rapids, Tommy went on to the meeting while I flew right back to Mooresville.

Arriving home shortly before ten that night, Sway was in the movie room with the kids watching a movie. She nearly pissed her pants when I said hello.

"Holy shit!" she screeched along with the kids.

"You're home ..." the kids were enthusiastic, as was Sway.

"I thought you were in Grand Rapids," she said, moving across the room to stand in front of me.

I chuckled.

"Tommy went for me," I moved closer, my arms wrapping around her waist. "He told me to tell you that you owe him a box of Krispy Kreme donuts."

"Oh, well that's definitely worth seeing you."

My mom came in the room behind me. "I'm here!"

"What are you doing here?" Sway asked her curiously.

Mom giggled. "I'm watching the kids while you guys get some alone time."

"We leave for Jacksonville Beach in the morning." Reaching down, I picked her up bridal style. "But for now ..." I left my mom with the kids, giggling in the movie room, as I carried Sway up to our room.

"Thank you," she whispered against my lips with more urgency than I expected. "I needed this. I shaved my legs, I'm wearing a bra, and I look like a fucking lady so take me to dinner."

"As did I, honey, and by all means, let's go to dinner."

I checked out those shaved legs, removed the bra, and took my fucking lady to dinner.

I wasn't sure I was ready for retirement yet, as racing was too important to me. But I was ready for a little relief. Tommy had expressed interest in taking over more responsibility with JAR Racing, so that was an option. We had enough help that I could easily step back and just race Cup and help out with Axel's racing. Sometimes you needed to back-out at times—to reevaluate and think about what's important. For me, that was this family and the woman currently in my arms.

I enjoyed the road and my lifestyle for the most part, but there were times, late at night, when I thought maybe where there was loneliness there would soon be adaption. What if I came home one day and it didn't seem as though my family missed me? What if they learned to deal with my absence and eventually had a life without me?

Cold Pits – This is when there is no racing activity on the track, and the pits are open to people other than team members and racing officials.

As the off-season progressed, testing and sponsorship commitments crushed me to the point where I was physically exhausted. Having never really been one who got sick ... well, I had one hell of a cold that I was sure had turned into pneumonia by the time early February rolled around.

While hacking up my spleen, I made my way into my office at Grays Harbor. It seemed I still suffered from problems with my lungs and was susceptible to pneumonia.

Mallory found me before I wanted her to. "Jameson, we really need to take care of this."

I nodded. Nodding was all I could do these days. I just didn't have time for any of this. Too much responsibility led to me having too much on my mind.

We had schedules to finalize for the season, get the insurance policies in order, and line up track promoters for the events. This might seem simple, but it wasn't. Track promoters were constantly trying to swing their own deals, and sponsors for events wanted everything under the sun.

For the last nine hours I'd been at the track with Axel and Casten, and I was ready to go home. I loved my kids, but I could only handle them for so long. I could only handle anyone for so long before my patience wore thin.

Currently Axel and Casten were watering the track with Spencer. The only problem with this situation was that the boys were helping by attaching inner tubes to the back of the truck with a rope.

They were water skiing in mud.

"*Idiots*," I muttered to myself, glancing back at the mountain of paperwork. One of them was sure to get hurt so long as Spencer was driving. Pouring myself a glass of whiskey, I had to laugh because there were *many* times when Sway and I did this when we were growing up. Our spaz children weren't much different.

Sighing deeply, I began looking through everything while sipping my much-needed drink. It was overwhelming, and if Mallory hadn't been there, I probably would have given up by now. I couldn't thank her, Andrea, and Jen enough for all the work they did keeping Grays Harbor running. Even though I couldn't be there as much as I wanted, I had absolutely no intention of selling.

Shortly before eight that night, Andrea came in the office with Macy following behind her. "Hey, Jameson, we are leaving for the night. Sway called and asked that you come home."

I nodded, focusing on a few insurance claims that had been filed last year by a driver racing in the street stock division. He was claiming we didn't tell him he had to wear gloves. In turn, his hands were burnt when his car caught on fire. You'd think some of these assholes would have common sense, but no. Those were the jerks who gave everyone the impression racers were dumb.

On the way home that night, after getting the boys cleaned up enough to get inside my car, we stopped by the Ranch House and picked up dinner.

I spent most of the drive home listening to Axel and Casten in the backseat.

"Well, damn ... I didn't think of that."

"No. No. There can't be a damn in this scenario. Take it back," Casten told Axel, his voice serious. This was alarming—Casten was never serious.

"Oh, yeah, well it's not that easy, Casten. Might I add ... this was your goddamn idea?"

Hearing my twelve-year-old and eight-year-old cussing was a little shocking. But, not surprising. By the time Axel was five, we had to "out" the money when cussing, or Axel would be a millionaire now.

"I'm aware of that," Casten replied with a chuckle.

"I want no part of this then," was Axel's response.

Casten laughed. "It's a little late for that."

"All right," I finally interrupted. "What's going on?"

"Nothing," they said together.

"Someone better tell me," I warned, eyeing them in the rearview mirror. The passing streetlights provided just enough light to catch glimpses of their eyes.

As I expected, Axel cracked after five minutes of silence. He didn't like to see me upset, in fear I'd take his race car away. "Casten," Axel began when his words were cut off by a grunt. I heard the punch Casten delivered to Axel's shoulder and Axel whisper, "You asshole."

"Casten *and* me," he corrected, "well ... we told Arie to, uh ... she was tired."

"And ..."

"Well, she was tired, and we told her to just sleep in the back of Spencer's truck."

"So?"

"Well, Spencer's not exactly going back to Summit Lake tonight."

I knew that already. Spencer had plans to drive up to Burlington tonight, and then he was heading to Canada for the weekend to go skiing with some of his buddies before testing began.

"Wait a second," by now, we had pulled into the garage. I turned to face the boys. "You're telling me that your sister showed up at the track today, without me *knowing*. You told her to get in the back of Spencer's truck to take a nap, and then didn't tell him or me that she was back there when he left."

"That's pretty much it," Casten nodded with wide eyes. Axel just stared at me in horror that I was going to freak out. And I did. My little girl was in the back of a goddamn truck in the middle of winter, going down the freeway with my reckless driver of a brother.

"You're both grounded," I told them, slamming the car door. They followed me inside the house with the bags from Ranch House. "And, another thing ..." they stopped dead in their tracks, knowing damn well what was next. "No Duel in the Desert."

Axel looked like he was going to cry, and Casten could care less. Even though he raced, he just raced because he enjoyed it, but he held nowhere near the passion Axel held for it.

"What's going on?" Sway came bouncing into the kitchen behind us.

Casten hopped onto one of the stools next to the island, digging through the bags from Ranch House for his dinner. "Dad lost Arie."

"I did not. You two did." I pointed to both of them. "I mean it—you're both grounded and will not race in Phoenix."

"What do you mean Arie is lost?" Sway began to panic.

Casten, being a complete mama's boy poured it on thick. "I'm sorry, Mama," he hugged her while batting his eyelashes; she was a sucker for that. "But look at it this way ... you won't have to drive her to those stupid dance classes anymore."

Sway slapped his shoulder. "Don't be a jerk." Her panicked eyes found mine. "Where is she, Jameson?"

By now, I was already calling Spencer. "Apparently, your boys decided to convince her to take a nap in the back of Spencer's truck."

"*Okay* ... so where is Spencer?"

"Burlington. Actually, he's on his way to Burlington and then Canada."

It took her about thirty-six seconds before she finally grasped the meaning behind this. "Oh, my God!"

"Now you finally understand."

She turned toward the boys. "That was not a very nice thing to do."

Emma walked into the kitchen with Noah following her.

"Why are you two here?" I asked, annoyed when Noah kicked my shin as he walked past. For being eleven now, he was still an asshole and even more dangerous around cars than he was at two. He was a little fucker.

"We came over for dinner. Aiden and Charlie will be here in a few minutes," she looked around the kitchen. "Is Arie with Lexi?"

"Nope," Casten replied. "She's heading for Canada, eh."

"Canada?"

"Yep," he nodded. "Axel's fault."

Axel's temper was exactly like mine. How do you think he reacted?

In a very quick movement, he had his younger brother on the ground and in a headlock while Casten screamed bloody fucking murder for Sway to rescue him.

Spencer answered so I let the boys wrestle around on the kitchen floor while Sway tried to get them away from each other.

"Spencer?"

"Yeah?" I could hear the faint sounds of his truck's engine in the background.

"Where are you at?"

"I'm just outside of Burlington, why?"

"Because ... Arie is in the back of your truck,"

"What?" he panicked. "How the fuck did she get back there? Jameson, it's snowing and has been for the last half an hour."

Jesus Christ!

"Pull over," I demanded. Now I was the one panicking. Sway was clinging to my side, trying to hear everything we said. Emma rushed behind her, knocking all three of us forward into the granite counter.

There was silence for probably close to five minutes while I heard Spencer getting out of his truck.

"Jameson ..." Spencer's said, amused. "Your daughter would like some words with you."

Shit.

Arie must have taken the phone because the next thing we heard was her screaming. "Those two better pray for their lives because when I get home," she growled. "I'm gonna ... I'm gonna kill those assholes!" Her voice was marred slightly by her shivering.

"Without a doubt ... you are your mother's daughter," I laughed at my daughter's use of words. We tried to teach them to not swear, but really, were we good examples? No.

I ended up having a conversation with Axel later that night after Arie arrived home, and we were sure she was all right.

"Hey, buddy," the door creaked open as I stuck my head inside.

Axel looked up with a furtive glance. "Hey Lil, I gotta go ... Dad's here ... yeah ... all right ... see you then." His cheeks flushed as she said something else. "I ... love you, too," he whispered and then hung up quickly.

Chuckling, I moved inside his room. "Love, huh?"

He shrugged, leaning back on his bed and tossing his phone on the nightstand. I noticed a picture next to his lamp of him and Lily when they were about four. "Why not love?"

"Love is a strong choice to use when you're twelve, buddy."

"I know that ... but it's true."

"Fair enough, *but* you need to be careful. You're young, and so is Lily."

He sighed, that same sigh I used. The one I used when someone warned me about Sway when I was younger. Sure, it turned out well for us; we'd just celebrated our twelfth wedding anniversary. I was still just as much in love with her as I was the day I said, "I do." I also knew enough about Axel to know his intentions with Lily were genuine. Without a doubt, he loved her.

"Do I really not get to race in Phoenix?"

"You need to learn there are consequences, Axel. You and Casten both. What you did with Arie today could have really hurt her."

"I know ... but Dad ..." he whined. It was difficult for me because if someone had told me at twelve I couldn't race ... I would have had a shit fit of epic proportions, no lie. I was pretty sure I actually did at one time or another.

"All right, buddy, *but* if you mess with Arie again ... I'm turning her loose on you."

"Oh, dear God," he teased with a smile. He knew damn well what she was capable of. Arie had repercussions down to a goddamn art.

Patting him on the back, I stood. "I say the same thing about my sister."

I found Sway in our room rubbing Arie's back as she slept in our bed. "How is she?" My hand ran up Arie's back, brushing her rusty locks to one side, her breathing slow and steady.

"She seems good. I called Dr. Sipher. She said to keep her warm and hydrated," Sway's eyes met mine, and I could see the weariness in them. "Her temp is 94.5 ... that's a concern."

Sway and I spent the rest of the night in bed with Arie, scrutinizing every shiver and breath she took. Something very strange happened when you became a parent. Suddenly, you were no longer focused on only yourself. There was this tiny human looking up to you for comfort, reassurance, care, and most of all ... love. It was a huge responsibility, and I thought being a NASCAR champion was hard. That had nothing on parenting.

It turned out Arie was fine. She did end up with pneumonia, but she was alive, and the boys seemed to have learned their lesson. We couldn't ask for much more than that.

Whether you wanted to or not, there came a point when you were interested in what the public thought of you. I didn't care who you were. At some point you would care. I did.

I didn't know why I had Googled myself, but when I did, I wished I hadn't.

It was times like this that I forced myself blind and only saw what I wanted to. It didn't matter. All I saw were lies, but then I started to believe them.

There was tons of hate websites on me *and* Jameson. There were pictures of my husband with other women and pictures of my kids. It made me sick. I wasn't worried about the other women, I had no need to. I knew it was happening; there was no way for him to get away from them at times, and, yes, photographs were snapped making it seem like he was with them ... I knew he wasn't. I would admit, though, when Jameson denied it was happening, it irritated me. Especially when it came to Nadia, a woman who was around him constantly, and there were many pictures of them together. I knew what the pictures represented, but he'd blown them off as though they meant nothing.

To me, they meant something.

Lying to me wasn't the answer. I knew why he did it, but *lying* was never the answer.

Even with those pit lizards and Nadia all over my husband and Jameson insisting it wasn't happening, what bothered me the most were the pictures of my children. It felt like an invasion of privacy. Like having your home broken into, only now the whole world saw. Free to judge your dirty laundry the way they perceived it. Only they based their theories upon lies.

Three cups of coffee and half a dozen donuts later, I was still on the internet.

Jameson called around four to tell me that he was on his way home from the shop. He and Justin had been preparing the sprint cars for next season, and he was set to leave for Daytona tomorrow night for the beginning of Speedweek. Every spare minute he had was spent at the shop with JAR Racing.

So by five, I was now wearing sweats and still on the internet while contemplating making comfort cookies or fudge, lots of fudge.

I couldn't believe some of this bullshit out there. The articles and debates about Darrin and Jameson were sickening. I knew what really happened, but the idea that there were assholes out there who were still caught up in it some twelve years later was maddening. I wouldn't lie. There was part of me that thought Darrin was still alive. It was the thoughts that scared me the most now that we had children. Those were the fears that screamed for me to convince Jameson to run away with me and never look back.

When Jameson had finally come home, my laptop was in pieces on the floor in the kitchen.

He smirked. “Did it talk back or something?”

“According to Wikipedia …” I began, but stopped when his eyes flashed with anger.

Jameson groaned and walked out of the room. “Not that again.”

I told him everything I had read, and all the sites that believed Jameson had killed Darrin, and all the crap about Darrin still being alive. He turned sharply on his heel to face me. “I don’t care what those fucking websites say. He’s dead as far as I’m concerned. Don’t Google that goddamn shit again,” his face was dark and demanding. “I mean it, Sway.”

Despite what the websites said, even if Darrin was alive, it didn’t matter. As Jameson said, as far as he was concerned Darrin was dead. We’d moved on, or so we thought. Everyone thought we had this perfect life because we made millions each year, and Jameson raced in an elite series every year, but we had problems just like everyone else. We fought just like every other married couple, over the same shit every other married couple fought about. But we had other pressures most didn’t see. Our lives were in the public eye.

“I won’t,” I finally said, nearly in tears. It’d been a rough day.

He sighed, knowing he’d hit a nerve.

“Honey, I just … I don’t *want* this. I want to forget about it, and … I can’t. I’ve *tried*, but I can’t. So please, help me by not bringing it up.”

I understood why he wanted to forget, but in the same sense, I didn’t really want to forget everything. It was something we needed to remember for the sake of our children. The moment we let our guard down with them was the moment something would happen.

Too many times I’d had to have Van rescue me at the track or a restaurant when a crazed fan took it too far. That was why I never forgot. It was a reminder of how hostile this world really was and how fragile the lives of our family were.

Jameson wanted to forget, and I would respect that because his was more of the violence. Regardless of what many people believed, Jameson was not a violent person and tended to shy away from conflict in racing if he could. But he did believe in his ability, and if someone questioned it, Lord help them.

Tommy stopped by on his way to Dog Hollow that night.

"Hey, Sway," he called out and then headed up to get Casten and Arie. I didn't pay much attention to him as he frequently took my kids for the night. Tommy may not be the most mature person I'd ever met, but for the most part, he was good with my kids, and that was all that mattered to me.

"I'm borrowing them," he told me before leaving.

Later that night, I apologized to Jameson.

"I'm sorry," I told him, crawling into bed.

He was on NASCAR's website checking out an article they wrote about him the other day.

He looked up for a moment and then back down at the screen.

"I'm not okay with you believing that shit they put on the internet," he said, keeping his focus on the screen.

"I said I was sorry."

"I know," his expression didn't seem like he knew, though.

"Are you mad at me?"

"No, honey," he sighed, resting his head against the headboard and pushing the laptop aside.

His arms wrapped protectively around me. What his expression wasn't telling me his arms did. He wanted to protect me and couldn't. But it wasn't that he couldn't, he just felt that he hadn't so far.

Jameson couldn't be with me every day and that scared him. Over the years I began to understand the feeling, but I would never truly understand what it meant to Jameson to provide a safe place for his children and me. It was a feeling only a man could understand.

Despite my feelings over what I found on the internet that day, I never brought up everything I found.

Tommy returned with Arie and Casten the next day and his new girl he'd met the night before.

She went on to talk about how she loved my kids and thought they were the greatest, especially Casten.

That was when I asked Tommy's intentions.

"Fire crotch," he quirked an eyebrow at me, and I smiled, knowing he hated that nickname. "Are you using my children to get women?"

He kind of choked. He kind of snickered. And, then again, he kind of laughed. All that confirmed my theory.

"Why would you think that?"

"Oh, I don't know, maybe because all these women seem to love my kids."

He shrugged and reached for a beer in the fridge and then sat down beside me at the table. I could see Arie and Casten talking with the new girl in the living room.

"Hey, I was thinking maybe they could come with me to Jacksonville for the weekend."

"No, Casten has a race and Arie has dance class."

"Oh, well, how about I claim them on my taxes then?" he blurted out.

"Why?"

"They spend enough time with me. It's only fair."

"Are you really that stupid?"

"Sometimes," he admitted and then caught a glimpse of Jameson walking down the stairs. He leaned forward. "Don't say anything to Jameson." He caught himself and then glared. "Never mind, you will."

"Oh, hey, Jameson," I grabbed his hand as he walked past. "Tommy wants to claim our kids on his taxes."

Jameson stopped and looked at Tommy. "Why?"

"That girl in there thinks our kids are his. He's trying to make it legit."

"I never said that," Tommy added and then wrinkled his nose. "It sounds horrible when you say it like that."

"Is it true?" Jameson asked him and then poured himself a cup of coffee. He looked into the living room at the girl and then smiled at Tommy knowing what he'd done.

"Yeah," Tommy hung his head in shame. "It's true. In my defense, they could pass for my kids."

"Why do you lie to these girls?" I asked Tommy, shaking my head in laughter as Jameson stared at him in shock. "What's not to love about an overly confident orange head with commitment issues?"

"I don't know why I subject myself to this torture." Tommy rose from the table, but grinned despite our verbal abuse and took another beer from the fridge on his way out.

Every year when our family was finally all together we took a big family picture. That meant everyone.

We had our family, Spencer and Alley, Aiden and Emma, and then Jimi and Nancy, including all the grandkids.

This was never a good experience in the ten years we'd been doing it. Something bad always happened. It was similar to the holidays we spent together.

So that morning around nine, we all met at the Carolina Beach in North Carolina.

Might I point out that Emma and Nancy arranged this every year? No one in their right mind, in our family anyway, questioned anything Nancy said, ever. And, Emma, well we just went with the flow, it was easier that way. It was like trying to control Axel and Casten's hair in the morning. If you messed with it, it was worse. Mess with Emma, life became hell.

Getting my family there without an argument was an ordeal.

It started in the car on the way there when Arie laid into Jameson about wanting to get her nipples pierced. I tried to warn her that today was not a good day to be asking him questions like this, but she never listened to me. I didn't why I thought she'd start now.

"Dad," Arie caught his attention, and he looked in the rearview mirror at her. That was when she went in for the kill with her pleading eyes and smile. "I was thinking that I would like to get my nipples pierced."

Jameson's nervous chuckle rang through the car at Arie's request. "She's not serious, is she?"

I shrugged and pretended to find my cell phone interesting. "She's your daughter. What do you think?"

"Dad, it's just my nipples. No one will see it but me."

"Or maybe you just want—" Arie's hand cut off her younger brother's remarks before they could be heard.

"Never mind," Arie mumbled, slumping back into her seat. "I never get to do anything."

"Oh yeah?" Jameson challenged. "Sway." He turned to me. "Who is that little girl you take to dance lessons each week?"

I laughed and that shut Arie up. I had a feeling I needed to school her on when to bring up this sort of thing. But if I was being honest with you, I wasn't exactly okay with the idea of my eleven-year-old daughter having a nipple pierced just because her cousin did. If Spencer only knew that his beautiful, blue-eyed only daughter had done this at ten.

Jameson was grumpy the entire drive because he had to catch a plan to Daytona in a few hours; his daughter talking about piercing herself wasn't exactly helping his mood.

He also claimed he had no time to be taking pictures.

Axel was being just as grumpy because he'd apparently changed out the rear end in his midget only to have it leak oil all night.

Arie was not thrilled about getting her picture taken either. Casten, well he was adding fuel to the fire. Any time he sensed his siblings annoyed in any way, he tried his hardest to send them over the edge. Nancy found Casten humorous because if you took Spencer, Emma, Jameson, and me and added all those personalities together ... you got Casten Anthony Riley.

"Leave me alone, asshole!" Arie pushed Casten on the ground when we got out of the Escalade. "You're such a little jerk."

"Arie," Jameson warned in his stern fatherly tone. "Knock it off."

I cringed at my little girl's use of words.

"He started it."

"I don't give a shit *who* started it. Just act like normal children."

Arie snorted sarcastically. "And how do normal children act, Dad?"

"How should I know," Jameson shrugged, checking his phone, and Casten chuckled at him, picking himself up from the pavement. "Where the fuck is everyone at? Let's get this shit over with."

And that was why my children cussed like truckers.

Casten started in with Arie again, and Jameson grabbed Casten by the collar of his shirt. "You're going to behave today," he told him.

"Yeah, sure," Casten laughed at his father's weak attempt at controlling him.

"I mean it. You fuck this up, and I'm sending you to boarding school."

Casten and I both knew that would never happen. I'd bail him out within twenty-four hours.

"School it is," Jameson glared at me. "And don't you think about bailing him out. I know you. He needs to learn manners."

Casten being the smartass I always knew him to be, smiled. "Oh, Daddy, please don't."

Jameson smacked him upside his head, and his rusty waves danced in the breeze. "I blame you for this."

After twenty minutes, everyone started to arrive. That was when the real fun began.

Van and Andrea showed up with the Lucifer twins who were practically adults. Lucas had just signed with the Pittsburgh Pirates to play professional baseball. So he was here, in body, much like Jameson, with his phone molded to his fingers. From my experience, this was the norm for any professional athlete.

Why?

Because there was an endless amount of emails, phone calls, Twitter updates, Facebook statuses ... it was how they stayed in touch with fans and publicists. As you could imagine, Jameson hated all of that.

Logan hovered around Jameson since he was now working for JAR Racing. Anything Jameson said, he now paid attention to. It still made me laugh when I thought about Logan duct taped to a chair, and Jameson eating cereal, acting as though there was nothing wrong with what he did.

Van and Andrea had just moved to the East Coast to be closer to us. With Van and Clint being with us pretty much non-stop, it was almost necessary for them to live near us. Clint lived about a mile away; he was single and took our safety seriously. He was the one who followed us everywhere. As he had his own family now, Van came when security would be an issue.

"What time does our flight leave?" Aiden asked Jameson as he approached him with Noah.

Jameson peeked at his phone. "Two hours ... we need to get this over with."

"Agreed," Lane said from behind us. Little Lane was no longer little Lane. At sixteen, he towered over me in height, looked identical to Spencer, except with blonde hair, and loved to race dirt bikes. Currently, he was racing on the WORCS series, which was the World Off Road Championship Series that ran once a month primarily on the West Coast.

"Hey, Jameson,." Lane nudged Jameson's shoulder. "Can I come with you to Daytona?"

All the boys in the family loved Daytona.

Because of the women. Daytona was notorious for half-naked women flitting around. For teenage boys, I learned this was a dream come true. Mine were still a little young for that. Thankfully, Casten thought it was disgusting, and Axel, well, he didn't see any of that. If it wasn't a sprint car or Lily West, he never looked twice.

Jameson laughed, shaking his head. "Just keep your dick in your pants, kid."

"Jameson!" Alley slapped his shoulder. "Don't say dick around my son."

"He's sixteen, Alley ..." Jameson looked up to glare at her. "He knows he has one."

"Regardless, don't say that around him."

"Mom ... Dad says *way* worse," Lane defended with a grin of his own.

Casten jumped on my back after that, smooshing his chubby cheeks into mine. "Let's go get me some ice cream, Mama."

"I don't think so, monkey, it's picture time."

"*I* don't think so. Don't want to get my picture taken today. Maybe tomorrow," he shrugged, letting his legs fall from around my waist to dangle with his arms wrapped tightly around my neck.

"Okay, everyone, let's gather by the water," Nancy called out, while Jimi gave everyone the eye. The one that meant you kids better behave. No one in their right mind crossed Jimi either. If our family was a kingdom, Jimi was the king.

Jimi was still racing on the Outlaw series with Justin, Tyler, Cody, and the new driver for JAR Racing, Rager Sweet. Jimi talked about retiring, but just like every other Riley in the family, racing was his life. I had a feeling he would only retire if he were forced.

Soon we were all lined up near the water, although none of us were actually looking at the camera. My kids were messing around, trying to throw Noah and Charlie in the ocean. Lane was helping them. Lexi was standing off to the side shaking her head at them. Lucas was on his phone as was Jameson. Van was trying to keep an eye on a group of women gathered a few hundred feet away taking their own pictures of us, stalking Jameson as usual.

Emma was screaming for Axel to put Charlie down. Aiden was helping Noah out of the water by now when Casten pushed him. Alley and Spencer were arguing about Lane going to Daytona with them. Nancy was smiling, glowing actually, and Jimi was glaring at everyone.

This was our family.

You couldn't get us together all at once, but what family all got along?

None that I knew of.

The off-season for us was a time to reunite with everyone. We were all so busy throughout the year and had little time to actually be a family. We learned though after a few years, that was how it was.

When the picture was finally taken, Jameson pulled me aside to say goodbye. "You'll be there on Wednesday, right?" he asked softly, his eyes searching mine. I knew he didn't want me missing the Budweiser Shootout.

"Yeah, Arie has her recital on Monday, and then we will head out."

He frowned. "Tape it for me?"

"I always do," my lips met his for a quick kiss. He had other ideas about that, pushing me against the side of our Escalade. His hands crept under my sweater, lingering around the waistband of my jeans. Leaning into his warm embrace, the cool, crisp air blowing in from the ocean caused me to shiver.

Sighing, I pulled his face closer, sweeping my tongue across his lips. My dirty heathen reacted. We might've been thirty-six now, but we still had that spark.

"I'm gonna miss you so much, honey," he whispered, pulling back after a few more kisses.

Casten beat on the window in the car. "Get a room, old guys!"

"He's a little shit," Jameson muttered. "I'll be waiting for you."

I smiled, taking in his sparkling green eyes, the tired lines forming on his face as he squinted in the sunlight. Taking my right hand that was wrapped around his neck, I leaned my forehead against his, running my hand over the stubble of his jaw. "I love you."

"As I love you."

Jameson left after that, and the life of the racing season began. There was one thing I learned from Nancy as I sat there in the parking lot watching my husband leave: you had to just go with the flow. It was all we could do.

We were racers' wives.

Darlington Strip – Term used in NASCAR when a driver gets into the wall at Darlington.

"Don't take it personal, Jameson."

I fucking hated those words. Despised them even. Anyone who said that to me at the track, they better be ready for my temper, and maybe a fist or two.

When I thought about my kids growing up, I thought about every meal I'd missed with them. I thought about every race of theirs I'd failed to attend. I thought about missing Arie's birth or Casten's first birthday. I thought about how many dance recitals I'd missed. I thought about Axel's first Dirt Nationals and the countless races on Sundays because I was racing. I thought about how many times I'd missed Sway's birthday since it was the same weekend as the Richmond race. Then there were the anniversaries that were interrupted by the award ceremonies.

All these things ran through my mind whenever someone spoke those words to me. So to say this wasn't personal to me was bullshit. This was personal. I put everything I had into racing, including my time away from my wife and kids.

Throughout the years I'd raced in the Cup series, I'd never had a problem with Paul Leighty—until the August Watkins Glen race. The heat wasn't the only obstacle that day. Patience was.

Back when I was learning to race, I had to draw a line. You wanted to go out there and give it everything you had, but there were times when you had to think, "How much will this set us back if I wreck? How much will a blown engine cost me?"

After that, you looked at everything differently. In turn, your driving style changed and patience played a key role. That patience, for me, was there now. Drivers like Paul, not so much.

Besides Colin Shuman and me, Paul was one of the most aggressive drivers in NASCAR. He wouldn't hesitate to trade paint with you each Sunday. Like I said, though, we'd never really had any run-ins.

Paul, unlike most, never faded. His three championships throughout his Cup career proved that. He was just as fast on lap two hundred as he was on the first lap. Being a soft spoken reticent, he never got into it much, until Watkins Glen.

Everyone said you couldn't go two-wide through the fast uphill esses there. Well, as it turned out, they were right. This season, Paul and I, both hungry racers, were fighting for position. I somehow clipped the inside curb, causing my back end to hit his left front. Before we knew it we were off the track and picking out a nice section of concrete to mark up.

I respected Paul. After all, we started the same season, and I also respected how he raced me these past thirteen years. So when we got back on the track after that, he pushed me up in to Tate, causing him to spin off in the grass and lose some ten positions on the restart. Not cool.

"Did you tell his spotter I didn't mean to hit him back there?" I asked Aiden. We frequently used our spotters to communicate with other drivers.

"Yeah ... apparently he didn't get the message."

That was evident by the hand gestures I'd gotten.

"How many laps is this thing anyway? I feel like I've been out here forever?" We crossed under the bridge heading back into turn one, Paul on my inside.

"There's room on the outside if you need it," Aiden added when we approached the outer loop.

Kyle chuckled. “Two thirty six.”

“Oh, geez. Did they increase it?”

“No.”

“Well it feels longer.”

Another thirty laps and bumping and banging with Paul, my air went out in my helmet. While temperatures rose, so did my car’s internal temperature. It was well over one hundred and thirty degrees in my car at that moment. All things considered, I was not in the best mood.

“I hate to say this, but my air just went out,” I grumbled. “It’s like a fucking oven in here.”

“Are you serious?”

“Do you honestly think I’d joke about that?” I laughed despite myself. “There’s no fucking way I can finish the race like this.”

We made a pit stop after that, and they gave me a hose that ventilated air coming in from outside the car. “What do I do with this?” I asked, looking at the hose during the last pace lap.

“Hook it up to your helmet. We couldn’t get it in there with the net and still get you out in time.”

After some negotiating and yelling at my helmet and lack of space in the car, it worked, but did nothing for my mood.

Paul and I were running second and third with just a few laps to go when he, once again, got on my bumper on a restart. After fishtailing briefly, I got it under control and managed to finish second to Bobby with Paul behind me in third.

Wanting to show Paul just how pleased I was, I nudged him on pit road after the race. In my mind, I got my point across. Done deal.

Well, NASCAR had its own theory on that one. They didn’t want other drivers getting into the habit of running into each other on pit road. It was dangerous. We could accidentally hit either a crewmember or an official doing that sort of thing. I knew that, and I wasn’t trying to hurt anyone. Honestly, I was going maybe fifteen miles per hour. It wasn’t like I hit him going full throttle and body slammed him. I had more respect than that. I wasn’t Darrin Torres. I was just simply expressing a little concern for his lack thereof on the track.

Like I said, NASCAR didn't see it like that and sent both of us to the hauler to hash it out.

Paul and I left the hauler without speaking, and it took weeks to talk about what happened in Watkins Glen. He tried to talk to me when Casten and I were leaving the media center after the Bristol race, but I wasn't having it.

"Listen, Jameson ..." that was not the way to start a conversation with me. "I just don't see why you're upset. You race everyone that way. *You* can't expect to run me off the track without me getting upset."

"I don't race *you* that way, that's the point," my eyes met his briefly. "I didn't hit you on purpose." I kept walking. Casten followed, paying close attention to what Paul was saying. Casten might've been the happiest kid on the face of the planet, but if you messed with his family, he threw down.

"Jameson, don't take it so personal, it's just racing. And if I remember correctly, you got the last hit on me," he said condescendingly.

"I'm leaving." I was thoroughly annoyed at this point and walked inside the hauler.

"That's right, walk away," he glared, holding my eyes for a moment before stepping back away from me.

"Fuck you, Paul," I added before slamming the door shut.

Most guys, I thought Paul was one of them, knew what to expect out on the track. We usually never meant anything by the bumping and banging each week, and the drivers who did usually didn't have many friends out there. Sure, we never forgot, but we didn't go looking for trouble each week, which was why I couldn't understand why Paul kept it up throughout the race. He knew I never intended to hit him in Watkins Glen, but he retaliated anyway.

As I headed back to my motor coach, Nadia caught me again. Nadia had caused just about every wreck this season and wasn't exactly on any drivers' good side. I'd been tangled with her a handful of times and usually got it turned around before the race ended—aside from Michigan when she took us both out just five laps into the race. Did I confront her?

No. I kept my distance.

"Not right now," I told her when she asked if we could have a drink.

I knew where that was heading and I wasn't in the mood for her shit again. In a season where she was barely hanging on outside the top twenty in points, she felt the need to get attention from the drivers, confirming Spencer's theories about her sleeping her way to the top.

"You know, Jameson," I actually acknowledged her and looked up. "Sometimes it's nice to have a friend. That's all I was wanting. Everyone hates me."

I couldn't tell whether she was serious or not, but given my shitty attitude for the night, I replied as I always would.

"Your temper is the reason you have every other driver on this series hating you."

"Something you know all about," it was meant to be sarcastic, and I knew that.

"I do," I told her with the same amount of sarcasm. "You need to relax out there before you kill someone."

"Also like you?"

I lost it.

"All right." I turned to her, stepping closer, and had her backed against the side of her motor coach. "I've tried to be nice to you, but you don't seem to get it. No one in this series will ever take you seriously, and no one will take it easy on you. If you wreck someone, you better be ready to defend that action, which is something I know *very* well."

I walked away then. I could have said more, but I thought I got my point across.

When he came in and slammed the door behind him, I had a feeling something happened, but with Jameson, it was best to give him room. If you pushed, he blew. Just like the coals in a fire when the wind blew, they ignited. The more anyone tried to control Jameson, the more he defied them.

I knew this had to do with Paul as it had been all over ESPN and SPEED the last few weeks.

For about an hour, I left him alone until he tossed his phone on the table and stormed back into the bedroom of the motor coach.

"Fucking bullshit news reporters," he grumbled as he pushed past me, his knuckles meeting the closet door. "Goddamn it!"

Casten smiled. "He's had a bad day."

Nodding, I followed Jameson, but before I did, I looked back at Casten and Axel playing video games. "I'd go find something to do outside of the motor coach if I were you."

They knew Jameson just as well as I did. They knew he needed space.

Both of them were outside before I got the bedroom door open.

Jameson was lying on the bed with a pillow over his head.

"Don't bother me," his voice was muffled from the pillow.

"Don't bother you, huh?" straddling his legs, my hands reached out to his.

"Yes, don't bother me," his tone was clipped and slightly edged the way he spoke with reporters. Not me.

And despite his shitty mood, his fingers wrapped around mine.

"I think I could improve your mood."

He let go of one of my hands to rip the pillow from his face. "What did you have in mind?"

"Oh, you know ... it's been a while since I did any micro polishing," my finger traced the line of his ready camshaft through his jeans. For being damn near forty now, Dirty Heathen and Mama Wizard had no problems with dyno testing.

"I think that might improve my mood," his hands moved from mine to behind his head. "Let's see what you got."

Lowering myself down his body, his eyes lit up when I got his jeans undone. They rolled back when I went to work, and they squeezed tight, his legs stiffened, and he squirmed a little when he met his rev limit.

When I finished, I was a tad breathless and crawling up him. "How's the mood now?"

Jameson chuckled, slightly breathless as well. I felt pretty good about my efforts there.

"Much better, honey," his arms reached out to pull me close to him, holding me tightly against his chest. He was quiet for a while before he whispered into my hair. "Every year ..." His head shook. "It never gets easier. It's the same shit. Same fucking story they always wanna print."

"Do you ever think about walking away?" Deep down, I knew he never did, but I decided to test the water. Stick a toe in, so to speak.

"No," his response was immediate. "I can't imagine not racing."

And he couldn't. When I thought about Jameson, I immediately thought of racing. The two went hand-in-hand.

The season went on much the way it had in the past, Jameson and Paul never getting any better at communicating. But every week we just chalked it up to two hungry drivers. That was all any of this was, and you couldn't read into it too much.

I'd pointed this out before, but pit lizards these days were constantly looking for new ways to get at me. The more I won, the worse it got. The older I got, the more they swarmed me. You'd think getting older would deter them. As rumor had it, I got better with age. At least that was what my wife told me.

So in October when I walked into my hotel room while in Las Vegas for the race, I wasn't entirely surprised to see a woman in my room. This wasn't the first time this happened. I once woke up with one naked in bed with me, only to find out my goddamn brother had bets with Colin Shuman she couldn't get into the room. It was a complete misunderstanding and could have been a disaster if Sway didn't believe me, but she did.

"Jameson, please," the woman begged when I told her to get out. "God, you are so hot!" She was completely naked, her arms wrapped tightly around my neck, her legs around my waist.

I struggled against her grasp, but I had to give her credit, she was stronger than she looked, which was probably how she got past security.

"You need to let go, now!" my arms fought to get her away. "Get off me."

"Just give in. Your wife will never know."

Oh, fuck!

Sway had the room key, and I told her to meet me in here. *Oh, goddamn it.*

"Get off me!" I roared at the woman and gave one final tug to her body as she crashed to the ground, naked. I quickly averted me eyes, not that I even found her attractive anyway.

"No, no, no, no." I gripped my hair. "This can't be happening."

"What's wrong?"

"Go away," I said with a shaky breath and knelt on the ground so that I didn't collapse.

"Did I do something wrong?"

"I said go away. You shouldn't have been in here!" My chest vibrated with such a growl I almost sounded like something from a safari. "Get the fuck out of my room, right now."

"You're a jackass," she huffed and stomped out, slamming the door behind her.

My breathing was to the point of gasping, and all I could think about was Sway.

Did I tell her?

What did I say?

I tried to shut the questions up in my head, but they kept coming. When I glanced up, I saw Sway standing in the doorway. "What happened in here?" she asked, her lips pursed as she saw the sheets and blankets ripped from the bed.

"Nothing," I answered quickly, standing from my place on the floor. "I just ... nothing."

Way to go dumbass, lie to your wife.

"Who was in here?"

"Just me."

"Jameson," Sway let out a deep sigh shaking her head. "I opened the door to the bedroom when you told that woman to get out. I heard you, and more importantly, saw her."

Goddamn it, I fucking did it again. Just like the girl in Texas and Charlotte. I lied because I thought she wouldn't trust me, when she had no need not to. I'd had more women thrown on my dick than Hugh Hefner these days, and not once had I ever acted on it. But I lied to avoid telling her it was happening. Obviously, this had backfired on me. I also knew my wife well enough—she wasn't stupid, she knew it was happening. How could she not?

"I need to go," she said, turning toward the door. "I can't keep doing this with you if you don't understand why this is important to me."

"Don't do this honey, *please*," I choked, following her. "I love you ... just don't leave."

"It's not about love, Jameson. That we have and always will," her tear-filled, reddened eyes met mine. "You lied to me." Her voice was soft, but her words stung because it was the truth. "I know you well enough to know that you had no intention of sleeping with her ... but you *lied* to me. Why lie about it?"

"I didn't mean to. It wasn't intentional."

"But you did, Jameson." She stopped to look at me for a moment. "All I have ever asked from you was honesty."

I hung my head.

"I never meant to hurt you by it. I thought ... I thought not telling you would be better. It looked worse than it really was."

"I know what it looked like," her lips pressed into a hard line. "I saw it with my own eyes."

Flinching at her words, I hung my head. It had to hurt her to see that, but I knew what stung worse was me lying to her face.

"I'm sorry," was all I could say.

"I can't keep doing this with you. I know you would never cheat on me, but you're constantly lying to me."

"I've never cheated on you, Sway. I never would."

"I know that, but you still *lie* to me," she moved toward the door.

"I never meant to hurt you."

"What about Nadia?" She remained facing the door, her breathing light and calm.

I felt like someone had just punched me as she spoke those words.

"What about her?"

Sway turned around, her eyes searching mine for an answer that would have her doubting my love.

"Have you ever been with her?" her body trembled as she reached for the handle behind her back.

My eyes darkened as anger spread throughout. It wasn't an anger like before. Now it was almost rage.

How could she ask me that?

"Are you honestly asking me that question?" my tone was bitter and sarcastic.

Her right hand quickly swept across her cheeks, brushing away her tears. She turned to face the door again.

I panicked and ran over to her. "Don't go."

"I can't stay right now," she said, quickly wiping her tears away again. "I need some time to think."

"What does that mean?" My voice was harsh, my eyes flared with anger. The thought that she would ever leave was real now, and I'd admit, it pissed me off because I didn't do anything. Yeah, I lied, but only to protect her. I never meant to hurt her.

She didn't say anything for a long moment, and I wasn't sure she was going to until she sighed. "I came to Vegas this weekend because I wanted to be alone with my husband for once. Just for one evening, I wanted him all to myself."

"Sway, I—"

She shook her head. "Jameson, I came up here to be alone with you, and I see another woman, *naked*, wrapped around *my* husband. I just ... I'm not leaving you—that's not me. I wouldn't do that. I know you didn't do anything with her, but you lied to me; you always lie about them. I just need some time to think."

"That's leaving!" I snapped back at her brusquely.

I stepped closer to her, reaching for the door, slamming it shut.

"Anyway you look at, if you walk out that door, that's *leaving* me."

"*This* is why I need to be alone. You're acting like a child about this," she pulled away from my grasp. I knew she was referring to my temper and my inability to control it when it came to us.

"We need to talk about this!" I shouted.

"We need to think about this before we say something we'll regret. I need to go," she replied calmly because I was inept in doing so, and then she left. This time I just stood there until her actions caught up with me.

"Sway!" I yelled after her, but she never stopped.

I think I laid on the floor for close to an hour before I realized I was lying in the middle of the hallway. Pathetic, yes, but if you knew our past and what lying to Sway meant, you'd understand my frustration with myself and my option to just lay there.

"Are you all right, Jameson?" the timid sound of Alley's voice made me look up from the floor. I shook my head at her question. I wasn't all right. I was far from all right.

Spencer, who walked in behind her, sighed, and put his hand on my shoulder. "Sway left."

She had every right to leave. I lied to her ... I yelled at her ... I deserved this. I was hardly the model husband here, and in the fifteen years we had been married, she came second to racing, and she never deserved that. I knew how Sway felt about these women, and she had every right to want the truth. I didn't know why I felt the need to lie because I'd never acted on one advance. I had nothing to lie about, but I did. I lied because I never wanted her to know how bad it really was.

My eyes fell back to the floor. "Did she say where she went?"

"Casten is racing in Williams Grove tonight."

"Shit," I scrambled to my feet. I remembered he asked me to come with him the other night.

"Go talk to her and see your son's race," Spencer squeezed my shoulder. "The longer you wait, the harder it will be."

Alley stopped me at the door. "Jameson, you have an autograph session in an hour, followed by an interview with ESPN. You can't leave."

"Fuck that, I need to see my son race and apologize to my wife."

"So you want me to call up Simplex and tell them what?"

"Jesus Christ!" I threw my arms up in the air. "I can't be in two places at once."

"I'll go watch Casten and talk to Sway," Spencer offered.

"I'd rather you didn't," I clipped. Spencer meant well, but I just wasn't in the mood. Besides, the last time Spencer intervened in an argument we had, I ended up doing more apologizing.

There was no way out of the obligations, and I knew it. If I cancelled, I had to re-schedule, and with everything else, I just didn't have time.

So Spencer, once again, went to Casten's race and to Sway. Spencer, Van, and Aiden saw my kids more than I did these last few months. I was once again battling for the chase this year, and time wasn't on my side.

I'd done a lot of fucked up shit in my time, but nothing compared to the way I felt knowing Sway didn't want me around. After my interview and autograph session, I flew to Williams Grove, but Sway had already left for Mooresville with Casten. On the way there, I called.

"Sway?"

"Jameson, what are you doing?" she asked in confusion, the hum from the jet caused static on the line, making it hard to hear her soft voice.

"Well, I tried to catch you guys in Williams Grove, but I just missed you. I'm on my way to Mooresville now."

"We're not there."

"Where are you?"

She was silent for a few moments. "I took Arie and Casten back to Washington for a little while."

"Then I'll come there."

"No, you have to be in Richmond on Wednesday. It's Tuesday. You don't have time."

"I'll make time," I quickly said. "Practice isn't until three."

Again, there was a silence on the other end before I could hear her sniffle. "Jameson, I just need some time to think. Stay in Mooresville for now."

"Sway," my voice broke as I tried to catch my breath. "Honey, please, I need to see you. I can't leave it like this."

"And I need to be alone right now."

"For how long?" I pressed, getting impatient. I was finding it hard to breathe so I leaned forward in the captain's chair. My hands obsessively ran through my hair. "How long?" I asked again when she didn't answer.

"I ... don't know."

"So that's it?" I snapped. "I don't get a say in this?"

"I told you why I needed to think, and as my husband, I hoped that you could see that."

"What does that even mean?"

"Okay, stop!" she snapped. "Stop being an asshole. I don't want to see you right now. You lied to me, again. I asked you if someone was in there, you said no. I saw her. All you had to do was tell me the truth. Just like in Texas when that girl kissed you. You told me she didn't, and then I see a picture of her kissing you. Or what about the time in

Vegas when you woke up with a woman in your bed? You denied it, and I later found out why she was in there. I know that wasn't your fault. Or what about the drink you had with Nadia in the bar that I had to hear about from her? I don't understand if you have nothing to hide, why do you lie about it?"

"Because ... I never wanted to hurt you."

"But you did! Lying to me hurt worse than knowing. You, of all people, should understand why that hurts me. I know you don't sleep with any of them. Hell, the entire time we've been together I've never seen you give another woman an ounce of attention, but you can't tell me the truth."

The line was silent for a moment before I finally made it worse. "I don't know what you want me to say. I said I was sorry."

"And I said I needed time to think."

"Think about what?"

"Everything,"

"Are you ... thinking of leaving?" The dead silence said it all. I lost it. "Goddamn it, Sway, answer me!"

I threw a water bottle across the cabin. I never meant to yell at her like that, but the thought of her leaving me was not an option.

"No, I'm not, but I shouldn't be treated like this."

"Sway?" I looked down at the receiver to see she hung up. I couldn't blame her.

I wanted to drown my sorrows. I wanted to numb the pain I was feeling, but I also knew that wouldn't solve anything. I had done that for years, and it had never worked in my favor anyway. This was all on me, and I needed to just face it.

Once I got home, I did have a beer, or two, or maybe it was three, but who cared?

Axel was home, which surprised me. I hadn't seen him in a few weeks and thought for sure he was supposed to be in Terre Haute this week.

"What are you doing here?" I asked, peeking inside his room.

He was sitting on his bed staring down at his laptop.

"I don't have to be at the track until Friday so I thought I'd sleep in my own bed. Spencer just dropped me off," he looked up from his computer. "Where is everyone?"

"Elma," I mumbled, stepping inside his room to sit on the beanbag in the corner.

"Elma?"

"Yes, that's what I said."

He looked at me, confused for a moment, and then raised his eyebrows. "Are you two fighting?"

"You could call it that."

"Care to talk about it?"

"Nope." I took another swig of my beer. "She made it pretty fucking clear what she wanted."

"And that was?"

"Space ... or whatever."

I eventually stopped talking. Axel didn't need to hear about my problems, and he especially didn't need to hear about my problems with his mother.

"How was your race in Grand Rapids?"

Axel shrugged. "Won my heat, dash, and took fourth in the main."

"Not bad." I nodded, taking another drink of my beer before setting it down on his nightstand. "I see you took over the points lead last week, though."

"Yeah, but Woods is only ten points behind me."

Smiling at him, I chuckled softly. "You'll get it."

I spent the majority of the night sitting in his room with him talking racing. Even though everything was so shitty with Sway, it felt good to be alone with my son. I hadn't realized how long it'd been since we were together that way, and eventually we found ourselves hovering over his car looking for things that could give him a little more edge over Woods.

I knew Sway simply needed some time to think. She never stayed angry with me, even when I deserved it. That wasn't Sway. But she did need space, or whatever.

Lapped Traffic – This refers to any cars that are not on the same lap as the leader.

Leaving Jameson in Vegas was difficult, but I needed to do it. The only way he was going to understand any of this was if I left him alone. Being around me, he wouldn't understand it.

I had my reasoning.

A few days after Arie, Casten, and I flew out to Washington, I was ready to go home. I made use of my time there, though, and took care of any loose ends at the track. I also visited my parent's graves, something I hadn't done in years.

Casten spent the morning at the track with some friends while Arie and I snuck off to their gravesites.

We sat in comfortable silence before Arie glanced over at me. "Does it ever get easier for you, Mama?"

"No baby, but the pain fades eventually."

Arie looked over at me, her eyes worried. "How old were you?"

"I was six when my mom died and twenty-three when Charlie died."

"I don't know what I would do without you and Daddy."

"I know ..."

When I thought about my kids and the childhood they'd had so far, I couldn't think of any time when they'd said they felt neglected or missed us. Jameson might've raced a lot and sure, we didn't see him for weeks at a time, but that was always been our life. They didn't know any differently, just like Jameson didn't growing up.

All the things I loved about my childhood—my mom, Charlie—I found those things in my life now ... with Jameson and our family.

I knew I shouldn't be mad at Jameson for lying to me. He was protecting me from the evil pit lizards. I understood that. But it hurt that he didn't feel he could tell me. Jameson knew me well enough to know I wasn't jealous of them. What made him think I couldn't handle it?

No one wanted a marriage to fail, who would? And, no, I didn't think my marriage was a failure at all. One thing was particularly important to remember: you fell in love in the first place. Remember why you fell in love. Remember that feeling you got when you knew you loved them, and remember the feeling you got when you knew they loved you back. That was what kept the marriage from failing.

I remembered the exact moment I fell in love with Jameson. It was in the pits at Knoxville. I also remembered when I finally realized he loved me back that night in Savannah.

Leaving probably wasn't the best answer given the circumstances. Jameson was over-systematical in everything he did. When I saw the results from the Richmond race where he blew a motor after forty laps, I realized he'd pushed himself into blowing his engine. He did this when he pushed himself too hard.

After a week in Washington, we flew home to face reality.

When I arrived back in Mooresville I stopped by the shop to make sure Katie, the payroll manager for JAR Racing, had gotten all the checks out to the boys on time. Last month she'd forgotten.

That never went over well, so I decided to make sure she hadn't forgotten this month.

She wasn't there, but I found the paperwork that said she'd taken care of it and even managed to get the rest of the staff on JAR Racing's payroll paid, too.

As I was leaving, Nadia Henley caught me. She was driving for Leddy Motorsports, whose shop just so happened to be across the street from us.

I wasn't blind to the women around my husband. Obviously. When Nadia started in the Cup series, I thought of her as just another driver.

I saw the attention Nadia invested into Jameson and his thoughts. She'd start off by asking for his advice at the track, which he was willing to give. Then casually, she'd touch him. It could be as simple as brushing her arm against his, but still, she was going out of her way to touch him. Something I didn't appreciate it.

When I asked Jameson about her, I didn't intend to accuse him of any wrongdoing. But in the heat of the moment, I asked anyway.

Now that I thought about it, it wasn't Jameson who I needed to talk to. If I had these feelings, I needed to go to the source, and that was Nadia.

"Hey, Sway, have you seen Jameson?" Nadia greeted me that afternoon.

I wanted to say, "Well no, we haven't seen each other in almost three weeks because I caught a naked woman in his hotel room."

I didn't say that.

"Yes, he's at home right now."

"Oh, Justin said he was flying back with Jimi today."

Well, fuck.

"He is."

Nadia wasn't exactly all brains, but she picked up on my lie and smiled.

"Nadia, I think we need to talk about some things."

She smiled again, her innocence showing, and I wanted to punch her. I knew it would be immature, but any woman in her right mind would want to resort to childlike tendencies when her children or man was being threatened. But I took the mature route.

"I know that you have been trying to tempt my husband," she started to interject, but I held up my hand. "Now, before you start defending your actions or saying he's attracted to you or whatever, I've heard them all before. The thing is ..." I tipped my head slightly, trying to find the best way to put it, and I decided I just didn't give a shit. There was no light way of putting it. She needed to know. "You seem to have this version of Jameson you've created in your head as a guy who would leave his wife. You see the version of Jameson who battles each week with other racers and gets in the faces of reporters who question his fighting for the win. You don't see the version he lets me see. The side that is broken, bare, and vulnerable to the words that can destroy him. I see that because I'm his *wife*."

Nadia looked at me for a long moment before her eyes shifted to the sign that read "JAR Racing" outside the parking lot.

Her gaze shifted back to me, wounded, but seeing what I intended her to see.

"Not many guys take a girl in racing seriously," she spoke softly. "He did. He raced me the way any other driver would and for that, I respected him. I just thought, well, I thought wrong. I'm sorry."

After a few more parting words, we went about our ways.

I honestly thought that'd be the last time I saw Nadia come on to Jameson, but it wasn't. She tried numerous times to get to Jameson, all with no success. For me, personally, I had to keep in mind that this sort of thing happened with this lifestyle. We would never be immune to it, just as there would always be rival drivers.

"What are you going to tell her?"

I just grunted in reply, and then realized who I was talking to, and that answer wouldn't fly.

"I guess I would say ..." I started to speak and then stopped.

For the past week, I'd been holding on and hoping not to fall apart without her.

When that didn't work, I just went about my day, praying she'd take me back. In my head I told myself I'd give her one more day before I'd call. Well, that was three weeks ago, and I still hadn't called because I didn't know what to say.

That was when my dad told me she was home. There I was, on the plane back to Mooresville Sunday evening, going over schedules for the next season, as well as sponsorships.

I wasn't surprised. Lately, I had been involved more with the business side of Riley-Simplex Racing, as I was with JAR Racing, therefore, my time was limited. Usually I preferred to just drive the cars, but I enjoyed my dad coming to me and asking what I thought of certain moves within the company. After all, our program had grown considerably in the last fifteen years.

The more I thought about what I'd say to Sway, the more I didn't know and just blurted out what I thought.

"That I love her and I'm sorry," I told him, handing him my recommendations on the third driver he was adding next year.

"Jesus, I thought you were smarter than that."

I wasn't sure if he was referring to my idea with Sway or my thoughts on his driver picks.

"And what would you say, old wise one?"

"For starters, I would try to understand *why* she's bothered so much by the lying."

Right, he was talking about Sway.

I didn't like that my dad was right, but he had a point. He always did.

That week after she left I called every day, but it went straight to voicemail. Van assured me she was fine, and I didn't press as to what she was doing. I said I'd give her time and that I did. That was a lie; I didn't agree to any of this, but what choice did I have? I fucked up, again.

There was only one way to fix this, and I needed her forgiveness and trust—which weren't things she just gave away.

When I arrived home in Mooresville that night, I was surprised and relieved to see Sway's car there. What surprised me even more was her crying in our bed.

Part of me, the paranoid part, envisioned her with a suitcase, waiting on the front porch.

That wasn't my wife, though. She was in this to the end. Just because we'd fallen off pace didn't mean she took the car to the garage and gave up home. She would be the one making pit stops to fix everything she could.

Sway had been ignoring my phone calls all week and now, worst of all, I had to listen to her cry. I had to listen to the woman who owned my heart cry, because I, once again, had broken hers. She trusted me with everything, and I had let her down. I knew it wasn't about the women. It was the lying, something we swore we'd never do.

I wouldn't be able to sleep until we spoke so I watched through the curtains in our room as the sky turned to a hazy pink and eventually her crying stopped.

Finally, she let me hold her, while she cried a little more. Her tears fell down her face, soaking my shirt. I told her over and over again how sorry I was.

Although my phone had been vibrating for the past two hours, I couldn't think of anything I'd rather be doing than holding and comforting my wife.

Sway groaned when she heard my phone vibrating, and her body shifted under the sheets, revealing patches of skin I hadn't seen in weeks.

She yawned. "We should get up soon."

"No, I want to stay here with you." Our bodies brushed against each others under the sheets.

Sway grumbled into the pillow, "I need coffee."

I knew I wouldn't be forgiven right away, but it wouldn't stop me from apologizing.

"I'm so sorry, honey. I never meant to hurt you."

"Do you understand why it hurts?" she finally asked.

"Yes, I do," I turned her around in my arms to face her. She blinked a few times, clearing the tears from her eyes. "I lied to you. Worst of all, I kept something from you because I thought it was best for you." Moving my hand from her waist, I cupped the apple of her cheek and leaned in to kiss her lips. She didn't hesitate to return the kiss. "That's exactly what Charlie and Rachel did to you." My eyes focused intently on her, trying to make her grasp the meaning. "I will *never* lie to you again."

"I know you won't," she said, leaning in to kiss me again. Our lips moved softly for a moment before she pulled away. "Please don't. I want to know. I can't take it when someone thinks they know how I will react."

That next morning, after showering, I walked downstairs to find Sway making blueberry pancakes, the sweet smell of syrup and my favorite fruit carried throughout our home.

All smiles when I stepped into the kitchen, my smile grew wider when I saw she was dressed in a pair of sweatpants and one of my very first Simplex t-shirts that had holes from where it caught on fire. I'd seen Sway in some of the most amazing dresses ever designed, but I preferred her just like this.

"I could get used to this," leaning against the island in the middle of the kitchen, I let my bare foot slide up her leg.

"Morning," she smiled, licking syrup from her fingers. She pushed a plate of pancakes toward me, motioning for me to eat.

"Breakfast is ready!" she yelled up the stairs for the kids. When Sway turned around, I had my arms wrapped around her waist, pulling her against me.

"You get that I'm sorry, right?"

"I do ... and I know you understand why." Though she spoke the words, her eyes showed the fear. Fear I was determined to make disappear, and that would take time. Anyone who knew me knew I was incapable of waiting. But for her I would. I made a vow when we married and for her, I'd keep it through whatever life threw at us.

Casten was the first downstairs, jumping up onto one of the stools.

"Thank God she forgave you," his eyes widened at the sight of pancakes as he pushed his hair from his face. Sway hated it, but he refused to let her cut it these days. "I thought we'd never eat again."

Sways slapped the back of his head. "I cooked for you in Washington."

Buttering two blueberry pancakes and pouring an ungodly amount of syrup on them, Casten raised an eyebrow at Sway. "I don't think—"

"You shut up." Sway laughed, smacking his shoulder. "At least you had food."

"I don't consider McDonald's food," Arie added, sitting next to Casten who looked over at her pajamas, shaking his head.

"You look ridiculous," Casten told her.

Sway and I just sat back and watched after that when Axel came stumbling down the steps sporting a black eye and a fat lip.

"And where have you—" Casten asked, but was cut off rather quickly by Axel pushing him off the stool onto the tile floor.

"Oh, my God, Axel," Sway balked. "Don't do that to him."

Casten, pleased that he'd gotten attention from his mom, added fuel to the fire and pretended to be hurt.

Turned out, while racing in the Silver Crown series, Axel got into a fight with some kid who thought Axel needed a reality check. I guess my little five-foot-three son showed him a thing or two because he broke the kid's nose and dislocated his jaw.

Axel, a tad sheepish, didn't have much to say. Just like me, his aggression frequently got the best of him, and then the consequences came crashing down. For the altercation, USAC suspended him from all three divisions for two races.

"Should you talk to him?" Sway asked when Axel left with Lily later that morning.

I had to leave for Charlotte later that morning, but I did plan to talk to him about it.

"I will. Just let him calm down. Right now, it wouldn't do any good."

"All right, just ... don't want this to turn into anything."

Kissing the top of her forehead as she reached for the plates on the island, I whispered into her ear, "Wait up for me tonight, please."

Her eyes sparkled with a sense of need, the same need I had.

"Don't be late," she tried to hide the smirk but couldn't very well. "You have some making up to do."

"I know."

"And take out the garbage."

"On it."

"And feed Rev," she added. "The last time I fed that damn dog he knocked me into the pool."

"I'm sorry. I'll make it up to you."

I was more implying about the way last weekend played out, but I was sorry about Rev. The dog outweighed Sway and thought she was his own personal chew toy.

Sway, well, she had other ideas about that.

"That's a long list there, champ."

"Well, then you'd better get a pen and start writing anything else you want me to do. I don't have all day."

Instead, she grabbed a sharpie from a drawer and wrote on the inside of my hand. "Be home by nine or else."

"Nine it is."

I did one better and was home by seven that night, making sure the kids had something to keep them busy. Axel was with Lily before he left for Terra Haute. Casten was with Cole at Spencer's house for the night, building ramps for their dirt bike track. And Arie was with my mom, shopping in New York. I was not thrilled with my daughter shopping in New York either. It was too yuppie for me, but whatever pleased my little girl pleased me.

"Sway?" I called out when Casten finally left with Cole.

"In the bathroom," she answered.

We only had six in the house so it took a few to find her.

And there she was, in the large sunken whirlpool tub in our master bathroom covered with bubbles. Her long, dark mahogany hair swept over the side, her legs were bent revealing only her knees. She was stunning and just as beautiful as the day I had met her. Only now, she was a woman, a woman who owned me entirely.

I took my time walking toward her, stripping away my clothes as I walked, my eyes focused on hers as she smiled up at me. The warm glow from the candles lit throughout the bathroom made her green eyes smolder. Or it could've been that we hadn't been together sexually in nearly two months between our schedules and her trip to Washington.

Glimmering flecks of light radiated from her as her legs moved under the water. "You gonna join me or just stare at me?"

"I'm taking off my clothes, aren't I?"

Before she could say any more, I was slipping into the tub with her.

Sway's head leaned back as my arms wrapped around her. Though I wouldn't say it, this reminded me of the time I accused her of sleeping with Mike. If there was an award for the worst husband of the year, or decade, I'd definitely be in the running for it.

"I went to see Charlie and Rachel's graves. Arie went with me."

"Mmmm ..." gently, I kissed along her collarbone, sweeping her hair away from her neck as my lips got closer to her neck. My left hand wrapped around her hair pulling it to one side to give me better access to her skin.

Sway melted at my touch, her body relaxing instantly as her head leaned back. It'd always been virtually staggering to me what just being in the arms of a woman could do for a man. Back in the day, I took it for granted, compared to now, where I couldn't get enough.

"Was it hard for you?"

Sway leaned her head to one side, her legs shifting in the water. "Harder than I thought. It never gets any easier for me." I kissed her shoulder once more, taking the sponge on the tile next to the shower and covering her chest with warm water as she spoke softly. "I just thought ... maybe it might get easier, you know?"

"It won't. I wish it would, but it will never go away."

Her hands reached for mine, her finger running over callouses formed from years of racing and engine work.

"I know that you never meant to lie to me."

"Good." My lips brushed over her shoulder once more. "I would never intentionally hurt you."

We laid in the tub until the water was cool enough that Sway was shivering worse than Arie was the time she spent four hours in the back of Spencer's truck.

Once in our room, I warmed her up physically after playing the piano for her. She insisted.

"I want this to be good for you," I said, kissing her cheek softly as I laid her in the middle of our bed. Her legs spread, allowing me the contact I wanted.

"Why wouldn't it be?" she seemed genuinely curious. "We're good at this. Make up sex is good for us."

I chuckled against her lips. "I have about two months of pent up sexual frustration. I'll probably only last thirty-two seconds."

She laughed at my admission, kissing my neck softly. "Don't worry ... it will be like my first time. Though that lasted about a minute so he's got you beat there."

I glared, she laughed. "I won't let that fucker last longer than me. Get me a stopwatch. I'm going for one minute, and one-tenth of a second."

Her response was to push her hips into mine, her hands finding my hair. "That is definitely not helping me set fast time or in my case, slow time," I told her, shifting away.

"Jameson ..." she whimpered, reaching for me. "You forgot it's been two months for me, too."

"Shhh ..." I whispered, kissing the path down her chest to between her thighs. "I need a sponsorship guarantee."

I did some of my best deburring during that time, and from her moans, I'd say she enjoyed it. Chuckling to myself, and quite proud I might add, I crawled back up her body and rested between her legs, preparing for some much needed align boring. "Now prepare for the best minute of your life."

After I returned home, it took Jameson a day or so, and he seemed to think he needed to apologize more.

That night, though incredibly emotional, was probably one of the strongest connections we'd had in a while.

I found him in the kitchen, staring at the lake through the sliding glass doors.

"Jameson," my hands crept over his shoulders as I pressed my chest to his back. "I don't want you to keep beating yourself up over this. You said what you needed to say. I said what I needed. Let's just move on from this."

He turned to face me.

"Stop," he breathed, parting his lips over mine and trying to calm the storm. "I know I was wrong, but I told myself I was doing the right thing." His lashes glistened as though they were diamonds.

The fault here lies within me. I shouldn't have left, and I knew that. Face the fear that drowns the light, was what I always told myself.

Did I listen? No.

His hands were restless, searching for himself between the shadow and smoke. He needed me, and I knew that. He never meant to hurt me.

The sun was setting over the lake, chalky orange smudging the sky. Standing against the counter, I looked over at him when no words were spoken.

"Will you go with me somewhere tonight?" he asked, flickering his gaze to mine.

I blinked slowly, the sight of him being so vulnerable brought back so many memories, and my heart ached for him, for us.

His smile was soft, slightly higher at one side of his mouth, and my heart stumbled as I was reminded of the child in him I once knew. It was reassuring when I saw that side of him comforted by the innocence.

I stroked his jaw and shivered, outlining the curve of his smile as my fingers moved to rest at his mouth.

Our lives, much like cars straight out of the hauler, were never perfect right from the start. They required adjustments along the way. This wasn't any different.

I followed him up the stairs to our room where he pressed me against the wall. The light shining through our room was soft just like his touches. Inside the room, he had "Purple Rain" playing softly.

My mind flashed to that first night in Charlotte and the way his hand felt on me as he asked me to stay with him. And here, in a roundabout way, he was begging me to stay again.

The moment got to me. This was his way of apologizing again. I made a strangled noise and turned my face away.

"Don't do that," he choked out, wrapping his arm around my waist, pulling me closer. "Don't do that, please. I'm holding on by a string right now and to see you cry ... I can't handle it."

He pushed my dress away, and his hands lingered, memorizing each curve, the fabric rustled as it descended. His shirt quickly followed while our mouths became desperate.

His hand slipped around my back, his other rising as he grasped my hair and moans swallowed us as I pushed and pulled and arched my way to his belt. With his buckle loosened and pants unzipped, I worked hard to get his clothing aside.

His strong hands trailed over my body, and then his voice brought me back to his face.

"Tell me you love me," he panted, shifting his position to look at me.

I pushed his hair from his forehead, my gaze lingering and holding focus with his eyes before my lips found his.

"I love you," I told him between kisses.

He kicked away the remaining barriers of clothing and moved from the wall to the bed, my head supported as he lowered me to the mattress. His knee was between my thighs, tongue between my lips, my hands greedy as they slid over his back muscles and squeezed his shoulders in an attempt to bring him closer. After weeks of separation, I needed him closer.

His look was long and hard, our loud breathing filled the room as his hands rested on either side of my head, and he pushed forward. His knees spread my legs; each movement was slow and so good.

He pressed his chest closer, warm skin comforting.

"Your heart is beating so fast," he murmured, staring down at me.

I brought my fingers to touch his lips, outlining their softness and feeling his kiss.

"It feels it's other half," I said quietly, the volume diminished under the intensity of his gaze.

He shivered, my hands grasping his hair as his head tilted back, and then his trembling lips found my neck. He swallowed thickly, his mouth returning to mine.

Trembling fingers found my heart. "I want to live right here," he breathed, his arms shaking as he held himself above me. "Always."

I tasted the tears at the back of my throat and assured him that he already did.

He exhaled and pressed his lips once more to my chest. He studied my body with his eyes and tongue. I gripped the sheets and urged for speed as his fingers curled into the pillow.

I made a noise when he entered me, and he stopped, waiting for me to respond.

"No, keep going."

And he did. Just his skin against mine calmed me and assured me I was the only one. I knew that already, though.

Nothing compared to this feeling, to the weight of his body as he groaned and pressed himself closer, filling me with his love. But it wasn't suffocating at all. It was finally being able to breathe. These moments of skin against skin were the only time I could really breathe.

"You're so fucking beautiful like this," he panted, focusing on my face. "Flushed and breathless beneath me ... because of me." He accentuated his words with a soft grunt, his breath hot on my cheek.

My lashes fluttered, but I didn't close my eyes. I wanted to see his face. The way his lids fell and opened, and the way his mouth parted. I wanted the noises that escaped and the feeling of being wanted. I wanted it all.

He whispered that he never wanted to stop, and I whimpered a plea that no space remained between us.

"Fuck," he breathed, his nose brushing mine as he traced my bottom lip with his tongue.

He raised himself, hands fisted in the sheets and pushed forward. My eyes found his, grass green, bright with desire and but clouded with lust. My fingertips grazed over his flushed cheeks and then over his shoulders and to his sides.

My nails dug into his sides, while I kissed from chin to temple and back as he cradled my head. My eyes drifted closed and took everything he was giving me, groans chasing whispers of desire.

I guided my palm to his heart.

"Let this always be mine," I pleaded. His eyes blinked heavy, and my words were low. "Please. Always."

He took my bottom lip between his teeth before pushing forward one last time, a low moan trapped against skin.

"It's *always* been yours, Sway," he murmured against my chest. "That will never change. Never."

I wrapped my arms around his neck, slick bodies meeting their limit and shadows lighted. Lines that had formed drifted in the wake, and hearts connected in their path. The fear of being alone faded with his embrace, and I knew then we'd be okay.

"Don't ever leave me again," he said, staring at me, holding my gaze with a fire that was still present and burning just as bright as the day we formed this sacred bond. "I can't do this without you. It would kill me if you left me."

The way he watched me, scrutinizing every breath and every blink assured me there was no bitterness there. He didn't hate me for leaving and forgave as unconditionally as he loved, with every fiber, every piece of himself that he gave to me. That was the way it always was between us.

Brake Caliper – The part of the braking system that, when applied by the driver, clamps down on the brake to slow the car.

Soon after Axel turned sixteen, we headed to Tulsa for the Chili Bowl. I hadn't been in three years and wasn't even racing this year; this was all about Axel. It was also strictly a "boys" trip.

Sway, Alley, Emma, and my mom took the girls to the Florida Keys for the weekend. This left me traveling with all the males in my family. Not something I enjoyed.

I had one order for my wife, though. No partying with my sister. She agreed, and I hoped she kept that promise.

Despite my concerns for my wife, all was outweighed by Axel's excitement.

The entire plane ride you could see the excitement in his eyes, but you could also see the nervousness peeking through at times.

The racing started with hot laps and practice on Monday and the final A-Main event on Saturday. Wes flew us to Tulsa on Sunday morning. Axel's midget was already there waiting for us, courtesy of Tommy and Justin's cousin, Greg.

After a half-assed continental breakfast Monday morning, we were on our way to the Tulsa Expo Center to get Axel registered.

My brother had other ideas and was acting like an idiot trying to get free bagels from the Embassy Suites where we were staying.

"Come on, Spencer," I groaned. "For once ... act normal."

I just wanted to get to the track, and my idiot brother, who was forty-three years old, was conning innocent hotel clerks out of ten dollars worth of bagels.

"Not possible," Cole, Spencer's youngest, guffawed with a smile. "He's incapable of it."

Still arguing, we all piled into a cargo van Alley rented for us.

"People are going to assume you're some kind of ... weirdo ... stealing bagels like that," Aiden told him, eating a package of peanut M&Ms he stole from the counter in the lobby. He wasn't any better.

"Oh, and what will they think of you?" Spencer snorted, angry he didn't get his bagels.

"Well, based on the tightness of these damn jeans, they are going to know for a fact that I am hung like a fucking horse. Where did these come from?"

"Your wife probably," Spencer replied, ripping the candy from his hands. "That's what you get for letting her buy your clothes."

Axel didn't say anything while all this was going on. Casten tried to provoke him, but he never responded. He stared out the window at the snow along the Interstate 44 while his iPod blared in his ears, his head bobbing to the beat.

I knew this was his distraction, so I didn't bother him and pulled his annoyingly entertaining twelve-year-old brother away from him.

"Why don't we give Axel a break?"

Casten smiled. "I don't think so. It's fun to get him mad."

"Fun for you or fun for him?" my eyebrow raised in question.

"Me, of course," he bounced up, snatching Axel's phone from him as he was sending Lily instant messages.

Axel snapped, yanking his headphones from his ears.

"Give that back!" he yelled, causing everyone in the van to look over at him.

"All right, boys," keeping my voice calm, I put my arms between Axel and Casten. "Casten, give him his phone."

"He should be concentrating on racing ... not Lily in a bikini," Casten snickered, holding the cell phone above his head, giving Lane and Cole behind him a clear view of Lily's modeling pose.

My first thought was, why she was sending him that kind of thing? My second was you weren't any better at sixteen. If a sixteen-year-old Sway had sent me a picture of herself in a bikini, you wouldn't have seen me for hours while I took proper care of bleeding my pressure valve.

Now that his little brother, as well as his cousins, had seen his half-naked girlfriend's body, I was sure Axel was irritated with Casten.

"You fucking jerk," he stood up, reaching for him once again. "Give that to me!"

If you thought I was protective of Sway, my son had inherited that side with Lily.

In one quick motion, Axel had grabbed him by the sweatshirt, dropped his shoulder, and punched Casten in the stomach with, I was sure, as much force as he had. Casten fell over, clutching his stomach, coughing, and then choking as he started crying.

I wasn't sure what to do, because really, if Spencer had done that to me, I would have punched him. "Uh ..." I stammered as I glanced between Axel, who had sat down now, having pulled his hooded sweatshirt over his head, and Casten, who was hunched over in pain.

There wasn't much of a size difference between the boys, and I figured that had to have hurt. I knew when Spencer punched me at that age I felt it. Axel wasn't big by any means; he was the smaller of our kids at barely five-foot-eight. Casten was catching him in size, but still, Axel put all he had into that punch.

This was one of those moments where I needed Sway; she'd know exactly what to do. Looking to Spencer and Aiden for advice did nothing. They couldn't believe he did that either and stared back at me with wide eyes. Axel had hit Casten before, but never like this.

Aside from Casten's coughing, an eerie silence spread over the van. Thankfully, he stopped the crying. My dad, who'd remained quiet this morning, nudged me when Axel took the sleeve of his black sweatshirt and swept it across his cheek, wiping tears aside. I knew he didn't mean to hurt his brother, but he was also already freaked out about racing in the Midget Nationals. He didn't need his little brother adding to his already jumbled mindset.

Oh, goddamn it. Where was Sway? Now I had two kids crying.

"Talk to him," he whispered, slouching in his seat, tilting his head toward Axel in front of me. "And, for God's sake, comfort the little one."

Both my parents were suckers for Casten, as most people were. I had to admit that Casten was adorable. He looked similar to Axel, but had Sway's big eyes, thick black lashes, chubby cheeks, and nose with my good looks. We had made some cute kids.

When he fluttered those sad, big eyes, *everyone* gave into him.

Casten had pulled the hood of his sweatshirt up over his head, as well. His tears were still streaming down his cheeks as he tried to shield them from view. I could count the number of times I'd seen either one of my boys crying, and it was usually earned.

Not that being punched in the stomach didn't warrant a few tears, but he had to understand if you provoked someone enough, they reacted. Maybe not in the best ways, but they reacted in some form. And you were usually not on the favorable side.

"Are you all right?" I whispered in Casten's ear, lifting his gray sweatshirt to see a swollen pinkish mark just below his ribcage on his left side. Axel had really nailed him. Already there were faint purplish bumps forming around the pink raised skin, indicating a bruise was forming.

Remaining slouched beside me, Casten didn't say anything and wouldn't look at me.

Thankfully, we pulled into the Tulsa Expo Center. It wasn't even ten yet, and already the day had turned to shit.

Justin and Tommy met us outside the Expo Center. Tommy, not knowing what just happened, grabbed Casten when he jetted from the van and threw him over his shoulder. Casten vomited down his back and then started crying again, but reached out with his foot to trip Axel as he walked by.

That started an all-out war between them, ending in Axel slamming Casten against a pillar outside, his hands fisted in his sweatshirt. Casten's head snapped back against the metal. "Leave me alone!" Axel pulled him forward and then pushed him back against the pillar once more. "I mean it, leave me alone!"

Tommy, Justin, and I intervened.

"Axel, Jesus, stop it!" I warned sternly, pulling Axel while Justin grabbed Casten, holding him against his side in a somewhat protective stance.

Casten's eyes were wide, filled with tears and fear.

Axel pulled his hood back over his head, grabbed his backpack, and headed inside with me following close behind him.

Reaching out, I grabbed the strap of his backpack, jerking him backward. "What the hell was that back there?"

"Nothing," he snapped, handing the registration desk his release forms and then handing the minor waiver to me. "Sign that."

I did and handed it to the lady behind the table, her eyes focused on me and my son glaring at each other. "It wasn't *nothing*. Your brother could be seriously hurt from that."

"Doubt it."

His phone beeped in his hand. He glanced down but didn't answer it, instead slipping it inside his jeans.

His chin came up, and his head tilted to the side. I could see so much of myself in him right then. "Keep him away from me today."

This was not what I had planned for today.

A fellow Cup driver of mine, Andy Crockett's, son, Hayden, came walking up to Axel. "Axel, you get registered?" he smiled when he saw me standing behind him. "Hey, Jameson, my dad's over there somewhere."

Hayden was already dressed in his racing suit, waiting for practice sessions to begin, and I could tell Axel was anxious to do the same.

From the time I had started coming to Midget Nationals with my dad when I was probably eight, the excitement of being at the world's largest midget race had never faded.

Chili Bowl Midget Nationals was the only event that took the best midget drivers from USAC, Badger (Midget Auto Racing Association), the Rocky Mountain Midget Association, USAC sprint car drivers, USAC Silver Crown drivers, and the World of Outlaws. All the best open wheel drivers in the world were put in one place for one weekend of competing for twenty-four starting spots in the A-Main. I honestly believed the racing at the Chili Bowl was some of the best in the world.

Too bad I wasn't racing this year. This year was about my son who was already strapping into his car.

Hovering over him, I handed him his helmet as he pulled his buckles over his shoulder one at a time.

"Stay relaxed out there, buddy. Just get a feel for the track and the way the car feels to you."

Axel nodded, his gaze fixed ahead of him. It was apparent now was not the time I would be able to talk to him. He needed to get out there and calm himself down.

When he reached for his helmet after pulling the arms straps tight, his hands trembled.

As his dad in that moment, I wanted to comfort him, but as a fellow racer, I knew he didn't need it. He needed the car.

The practice sessions were formatted differently for national events like this. You received a number when you registered, and that designated which was your first practice session. Axel was in the seventh session. This was good because it was later in the afternoon and a good amount of rubber had been laid out on the clay.

Midgets had a starter in them with an in-line clutching system, which meant they had one gear just like sprint cars. The only difference was that the driver could take off at will as opposed to a sprint car where you needed a push to get going.

Justin found me after his practice session, his expression both uneasy and frankly, a little annoyed. "What's with him today?"

We took a seat in the pit bleachers.

“I don’t know,” I shrugged. “Nerves I guess.”

Justin seemed to contemplate this for a minute. “Yeah, I guess this is the biggest race he’s been in, huh?”

Nodding, I examined Axel’s first few laps on the track. In his practice session he had Hayden, Tyler, Cody, Ryder, Brett Lucan from the Badger division, Travis Quinn from the Rocky Mountain Midget Association, and, worst of all, my dad, more importantly, Axel’s grandpa ... the king of the open-wheel ... racing on dirt.

“This oughta be interesting,” Spencer said, a hotdog in one hand and a plate of nachos in the other, taking a seat on the other side of Justin.

“Do you ever stop eating?” I asked, stealing a cheesy nacho. “No, do you?”

“No.”

The official waved the green flag for the start of the hot laps. Jimi started midway through the field and hung out toward the rear, getting a feel for everything. Axel seemed to do the same for the first three laps of the twenty-lap session. Coming out of turn three on the fourth lap, he went up high on the berm, passing by Tyler and Cody in turn four, leaving him in some clean air.

Axel spent countless hours watching racing and learning from some of the best around the world. He knew how to race, and I knew damn well he could win this race if everything lined up. You couldn’t just have talent, not at these events. Engines blew, drivers misjudged, and race officials made shitty calls at times. It wasn’t about talent all the time. Mental awareness was the key and knowing what could happen was half the battle.

But the most import aspect of winning was keeping a clear head, and that was something that Axel did not have right now.

Brett Lucan of the Badger Division was an eighteen-year-old kid who Axel hated.

Probably as much as I hated Darrin back in the day.

Brett was always looking for a fight and constantly sought out Axel on the track if he could. Keep in mind this was the same kid Axel got suspended over last year. This was also a reason why Brett raced the Badger series now. Even though Axel was suspended, the Riley family did hold a certain bit of weight with USAC.

Usually the kid couldn't finish a race without ending up in the catch fence so it was rare he actually got to Axel during a race. It was generally after the race or at national events when their paths crossed again.

As I said before, this was a practice session. It wasn't a time to be battling for position with anyone, and Axel understood that to an extent. Lucan did not.

When Axel came out of turn two on the eighteenth lap, Lucan swept down under him, pushing him up into the wall and then back down on the cushion. Usually that was a move by another racer saying, "Hey, I'm down here and have position on you." In open-wheel, it was easier to see another driver as opposed to stock cars, but you still couldn't see *everything*. That was where we usually relied on small taps from other drivers. That was not a small tap and ended up cutting Axel's tire down and breaking the front control arm.

Axel sat up near the wall on the backstretch when they threw the caution and ended the practice session early to clean up the mess. He stayed in the car, which was probably a good thing when we heard the engines of the cars filing off the track beside us. My dad's car pulled up right beside Lucan's car. Dad revved the engine twice, before waving, pointing to the track, and then throwing his arms in the air. This was racer talk for, "What the fuck was that?"

Tommy was down on the track helping Axel, when Justin, Aiden, and Spencer broke out into laughter at our sixty-three-year-old father picking a fight with an eighteen-year-old kid over his grandson.

Drivers who have watched Axel from the time he raced his first USAC race at age four also got in on the "What the fuck, Lucan?" action ... drivers like Ryder Christenson, Cody Bowman, and Tyler Sprague just to name a few. Sure, these were my boys and thought of Axel as their own, but that was how racers worked.

Let's just say Lucan never made it past the second night of racing;

he had no friends after pulling that move. No friends on a track was bad news any way you looked at it.

Keeping Casten and Axel separated the rest of the evening was easy. Casten and Cole were quite the pair together and spent the majority of the week in Ryder's pit—Casten thought Ryder was the greatest ... probably because Ryder and the boys had about the same maturity levels.

After the wreck with Lucan, Axel's patience was non-existent.

Tommy and Greg went to work changing out the right control arm and gears for tomorrow's heat races while Axel stood just outside the hauler signing autographs.

Most of the people surrounding him were the same who surrounded my dad and me, but I noticed a girl standing awfully close to him who I didn't recognize. Van was here with us, keeping his distance, but I could tell he was aware of the situation.

"Who's that?" Justin asked, nodding in the direction of the girl.

"I don't know. Fan maybe ..." my voice trailed off when the girl leaned over and kissed him on the cheek. Axel flinched away from her indicating the kiss wasn't wanted.

"Looks like he's got the Riley charm with the girls," Justin snorted, walking away.

There was one bad thing about your son dating your best friend's daughter—what if he broke her heart?

Knowing Axel, he had no intention of ever hurting Lily, but then again, I never had any intention of hurting Sway. I'd like to think that Justin understood that, after all, we'd become pretty close over the last sixteen years.

I watched for a little while as fans and the media continued to crowd around Axel. He had just turned sixteen in December, which meant he was the youngest driver here and that was news.

A group of girls around seventeen, maybe eighteen, shuffled past me, smiling. I knew what they wanted when they pushed their programs in my face.

"Is that your son?" the shorter black-haired girl asked with a small smile.

Without looking up, I nodded. "Yeah."

"Wow, you look too young to have a son."

My eyes met hers for a moment before handing the program back to her with my autograph spread across the cover. "I'm damn near forty. I'm old enough."

The blond one giggled. "You still married?"

Jesus, she's bold.

I laughed. "Yes."

"What about your son?"

"He's dating someone."

This wasn't the first time someone asked about Axel's dating status. I actually got that a lot around the time he turned fourteen and won the Hut Hundred. There was no way around it now, my little spaz son was famous and sought after by women—women Sway and I wanted to keep away from him.

Before Axel could get completely swamped by fans, I pulled him aside to get some food, *alone*.

We ended up at El Guapo's Mexican restaurant in downtown Tulsa.

Axel was quiet until midway through dinner when his phone kept vibrating.

He finally shut it off and sighed.

"Girl problems?" I hinted, taking a drink of my beer.

"You could say that ..." he nodded, pouring salsa and sour cream on his nachos. After another few minutes of silence he opened up to me. "Lily ... well, I *think* she wants to date other guys, maybe closer to Hillsboro."

Justin and his family still lived in Hillsboro, Indiana. It was easier for them with the majority of the Outlaw races taking place in the Midwest. This was not ideal for Axel and Lily, but over the last sixteen years, they'd remained best friends and eventually began dating. Most of the time they went weeks without seeing each other, but there was also a great deal of the USAC races that took place in the Midwest enabling them to reunite.

Time wasn't about to get any easier for them and probably never would with Axel's desire to race. This coming season he was set to race his first full season in all three of the USAC divisions. Time would definitely not be on his side.

"And how does Lily feel about this?"

Axel glared. "She's with some kid named Brian tonight. She says he's just a friend."

"Just a friend?" My eyebrow raised in question.

"So she says," I could tell Axel did not think Brian was just a friend.

"Is that why you shut off your phone?"

"No ... yes. I just ..." He sighed, pushing his half-eaten plate of nachos aside. "I just feel like I'm being pulled all over the place, and she doesn't understand that. I thought she understood, but now, I just don't know."

"I'm sure she does, buddy. She's grown up around it as well."

"I know."

The waiter brought by another beer for me and refilled Axel's Pepsi. "Did you talk to Casten?"

"No." His eyes met mine. "I never meant to hurt him, but *Jesus* ... he's got to stop sometimes."

"He's twelve, Axel, and he will always be your little brother. He doesn't always know when to stop. Look at my siblings ... they still piss me off daily."

He nodded but didn't say anything.

"Axel ... you need to think before you react with him and Arie. They're your family. *And* on the track, well, the sooner you realize how mental this sport is compared to how physical it is, the better off you'll be."

Axel chuckled. "Grandpa tell you that?"

"Yeah, some of his timeless wisdom."

When we headed back to the hotel, Lily sent him another text message, telling him she loved him and wished him good luck tomorrow. "See, I don't get it." He showed me the message. "She tells me she's hanging out with other guys, and then she tells me she loves me ... what the hell?"

"Just give her space. Being sixteen is hard enough. Then you add on having a boyfriend who is a professional race car driver, and that's a lot to handle. Think about how she feels with girls all over you?"

"She hates that," he groaned. "Mom does too, huh?"

"I'm sure Lily does, but your mom is different. Before being my wife, she was my best friend and understands what I go through every day. She's seen it from the beginning."

Axel nodded again, buckling himself into the front seat of the truck we drove here. He looked like he was going to respond to the message Lily sent him, but he stopped and slipped the phone inside his coat pocket.

"Do you know that girl who kissed you on the cheek?"

He didn't look over at me, but just stared out the window as I pulled out of the parking lot. "Yeah, that's Shaylee. Her dad is a sponsor rep for Wyle."

"Do you know her well?"

"Not really," he shrugged. "She's at most of the races, but we don't talk that often."

"Be ... careful."

Again, he didn't say anything, and part of me wondered if something had already happened between them.

I made a mental note to talk to Sway about this. She'd know what to say.

The rest of the week through all the heat races, Axel kept advancing. They had two hundred and sixty-three drivers here this year with ten main events planned for Saturday. The fastest four qualifying cars were in the A-Main with the top two cars from each main advancing to the next main.

Since Axel broke the control arm in practice Monday, we had

some trouble getting the setup to the point where he felt comfortable, so he ended up starting in the D-Main event.

Lily showed up on Friday night improving his mood greatly.

Looking back on the way I acted at events like this when I was his age, Sway was always what I needed. It wasn't any different for Axel.

Casten made an appearance shortly after Lily arrived. He smiled, but surprisingly didn't say anything.

Tommy and Greg were changing the gears on Axel's midget before the last heat race when Axel pulled Casten inside the hauler, leaving me and Aiden standing in his pit wondering if we should follow them after what happened Monday.

Even though you fought with your siblings, there was never a time when I didn't love them. Yeah, I'd hated them on occasion, but I never wanted to hurt them. And I knew Axel never wanted to hurt Casten.

After about three minutes, they came walking out and went different directions.

"What was that about?" I asked Casten, making sure he was all right. Since he and Axel had gotten into it on Monday, he hadn't been the high-spirited little boy he usually was.

Casten shrugged, retrieving a Gatorade from the cooler beside the hauler and sitting down in a pit chair. "He told me he's sorry."

"And you said?"

"He better be."

"Casten ... if I remember Monday morning at all—I remember you actually started that."

"So ..." he gave me a blank stare.

I kicked his leg. "You should apologize, too."

"Geez, Dad," he groaned, throwing his head back, annoyed. "What do you take me for, some kind of idiot? I said sorry."

"Good," I picked him up out of his chair and threw him over my shoulder. "Now ... let's go cheer on your brother."

He laughed.

"Put me down," he wiggled laughing again when I squeezed him harder. "You look ridiculous, put me down. I'm not a toy."

My right hand scooped him into a headlock before setting him safely on the ground. He smiled but rolled his eyes and straightened his hat. "Have some dignity."

"Do you even know what that means?"

"No, but neither do you apparently."

Everyone filed into the stands when the cars lined up. Aiden, Spencer, and Van made their way to us with Lane, Cole, Logan, and Noah close by. Who knew where Charlie had disappeared. Between the two of Aiden's boys, Charlie was the worst. Whenever Charlie was a handful for Aiden, Dad stepped in and laid down the law with them. Most of the grandkids were petrified of Jimi, for good reason.

Dad set fast time and was locked into the main with Justin, Ryder, Cody, and Tyler. By the time the B-Main rolled around, there were four positions open. Axel wanted one of those positions.

The stands were packed with fifteen thousand fans all eagerly awaiting to see what this sixteen-year-old kid from Mooresville had to offer the greatest midget racers in the world.

The race got off to a rough start when Shane Jennings flipped on the second lap, bringing out the red flag for ten minutes while they cleaned up the mess. That was when the real fun began.

On the front row, Axel was lined up against an Australian driver, Dylan Cottle.

Cottle had won events like the Hut Hundred, Turkey Night, and the Cooper Classic last year. He was tough competition, but I knew Axel had the talent and patience to outrun him.

Off the track Axel was like me, impatient as hell. On the track, he showed fortitude in situations like this.

"He's gonna choke," some kid behind us said. Spencer and Casten turned to look back at the kid, glaring. "What?" the kid asked. "He is."

Casten took Spencer's fries, loaded with ketchup, and tossed them back at the kid, ketchup spraying him in the face. "Looks like *you're* choking now."

That was my boy.

Turned out, Axel didn't choke as he stayed right with Dylan all twenty laps and locked in a spot in the A-Main tomorrow night.

I called Sway to let her know, and she told me Arie got a tattoo. I was not impressed by this at all. My little angel was fourteen; she didn't need a tattoo. Apparently, it was small and on the inside of her ankle, but still, this was not *good* news to me. It just meant she was growing up, and that depressed me.

Back at the hotel that night, it took a good hour to get my hormone driven sixteen-year-old son away from his girlfriend. They must have spent a good twenty minutes in the parking lot making out.

This time Justin was not impressed.

"This is not good," Justin sighed, closing the curtains so he couldn't see them any longer. His hotel room was right next door so we decided to open up the mini-bar. "Your son better not break her heart."

"I have no control over that."

His eyebrow arched as he chucked an airplane bottle of rum. "Regardless ... put yourself in my shoes ... think of that as Arie out there."

I leaned out the door of the hotel room. "Axel, get your ass in here!"

Justin started laughing, tensely throwing back another bottle. "My point exactly."

The next morning, it was back to racing.

"You beat me ... I didn't make it out here until I was nineteen," I told Axel.

"How'd you do?" Axel asked as we walked into the Tulsa Expo Center around seven on Saturday morning.

I pointed to the plaque on the wall. "You tell me." My name appeared on the wall seven times—the first being in 1999 when I won the event, my first time there.

Axel was calm and withdrawn that morning. Much like me, he

retreated when he needed to focus, spending much of his morning inside the hauler away from everyone. Lily made her way in there for a few minutes, but eventually she knew he needed to be by himself.

About an hour before driver introductions, my dad and I made our way inside the hauler to check on Axel. He was sitting at the table, his head resting on his arms, hiding his face.

"You ever coming out of here, boy?" Dad asked him, pushing him over so he could sit next to him. "I need some healthy competition out there."

"I'm hardly competition for you, Grandpa." Axel answered, his face still out of sight from us.

Dad nodded toward him and then the door before rubbing Axel's back once. "See you on the track, kid."

Axel didn't respond, just kept his head down. We sat there in silence before he finally looked up at me, "I'm ... scared," his voice was soft.

Instantly I saw the little boy I saw before his first Dirt Nationals, looking to me for advice and more than anything, reassurance. I knew then everything my dad tried to warn me about when I was Axel's age. Talent could only take you so far, he was right. Confidence, determination, and a clear level head was what won races and championships. To do that, you couldn't be second-guessing yourself. Something I never did, of course, but Axel, he worried a lot about what others thought and turned to them for comfort.

"There's not much I can tell you that will comfort you, buddy. I know you can do it."

His eyes met mine, his expression wary. "With Grandpa out there?"

"Every race I've ever won, I've looked at my competition. To be the best racer you can be, you want to beat the best. Personally, if I won a race where Grandpa or Justin and Tyler were in it ... I would feel like I *really* won."

Axel seemed to understand but still held some nervousness.

"You got the talent, buddy. I've seen you do it before, just keep that in here," I tapped the side of his head.

We didn't have much time, but as we made our way outside so he could get to driver introductions he hugged me. Really hugged me. Both arms wrapped around me tightly.

Kissing the top of his head, I returned the hug. "Go get 'em, buddy."

When the race started, Axel lined up behind Dylan Cottle and Cody Bowman in the fifth row beside Shane Jennings, a fellow USAC midget racer he'd raced with since they were nine.

After a four-lap yellow in the beginning for a few tangled cars on the start, Axel began moving up the field from his tenth starting position. He hugged the inside edge of the track, protecting his position, at times driving up on the berm for the first fifteen laps.

With eighteen laps to go, he passed Cody for fourth. With fourteen to go, Travis Quinn flipped, bringing out the caution. When the race restarted, Hayden went airborne just before the start-finish line and was, in turn, hit by Shane Jennings, who also flipped.

After the yellow, the race was on with twelve laps to go. Axel was running fourth with Ryder, Justin, and Dad in front of him. He shot down low with nine to go and got past Ryder for third.

He bobbled a little on the backstretch allowing Ryder to catch him again, only to pass him on the front stretch.

"I think he can pull this off!" Tommy said, nodding.

I couldn't say anything. I was too busy biting my nails. Yeah, that's right. Twelve time NASCAR Cup Champion biting his nails over his son racing in the Chili Bowl.

Justin held his ground for two laps before Axel swept past him on the line. He was right on Dad after that. Every move he made, Dad blocked him just like he should. It was going to take more than just talent to get past old Jimi. Axel finally understood that when he pulled back about a car length and followed every move he made, waiting for his opening. With one lap to go on a quarter-mile track, everyone, including Tommy and me thought Jimi had the win.

I looked down for just a brief second as the cars came out of turn two; the fifteen thousand fans went into an uproar, as did Spencer and Tommy beside me. Looking up, I saw Axel shoot up the track into the cushion, bounce off it and the inside rail, only to slingshot forward into Jimi, their nurf bars banging. They came out of turn four side-by-side, and Axel simply drove away as if it was no effort.

My son learned the art of patience.

He had the car to beat his grandpa all along. But he knew if he made his move too soon, he'd spend the next few laps holding him off and eating up his tires, potentially allowing Jimi to get back by him. This way, Jimi was the one who ate up his tires holding Axel off.

I nearly cried.

All those times my dad told me how proud he was of me, and how seeing your child living their dreams meant far more than winning yourself, made sense to me now.

Tommy and Spencer hugged me, Van and Aiden hugged each other. Casten was screaming with Lane, Cole, Noah, and Charlie as we watched our own bring home the victory.

My dad stopped in the middle of the infield, just like he did when I won this event back in '99 and ran over to Axel.

Axel was the youngest driver in the history of the Chili Bowl Midget Nationals to win. Three generations of drivers had finally been placed on the wall.

The party in Axel's pit was similar to the one that took place when I won back then. Axel had his first beer. Casten told everyone his brother won, while Lane and Logan took advantage of all the girls swarming around.

There was a smile plastered upon everyone's faces that night, including mine and my dad's.

"He was strong out there," Dad said, drinking a beer beside me as we watched Lily congratulate Axel with a kiss that made me a little uncomfortable.

"He had patience," I agreed, slinging my arm around him.

Dad smiled. "Something you still don't understand at times."

"I resent that."

"You would ... now go party with your son. I'm exhausted."

I knew I had patience. He was full of shit. I sat back out of the spotlight that night. This was Axel's time, not mine. I declined to sign anything for the fans, only to push them toward Axel. "He's the talent," I would tell them. No one seemed to be overly offended by it. I just wanted them to understand what this meant for him. It meant everything.

The next morning was the first real conversation I was able to have with Axel without someone around.

"How does it feel?" I asked him over breakfast before we headed home. Sway was already planning a party with Emma to celebrate his win for when we got back. Now just might be my only time to talk to him alone for a few days.

"I'm not really sure ..." He smiled wide. "It hasn't really sunk in yet."

Pushing the front page of the *Tulsa World* toward him, I smiled. "This might help."

Spread across the front page was a picture of Axel standing on the roll cage, his fist in the air with my dad beside him. The title read: The kid dominates the legend.

He smiled while reading it and then pushed it aside, looking up at me. "Thanks, Dad."

"For what?"

His eyes stayed focused with mine as if he was trying to make me see before shrugging.

"For everything."

Poppet – Valve mechanism that continually opens and closes in response to variation in pressure.

Not long after the season began that year, my sponsor, Simplex, was promoting a driver challenge at Eldora with a few Cup, Outlaw and Truck series drivers.

Simplex had been promoting the event for months, and we'd finally strung up twenty-three of us to race in the event the weekend after the All-Star Race during the bye week before the Coca-Cola 600.

After doing press on Charlotte Motor Speedway, Casten and I were on our way to Eldora for the two-day event with Spencer, Bobby, and Tate. Axel and most of my sprint car team was already there waiting for us with our cars. Now we just had to get there.

About twenty minutes outside of Eldora, my phone started ringing.

Most of the calls were from Alley. When I didn't answer, she called Tate and then Bobby.

Casten, who was sitting next to me in the front seat, turned down the stereo and looked back at Tate who shrugged. "What's up?"

"I'm not sure. Here." I handed him my cell phone and tried to keep the truck on the road. "Check the messages for me."

He did and immediately turned rigid. His face lost all color, and his eyes widened, the alarm shining back at me.

"Dad, you should pull over," he spoke softly, handing me his cell phone.

I looked at the screen to see that Sway was calling.

"Honey, what's up? I thought you were on a plane to Elma?"

"I was ... I, uh, we landed, and then I saw on the news ..." My wife's hysterical response broke through. "Oh, God, Jameson, I thought you were on that plane!"

"What plane?"

"The one heading to Eldora."

"Well, no, Casten and I decided to drive with Tate, Spencer, and Bobby. We are meeting the team there. What's going on?"

Sway was silent for a moment as I watched Casten dig out his iPad to look at the news. The guys observed over his shoulder.

Sway fumbled through a string of words that took me a moment to decipher, and then it hit me what she said ... plane crash.

"Honey, please slow down, what are you talking about?"

My mind raced to comprehend. Adrenaline jolted through me, sending a sharp pain through my bones.

Pausing to control herself, her voiced evened out. "Jameson ... your team plane crashed outside Lancaster, Ohio, on its way to Eldora."

My stomach dropped. I had just watched half the team load onto that plane in Charlotte.

Gentry. Ethan. Jeb. Wes. Cal. Andy. Trace. *Oh, God.*

Half my team and Tate's team was on that plane, and I was supposed to be along with Spencer, Casten, Tate, and Bobby, but we drove because we got caught up in press after the race.

My wife's voice drew me from my thoughts.

"Jimi just called and said Eldora cancelled the races this weekend. He asked that you guys just come home."

I couldn't form a reply. Sitting there staring off at the highway, I couldn't reply.

My fingers clamped over the wheel, knuckles paling, and I dropped the phone. Casten quickly scrambled beside me to retrieve it.

I couldn't focus, much less drive, so Spencer took over.

I called Alley, who was already doing damage control to see what she knew. Sway stayed in Elma until I told her where I was going. I knew one thing. I needed to get to Charlotte as that would be where most teams would be gathering.

"Jameson," Alley answered right away. "I need you guys to head back to NC and stay in Charlotte tonight. There will be a press conference held in the morning, and they will announce the plans from there."

"What plans?" I motioned for Spencer to pull over so we could turn around and head to Charlotte.

"You do realize who was on that plane, don't you?"

"Well, mostly my team and Tate's, but Andy, too."

Alley was silent.

"Alley?"

"Jameson, at least three of the Truck series drivers were on that plane, along with Andy, Colin, and two Nationwide series drivers."

"Oh."

It was my plane, and I knew most of the guys boarding it when it left, but I had no idea all those people were on it. Wes frequently gave guys rides when they needed it, and he knew I would never object to it. But the fact they were on a plane I owned, and it crashed, felt as though it was my fault.

Our community, my racing family, had lost members of their family today, and though I knew deep down it wasn't my fault, it didn't stop it from taking a piece of me.

Just as a reciprocating engine was made up of systems that kept it running, so was the racing community. There was one that kept the pistons moving, one that kept the belts moving, and one that kept oil flowing and one that created spark. They were all connected. Take one out of the equation and guess what, that engine that kept you going was no longer there and everything fell apart.

Take drivers from the series and you felt it.

That checkered flag you saw in the distance became a yellow flag. Until they failed, or one was taken from the equation, you didn't realize how much you depended on those pistons, cylinders, belts, and oil.

Death was such a surreal thing to me. It waited under the surface—waited to consume. It was noticeable, but hovering and ready to take victim at any moment.

I didn't waste time in Elma after I heard about the accident. Arie and I flew back to Mooresville that night and helped with the devastation. I knew I couldn't offer much, but I'd help in any way I could. Those drivers, those crew members, and pilots all had family, and I could be there for them.

Tate's teammate, Andy Crockett, one of the drivers on the plane, was married and had kids the same age as Arie and Casten. My heart ached for his wife, Erica, and I wondered how in the world she was managing right now. I couldn't comprehend the feeling I had when I thought that Jameson was on that plane, and the relief, though incredibly reassuring, was immediately forgotten when I realized that just because Jameson, my world, wasn't on that plane didn't mean there wasn't a handful of others on it who had family.

When I got to the shop where Alley told me Jameson was, I heard the sounds of screaming and destruction coming from inside his shop. I could hear things being smashed and destroyed over his pain.

Opening the door, it pushed open, but with resistance from the parts that had been hurled against it.

He stood in the middle of the shop, bent forward with his hands resting on the wing of a sprint car.

He turned slightly, his body remained in line with the car, and just his head moved at the sound of the door. His brow furrowed, lines forming in the outer corners, his expression bordering painful, his eyes dark to match his lashes.

When he noticed it was me, he turned to meet me walking toward him. He was scared, and he was angry. He also had every right to feel both.

"Honey, you really shouldn't be in here." His voice was firm but breakable as he stared down into my eyes, his face an unreadable contrast to my own. He scratched the back of his neck slowly, his head hung in defeat. Regret and sadness were easy. Moving forward wasn't. I knew that, just as Jameson did. But I'd be here for him.

Just the same as I'd heard those very words back in California all those years back, I ignored them because he was a man, my husband, needing me again.

When I looked at him, I could see the same fire I'd always seen, but it was trying to go out with the winds created.

I felt him lower his face to mine, his breath hitting my lips.

Jameson's lips trailed across my jaw stopping in their path to kiss my lips and forehead, his nose delicately nudging against mine.

His lips were there next, brushing lightly against mine, soft and feather-like.

When he finally closed the distance, pressing gentle kisses to my lips, a sigh of contentment and relief fell from me.

My hands soon found their place in his shirt, immediately fisting it in my hands.

"I love you," I told him over and over again. My words felt pathetic; they meant something, but nothing of comfort or even an answer for him.

I told him this because that was what he needed to remember. He needed to remember that I was here for him despite his pain and anguish.

Tears were streaming down my face with an unstoppable force along with choking, bone rattling sobs.

"I love you, too. You can be sure of that," he assured me with steady palms cradling my face.

We both dropped to our knees, and he was offering me anything he could to provide for me—comfort me in any way he could. But it wasn't me he needed to comfort. I was crying for him. For his suffering that he wouldn't show.

He tried to detach himself from it, but not feeling anything was the last thing he needed right now.

"It's going to be okay," I whispered to him, finding a place against the rear tire of the sprint car.

"Sway," his voice cracked, eyes glistened with remorseful tears. "My team and members of my racing family were ..." his eyes shut, trying to stop the few tears that slipped by. "So you see," he continued, refusing to look at me. "Nothing is as easy, or as simple, as it should be."

He lifted me up, setting me on his lap to wrap his arms around me.

"It will be okay, Jameson." It was the only answer I had for him.

"You say that now, but, I can't say the same." The sadness swirled with the green and almost took my breath away.

He'd just lost friends of his, and I couldn't blame him for feeling this way.

"Your friends, your team, they would want you to be the champion you've always been. They would want you to be strong."

Jameson didn't answer right away, just stared, and fear prickled my skin, his silence only scared me.

"I don't know," he finally replied slowly, his voice echoed throughout the room.

Later that night, Alley showed up, and we went over the press conference that was set for ten the next morning where Jameson, Jimi, Tate, and Bobby were requested to speak.

With something so tragic, they wanted answers.

"I don't know what to say to them," Jameson said, sitting inside the small conference room we had at the sprint car shop. Thankfully, Jameson hadn't touched this room in his earlier rage.

Alley sighed, reaching for his hand across the table. "I know it will be hard, Jameson, but I think out of anyone right now, you will know what to say."

Alley was absolutely right. She knew that when pressured for words, Jameson knew what to say—he always did. He could respond regardless of the circumstances. He might not always say what others wanted him to say, but he spoke the truth, and he spoke from his heart.

It was times like this when the truth behind what you knew and what you felt gave way, and you were left with what you needed. What you needed to say. What you needed to feel. And, more importantly, what you needed to believe.

There was also a point when you've had enough. Enough pain, enough sadness, and enough loss.

The morning brought with it grief and regret for what happened, but also answers as to what might have gone wrong.

My private jet that was carrying twelve passengers and two pilots crashed outside Eldora in Lancaster, Ohio. Other than that information right there, I didn't pay much attention to the news report because I knew each and every person on that plane. More importantly, I knew each one personally. I wasn't going to say I didn't feel regret because I did. I felt more regret than I should have.

It was times like this that you looked at yourself, your life, your family and wondered why.

Why them, why us, why you, why not him?

You looked at everyone and anything for an answer that would never come.

I wasn't sure whether I believed in God or whether I didn't. But at times like this, I wondered who made the decisions for us. Who took lives and left others to face the unknown and life without them. I wondered why.

Everyone on that plane had a family. They had loved ones; wives, kids, aunts, uncles, and they had someone who hung on their every word, and maybe even someone who hated them.

Why?

My wife—my wonderful understanding and supportive wife—stood beside me, watching the crowd gather. Each one of them was asking themselves what I couldn't answer.

Why?

Racers like me were used to deciding their own fate on a track. That wasn't to say outside factors didn't play a role, but usually, your destiny, which is dependent on the outcome of a race, was held in your hands.

As a racer, your home was the track. It was where your love for racing was formed and where you cultivated it into something great. It was where nothing else mattered but the dedication, passion, confidence, and ambition. These were the only traits I believed set a racer apart from others. Until today.

Patrick Maddens, CEO of NASCAR, took the podium first and explained the details surrounding the crash. Through it all, Sway held my hand.

"The King Airjet of NASCAR Cup driver, Jameson Riley, took off from Charlotte, North Carolina, at nine AM, Eastern time, carrying fourteen passengers. Among those were several NASCAR drivers, including Sprint Cup drivers, Andy Crockett and Colin Shuman; Nationwide drivers, Kevin Millan and Jack Burwell; and Camping World Truck drivers, Stacy Ewing, Terry Williams, and Carl Baker. Other members on the plane were Gentry Wade, crewmember for Jameson Riley; Ethan Norton, back-up spotter and driver of the number nine transporter for Riley Racing,; Jeb Erickson, spotter for Bobby Cole; Cal Porter, team member and driver of Jameson Riley's personal motor coach, and pilots Wes Turner for Riley Racing, and driver of the No. 9 Simplex Ford Jameson Riley and David Cates, pilot for the Leddy Motorsports.

"The plane was en route to Eldora Speedway where Simplex Shocks and Springs was holding a drivers challenge among NASCAR Sprint Cup, Outlaw, and racers in the Nationwide and Camping World Truck series. The plane piloted by Wes Turner and David Cates was reported missing at 9:36 AM. After an extensive search by a ground team, the wreckage of the plane was found. It was reported that no one on board survived." Patrick looked into the crowd of reporters and closed his eyes for a brief moment. "NASCAR asks that you keep those affected in your thoughts and prayers and respectfully requests that privacy be considered throughout this difficult time."

That was when Patrick looked to me, and every eye shifted from him, to me.

Racers were not born racers.

Sure, you may have had some innate ability within you that drove you down this career path, but it wasn't a gift. It was a natural inclination for speed, competition, and tact—for pushing yourself beyond your comfort zone, taking risks, and striving to be the best.

Over time you nurtured these to become a champion in the sport that had consumed your entire life. Success and respect in the industry wasn't just handed to you.

I was a champion. The racing community was looking to me for answers. They wanted me to help them through this tragic time.

But could I?

Lisa approached me, and the tears in her eyes reflected what the racing community was feeling.

"Jameson, can you speak to the media?"

This was something countless hours on the track and in the garage never prepared me for. Consequently, I realized that titles, trophies, and driving abilities, were not, in fact, what set a champion apart from other racers. The true test was now.

You see, every now and then, a racer comes along and his talent isn't defined by the trophies or by his ability. What sets him apart is what defines him in the blaring spotlight.

It was ordinary men doing extraordinary things.

Still, the questions remained.

Could I?

I thought back to what my wife said to me this morning about speaking the truth and realized I should just speak the truth.

My dad stood next to me, his head tipped to the microphone. "It's all you, Jay."

I smiled when he used the nickname my grandpa used to call me, and then I thought about the words of wisdom old Casten used to provide every now and then. In a time like this, he would probably tell me, "It's not the fiery disposition of the driver that can rattle even the toughest. It's what he does with that fire that defines even the dullest."

With Grandpa and my dad, you had to look between the gaps in their statements and decipher what you could, and now I understood what he meant.

"I was hoping that I would never hear this. I feel like half my family was on that plane, and, in reality, they were. I've known Wes my entire life, and those boys on my team, well, they were like my brothers. It's a very sad day for me."

I wasn't lying when I said that. This was and always would be a very sad day for me.

The media, as they always did, wanted every side they could get, and if there was a story to be written, well, they were there to find it.

"Jameson, do you think this could have been pilot error?"

I wanted to scream at them and tell them not to push the blame on something they didn't know, but I went for the subtle but harsh approach.

"The National Transportation Safety Board is investigating the accident. None of us were there. Don't place the blame on something you don't know."

And with that, I walked away from the podium. Was that a championship speech? Probably not, but I spoke the truth. Something they knew very little about.

Tate and Bobby stood to the side not wanting any interaction with the press. Tate had lost his teammate, pilot, and cousin in that crash. Little words were spoken between us or anyone else.

Kyle had lost his younger brother, Gentry, and wasn't here at the press conference. I couldn't blame him. I couldn't blame anyone who was with their families today and not here.

For the first time ever in the history of NASCAR, aside from September 11, 2001, they cancelled all three divisions that weekend in NASCAR, as well as other NASCAR-sanctioned tracks around the world to pay respect to those who were lost.

In my mind, that was a championship call by NASCAR. Every single one of those people who were lost that day deserved to be remembered with dignity and in a way that was respectful. They didn't need to be asking who did what wrong.

As for my team, I lost Wes, my pilot, two members of my crew and fellow drivers.

That didn't just go away. You remembered in ways you never thought you would. When I looked at a spark plug, I thought of Ethan and him buying lawnmower spark plugs. Every time I made a pit stop, I thought of Gentry. I saw a plane and immediately thought of Wes. Walked inside my motor coach and thought of Cal. Looked at the number four and saw Andy's face. It was hard. So many lives were lost that it felt wrong to be here.

Was I afraid to fly after that?

I'd be lying if I didn't say that every time I boarded a plane I didn't think of it.

Wes had been flying around the world for over thirty years. To me, this was just an accident. There was no sugar coating it or blaming, it was an accident.

I learned, and though it was taking me some time, things like this happened. I never wanted them to, but they did, and that was when I began to understand what it meant to be a champion, on and off the track.

Panhard Bar – A lateral bar that keeps the rear tires centered within the body. It connects the car on one side and the rear axle on the other. This can also be called the track bar.

Over the years, I'd like to think I'd grown just as much as this sport. It was time to mend with Paul. It wasn't fair being teammates now to have that sort of hostility. With everything that had happened in our sport over the last few months with the plane crash, I couldn't have a racing relationship like this with Paul.

Turned out, my dad took my recommendations despite my arguments with Paul over the years and hired him as the third driver for Riley-Simplex Racing. Bobby transferred to another team this year while Paul Leighty took his position.

"I don't say this very often so believe me when I say it ... I'm sorry," I said to Paul one night after the June All-Star race.

Paul laughed, walking with me to our cars. On races like this, we just drove to Charlotte since it was such a short drive back to Mooresville.

"I wish I recorded that."

"Fuck you," I laughed. "You're never getting another one. Ask Kyle. I think I've said it to him one time."

Paul nodded but remained smiling.

"I've never met someone like you before, Jameson," he said conversationally.

"I assume that's a good thing?"

He snorted. "It can be when I'm on your good side. I will say this ..." he paused, closing the trunk of his car after tossing his bag in it. Leaning against the bumper, he looked past me toward the track. "You're one of the only drivers I know in *any* division who knows exactly when to turn on the aggression and when to turn it off."

I thought about his statement for a minute, decided it was actually true, and smiled. "It didn't come without practice," I said with a stoic seriousness that even Paul remained focused on.

Every driver who was in the series around 2003 remembers the problems with Darrin and me. They also remember I nearly walked away that season because of him.

If it hadn't been for Sway, I would have.

When I got home that night, Sway was waiting for me, receptive as always and welcomed me in ways I found extremely satisfying.

The next morning, though, she made me do something I'd hoped I would never had to do as a father.

The sex talk.

"Jameson, I'm serious, you need to talk to Axel about it."

It wasn't a request either. She had basically *told* me I was doing this.

"I don't think so ... it can wait. They're only sixteen. I doubt they're ready for *that*."

Sway slapped me. "Are you a fucking idiot?"

I glared, but then looked back to my coffee cup.

"No, I just don't think they're doing it."

That was a lie. I walked in on them, on more than one occasion, with their hands in places they shouldn't be, and in one instance Lily was straddling him on his bed. At least their clothes were still on?

"And what would make you think that?" she challenged, placing her hands on her hips. "I lost mine at sixteen."

"I just don't," I shrugged. "And if you want me to remain in a good mood the rest of the evening, don't bring up Dylan Grady again," I warned.

"You're cute when you're jealous," she laughed.

"I'm dangerous when I'm jealous."

"Ain't that the truth." I reached for her ass while she slapped my hands away.

"We have bigger issues at hand here."

"Doubt that."

She turned on her heel sharply and went to the laundry room and pulled his jeans out of the hamper. "Really?"

"So the boy wears jeans ..." I chuckled.

"Jameson!" she yelled and pulled a condom wrapper out of his pocket. It was empty, just the wrapper.

"Well ... shit," was my only intelligent response.

"I don't think he's doing anything," she mocked and stomped away. "Go!" she yelled over her shoulder.

Damn. I should have thought of this sooner. He was young to be sexually active, wasn't he?

How old was I?

I remembered taking interest in masturbation early on—around twelve I thought. But sex, *Christ*, I didn't lose my virginity until I was seventeen. He was sixteen, I was sure he'd thought of it by now.

After some convincing of myself, with some Jack Daniels, I made my way outside to the race shop where I knew Axel was.

Of course, Lily was in there with him, sitting on the counter while he was standing in front of her, between her legs, with his hands in places they shouldn't be.

I chuckled when they jumped away from each other.

"Axel," I smirked, sensing he was uncomfortable. "Can I talk to you for a minute, alone?"

He nodded, and Lily scrambled away.

"Sorry," she mumbled, passing by.

"Don't be sorry," I told her. "You didn't do anything wrong."

She smiled, pink flushed cheeks and slipped out the side door.

They didn't do anything wrong. They were kids and having natural reactions to their bodies. It wasn't wrong for them to feel this way. It was completely normal.

Axel fumbled with a spring off his sprint car. "What's up, Dad?"

I chuckled nervously. I had no clue what to say to him.

When I was thirteen, my dad had the talk with me sometime after we came home from Mexico, and he caught me speed bleeding to a picture of Sway in a bikini.

His advice: "Stop spending all your time bleeding your pressure value and take the girl on a date."

I never did, well, until much later. Jimi thrived on embarrassing the hell out of me in situations like that and told my mom, Sway, and *Spencer* at the fucking dining room table that he caught me. I made it a personal note to wreck the bastard the next time we were on the track together back then and I did.

Anyway, back to the nervous teen sitting in front of me. Poor kid, he was sweating profusely.

"So, buddy ... I, uh ... wanted to talk to you about something," I leaned against the side of his sprint car.

"Yeah ... I kind of figured that."

"Do you know why?" I hedged.

"Yeah ... I think I do." He sighed and buried his head in his hands. "About Lily and me and ..." he motioned south.

I had to laugh when his cheeks turned pink. "It's nothing to be embarrassed by, buddy."

"I know, I just ... I don't ... *urggg* ... this is so stupid," he groaned, leaning his head back so it was resting against the side of the tire. He reached up and tugged at the ends of his hair.

"What's stupid?"

"I don't know what I'm doing, did you?"

Another laugh. "Not really ... have you had sex with her?"

All the color left his face instantly as he gaped at me in horror.

"I, um … eh … what?" he stammered.

"Are you already having sex with her?" I asked again, trying to avoid any type of reaction that might scare him.

It took him a while, but eventually he answered with a nod of his head.

"So … are you using protection?"

Again, he nodded. I could tell he wanted to ask me something, but he was afraid. "Do you have any questions about it?"

His eyes that were fixated on the spring in his hand again slowly met mine.

"What was uh … your first time like?"

Wow, wasn't expecting that question, but the poor kid was looking for advice so I decided to be honest as I always was with him.

"My first time was conceivably a mistake and with the wrong girl," I chuckled. "It was over pretty quick, I remember that much."

"How old were you?"

"Seventeen, almost eighteen."

"Do you think I'm too young?"

"Yes … and no … I know you love Lily, and I know she loves you. I also know that she's not in it for the fame, and she's a good girl for you."

He smiled lightly. "I do love her."

"That's all that matters then, treat her right."

After a few moments of silence, I thought my work here was done when he spoke again.

"Dad, um … is it normal not to last very long? Is that bad? Am I doing something wrong?"

"Oh, it's normal all right," I chuckled. "It's just not very pleasurable for the girl."

"How do you know … last longer?"

"Dirty engine talking."

"What?" He looked at me with a blank expression.

Jesus, shut up, I told myself.

It was clear I was in over my head.

Is this appropriate? I thought to myself.

Shit, where was Sway when I needed her? Or Spencer. I know he'd had to have this conversation with Lane by now.

"Well," I began, still glancing around the room as though someone was going to rescue me at any moment. "With practice it gets easier to hold back. Listen." I sighed. "I feel weird giving you advice about this sort of thing, but I'd rather you get it from me than someone else, especially your moron uncles. How does Lily feel about this? Did you pressure her into this?"

"No," he answered immediately. "Not at all ..." His eyes once again sunk to the spring he was holding. "We were at Williams Grove a couple weeks ago when you guys were in Darlington ... after the race Justin let us go out to get some dinner. When we got back, he had left us a note saying he'd be back later. I was ready to go to bed, but Lily, she wanted to try having sex. She's been wanting to for a while, and she wanted me to be her first. We've done everything else, so I thought it was time to do it," he shrugged. "It was over in like a minute, and I was embarrassed, *really* embarrassed. We tried it again a couple weeks later, and the same thing. I know it's supposed to be pleasurable for her, but I can't last long enough. Is that bad?"

Noticeably, I was not prepared for this. I was sweating worse than him now.

"Like I said, it gets easier to control yourself," I choked out. "Axel, buddy, you need to be careful, okay?" He only nodded. "You don't want to be a dad this soon ... everything you've worked for would put on hold, you know that, right?"

"I do; she's on birth control and I used a condom."

"Okay, well good."

"Did you have sex with a lot of woman before you met mom?"

"What?" it was my turn for the color to drain from my face. "Axel, have you had sex before Lily?" I asked, alarmed and feeling like a horrible parent for not knowing my son was sexually active.

His face turned a shade darker than his red sprint car. "I, uh ... shit," he sighed.

"Damn, kid," I laughed. "I'm really late at this, huh?"

"I wanted to tell you ... but I thought you guys would be mad at me."

"Why would we be mad at you?"

"I don't know ... I just thought you would be."

"How many?"

I was almost afraid to know the answer now judging by my own background, and I knew the way women acted around race car drivers, let alone the kid and grandson of two well-known racers.

"Just one ... you remember Shaylee, right?" I nodded, remembering the girl in Ohio we met at the Chili Bowl earlier in the year. She reminded me of Chelsea, and I distinctly remembered warning Axel about her. "It was awful, and she told everyone about it, including Lily.

"How'd Lily deal with that?"

"She cried ... that's the night we had sex for the first time."

This was worse than I thought.

"Okay, so you slept with another chick and then told your girlfriend about it and took her virginity the same night you told her?" I slapped the back of his head. "What the fuck is the matter with you, taking lessons from me?"

"I hurt her ... I felt awful. I don't even know why I did it ... I wanted it to be with Lily, but she didn't want to at the time, and Shaylee did."

"Think with your head, kid, not your dick."

He chuckled sarcastically. "Thanks for the *late* advice."

"Hey," I said defensively. "I had no idea you were sexually active, or wanting to be."

"Really?" His eyebrow arched in question. "Are you an idiot? Do you not even realize how much time I spend in the bathroom or touching Lily? I'm all over the poor girl. I think I remember you actually walking in on us."

"Oh, I saw ... but I didn't think you were *acting* on it. If I remember, your clothes were at least on."

"It's a little hard not to think about sex when girls throw themselves in your lap after races, and Lily, well she's innocent," he groaned. "I can't believe how bad I messed this up with her."

"What do you mean? I saw you guys when I came inside."

"I'm trying to convince her I love her and that I am sorry. I never meant to hurt her. It's like the only reason she wanted to have sex with me was because she thought that's what I wanted. This is so messed up and not what I need right now."

"Story of my life ... do you know how long it took for me to figure things out with your mom?"

He shook his head. "I met mom when I was eleven, completely infatuated with her, but thought it was only physical attraction ... anyway, we did the whole friends with benefits thing after I pretty much slept with every woman who was thrown my direction. Broke your mom's heart, and then finally, when I was twenty-three, I wised up and realized how much I loved her."

"So you slept around a lot."

My turn to groan, "More than I care to admit; don't do it by the way."

"I don't plan on it. Shaylee assured me of that. I didn't feel anything but disgust afterward." He was silent for a few minutes. "What should I say to Lily?"

"For one, don't lie to her, *ever*," I warned. "They don't like that. And don't sleep around. If you're serious about Lily, which I think you are, treat her right. Tell her how you feel, and if she's not ready to have sex anymore, don't pressure her."

"I didn't. Like I said, Dad, she practically attacked me!" he said defensively.

"Regardless, sex complicates things sometimes."

"You're telling me."

"Don't be stupid either. Keep using protection. I'm not ready to be a grandpa. I can't even handle you three, let alone another *you* running around."

"Really?" he challenged. "It's not me you need to worry about."

He had a point there. Arie was the troublemaker, and the fact that

I thought she was an angel made it worse. Casten, well he could potentially be a problem, but at his age, we still had time to steer him in another direction.

When I walked back inside the house, Sway was sitting on the kitchen floor with a bowl and a spoon eating fudge she'd just made before it settled. "Please tell me he's not a man now?" she wailed, her tears mixing with the chocolate over her lips.

"I wouldn't say he's a man, but ..." I let my voice trail off, trying to tell her without telling her.

"Oh God!" she cried out, stuffing another spoonful of fudge in her mouth.

Sitting down beside her, she offered me a spoonful of fudge, which I took. It'd been a rough day. "I probably should have talked to him sooner."

"Go talk to Casten about it, right now!" she ordered.

"Honey, he's twelve ... I—"

She held up her hand. "You're in no position to decide that, now are you?"

"Point taken," I grumbled, hoisting myself up from the tile floor. "But you're talking to Arie about sex. I can't do that."

"I already have."

"She just turned fourteen!"

"Yeah, but it's important. Besides, she was curious because Lexi started her period when we were shopping one day. It was a fucking disaster! I had to explain, since she thought Lexi was dying."

"You couldn't just say that once a month you bleed?"

"I'd rather educate her on it," she shrugged, pouring hot water into the fudge bowl. I leaned against the counter and sighed. This parenting shit was hard, exhausting work. "I mean, my dad just told me that he wasn't qualified for that sort of thing. I ended up having to ask the kid behind the counter at the Texaco in town how to use the goddamn tampons."

"Who the hell was the kid, and why didn't you ask my mom?"

She pushed me down the hall. "It doesn't matter. Go talk to Casten."

Let me tell you something about Casten. Everything was funny to him. He was just like Sway in that regard, but worse. It might not be funny at all, but Casten would laugh. When he was little, he used to think that if you screamed in pain, that was funny. So after my conversation with Axel, my wife's nervous breakdown, and finding out my fourteen-year-old daughter already knew about the align boring process, I wasn't really in the mood to be talking about this with my twelve-year-old son, who would more than likely laugh at me.

Casten was outside with Cole and Lane setting up new jumps for their dirt bikes.

He wanted to show me a new jump they made so we walked toward the back of the property while Lane and Cole continued with the track.

"Why are you sweating?" Casten asked, kicking dirt around.

"It's hot out here."

"No it's not. It's like sixty."

"It is too hot," I stopped walking and looked over at him. "I need to talk to you about something."

His eyes widened in panic. "I told her I'd buy her a phone."

"What?"

"Arie ... I told her I'd replace her phone," his eyes scrunched. "Wait a second, what did she tell you?"

"Nothing, but now I want to know. What did you do to her phone?"

"Nothing." He laughed lightly before tossing the rock he'd picked up and sat down on the bleachers we installed last summer.

"Bullshit," I sat next to him and leaned back.

He held out his hand for money.

"I don't think so. You're not five any longer, and you cuss worse than I do."

He smiled. "What did you want to talk about?"

I thought about my approach for a moment.

Tommy was out on the track with the boys before he fell down and then just laid there and looked up at the sky as though that was a comfortable spot to lay. Only problem was he was right under the double jump they had out there. That's when he brought the spray bottle to his mouth again.

"I'm beginning to think that spray bottle is not water."

Casten tipped his head as if he was looking closer. "Nope. It's vodka."

I nodded and then decided on my speech for my youngest.

"So, um, well ... I ... have you had the birds and the bees talk in school?"

Like I expected, he started laughing.

"Geez, Dad, you look like you're about to have a heart attack," he laughed again before I pushed him off the bleachers.

He landed on his ass, still laughing.

"Don't have an aneurysm," he chuckled.

"Just answer the question," I huffed, wanting to end this.

Casten loved fucking with people. He lived for it.

"Birds 'n' bees, huh?" He smirked. "I'm not sure I know that term."

He wanted me to say it, and I refused to. But then again, I'd be here all night if I didn't.

"Sex, do you know about it or not?"

Once again, he laughed.

"Was that so hard?" he teased.

"If you want to continue living in my house, you'll stop making fun of me," I snapped.

He thought this over for a moment.

"Fine." His amused eyes met mine briefly before his cheeks flushed. "And, yeah ... Lane told me. Logan may have said something once, too."

This could be bad. "And what did he tell you?"

"He said ... uh, that you do it when you love someone."

"Anything else?"

"Always wear a condom."

"Good."

I'd have to thank Lane and Logan for this one. I couldn't understand why this was so hard for me but easy for him. I mean, Christ, he was twelve. My parents never had this conversation with me. I walked in on Spencer and a girl when I was twelve and put a few things together from there, but anything else I learned from his porno stash and health class. I guess I thought my kids would do the same. I never anticipated actually having to talk with them about it.

"You're not having sex, are you?"

He gave me this blank stare.

"I know you're eleven ... or twelve ... or whatever," I ran the heels of my hands over my eyes. "I just want to make sure you're safe."

"Just so you know my real age, *Dad*, I'm twelve," he replied, looking up at me as though I was completely crazy.

"So that's a no?"

"That's disgusting." He shook his head and side-eyed me. "I'm not going to have sex. I don't even like girls."

"Come talk to me when you're fourteen, and I guarantee that will change."

"Doubt that."

"I think I'll bet you on that. I bet you five hundred dollars by the time you're fourteen, you'll spend the majority of your time in the bathroom."

"Why, will I be constipated or something?"

"No, you'll be distracted by *something*."

"Well, then I will stay eleven ... or ... twelve," he acted as though this would not be a problem. "And deal on the five hundred. I could use some extra cash these days."

I laughed. "Now back to Arie's phone ..."

"Shit," he muttered with another laugh.

Sway freaked out about Axel being sexually active. She knew after my conversations with her, but the dumbass got careless and left his bedroom door unlocked one afternoon that summer. Needless to say, Sway walked in on them. I was on my way home from Sonoma when she called crying while eating ice cream.

"What did he say?" I asked when she told me.

"Nothing," her voice muffled by the full mouth of ice cream. "He didn't notice me. I saw and immediately closed the door. I didn't want to see any more than I already had. At least they had blankets on them, so this could have been worse."

"I'll talk to him."

"Okay ... when will you be home tonight?"

"Around six, I'll talk to him then."

I managed to get her off the phone after that and decided to call Axel on my way home. He was on his way to Lernerville with Tommy.

"Hey, Dad, what's up?"

"Your mom walked in on you and Lily," I had no intention of sugar coating it for him. He needed to learn about these things.

He chuckled casually. "That sucks for me, huh?"

"Pretty much."

"Sorry," he offered.

"Just lock your door, kid. No one wants to see that, especially your mom."

"Noted."

"It better be more than noted, buddy, more like remembered."

"All right, lock the door."

"Good, now how was Grand Rapids on Wednesday ... you took first in the Silver Crown and Midgets, right?"

"Yeah, something is missing with the sprint program. We're forty points out of the lead behind Shane, and I just don't see what we're doing wrong."

We got talking about racing after that, and I gave him what pointers I had. More than anyone on this, Tommy was where the brains were—hints why he was always with Axel these days.

When I got home that night, Sway was crying over her children growing up. Casten, who faithfully said goodnight to Sway, went to bed without saying anything to her when he got home from his midget race.

"Let's have another baby?" she said to me as we laid in bed that night.

"No, I don't think so," I told her firmly, rolling away from her. "I'll get you a puppy."

"Not the same."

"Sure it is. And, best of all, they don't talk back."

I had a feeling this wasn't over, but for now, she fell asleep. Poor Sway hated the kids getting older and becoming adults, especially the boys. She wanted to baby them.

I knew how she felt—I hated it, as well. I missed the times when they were babies and learning to speak. Now they talked back, and I could live without that.

"Let's get away for the weekend."

"Get away? You're kidding, right?" He threw his arms up, and papers scattered across his desk with the motion. "Do you not see all this shit?"

"I see it," my voice was timed, trying not to set him off any more. "I just think you need a break."

It took me a good week after that to convince Jameson that we needed to get away, but the week after Christmas, he agreed.

We decided to keep it simple and just head to our house that we purchased in the Florida Keys after I had gone there last winter with the girls.

The house was simple, only three bedrooms, but it was right on the water and very romantic.

Knowing how our vacations or trips in general usually went for us, how did you think our time went?

Let's face it. Jameson and his moronic ideas had gotten us both in our fair share of compromising situations before. Now wasn't any different.

We got a speeding ticket on the way there because we drove, which was a stupid idea, by the way. I got food poising from some gas station food, and by the time we got to the beach house neither of us was in the mood to do anything besides sleep.

All that ended around three in the morning the next day when I felt better.

I woke him up with a little micro polishing and finished with some of the best press forging we'd ever done.

Jameson sighed against my shoulder, his breathing harsh.

"Jesus Christ, I think I pulled a muscle."

Laughing, I rolled over on him again. "So, that's a *no* on round two?"

"I'll try, but damn, turning forty has really done a number on me. And I thought thirty was bad."

"Just imagine when we turn fifty."

"Oh, dear God, don't remind me."

We laid in comfortable silence before he turned toward me, his fingers running over my lips. "I was good at the *woo* once upon a time."

"You still are," I whispered against his lips. "It's been one hell of a fairytale."

And that it had been. That weekend we celebrated our seventeenth wedding anniversary, and, as always, Jameson showed me just as much love and woo as he did the first year of our marriage, along with lots of press forging, deburring, reciprocating motions, piston stroking, and some align boring. It was a good time as always.

Returning home, Jameson was stressed, and Speedweek was just around the corner.

As we were sitting in the kitchen at Jimi and Nancy's house one morning before he left for Daytona, I tried to distract him.

"I think dyno testing cures all. What are your thoughts?"

I couldn't help but smile as my husband's head shot up from his phone. "Are you wanting to do a little micro polishing right now? In my parent's kitchen?" he asked with a smirk.

"Wouldn't be the first time, would it. Will it make you happy?"

"Fuck, yeah, it would make me happy, but I'd still have all this shit on my mind."

"What are you guys talking about?" asked Nancy as she walked into the kitchen, holding Logan's newborn daughter, Madison. Hard to believe the Lucifer twins were of reproducing age.

"I offered to micro polish Jameson's camshaft to reduce the friction in his engine," I admitted without shame to Nancy. Glaring, Jameson kicked me under the table.

"Don't tell my mom that," he groaned, watching me rub my shin where his foot smacked.

"Oh, sweetie," Nancy looked confused. "Is the engine in your sprint car running badly?"

So clueless.

"Come on," Jameson ordered, pulling me outside and to the car. "No more teasing me."

And just like that, I was showing my dirty heathen a good time again.

Regardless of his mood, I knew my husband and always knew how to make his life a little easier, even if it was just bleeding his pressure valve at times.

As I'd said, Sway had a hard time with the boys getting older and becoming adults. When a twelve-year-old Casten came home with his first girlfriend, I, for one, was five hundred dollars richer, and Sway was a basket case again.

My own nervous breakdown came when Arie got her first broken heart.

Being a father was hard, evidenced by the gray hairs I kept pulling out. And being a father to a fifteen-year-old girl was so much worse than boys.

I rubbed my forehead, ignoring my ringing phone until I realized it was Sway. Immediately I picked it up.

While I was in Talladega, Sway was in Knoxville with Axel and Casten. Arie was with Emma and Lexi at home.

"What's up, honey?" We'd just gotten off the phone with each other so I was surprised she called again so soon since I was on my way to Knoxville to see them.

"I need you to go home instead," she told me.

"Why, what's wrong?"

"Arie ..." She sighed. "Emma called. Arie locked herself in the bathroom. She's been crying for the last four hours. She wants you."

Sway and I never smothered our kids. If they wanted to talk about something, they came to us. This had its downsides. Arie was the downside.

Axel was our levelheaded kid, patient and thought things through, *most* of the time. Casten was out of fucking control most of the time, but he was a good kid and happy, so that was all we could ask for. I did wonder where he got all his energy, but then I looked at Emma and Spencer and chalked it up to something he may have inherited from them.

Arie, well, she was secretive. If she wanted you to know, she'd tell you. If not, you'd never know.

This was why we weren't aware she even had a boyfriend.

I did not like the idea of her having a boyfriend, for the simple fact that I was a teenage boy once, and all I thought about, aside from racing, was my dick. I wondered how the hell my parents put up with Spencer, Emma, and me as kids.

So I went home instead of to Knoxville to deal with Arie and this mysterious boyfriend.

When I walked inside, Emma was on my couch eating ice cream.

"She's in her bathroom."

I slapped the back of her head when I walked past. "That shit will make you fat."

"Fuck off, asshole," she mumbled with another spoonful of ice cream.

Making my way up the stairs to her room, I could hear her crying from outside the door.

"Arie," I tapped lightly. "Sweetie, it's Dad."

"Go away!"

"Nah, I think I need to come in there."

It took me about an hour to get her to finally open the door. When she did, she was sitting on the floor next to the tub with the sleeves of her sweatshirt drawn over her hands, her face against her arms and her knees pulled up to her chest, crying.

"Do you want to tell me what happened?"

She didn't say anything before she showed me her cell phone with a picture of said boyfriend, kissing Shaylee, that same girl Axel knew.

Sighing, I sat down next to her. "Who's the guy?"

"Ricky Hagen," she answered softly, her tears coming once again. "I thought he ... after we ... well now apparently that meant nothing."

Her phone cracked under my hands. *That motherfucker.*

"Dad, you broke my phone!" she ripped it from my hands, only to have it fall apart. "Damn it, I just got that one."

I tried to remain calm and collected and not like I wanted to find this asshole kid and show him just how scary Jameson Riley could be. Stupid little shit.

Arie moved closer to me, her head resting on my shoulder. "I'm sorry, Dad. I know I'm too young for this sort of thing."

"You didn't do anything wrong, Arie. He did. He's clearly an asshole, and you can do better than that."

"Why do all the guys go for the sluts?"

How the hell did I answer that one?

I thought I knew how Sway might have felt knowing I slept around before her, but hearing those words from my daughter made it that much more real to me. I was just like Ricky when I was his age. I went for who was easy and less likely to have strings attached. Ricky was a racer, too, as he was more than likely playing by those same rules.

Rules I didn't want my little girl knowing even existed, but they did.

"There's not much I can offer you on that, sweetheart. Guys are jerks. Do you want me to beat him up?"

"No, you'll get arrested. Besides ..." she smiled softly, her green eyes brighter from her tears. "Kale broke his nose anyway."

"Kale ... Justin's boy?"

"Yeah, he's a nice kid."

A small laugh escaped me before I threw my arm around her. "Good for him." I honestly didn't think that little runt had it in him. "It doesn't make the pain go away, though, does it?" I remembered comforting Sway this very same way when that jerk off Dylan Grady broke her heart and hated the similarities my kids were now facing with their own lives.

She shook her head. "No. I just want to be grown up now." I watched her brush some hair behind her ear, her face one of sadness and resignation. She clearly believed this pain would hurt forever.

"Don't rush it," I told her. "When your childhood is gone, it's gone forever. You can't get it back."

"Mom says I'll remember, though."

"Yeah ... you will, but just live for now. That's something I never did."

"You've always lived this lifestyle, haven't you?"

I nodded. "I have, but it's what I wanted."

"Do you ever think of retiring and spending more time with Mom?"

"I think of spending more time with your mom, but not about retiring. Racing is what I love. And I love your mom and you kids, but racing for me is much more than I can ever explain. Mom understands that."

Arie and I sat there for close to an hour before she said she was tired and went to bed. Making my way downstairs, I checked my phone to see when Sway would be home.

Emma was still on the couch, now watching *Top Gun.*

I threw myself down in one of the leather chairs across from her, glaring at the television on the wall. "I hate teenage boys."

"That would mean you hate yourself. You act like a teenage boy," Emma replied, gazing at Tom Cruise on the screen.

"Don't you have a home to go to?"

"Yeah, but my asshole sons are there with their stupid girlfriends."

"Don't like the Double Mint twins?"

"Fuck no," Emma sighed, her eyes remaining on Tom Cruise. "Fake little bitches."

Charlie and Noah were dating twins. They were blonde, annoyingly superficial twins who nearly everyone in the family couldn't stand.

Apparently Charlie and Noah could, though.

"Am I still cool?" I asked, kicking my legs over the ottoman. "I used to be cool."

I wasn't sure why I asked Emma. I knew she'd give me a response I didn't want, but I asked anyway.

"No, you're not cool. You're old," Emma replied with no regard to my feelings.

Grabbing the remote, I turned off the television. "Go watch TV with the Double Mint twins then."

"You're an asshole, too!" she yelled after me as I stomped back up the stairs. "Just remember, mall appearances!"

Emma was constantly threatening me with mall appearances knowing I had a phobia about malls. It was nearly as bad as my phobia about sand on my skin.

Later that night when Sway got home, I pulled the boys aside.

"Axel, do you know this Ricky Hagen kid?"

"Yeah, he races USAC Midgets on the Western circuit," he looked confused. "Why?"

"Apparently he broke Arie's heart."

Axel looked at me and then Casten. "Did you know about this?"

Casten's brow furrowed. "I knew she liked him, but no, I didn't know much else."

"I need to talk with this kid," I told them.

"Apparently we do, too," the boys said, walking upstairs into Arie's room.

There was one good thing about my kids, they stuck together. About a year ago now, Axel had gotten into a fairly bad wreck in Terra Haute that landed him in the hospital overnight. Arie and Casten never left his side.

"They're good kids," Sway said, closing the door to Arie's room; all three kids were on her bed watching a movie.

"I can't believe she fell for a racer."

Sway smiled. "Did you really expect anything less? Look at her family."

"Did you hear Kale broke Ricky's nose?"

"Actually I was there when it happened. Kale sure does have a thing for Arie."

"Great," I groaned. "Now I have to hate Justin."

"And how do you think he feels about you? Your son took his only daughter's virginity."

"Don't say it like that. That sounds horrible."

"I'm not going to sugar coat it for you."

No, Sway never sugar coated it for me. Throughout our entire lives together, she told me the way it was. I needed that. Too bad parenthood wasn't that way. I needed sugar coating on that, I couldn't handle this whole truth shit.

It sucked seeing them get older and making the same mistakes you made, but it would hurt if you never got to see that. You couldn't tell them what to be or how they should act. You had to let them be who they wanted to be. When they became their own person—that was what made you a proud parent. All that shit you didn't want to know became worth it because you did something right.

You raised your kids to be their own person.

Hairpin – A slow 180-turn which exits in the opposite direction the driver enters.

Toward the end of every season my life felt like I was going two hundred miles an hour down a straight stretch, and I was praying for a left turn in sight.

That year, after the plane crash and parenting, and racing, it couldn't have been truer.

With everything that was happening with racing, sponsors, team changes, media, kids, my wife ... I just needed ... me time.

Was I ready to retire?

No.

I needed to relax and step back.

I couldn't do that by just simply relaxing at home. That wasn't me.

Naturally, I went sprint car racing.

The methanol, the dirt, the Saturday night lights ... this calmed me in ways fishing or golfing might do for someone else my age. I needed the adrenaline to feel alive.

As it turned out, for turning forty-three that year I still had it in me. I won.

Life got to you at times, and you couldn't help it. For a while you were going along thinking everything was good and then a plane crash happened or your daughter lost her virginity to an asshole. You were dealing with life the best you could and it was working for the most part.

Then it hits you that you were just like everyone else, trying to make it through each day. The only difference was that I was a race car driver. My life was constantly going two hundred miles an hour. It never stopped until it stopped you.

As a racer, you couldn't just walk away. It was in your blood to keep coming back to what had been your life all those years.

Look at Bucky Miers, the man who took a chance on an eighteen-year-old kid. He retired last year only because he had a heart attack.

Look at Andy Crockett. He'd been at the peak of his career when he died. And Colin Shuman was a kid taken much too young. I didn't always agree with Colin, but still, the kid had talent and his career was ended suddenly.

I don't know. Maybe I couldn't figure out where I was going with all this but my point was that you're going along in your life the way you know how and my way was at 200 mph. I knew that no matter what direction your life was headed sometimes it took a hairpin turn the other direction. I had a feeling that turn was coming my way soon.

Like I said, you didn't just walk away completely. Bucky was still at the dirt track every Saturday night, except he wasn't in a car. You could take the racer out of the car, but you couldn't take him off the track completely.

I knew the possibility, that each Sunday could be my last, but I also couldn't think about it that way. The moment you were scared was the moment you *needed* to walk away. There was no room for fear.

The race season had gone on much like it always did, but there was a void that year for everyone we had lost. With my team, it wasn't the same anymore. A part of Kyle was gone, a part of our family was gone, and that affected us in every way. We struggled each week in the pits, though we kept it together. Our romance was gone, and I knew it'd take some time to find a groove again.

In November of that year, right before the last race of the Cup season, Axel raced in his first World of Outlaw race in Charlotte at the World Finals. He'd raced Outlaws before, but never in a sanctioned point race.

This was also the first race where three generations of drivers ever started a World of Outlaw race together.

Nothing exciting happened. I started midway through the field and ended up blowing a tire with six laps to go. My dad started fourth, snagged a third place finish, but what really made the night for us was Axel.

He started last when he wrecked in his heat and charged through the field of twenty-four cars to win his first Outlaw race.

My dad and I let him have his spotlight with the media, laughing when Lane dumped a cooler full of ice down his back.

"There was a lot of talk during the break on whether or not we should change out the gears, but it looks like the call was right," Axel told the reporter in his face.

I smiled.

My son had just won his first World of Outlaw race. Much like my own dad when I won some of my first races in my professional career, I didn't have many words. It was kind of like his first Chili Bowl Midget Nationals win.

My dad sighed beside me, limping back to the haulers.

"Can you make it or shall I carry you, old man?"

He pushed me, knocking me sideways.

"Carry me?" he repeated with a snort. "Son ... who finished ahead of you tonight?"

"I blew a tire," I defended, watching the boys in the distance.

"Still, I beat you," he laughed and rubbed the shoulder he had surgery on last winter. "I'm sure that's all that matters."

"Come on, old man," slinging my arm over his shoulders, I pulled him into me. "Let's go have a beer."

Back at the hauler, we relaxed and threw back a few beers while Axel and his boys celebrated in victory lane. I enjoyed times like this with my dad. It reminded me of when I traveled with him when I was younger, and we'd sit around after the races, and he'd tell me how he thought I could do better.

Now it was different, though. Times like this we just enjoyed the company. That wasn't to say we didn't have the smart-ass comments from time-to-time, but it was nice.

Jimi tipped his beer toward me, his eyes tired.

"I'm getting too old for this," he rolled his neck to one side. "It's wearing on my body."

"I feel you."

Injuries have a way of catching up with you, too. In sprint car racing you could get in some of the most violent wrecks that did damage to your body. With Jimi pushing seventy soon, everyone expected him to announce retirement any day now. I knew it was coming, but as a fellow racer, you didn't bring up retirement.

As a racer, Jimi couldn't just walk away. Not without regrets.

"Hey, Jameson," Tommy yelled from the back of the pit bike Lane was riding. "Can I get a ride with you back to Mooresville tonight?"

"Yeah," setting my empty beer down, I jumped up to push Lane off the bike only to have him roost me in the face with gravel.

"Asshole!" I yelled after him.

Spencer, who ran up behind him, tried to knock him off, too, only to have Lane do a wheelie through the pits. He loved to show off these days and did so more often around his dad. It wasn't like Spencer didn't think he was something special because he did.

Lane laughed as we all took turns trying to knock him from the bike and grinned the same grin he had when he was three.

Lane was quite the racer on dirt bikes. He was racing in the GNCC which was the Can-AM Grand National Cross Country series, America's premier off-road racing series. They ran a 13-round series, which raced on a wide variety of terrain that included hills, woods, mud, dirt, rocks, and motocross sections. They're a test of survival and speed, two things any Riley was good at.

He'd just won the XC1 Pro Bike Class this year and had a very promising career ahead of him.

He circled around the pits and came back by me as I was walking to my car.

"How's that dirt taste?" he smarted off with a smug grin.

"How's that car taste?" I asked just as smugly as I kept my eyes forward so he wouldn't notice the amusement. He was hardly paying attention.

"What ca—" he smacked right into the side of my dad's truck, sending him flying over the hood.

"That car."

Walking around the side, I laughed at him sprawled on the ground.

"Not such a hotshot now, are you?"

Glaring, Lane didn't say anything.

"Lane!" my dad yelled. "Come back here, you little shit. You're paying for that!"

Lane's eyes got huge. "Hide me!"

"No way, kid. You're on your own."

Axel ended up partying all night with his friends and cousins while the old guys went home to our beds. I tried staying up when Axel won the USAC Triple Crown last year and ended up lying in bed for two days straight with the worst hangover ever. I was not meant to be a party animal any longer; those days had passed me by.

Funny thing was, I was okay with that. I had something much better waiting for me in bed. I may not be able to party like a rock star any longer, but I had no problems showing my wife just how much life my camshaft still had.

I was able to sleep in my own bed that night before I left for Homestead to finish out the season.

Sway was packed and ready to go with Casten and Arie when my phone wouldn't stop ringing.

Glancing through the numerous emails from Alley and Emma, there were about ten calls from Justin and four from Tommy.

I panicked, thinking something happened to Axel last night. Trying to keep myself calm and guarded from Sway and the kids, I excused myself and stepped back inside the house to call Justin.

He answered, his voice rough and drained from any emotion.

"Did you call me?"

"Yeah, did you hear about Ryder?" There was a distance in his voice that I hadn't heard in a long time. At least not since the plane crash.

"No—why?" I stopped for a second and then panicked. Ryder wasn't always the best influence on Axel and had gotten him in trouble on more than one occasion. "Hey, is Axel with you?"

"No, he's with Lily celebrating. I heard something about them going to Jacksonville."

"Oh, all right. What happened to Ryder?" Ryder was still racing in the USAC Sprint Car division and swore up and down this was his last season.

There was a long pause before he mumbled, "He wrecked at Perris Auto Speedway last night ..." There was another long pause. "He died this morning from head injuries."

I felt a sharp stabbing pain in my chest. Instantly I felt like I couldn't breathe.

"Are you serious? Please tell me you're not serious."

I couldn't understand why again.

Why did this keep happening? Couldn't we catch a break?

"Justin," I begged. "Jesus, please tell me you're not serious?"

"It's not something I'd joke about, Jameson."

I didn't say any more.

What could I say? Sorry? No, sorry wouldn't do this justice. Justin and I grew up with him and Tyler. We made our way through the ranks together. Sure, most of us went different directions, but still, a bond had formed back then that was still there today and always would be.

We had always known the dangers; but there was also something about those dangers that urged us to put it all on the line. The danger fueled the adrenaline.

Justin said he was flying to Knoxville where Ryder had been living for the past few years to see his parents. I couldn't, though. I had to be in Homestead tonight.

"Give his parents my best," I told Justin before hanging up. With the Outlaws finishing up their season last night, he was free to go if he wanted, as no more races were scheduled until January.

"I will. I haven't said anything to Axel. I thought you should be the one to tell him. Ryder's dad just called me about an hour ago, which means it will be hitting the news any minute now. You might want to call him."

"Thanks Justin ... I will call him."

Sway walked in just as I hung up with her cell phone in hand.

She held the phone out. "Axel is looking for you." Her eyes glazed with tears as she eyed me cautiously. She knew.

"I'm *so sorry*, Jameson," she offered, wrapping her tiny arms around me.

Inhaling a deep breath, I pulled back to look at her. "It's all right. It happens in this sport."

My eyes focused on hers.

She didn't even need to say it back, I already knew she wanted to comfort me, tell me everything would be all right.

"I love you," she told me, running her consoling hand down my cheek. "I know that it happens too often, but it doesn't make this any easier. Especially not when it's a good friend of ours."

Leaning into her touch, I dropped my head to pull her into a hug when Casten came inside.

"What's the deal?" he threw his arms up. "I thought we were leaving."

"Yeah, let's go," Arie added, stepping inside behind him. "It's hot in the car."

The kids took in our embrace and looked between each other knowing something was wrong.

"Is Axel okay?" Arie asked, her brow scrunched in confusion and nervousness.

"Yes, sweetie, Axel is fine," Sway told her, walking over to them. I nodded when her eyes met mine and then slipped inside the bathroom down the hall to compose myself a little. Though I didn't cry, I needed a few minutes before I told Axel.

I heard Sway through the door telling Arie and Casten what happened.

"Ryder wrecked last night at Perris. He died this morning."

Neither of the kids said anything. Just like me, they knew the dangers. Again, those dangers didn't make this any easier. It almost made it harder to accept the fact that it was happening because your mind was in denial that it could happen.

I must have sat in that bathroom for a half hour, just staring at the wall, trying to find the courage to call Axel. Over time, he and Ryder had shaped a bond together. They'd raced in the same division for close to ten years now. Ryder was not only a fellow racer of his, but someone he looked up to. Just coming off a World Final win last night, this was not something I wanted to tell him. But I also didn't want him to hear it on the news or from someone else.

He answered on about the fourth ring with a groggy voice. "What's up, Dad?"

"How are you feeling, buddy? Get any sleep last night?"

"Yeah, I got a couple hours once we got to Jacksonville. I was gonna head to Perris today, though. Shane sent me a text that Ryder got in a wreck there last night. I wanted to check on him."

I couldn't get the words out before he asked.

"Are you still there, Dad?"

"Yeah ... uh, buddy ... Ryder didn't make it. He died this morning from head injuries."

There was a sharp intake of breath from him followed by a deep shaky sigh before he asked, "Are you sure?"

"Yeah."

I wasn't positive, but from the sound of the television in our family room, it was all over ESPN right now.

"You're coming to Homestead, right?" Axel asked after a moment of silence. I could hear Lily crying in the background.

"Yeah, I need to leave now."

"I'll meet you guys there."

"You don't have to come, buddy. Just ... enjoy some time off."

"No, I need to be with my family right now," he said this as though it was the only option.

I thought I'd said this before, but on the track, everything was up for grabs. Tempers flared, friends you thought you had no longer gave you room and would do anything to get a jump on you.

Off the track, the racing community was like your family. They'd do anything for anyone. That never changed. With the plane crash earlier in the year, we had all pulled together and did what we could do to go on, and now with Ryder, I knew we'd go on, but it didn't stop it from hurting. We needed each other.

When Bobby cheated on his wife, multiple times, no one agreed with it. But when she left him, who do you think was there to offer him a beer?

Yes, guys like me and Tate who were fellow racers.

Then there was the time that Wade Simmons, a nineteen-year-old rookie NASCAR driver, was killed in Texas last year during happy hour. We all gathered together and made sure his young wife and little girl would forever be taken care of. We came together when we needed to.

Tate, Bobby, and I made sure those families, who lost their loved ones in that plane crash in May, were taken care of and had nothing to worry about financially. The heartache alone would be enough. They didn't need to worry about trying to make a home for their family and deal with that. This was what made us champions in our sport. Sure, winning them defined the trophy, but being a champion, there was a difference between earning the title and being it.

Now wasn't any different. After the Homestead race, about five hundred fellow racers attended Ryder's funeral in Knoxville to pay their respects for one of the greatest drivers the USAC division had ever seen. Not only had Ryder won the USAC Triple Crown ten times, he'd won events like Chili Bowl Nationals eight times, Turkey Night, the Hut Hundred and the Cooper Classic, just to name a few. Basically, every race I'd ever won in a sprint car or midget, Ryder Christensen had done, too, only multiple times.

As a racer, you never wanted to attend another racer's funeral.

It made the possibility of it happening to you and your family real. You saw it. You saw the family suffering and knew that it could have been you. Death was suddenly right there in your face, taunting you. It reminded you just how precariously you were balancing on the edge of disaster.

Here was the thing about warning a race car driver. We did not listen.

We never listened, or ninety percent of the time we didn't listen. Just like an engine light in your car. Most waited until they were left stranded on the side of the road, cursing themselves for not taking that damn orange light seriously. We were no different when racing. Dangers, well, they didn't exist to us.

A few months after Ryder's death, a little too late I thought, he was inducted into the National Midget Auto Racing Hall of Fame.

Too bad he wasn't around to give his standard humble response, "Ah, well, I'm not that good. I just know how to go fast and turn left."

I heard those exact words from him a lot over the nearly thirty years I had known Ryder.

Ryder's death took the biggest hit on Casten actually. He quit racing altogether after that. Casten never really showed as much interest as Axel did anyway, but after Ryder, he just said it wasn't fun for him anymore. He never set foot in a race car again. I thought part of the reason was because the midget he'd been racing was one that Ryder owned. It didn't feel right to him anymore.

I respected his decision, because like I said, if you were scared ... you had no business strapping into that car.

For the past few years, it seemed our entire family was spread across the states and even into different countries for the holidays. But that Christmas, after all the loss we'd suffered, everyone was home. Our championship team was together and pulling through this as a team.

This was both a good thing and a disaster.

Sway loved having everyone together at our place. I couldn't understand why it always had to occur at our house, but I kept my mouth shut when I saw how happy she was.

Christmas morning started simple enough. The kids opened presents with us, and I gave Sway her gift, alone.

For a while, I'd been thinking about what I would get a woman who had absolutely everything she could ever want. With the help of my mom, I found a picture of Sway and me when I won Knoxville Nationals during our summer together in 1997. Sway had always been fond of the picture and told me that was the night she knew she'd fallen in love with me. The picture was the one they had used on the front page of the newspaper the next morning, but from at a slightly different angle.

I was still sitting inside my sprint car, leaning toward Sway, who was leaning inside the car. Her arms were around my neck with one of my gloved hands touching the side of her face as we kissed. Up until a couple weeks ago, I'd never seen the picture.

My first thought: Wow, look how young we were.

My second: She was just as beautiful so many years later as she was that night.

Though my early years of racing were becoming vague, I still remembered that race and the feeling that washed over me when I saw her waiting for me.

I thought deep down that was the night I realized what her being there for me meant. I wouldn't say I knew I loved her then, because I did love her, but my realization didn't come until a few years later, having been too caught up in racing to see anything past that. But I did love her back then.

Sway would never understand what that summer meant to me. You could say it was just the summer I made a name for myself, but back then, it was more than that. We were all just a bunch of kids, but you honestly couldn't tell any of us that.

For Christmas, I had that picture transferred into a canvas painting and hung it above our bed as she slept that night. When she woke up Christmas morning, naturally, we made love. Carefully, I pulled her on top of me, and she straddled me for a better angle. Her head tipped back and she saw the picture.

"Holy shit, Jameson. Where did that come from?"

She remembered the picture. I was sure of that when a smile tugged at her lips. "That's the night," she whispered so softly I had to strain to hear her. "How did you ..."

"My mom found it," I told her, leaning forward to sit up. My arms wrapped around her backside, pulling her closer as my lips found her collarbone. "Merry Christmas, honey."

"Merry Christmas to you, too," her lips met mine with a sudden sense of urgency.

Though we were good at the dyno testing and align boring, that morning in bed with my wife of the last eighteen years was all about love. The love I'd felt for her our entire lives. It was slow, passionate, and all that storybook love you read about. Over the years, I would like to think I provided Sway with the fairytale fantasy she wanted to remember. Now I knew I had.

There was no doubt, looking at that painting, and then looking at us now, we had something noteworthy of a fairytale.

After we made our way back downstairs, Lily was there along

with Kale, her younger brother who was convinced he would marry Arie someday. I had a feeling my headstrong little girl liked him, but wasn't ready for anything serious after what happened with Ricky.

Kale cared about none of that, and he claimed he'd wait for forever.

Today was also Axel's eighteenth birthday.

And where was my son?

He was flying home from Australia, where he'd been racing for the past few months.

Much like me at his age, he lived to race. And since our weather here didn't permit winter racing, he flew to Australia where it was. I'd spent many winters racing down under, but these days, I enjoyed the time away. Every January, though, I was itching to get back to it. That was how I knew retirement wasn't near.

Axel ended up arriving shortly before the rest of the family arrived with a big smile on his face when he saw Lily had made it.

The real fun began when my sister's asshole children showed up with the Double Mint twins, and they started hitting on Axel. Up until that night, I had never heard Lily swear.

But when the Double Mint twins cornered Axel, she got her point across.

"Most guys may fall for your fake breasts and your bleached out hair, but Axel's different. Leave him alone," she told them in a civilized manner. Listening to them around the corner in the family room, Sway, Casten, and I stood in the kitchen.

Casten giggled, and that was when Sway slapped her hand over his mouth and pulled him to her.

"Shhh," she urged, trying to suppress her own giggles.

"Maybe he needs more than just a small town girl from Hillsboro," one of them snarked back.

Lily laughed. "Yeah, because being from LA is so much better."

Axel interrupted.

"You guys should leave," he told the girls.

That caused an actual fight between him and his cousins, which

Aiden and I had to break up. Axel was not a big kid by any means. Noah and Charlie looked more like one of Spencer's kids with their burly builds.

Axel didn't stand much of a chance, but when Lily was involved, Noah and Charlie didn't stand much of a chance.

Axel ended up breaking Charlie's nose and gave Noah a large, gaping cut just above his eye before we got to them.

See, I told you our family gatherings never went well.

Emma got upset with Axel, which made Lily even madder. "If your sons would keep their fucking hoes under control, this would have never happened."

Emma stood there, dumbfounded, because she knew her sons were jerks and couldn't say much about their girlfriends. She hated them, too.

Sway laughed and stepped in between them. Slinging her arm around Lily she pushed a plate of brownies toward Emma.

"You're going to fit in nicely with this family," she told Lily.

The rest of the night seemed to go smoothly, which was a nice surprise. With Speedweek just around the corner, I needed smooth and relaxed.

The rest of winter went by quickly as usual. Sway and I managed to sneak away to our other home in the Florida Keys a few weekends, but most of the off-season was spent restructuring Riley-Simplex Racing.

Jimi Riley was hanging up his helmet after forty-three seasons with the World of Outlaws. Though he was keeping his position as the owner, he was no longer racing in the Outlaw series.

So he said at least. We all knew him well enough to know he wouldn't be able to stay away completely. I had a feeling if it was me, I wouldn't be able to either. He would still be the owner of the Cup team and his sprint car team as well, so he wasn't walking away completely. He'd still be around to tell us how badly he thought we were fucking up his business.

I wasn't retiring, though; I was on top of my career right now. Having just won my fifteenth career championship, I felt like I could still give this sport a run. I was a champion, and in my mind, I could be that legend everyone was pegging me to be.

With Jimi retiring, guess who he hired to take over his position?

The kid.

Axel would be racing his first season in the World of Outlaws.

I had mixed feelings about this. Though USAC resembled NASCAR with its frequent rule changes and drama, the Outlaw series was where the big money was at in sprint car racing. When drivers entered into that series, they usually stayed. Axel and I had a long talk when my dad came to me with his plan.

"Did you know what series you wanted to run in right away?" he asked me one day when we were at the sprint car shop. I was finalizing the schedules for appearances for the guys and going over any sponsorship appearances we needed to attend.

"I knew I wanted to race. That's all that mattered to me," I told him, pushing my laptop aside to look at him sitting in front of my desk. "I did look at everything from Indy to even drag racing. In the end, I looked at where I could get the most exposure and that led me to NASCAR. It wasn't about the money for me, it was about being *me*. My dad raced sprint cars, and while my love for racing will always be related to sprint cars, NASCAR gave me the opportunity I was looking for."

"Was it hard for you being his son?"

I thought about this for a moment because any pressure I ever felt from being Jimi Riley's son, Axel felt, but doubled. He not only had everyone telling him how good his grandfather was, but then they told him how great his dad was.

"It was hard, but I think if anyone, you understand that feeling."

That legendary bloodline just added that much more pressure to what you already felt.

Axel sat there in the leather chair across from me, twisting a spark plug around his fingers. “I want to race sprint cars,” he said after a few minutes of silence. “I think that’s where I’ve always belonged.”

I knew that already. Even when USAC went to asphalt, he hated it. Much like me, his love for dirt would always be there. Both for different reasons. Asphalt scared Axel; I don’t know why, and neither did he, but some of his worst wrecks occurred on asphalt tracks. Dirt felt comfortable for him.

For me, dirt was home. It reminded me of the greatest summer of my life, both frustrating and exciting. When I got inside a sprint car on dirt, to me, it was like coming home.

“Do you think I can do this?” Axel asked when I smiled at the picture on my desk of us when he won the Chili Bowl.

“I do, buddy. Without a doubt, I know you’ll be good in whatever series you run. Go with your gut instinct.”

His gut instinct was to race.

“Have you ever felt pressured to race?” I asked him after a moment.

Sway and I always worried the boys felt as though they had to race, given my profession and my dad’s. While we knew where Casten stood with it, I wasn’t sure about Axel. Maybe that was why he constantly needed reassurance that he could do it.

“No, I’ve always *wanted* to race,” he smiled, remembering why he did. “I don’t remember how old I was, but I think Mom was pregnant with Casten. I just remember watching the memorial race for Grandpa Charlie ... I remember standing in the flag stand holding the flag when you, Grandpa, Justin, and Ryder came by on the front stretch four wide, engines rumbling ... From then on, that’s what I wanted to do.”

“That sound gets most people.” I nodded with a smile, remembering the thunderous rumble from my childhood and watching guys like my dad and Bucky Miers.

“What made you want to race?” he asked, glancing at the other picture on my desk of Sway and me on our honeymoon in Rio right after he was born. I had to chuckle as it was one with my leg bleeding and her with the jellyfish sting.

"Same as you," my gaze shifted to the photograph beside that of Sway and I at Elma last spring. "I grew up watching Grandpa race, just like you."

My eyes shifted to a photograph of my dad. It was the one of us singing "Barton Hollow" by The Civil Wars at a bar outside of Williams Grove after a race. That was when I felt the pain in my chest that he was hangin' up his helmet, something I thought he'd never do.

"Racing has always been there for me, and after a while, it was just the natural way to go." I smiled at my son. "I could never imagine my life any other way than inside a race car."

Axel knew exactly what I was trying to say without me needing to go into any more detail. Like I said, racing was his gut instinct, just like mine was.

He left after that, and I sat there in my office looking over the pictures Sway and I framed over the years. It was hard to believe how quickly that last twenty years had gone by, but I never regretted this lifestyle. It was me. I gave this sport what I gave to racing. Myself.

A racer couldn't be labeled or molded.

Most guys in the garage area would agree with that statement.

A racer didn't race for anyone but himself.

Another statement most would agree with.

Some had different theories, but really, the victory was what you raced for. Now that victory could be, and was, owed to more than you, but to get there, to get inside the car and decide to race, came from within.

At some point, you were nothing, until one day, you were suddenly something. Worshipped by millions for something you did for yourself. Why was it that they suddenly thought you were different?

What made them love you now when they didn't before?

I could tell you why. You had the balls to do what they never did. You got inside the car and pushed yourself to be the best. You did that. No one else did.

What they didn't understand was that there would always be confessions that bared no sound and lived inside my head, my heart, and were my own desire. They were my own aspirations and something they never took the time to discover.

I raced for me. It wasn't selfish. It was me being me.

I did it because that's who I was and who was embedded into every fiber of my being.

I raced for the adrenaline, the power, the rumbling in my chest when behind the wheel. The sense of belonging in a sport that was quick to prove you were nothing, but still, I raced for me. That was what defined me.

I couldn't say every racer was the same, but for the most part, they were.

So now, with time, as one career was ending, another was just beginning in a sport that was forever changing.

Throughout death and despair, our family had once again kept it together. Through the birth of our kids, season after season of the same rival drivers, doubts, marriage troubles, loss and life changes, we did it. We were, just as we always had been, a woven mesh window net holding it together. It was funny how your life, or maybe just mine, went similar to a race. You got the laps of happiness, laps of sadness, laps of success and laps of hardship. No matter what lap you were on or what stop you were trying to make it to, gambling with fuel mileage, or holdin' on with worn tires, you could count on your crew to get you through it. I could do that.

In my mind, we were a championship team who kept together no matter what. Maybe there'd be more races like the last eighteen years, but I was ready for that. As a champion, I was ready for that.

But I wanted to be a legend, not just a champion.

First they ignore you, then they laugh at you, then they fight you, then you win.

-Ghandi

Shey Stahl is the author of the Racing on the Edge Series. She enjoys spending time with her family at the local dirt tracks. You can follow her on the links below.

Facebook: https://www.facebook.com/shey.stahl.9
Website: www.sheystahl.com

Website & Social Media:
www.sheystahl.com
Facebook: Shey Stahl

Novels by Shey Stahl:
Racing on the Edge:
Happy Hour
Black Flag
Trading Paint
The Champion
The Legend
Additional novels coming soon:
Hot Laps
The Rookie
Fast Time
Lapped Traffic
Behind the Wheel - Outtakes

Everything Changes

Waiting for You

Delayed Penalty

28538416R00276

Made in the USA
Charleston, SC
15 April 2014